SCENT OF FEAR

TONY PARK

PAN BOOKS

First published 2018 by Pan Macmillan Australia Pty Ltd

First published in the UK 2018 by Pan Books

This paperback edition first published in the UK 2019 by Pan Books
an imprint of Pan Macmillan
20 New Wharf Road, London N1 9RR
Associated companies throughout the world
www.panmacmillan.com

ISBN 978-1-5098-7657-0

1 3 5 7 9 8 6 4 2

A CIP catalogue record for this book is available from the British Library.

Cartographic art by Laurie Whiddon, Map Illustrations

Printed and bound by CPI Group (UK) Ltd, Croydon, CR0 4YY

Visit **www.panmacmillan.com** to read more about all our books
and to buy them. You will also find features, author interviews and
news of any author events, and you can sign up for e-newsletters
so that you're always first to hear about our new releases.

SCENT OF FEAR

Tony Park was born in 1964 and grew up in the western suburbs of Sydney. He has worked as a newspaper reporter, a press secretary, a PR consultant and a freelance writer. He also served 34 years in the Australian Army Reserve, including six months as a public affairs officer in Afghanistan in 2002. He and his wife, Nicola, divide their time equally between Australia and southern Africa. He is the author of fifteen other African novels.

For Nicola

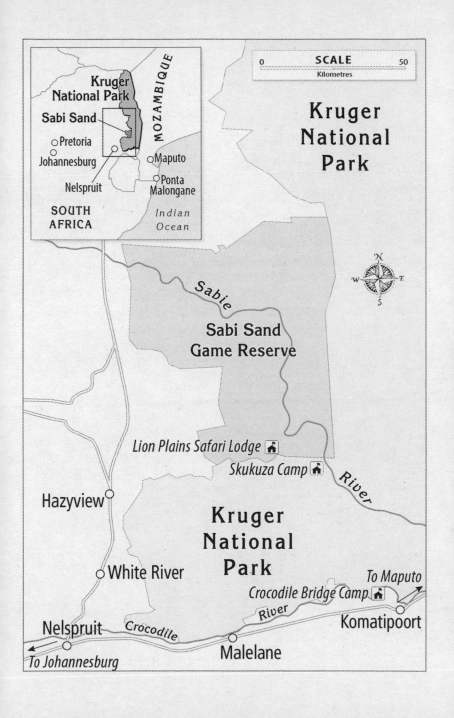

SCALE

0   50
Kilometres

Kruger
National
Park

MOZAMBIQUE

Kruger
National Park

Sabi Sand

○ Pretoria
○
Johannesburg

Nelspruit

SOUTH
AFRICA

○ Maputo

○ Ponta
Malongane

Indian
Ocean

Sabie

Sabi Sand
Game Reserve

N
W   E
S

Lion Plains Safari Lodge

Skukuza Camp

River

Hazyview ○

Kruger
National
Park

○ White River

To Maputo

Crocodile Bridge Camp

River

Nelspruit ○

Crocodile

Komatipoort

To Johannesburg

○
Malelane

Prologue

Sabi Sand Game Reserve, South Africa

I hate cats.

Don't worry if you're a cat person. I'll win you over. I tend to grow on people. Sure, I have my faults. I'm messy, my farts stink, and my best friend says that all I think about is eating and chasing tail.

And work.

I love my job. I'm good at it, which is why I'm alive and still working today. My idea of hell is to be cooped up indoors somewhere, or unemployed. It's cool if you like to have your nails done, your hair fixed, to get a new outfit or a new toy every week. If that's your thing, that's OK. But it's not mine.

While I like my job, I like my sleep even better, so I was annoyed at being woken by the cat. I was having a dream, and it was a good one. I was chasing pussy. I like that, as well.

Did I tell you I went to war?

Want to know the truth? I liked it.

It's not for everyone; not for those who need gourmet food, a

1

comfy bed, endless amusement. Not for the ones who need to be carried through life, or adorned with jewels or taken to the doctor at the drop of a hat for a check-up.

But it's not all fun.

War is crazy. Mad and bad. I lost a couple of friends and that was sad. I howled. I got hit, took some homemade shrapnel from an IED, an improvised explosive device, they call it. Me, I call it a big fucking bang, worse than any firework you could ever imagine.

That's another downside of war, too many bangs.

But on the whole, the chow was good, the work was fun, and I made some great friends. Buddies for life, in fact, and that's how I ended up back home, in South Africa.

I knew Africa, as soon as I came back. One time, when I was on a helicopter – I hate them, too, by the way – I thought about grass. Not marijuana, though there was plenty of that in Afghanistan (I can sniff that shit out half a mile away), but the kind you roll in and like to feel under your feet. I was so damned used to walking on rocks and dirt and sand, and through mud and crap and ice-cold rivers, that I almost forgot what it was like to walk on grass.

It was after the IED had gone off. I had a metal screw, part of the bomb, stuck inside me, near an artery, and I was bleeding bad. A US Army Special Forces medic had put a field dressing on me and inserted an IV to keep my fluids up. He saved my life and he was crying as he worked on me. Sean was next to him, holding me still, and he was crying too. I have that effect on people – told you that you'd grow to like me.

As I passed out, from loss of blood, the last thing I thought of was grass. I remembered the summers, when I was small, when the grass was green and soft, like running on velvet. By the time I finished training it was the end of the dry season and the grass was the colour of gold, brittle, dry, spiky to the touch. Still, it was better than dirt and rock.

I woke up in the hospital and I freaked out. I hate going to the doctor, always have. Give me gunfire and explosions any day, but there's nothing that makes me whine and cower and hide under my arse more than the prospect of a trip to the sawbones. It's the smells, you know? All that disinfectant and piss and drugs, and that look in the eye of the person taking you there. You just know it's going to be bad.

I survived Afghanistan, and so did Sean. Got me a scar where the hair won't grow to this day, and a promotion, to US Army corporal, honorary of course, and a medal. I saved a guy, my buddy Sean, and a whole bunch of American GIs. It didn't really mean anything to me; I was just doing my job.

I can sense it, you know, when there's danger. It's what the guys liked about me.

They came to visit me in the hospital, brought me food, and even a beer, though the alcohol-free kind. I lapped it up and I wolfed down that hamburger like it was the best meal of my life, the best day ever. It was both of those things. It took a while, but I got back to work, and so did Sean.

But where was I? Oh, yeah, cats. Right.

Hate 'em. I can hear the one that woke me up, right now. It's just outside my place. I live back in South Africa now. Different job, same rank. I'm still a corporal, although now instead of looking for Taliban and bombs, I'm hunting poachers. There are no IEDs, but that doesn't mean it's not dangerous, or scary; it's both.

The cat's calling, keeping me awake and pissing me off, because I'm on duty and I need my sleep. I can be called out at any time, day or night. Poachers don't keep regular hours, but that's fine by me.

It's like the war, you know? You train a lot, and that can be fun, but the real excitement comes when you get a callout. There's nothing like it, that thrill of the hunt, running through the bush or finding a bad guy. And like in the war, you sleep when you can.

I heard a stretcher creak, and rolled over. Sean was awake. 'Howzit, *boet*?'

Like me, Sean was born in South Africa, in Durban, but we both ended up working for the US Army in Afghanistan, as contractors. He calls me his *boet* as we're brothers, inseparable.

I didn't say anything, but he could tell from the look on my face I wasn't happy.

'I know. Bloody cat.'

I sighed. He picked up his phone off the upturned box that served as a side table in the permanent safari tent we shared and checked the time. 'Middle of the night still.'

He stretched and yawned, and I did the same. It was cold, and the full moon's watery light seeped into our room.

We both heard the sound of gunfire.

'Shit.' Sean switched on the tent light.

I jumped off the stretcher.

Full moon nights used to be really busy, but it had been some time since we'd been called out.

'That's near.' He cocked an ear. There were more shots, and they were very close. Sean pulled on his boots and was buttoning his bush shirt when his phone rang.

'Howzit . . . OK,' he said into the phone, then ended the call and turned to me. 'We're on, Benny.'

I was ready to go. Couldn't wait, in fact. I hadn't slept much – the cat had seen to that – but I was awake and alert and ready to do my job. It was a cold, clear night, but the chill in the air was nothing compared to the sleet and snow in the mountains of Afghanistan.

Sean opened his mouth to speak, but as I looked up at him – he's much taller than me – I already knew what he was going to say. At that very second, when I heard the noise, that dull *thwap-thwap-thwap* of rotor blades bouncing around the night sky and heading our way, I wanted to turn tail and hide under my blanket. In fact, I got up and started to move.

'Benny. It's OK, boy. How many times do I have to tell you, it's only a chopper?'

Only a chopper?

'Quit your whining, Benny,' he said. 'You're a dog, not a pussy.'

I was reluctant, but I followed Sean outside into the cool night air. Swivelling my head in the direction of the noise, I saw the reflection of the landing light rippling its way along the surface of the Sabie River in the distance.

Only a chopper. And people call me a dumb animal.

Chapter 1

Sean Bourke slung his LM5 rifle over his shoulder and grabbed Benny by the scruff of the neck. He buckled Benny's green nylon webbing tracking collar on him and the dog's alert status instantly ratcheted up a notch.

Benny knew that when his collar came on it was time to go to work, that this was not play. However, as much as Benny loved working he did not like flying, and he started to whine again.

Sean clipped on Benny's short lead and held him steady as the anti-poaching helicopter settled into a hover, and then touched down on the cleared landing pad adjacent to the anti-poaching camp hidden in the bush not far from the luxurious Lion Plains Safari Lodge.

'*Eish*, man, you're getting heavy,' Sean said to Benny as he picked him up and headed to the chopper. 'Too much biltong.'

Benny was a Belgian Malinois, and when Sean described him, and the breed, to people who didn't know them, he usually said his dog was like a compact German Shepherd and faster than the bigger dog. He had a black muzzle and a deep tan—coloured coat.

Sean screwed his eyes shut against the wave of dust and grit that washed over him as he jogged, hunched over the dog, then turned and slid, butt first, into the helicopter. He was barely in when Francois, the pilot, started lifting off.

Like all dogs, Benny loved riding in cars, even when confined to his travel kennel or a cage, and he was fearless in the bush, but flying reduced him to a terrified, whining mess. It was hardly surprising. Sean wasn't mad about helicopters either.

He hugged Benny closer. 'It's all right, my boy. We'll be on the ground soon.'

There were two other green-clad men in the chopper and when Sean had found a seatbelt and fastened it on he nodded to Charles and Oliver. They were armed members of the team who accompanied the dogs and handlers, providing extra firepower. When they were rostered on duty, Charles and Oliver stayed in the same camp as Sean, but this evening they had gone out on patrol at dusk and, once it was dark, had set up a night obser-vation post on a *koppie*, a rock-studded hill that overlooked a large chunk of the reserve. Both were good trackers in their own right. The leader of the anti-poaching unit, Craig, who doubled as another dog handler, was off duty. Charles smiled and waved to Sean; Oliver stared out the open side door of the aircraft, watching the ground.

Benny barked and writhed in Sean's embrace and it was only when Sean followed the dog's gaze that he saw there was some-one else on board, a woman, on the far side of Oliver, and another dog. Sean didn't recognise the mouse-grey Weimaraner or the other handler, partly because she was all but obscured by Oliver's bulk.

The other handler on their team, Musa, had left the previous week to take up a job closer to his Zululand home, at the Hluhluwe-iMfolozi Park, and the team had been expecting a replacement who they knew had just finished training at a place up at Hoedspruit, north of where they were. Sean had met women handlers in the police and the military and working in war zones overseas, but females were still something of a rarity in this particular role.

Sean leaned as far as he could past the two men and waved to her. He yelled his name.

He couldn't hear what she said, but guessed she was introducing herself. She didn't need to speak for him to recognise her fear. Her uniform was so new it was shiny, the creases factory-fresh. He looked down at her boots. They were spotless, still gleaming from weeks of spit-polishing during her basic training.

Benny sniffed and his tongue lolled, his fear of flying overcome by his curiosity over his fellow passenger.

Sean nodded to the Weimaraner. 'Female?'

The woman must have heard, or read his lips. She nodded vigorously. 'Gemma.'

The dog looked in good condition and her handler was pretty, big eyes, luscious lips, and Charles obviously thought so as well, because he started talking to her and whatever he said made her laugh.

Sean looked out through the perspex windscreen of the cockpit. Francois was pointing. Sean unclipped a spare headset from the bulkhead and put it on.

Oliver, who was also wearing a headset, tapped Sean on the arm, and also pointed ahead. 'Francois has spotted the carcass.'

Sean craned his neck and saw the inert mass on the ground, lying in an open grassy *vlei*. 'Downwind of the carcass, please, Francois.'

The pilot nodded. The dogs, Benny and Gemma, would initially be trying to air-scent, to pick up the trace of the people who had done this or their weapons and ammunition from their targets' smells, tiny particles blowing in the night breeze. For this reason, they tracked, where possible, by walking into the wind to give the dogs' noses a better chance of success. There was a large waterhole not far from where the killing had happened and they could all see the directions of the ripples caused by the wind on the moonlit surface.

Francois knew the drill. He brought the helicopter down, flaring the nose. Sean undid his seatbelt, and the moment the skids touched the earth he and Benny were out. Oliver freed himself of the headset and he and Charles jumped out after them. Sean set down Benny, who was tethered to him by his lead, which was fixed to his webbing harness with a D-ring, and used his left hand to yank back the cocking handle of his LM5. He let the working parts fly forward, chambering a 5.56-millimetre round. The simple action triggered a shot of adrenaline, charging his senses and readying him for the pursuit to come. Benny also knew that sound and was ready for action, nose up, sniffing the breeze. Charles was kneeling in the grass next to them.

Sean would have set off, but the helicopter was still turning and burning behind him. Francois should have been gone by now, Sean thought. He looked around and saw that the young woman and her dog were still on board. Oliver was on the other side of the chopper, yelling at the woman. Was she scared? Sean wondered.

He unclipped the D-ring securing the leash and Benny bounded away, then stopped and looked back at Sean, tongue out, eyes bright, waiting for him to follow.

'Sit.'

Sean ran around the front of the helicopter. He saw the problem immediately. The other dog, Gemma, had got her lead wrapped around the woman's legs and the handler herself was having trouble getting out of her seat.

Oliver was swearing at her.

'It's OK,' Sean said. He brushed past the male ranger, looked in, and assessed the situation. Gemma's leash was knotted into a loop and the woman had somehow threaded her seatbelt through the loop. He reached in, found the belt's buckle, which was hiding under one of her ammunition pouches, and undid it. Next he unthreaded the lead. Gemma, confused and also panicked, jumped down and ran towards Benny, the lead trailing behind her.

Sean took the woman's hand and helped her out and down. He saw now that she was young. Francois, shaking his head, lifted off.

Silence returned, but Oliver started his tirade, albeit in hushed, urgent tones.

'What do you think you're doing, you stupid girl? We have important work to do.'

'Chill, *bru*,' Sean said.

Oliver glared at him. 'Don't tell me what to do. Get your dog, start working.'

Ignoring him, Sean turned back to the woman. 'You all right?' She nodded, but he could see she was biting her lower lip. 'Come.'

She nodded again and followed him, and Gemma returned to her side. Benny looked back, eager to get on with the job.

'Check, Benny.'

On that command Benny went towards the dead rhino, sniffing. It was big, probably a bull, Sean thought, and its blood was a dark stain on the ground. Its horn had been taken off, down to the white bone. Benny circled the dead animal, nose down, then he stopped. He went tense, instantly even more alert. His body language told Sean he had picked something up.

Sean came to him and looked down and ahead of where Benny was sniffing. The grass had been trampled and further on some low branches had been broken off a sapling.

Sean shrugged off his twelve-kilogram backpack. Amid the six litres of water – four of which were for Benny – first aid kit, marker panel to signal a helicopter, food, toilet paper, GPS, handcuffs and extra ammunition, were Benny's tracking harness and a six-metre long lead made of stout nylon cord encased in rubber.

Sean quickly fitted the harness and this act, like attaching his collar, told Benny that they were about to get serious. Benny strained against him, eager to get on the trail. Sean stowed his gear and Benny's short lead, but tucked the long lead behind the pouches fixed to his webbing, across his chest.

'Benny, *soek*,' Sean said, giving the command to seek, or find. Benny set off.

The woman had done the same thing, but had attached a tracking lead to Gemma's harness. 'You're working your dog off-lead?'

Sean nodded.

'I thought we're supposed to keep them on-lead at night-time,' she said.

She was clearly fresh out of training. He shrugged. There was work to do. 'Full moon, plenty of light, and it's Benny. He's smart and experienced. Stick close to me and keep your dog on-lead.' He began to follow Benny at a jog.

'*Yebo*.' Her rifle dwarfed her and her gear rattled as she ran to catch up with him. He would talk to her about the noise later, when they were done.

Thorny branches scratched and snatched at him as Benny led him into the bush surrounding the *vlei*, towards the Sabie River. It was the dry season and the water level was low. Above them, Francois was flying a circuit. He would be checking the FLIR, the forward-looking infrared camera on board, seeking out the man or men's heat signatures.

For all the high-tech wizardry employed in the fight against poaching in South Africa, it was down to teams on the ground and, increasingly, dogs, to catch the people that the gadgetry sometimes detected. A hippo honked from the river, a reminder that humans were far from the only danger waiting for them in the gloom.

Charles and Oliver kept pace with them. Then Benny gave a growl and Sean held up a hand to stop them all. Oliver muscled between Sean and the woman and Gemma, effectively pushing her to the rear of the patrol. Sean didn't know whether he was trying to shield her from potential danger or cut her out of the action.

Benny was sitting, ears up, tail sticking straight out behind him and resting flat.

'He's indicating,' Sean said quietly, dropping to one knee. 'Found something.'

'Make him attack.' Oliver pointed to a thicket of raisin bush. 'There is probably a poacher hiding in there.'

Sean shook his head. The hairs rose on his arms. 'No, it's something else.' To the right of the bushes was a game trail, a hippo highway visible between a pair of giant jackalberry trees and leading down to the river.

As they took it in, there was movement behind them and the Weimaraner ran past them, almost towing her handler behind her. The woman's rifle, slung across her body, bounced on her back and swung around to her front as she stumbled and nearly fell.

'Come back.' Sean realised he still didn't even know her name.

The woman looked over her shoulder. 'Gemma's picked it up as well.'

Benny whined and looked at Sean as Gemma and the woman passed them.

'No!' Sean stood and ran. 'Stop!'

On the game trail there was an irregular object, something that didn't belong there, and Sean knew it was this that Benny had detected.

'Benny, come.'

Benny stood, seemed to hesitate, but then turned and started to come back to Sean.

'Stop!' Sean called again to the woman, but either she didn't hear him or Gemma was pulling so hard on her lead that the handler was concentrating all her attention on her dog. Gemma followed the scent all the way to the object in the pathway, with the woman in tow.

'Hey.' The woman stopped, at last. 'It's rhino horn. Right here, in the middle of –'

The night exploded.

Chapter 2

Sean couldn't work out how it had happened, but he was back in Afghanistan. The dust, the smells, the light; Benny, curious as ever as he worked off-lead, sniffing the rock wall that ran alongside the pathway that cut through the fields.

Why? he asked himself. Why had he gone back when he'd sworn he never would? Craig was there as well, ahead of them, with his dog, Brutus, just entering the outskirts of the village and approaching the first flat-roofed mud-brick family dwelling.

No! Sean tried to yell the warning, but the word wouldn't form and he couldn't stop Craig and Brutus before the wall of the compound beside them erupted, just as he had known it would. Sean saw the flash of light, felt the thump in his guts and the storm of heat, dirt and rock wash over him.

Sean was on the ground, Benny was barking, Craig was screaming. Sean knew he had to get up, to go to his friend, who had been wounded. At the same time, experience told him there would be another IED planted somewhere nearby, and an insurgent watching, waiting for someone like him to move forward to help Craig. They hated dogs, these people, feared them for their effectiveness. To kill two dogs in one day would be a victory.

Behind them an American was yelling into his radio. 'Troops in contact, troops in contact!'

'Medic!' someone else called.

Benny was up first, and even though he hated loud noises, he knew his job. Sean got to his knees, then his feet, and stumbled forward. Benny worked, all the time, sniffing the wall, oblivious to the chaos. Dogs were like people; some were better at their jobs than others. The Americans liked Craig; he was confident and outgoing, and unlike Sean, a natural leader. However, while Brutus was a good dog, Craig always said, not bothering to hide his envy, that Benny was a brilliant explosive detection dog.

Sean knew that if it were him lying bleeding and screaming in the dust, Craig would not have hesitated to charge forward, but as Sean started to jog, his feet felt encased in lead, the fear of the probable imminent explosion almost crippling him.

Benny, who was in front, stopped sniffing and sat down, ears up and tail pointing straight. He was passively indicating, silently watching a spot in the dry-stone wall where he had, no doubt, detected more explosives.

Shit, Sean thought. As he had suspected, there was another IED there, waiting for them. Somewhere, someone had a mobile phone or a garage door remote, waiting to press a button to detonate it. Sean knew he should stop, get a metal detector and check the wall, but Craig was writhing in pain in the dust. He had to get to him.

Sean ran to Benny and briefly ruffled his neck, rewarding him for making the find that might now kill them. 'Here, boy, come.'

He braced himself for the explosion, but nothing happened, and Sean ran past the spot where Benny had indicated and dropped to his knees beside Craig. 'You're going to be OK, *boet*.'

Benny trotted away, but Sean was preoccupied with his

comrade. He ran his hands over Craig, checking him and trying to still him. Sean ripped open the remains of Craig's shirt and unwrapped a shell dressing. Craig's chest was peppered with shrapnel and there was a larger hole in his side that was oozing blood.

Benny growled. Sean looked back over his shoulder and saw a man wearing a black turban climbing over the rock wall.

'Benny, rim hom!' Sean yelled, giving the command for Benny to attack. His dog's demeanour changed instantly as he switched from curious detector to attacker and launched himself up and into the Taliban gunman. Benny's jaws latched on to the man's arm as he was trying to bring his AK-47 to bear.

Sean turned and reached behind him, scooping up his M4 carbine from the dust and swinging it around. He thumbed the safety catch to fire and pulled the trigger.

Nothing happened.

*

Sean sat up on his stretcher, his bare torso drenched with sweat. For a moment he didn't know where he was. When he realised it wasn't Afghanistan, and that he had been dreaming, relief flooded through him. But it was banished just as quickly by the reality of the memories that plagued his sleep and, sometimes, his waking hours.

The nightmare was true. In real life, however, Sean had shot the Taliban insurgent, killing him with a bullet to the head as Benny had continued to savage him, but a second later the man's accomplice had rectified whatever fault there'd been in the remote detonating system and the rock wall had exploded, injuring Benny. The medics had worked first on Craig and then, while they waited for the evacuation chopper, on Benny. Sean had been left with the blood of his friend and his dog soaking into his uniform.

He knew why this memory had come back to him. He saw again the flash of light and felt the thump of the explosive shock wave that had shattered the peace of the African night, and he heard again the young woman's screams. Tumi. He had learned her name as he'd knelt beside her, holding her hand as they waited for the helicopter. While Charles had provided first aid for Tumi, Sean had worked on Gemma, her dog. The Weimaraner had taken the brunt of the blast and she was lucky to be alive, but he was not sure she would make it. Gemma's left front leg was a shattered mess of skin and exposed, jagged bone and her body had been peppered by shrapnel. Her left eye had been bleeding. Both Tumi and Gemma had left on the chopper while the rest of them waited for Craig to arrive in the *bakkie* and extract them. Sean had sat there, while they waited, hugging Benny. The past and the nightmares he had long sought to escape and subdue had vividly returned to his present.

Sean screwed his eyes tight. The permanent safari tent he lived in at the anti-poaching encampment was baking. He swung his legs over the side and, too late, remembered the broken glass. He felt the prick on the sole of his foot and snatched it back. Sean lay down again, closed his eyes and his head started spinning.

He rolled over on his side. There was no way he would make it across the glass-mined floor and out to the ablutions. He vomited on the cement slab floor of the tent.

At least Charles and Oliver, who had been dismissed to their homes in the nearby communities, were not around to see the state he was in. It was Sunday and, he remembered, he had a *braai* to go to, at Christine's house, which had once been his home. His stomach flipped. Every time he saw her it was silently wrenching for him, inevitably bringing back memories of the brief but happy times they'd had together and making him feel again the shame of their break-up and the emptiness that had followed it. He took a look at the mess in his tent and grimaced at the smell of alcohol. At least the nearly finished bottle of Captain Morgan rum wasn't broken.

He surveyed the floor. The mountains of Afghanistan, when he'd flown over them in helicopters, had reminded him of broken beer bottles, the kind people stuck on the top of breezeblock walls in the old days, before razor wire. Sean felt stupid about breaking the glass, and throwing up. He didn't binge drink very often, as he couldn't handle it; alcohol was not his preferred method of escape from reality.

Sean mapped a route through the glass and tiptoed outside. He walked barefoot to the ablutions, urinated, and found a mop, broom and a bucket. Benny's ears pricked up and he stood and came to the gate of his enclosure. Benny slept with Sean in the tent most nights, but thankfully Sean had locked him in his kennel before he got too drunk. Sean had wanted to drink himself to sleep without Benny trying to get on the stretcher with him. The dog's night home was spotless and roomy and fronted on to a grassy yard that was also fenced.

'You always look happy, even when I lock you in the doghouse.' Benny grinned and panted. 'How do you do it, my boy?'

Sean went to his tent and did his best to corral and sluice out the mess. He gagged more than once as he worked, feeling disgusted with himself. That wasn't new. He rubbed his chin. He should shave and shower before he went to the *braai*. Benny would enjoy the outing. Sean just needed to try to stop thinking about the girl and the dog lying there bleeding. Maybe he would drink again today, just not as much as last night. It was better than the alternative, and he was glad he had agreed to go to Christine's place, and not spend his weekend in Nelspruit.

'One day at a time,' he said to himself as he mopped.

Sean knew there would be more questions, from the police and the national parks hierarchy. The media would already be clamouring for people to talk to; he had deliberately not checked his phone or laptop to see what was on social media about the bomb.

His mind started to turn and he knew he would regret the path he was taking, even as he took the first steps. *What if I had gone ahead?*

Right now, he knew what he wanted, what he needed to soothe the tremor in the hands that held the mop, to banish the thoughts of the explosion and the blood from his mind. He needed the tinkle of the digital bells, the soft snickery sound of the cards leaving the shoe, the clack of the chips in his hands.

Sean wanted an escape to dull his emotions, but at the same time he gave silent thanks that he would not have an opportunity. He felt the quiet rage bubble inside him.

Benny barked.

Sean went outside the tent and looked around. Benny could use a wash after last night, and Sean definitely needed to shower. Also, the tent was still far from clean. He filled a bucket and walked towards the enclosure.

Benny's eyes widened in terror.

'Somehow, you always know when it's bathtime.' Sean laughed and tipped the water into a cut-down drum. He found the bottle of dog shampoo nearby and squirted some in.

Benny cowered in the far corner but Sean strode into the enclosure, cornered him and grabbed him. As he lifted his dog he heard a rasping sound like a saw cutting through wood.

Sean stood still and Benny whimpered and looked to him.

'Hush, boy. I know that cat scares you, but you're safe in here.'

It was unusual but not unheard of for Mbavala, the neighbourhood cat also known as Vin Diesel, to be calling in broad daylight.

Sean set Benny down in the water despite the Malinois doing his best to prevent any of his four paws getting wet. Once he was in he settled, marginally, but kept looking around, eyes and nose searching for the leopard.

The big cat ruled this part of the Sabi Sand and his territory included part of the Kruger Park across the river and along the watercourse to the Hippo Rock Private Nature Reserve, where people had holiday houses. He was the size of a lioness, a huge specimen, with muscled legs and a bullish neck that had earned him his nickname, after the solidly built American actor, Vin Diesel. His other name, Mbavala, meant bushbuck, in the local Shangaan language, in honour of his favourite prey.

Leopard, Sean knew, generally made their distinctive call when looking for a mate, and Vin/Mbavala had sired a few generations in his time. However, Sean suspected the big cat might also just be taunting his canine neighbours, who had moved in to their new home near Lion Plains in the Sabi Sand Game Reserve as rhino poaching had increased.

Sean scooped water over Benny's back and lathered him with shampoo. 'He can't get you in here.'

Benny didn't seem reassured and Sean knew just how cunning leopards were, and how highly they rated dogs on their menu.

Vin Diesel must have had sex on his mind, because they didn't hear the cat again. Sean finished cleaning Benny and lifted him out of the tub. For his efforts Sean was showered with a spray of water as Benny shook himself dry. Sean filled the bucket again and went back to his tent to finish cleaning. When he was satisfied that he had made the tent presentable again he set off to rid himself of the doggy and boozy odours that emanated from his body.

Sean stood in the outdoor shower and looked up at the perfectly clear blue sky. He had seen death, in Afghanistan, but he had hoped never to see again the terrible aftermath of an improvised explosive device.

There had been near misses in the past; poachers had been known to place a hand grenade with the pin removed under the carcass of a freshly slain rhino so that when the anti-poaching

rangers or police arrived to investigate they might be killed or
injured when they shifted the dead animal.

But this was different. It had been a properly designed IED,
similar to those he and Benny had encountered in Afghanistan,
that had injured Gemma and Tumi. This was a first for the war on
poaching, and while it had dredged up the traumas of his former
life, he wanted to take the fight to the enemy. Sean knew that as
Benny was the best EDD – explosive detection dog – in this part
of South Africa, they had important, dangerous work ahead of
them. The Lion Plains dog unit's primary role was to deter or
catch poachers and detect rhino horn and guns and ammunition.
None of the other dogs had been specifically trained to detect
bombs, like Benny had been in Afghanistan, and it would take
time to get them up to speed. Sean felt frustrated; he would have
liked to be out in the bush helping search for clues or evidence
about who had planted the bomb, but the police had told them
all to stay clear of the crime scene for now.

Sean shaved in the shower, rinsed off and dressed in shorts,
a T-shirt and sneakers. He took his car keys from the pocket
of his green uniform trousers and whistled to Benny, who had
retreated to the fence in order to keep a watch out for the neighbourhood cat.

'He's gone, Benny.'

Sean went to his Hilux *bakkie*, got in, whistled again, and
Benny jumped up next to him on the passenger seat.

*

Christine Glover held up the blue sundress and looked in the
mirror.

It matched her eyes, but she wondered if it was too short. She
surveyed her body and pulled in her tummy, just a little. She told
herself she was still in good shape.

She pulled the dress over her head, tugged it down over her

22

hips and zipped it up. She looked in the mirror again and sighed.

From the top of the chest of drawers next to the mirror she took her rings. As she slid them on she looked at the picture of her ex-husband Sean and his best friend Craig in Afghanistan.

They both had beards and wore tan baseball caps. Craig was in full camouflage gear while Sean wore a black T-shirt that moulded to his muscular upper body. They carried American M4 rifles, and their dogs were next to them. Benny was by Sean's side and poor Brutus was with Craig. Behind them was a building made of mud brick that would not have looked out of place in an illustrated version of the Bible. There was even a donkey in the corner to complete the scene. The men were grinning, arms around each other's shoulders. Benny was looking up at Sean, adoringly, maybe even a little jealously.

Christine touched the picture with a fingertip. Like the two men who had shared her life she had been to Afghanistan and was no stranger to death, but the bomb that had hurt Tumi and Gemma had shaken her. If someone was deliberately targeting dogs and handlers then that was a direct threat to her livelihood, her staff and the people closest to her.

Christine heard a car engine outside and went to the front door.

Craig drove his Land Cruiser up the long driveway of Christine's farmhouse and turned off the engine. She paused before going out to greet him. He stayed sitting in the vehicle, gripping the steering wheel for a few moments, then got out.

Christine drew a deep breath and walked out to meet him. 'How did it go?'

'Tough. I've been with the cops last night and all this morning, not to mention the Sabi Sand's warden and national parks public relations people. Everyone's worried about the use of a bomb.' They hugged and he kissed her on the mouth. 'You look beautiful.'

'Thank you.'

He smiled. 'I need to have a shave and get cleaned up.'

They walked into the house together, to the master bedroom. Craig unbuttoned his shirt, took it off and tossed it on the bed. He went into the en suite bathroom and turned on the sink tap. His torso was lean and hard, the muscles in his back well defined. Christine's eyes were drawn again to the picture on the chest of drawers.

Craig looked over his shoulder and followed her gaze before she had time to meet his eyes. 'Are you OK?'

'Yes.' Christine nodded decisively. 'Probably not the best day for a *braai*, though, after what's happened.'

He shrugged and lathered his face with shaving cream. '*Ja*, we're going to have our work cut out for us, but at least the guys can blow off a little steam. It might help them and they can talk about what happened.'

'That's what I'm worried about.' Christine sat on the bed. She could see he was tired, but she needed to be kept up to date. 'What *did* happen?'

'From the preliminary investigation it looks like the IED was command-detonated,' he said.

'You mean someone was there, waiting, to trigger it via remote or something.' She knew the terminology. The thought that this had been a deliberate ploy to take out a dog and/or a handler chilled her.

'Yes. The national parks PR people are predicting there's going to be a huge amount of interest – probably more about the dog than Tumi.'

Christine shook her head. 'Tumi's OK?'

'Yes,' Craig said. 'I know that Julianne Clyde-Smith thought that Tumi might be of interest to the media as our first female anti-poaching dog handler, but not this way.'

Christine felt a flash of anger. 'Well, Julianne Clyde-Smith may own Lion Plains and hold our contract, but this is *my* anti-poaching unit and I decide who gets the limelight. We need to protect Tumi.'

'I agree,' Craig said as he shaved. 'I think that with this new threat we have to keep her away from the press. If someone's out to get us and our dogs we don't want to make Tumi a bigger target than any of us is already.'

'Good. Sorry, I didn't mean to raise my voice,' Christine said.

'Perfectly understandable.' He put down his razor, flashed her a smile, then rinsed his face. 'It's a trying time for all of us. There'll be questions in the days to come about her level of training, and about this change in tactics by the poachers, but we don't want whoever is targeting us to learn more about us than they already know.'

'Yes. As operations manager I want you to be our main media spokesperson. Let the others know to keep quiet if the media contacts them.' Christine stood and went to Craig and handed him a towel from the rack. 'How is Gemma doing?'

'I called Graham and he drove down from Hazyview in the middle of the night, collected Gemma from Nelspruit and took her back to his surgery,' Craig said. Graham Baird was a local wildlife and domestic animal veterinarian who had recently moved his practice from Hoedspruit to nearby Hazyview. 'He had to amputate one of her front legs and she's lost the sight in one eye. The blast shook up her internal organs. Graham's not overly optimistic but he said the fact she's still alive at all proves she's a fighter.'

'Let's hope she makes it,' Christine said. 'I'll also need you and Sean to give the dogs some training in explosive detection. Other than Benny, none of the dogs can detect anything bigger than a bullet.'

'Good idea, but you know that could take three months or more.' Craig hung up the towel. 'I can work that into our selective detection training program, dig out some explosives for them to find while they're busy ignoring my dirty socks.'

'I wish I could ignore the smell of your dirty socks,' Christine said dryly as he went to the bed, sat down and unlaced his boots.

While Craig occasionally went on patrol, his primary role was managing the anti-poaching unit and, as a partner in Christine's business, he was also responsible for recruiting and training operators and dogs. Lately, he had been training all their dogs to differentiate between different human smells. Guides from the Lion Plains lodge sometimes took their guests on walks in the bush and Craig had explained to Christine that the dogs needed to be trained to not just follow or be distracted by any human scent they picked up, but to focus on the trail their handlers wanted them to follow. He had been using his own socks and clothing from the other team members as decoys while training the dogs.

'In the meantime,' Craig said, 'Benny's our only qualified explosive detection dog, so he and Sean are going to have to work overtime.'

'How is Sean?' She tried to make the question as casual as possible, but she knew that Sean, a sensitive soul despite his years of paramilitary service, would have been affected by the explosion that had wounded Tumi and her dog.

'I'll keep an eye on him.'

The reply was noncommittal, but Christine didn't want to push it. They had discussed the fact that Sean would eventually learn, if he hadn't guessed already, that Christine and Craig had become more than just friends and business partners. Christine had told Craig that she wanted to wait a little longer before he or she told Sean, maybe once they knew Sean was in a better place, mentally. In fact, Christine was waiting to see how things panned out with Craig, and whether what they had was going to be a lasting relationship instead of a rebound fling. It was difficult – Craig wouldn't be human, Christine thought, if he didn't also feel some discomfort over sleeping with his friend's ex-wife.

'You'll need a shower as well before the *braai*,' she said, keen now to change the subject.

After Sean and Christine had split, Craig had come to her financial rescue, investing in her farm and business, and she had given him the old farm manager's cottage to live in. He nominally lived either there or in a tent at the anti-poaching camp on the Lion Plains property in the Sabi Sand Game Reserve, forty kilometres away, but lately he'd been keeping his toothbrush and a couple of changes of clothes in the big farmhouse, where Christine lived.

Craig finished taking off his boots and socks and stood. Even as she watched him undress her eye drifted back to the picture of him and Sean. He stepped back from her and out of his trousers. If he noticed her looking at the picture again he made no mention of it. He raised an eyebrow. 'We've probably got time before everyone arrives. Let me shower first though, please.'

She nodded. He went into the bathroom, ran the water and stepped under. She didn't join him, but by the time he had finished and towelled himself dry she had stripped down to her bra and pants. She wanted sex with him, loved his chiselled body, but the news of what had happened was threatening to unravel her. She forced a smile.

'What's wrong?'

She shrugged, then looked up at him, realising her brave face had slipped. 'I don't know. Everything. Nothing. I'm always worried when people – you – are called out at night. You and your guys have done such a good job at Lion Plains that you hardly ever have to deal with poaching incursions any more. I've got used to having you around, safe and sound, Craig.'

He went to her and put a hand on her shoulder. 'It's all right. Sean will be OK. Tumi is going to be fine. Shame about Gemma, but she might pull through.'

'Yes. Shame,' she said. 'Audrey, the English volunteer who was staying here last month said she was amazed by the way we South

Africans use that word. She pointed out that it covers everything from a broken fingernail and a term of endearment for a cute baby to a death in the family.'

He took her in his arms and kissed her. 'Shame, but I love you, my girl.'

She sighed. 'Same. Hold me, please.'

He did, and didn't try to stop the towel from falling from his waist. He undid her bra strap as they kissed some more and ran his hands down her back, over her bottom and inside the flimsy material of her underwear. Most days she wore plain khaki bush clothes on the outside, but she liked nice lingerie and she had put the dress on for him as well. She was trying to make this work, to forget about Sean.

While she wasn't sure how much she loved Craig, she was level-headed enough to know she needed him. Now. Goddamn Sean; he had hurt her. Craig had rescued her.

He squeezed the soft skin of her bottom and she pressed herself harder against him.

For a moment she forgot Sean, the bomb, the injured dog and handler, and surrendered to the pure physical joy as he touched more of her. They moved to the bed and Christine lay back.

Craig rested a hand either side of her and looked down. 'You're beautiful, Christine Glover.'

Christine reached up and stroked his cheek. 'I needed to hear that, Craig Hoddy.'

He smiled. 'I'm glad I found you.'

'Me as well. Kiss me, please.'

He did, on her mouth, each of her breasts, and then where the warmth told him she wanted him as much as he needed her. Craig kissed the inside of her thighs as he slid her sheer pants off.

She put her hands on his shoulders and brought his face back to hers and when he entered her it felt like he was taking her away. Their first time, two months earlier, had been charged with the feverish excitement of something illicit, even though she and Sean were already divorced. Afterwards, she had felt guilty, and she had told Craig it felt like she was cheating on Sean. Craig had assured her that she was not, but that he thought it might be best if they kept their relationship from Sean for a while longer. Christine had agreed, both because it was easier for her and because, if she was honest with herself, she feared that his knowing about it might lead to Sean leaving her life completely. If they could not be together, she at least wanted to know that he was OK.

Now, as Craig slowly brought her closer to finishing, they moved in unison, both wanting to prolong this journey almost as much as they wanted it done. Christine cried out, the noise as much of a release as the act.

'I love you,' he said, as he rolled onto his side.

She propped herself up on one elbow and stole another kiss. 'Yes, I know.'

From outside they heard the honking of a horn.

'Shit.' Craig laughed, and Christine joined him as they both jumped up. As she reached for her dress and Craig rummaged through the drawer where he kept his things, Christine told herself to be pleased that she had lost track of the time.

*

Tumi Mabasa took a deep breath and knocked on the door. There was no answer.

She heard music and laughter from the rear of the house. It looked like a nice place from the outside and she guessed the *braai* was in full swing out the back. She walked down the driveway to a fence and peered over. She was stiff and sore, but other than some abrasions where a storm of rocks and dirt had blasted her exposed skin, and a nasty cut and bump on her head which had bled all over Sean, she had survived the explosion without serious injury. 'Hello?'

Craig appeared from around the corner of the whitewashed single-storey stone farmhouse. 'Tumi? What are you doing here? The doctor told me you were going to stay in the Mediclinic overnight?'

She forced a smile and instinctively touched her right side, where she had landed hard after the blast. 'He said I was fine to go, after all.'

'But surely you should be resting?'

Tumi shrugged, and that hurt as well.

'Anyway, come through, please.' He opened a gate for her and led her through.

Tumi saw from the number of empty beer cans and bottles that the party had been going for a while. She was acutely aware of the way the conversation stopped as Craig led her into the grassy yard. Benny walked up to her and sniffed her crotch. She pushed him gently aside.

Oliver Baloyi and Charles Dlamini watched her. Oliver didn't even try to hide his scowl, but Charles's look of wide-eyed surprise was punctuated with a big smile.

Charles jumped to his feet, too quickly. 'Tumi! How are you?'

'I'm doing OK, mostly thanks to you, Charles.'

'Oh, I just put on a couple of sticky plasters,' he said.

She felt self-conscious, embarrassed almost. Sean set down a bottle of Miller beer. His look was devoid of all expression. He walked over to her.

Tumi was scared. She knew of Sean Bourke mostly by reputation. She felt a fool now for the mistakes she had made on her first real-life patrol. Sean and Benny had, it was said, been responsible for the arrest of more poachers in the Sabi Sand Game Reserve than any other team of handler and dog. He had also killed men, she'd been told, in the course of his duty.

Sean came to her and stared at her with green eyes that would have been pretty if they hadn't been so devoid of any recognisable emotion.

One hand was behind his back. 'On my first patrol, in Afghanistan, with the US Special Forces, the first time me and Benny tried to cross a river, he panicked and went underwater and somehow went between my legs. He was on-lead and we got tangled up with each other, just like you did, on the chopper.'

She swallowed hard and, unbidden, felt her eyes start to prickle with tears.

'Difference was,' he went on, 'I almost drowned. But I learned a lesson.'

'I've been turning over what happened in my mind. You tried to get me to stop.'

He nodded, slowly. 'Can you learn from your mistakes?'

'I can. I'm so sorry, Sean. I was so focused on Gemma, and she was pulling me so hard that I didn't pay attention to what was going on – I was letting her control me, not the other way around, and . . .'

He held up a hand, and his solemn stare told her to be quiet. A second later his face broke into a broad grin and his eyes seemed to come to life and twinkle at her. From behind his back he produced a Savannah Light cider and a Red Square vodka drink. She took the Savannah.

'All I ask is that you learn, Tumi. Now, welcome to the team, and, ladies and gentlemen, raise your glasses, please.' Sean raised his beer. 'To Gemma, who took most of the blast. May she recover.'

'To Gemma,' the others said.

'And,' he held his beer high again, 'to Tumi, who will from this day forward be known as "Lefty" because of her two left feet.'

There was laughter from all of them except Oliver, and a clinking of bottles and glasses. Tumi smiled and gave a little bow.

'Come, let me introduce you around,' Sean said. Benny came up to her and sniffed her again. 'He likes you.'

Tumi took a sip of cider. 'I miss Gemma. I feel responsible for her nearly getting killed. She might still die.'

'It could have been you,' Sean said. 'I know it's hard, but you have to put it behind you. In addition to the police investigation we're going to do everything in our power to find out who planted that IED, Tumi.'

Tumi nodded. Just then, a woman she recognised from the K9 Force company website emerged from the back door of the house carrying a bowl of salad.

Sean turned towards her. 'Tumi, this is Christine Glover, the head of the company.'

Christine set down the bowl and came to Tumi, took her hand and gave her a kiss on the cheek. 'Howzit, Tumi, I'm so pleased you're with us today. Because Craig's responsible for recruiting and training I don't always meet our new employees before they start, but I'm sorry that in your case it had to be after this terrible thing happened. I did hope for you to go through some familiarisation training with the rest of the unit before we sent you out on your first call, but last night took us all by surprise. So, please accept my apologies for literally dropping you in it. We're all holding thumbs for Gemma.'

Tumi's lip trembled. She was almost overcome by Christine's gracious welcome. 'I'm . . . I'm sorry I let you down.'

'No such thing. We're just all glad that you're OK, but you must rest if you need to.'

Tumi nodded and saw a blonde woman, much younger than Christine, perhaps about Tumi's own age, also emerge from what appeared to be the kitchen.

'And this,' Sean said, 'is Zali Longmuir, who manages Lion Plains's Jackalberry Lodge. I'm not sure how much you know about where we work, yet, but the Lion Plains property, which we patrol, is located within the Sabi Sand Reserve and has two luxury safari lodges, Jackalberry and Ivory.'

Sean was right; Tumi was still trying to get her head around all the names of the places, and while she had studied a map of the Sabi Sand Game Reserve and checked out Lion Plains and its owner, the wealthy British tycoon Julianne Clyde-Smith online, her situational awareness was still pretty limited. Julianne owned the property, Christine had the contract to supply anti-poaching rangers and dogs, and Zali, it seemed, worked for Julianne. Tumi was pleased she could show Zali that she was fit and ready for work.

'Hi,' Zali said. 'Welcome, and nice to meet you. I'm relatively new, as well, I only started at the lodge three months ago. Shame, but you're very brave to check yourself out of hospital.'

'I don't know about brave, but thank you.' Tumi thought Zali was overdressed for a *braai*. She wore a red dress with a zipper that went all the way up the front from top to bottom and high, strappy black heels. She was very pretty, but looked like she was out to snare a man. 'You're not working today?'

'No, thank God.' She ran a hand down the front of her dress. 'This is my escape outfit. I *love* working at Lion Plains in the bush, but sometimes I just want to go to town – even if town is Hazyview – and wear something other than khaki, if you know what I mean.'

'I do.'

'I had my hair and nails done at Perry's Bridge this morning. On a day off I like to channel my inner girly-girl.'

'I hear you, *sisi*. I'll have to get the number of your hairdresser, you look amazing.' Tumi raised her bottle in a salute, but really she was just humouring Zali. Tumi was not a 'girly-girl' and all she really wanted to do was work with animals in some way and do something meaningful to help conserve wildlife. Getting her nails done was not a priority.

'Just wait until you've been out in the bush for a couple of months. You'll be *dying* for a pedi.' Zali turned to Christine. 'I don't know how your boss lady here manages to keep herself looking so perfect, what with tending to her cats and dogs every day. By the way, Chris, I'd love to see your lions some time.'

Christine's smile was thin and tight and Tumi's radar came on. Despite the apparent flattery she wondered if there was some animosity between the two women. 'Sure, Zali,' Christine replied. 'You're welcome to come for a tour any time. Same for you, Tumi.'

'Thank you,' Tumi said.

'So,' Christine said, 'where are you from, Tumi? Are you a local girl?'

'No, I actually grew up in Joburg.'

'What part?' Christine asked.

'Illovo,' she said.

'Oh, a rich girl in our midst,' Zali said, 'and here I was telling you about the decadence of Hazyview's spas.'

Zali laughed, and Tumi was sure she wasn't trying to be mean, but she did not want to be seen as the privileged rich girl out slumming it. 'My folks grew up in a rural area, near Mkhuze in KZN, but they've done OK for themselves.'

'Good for them,' Zali said.

Tumi's family were from KwaZulu-Natal – KZN – originally and were Shangaan, like the people who lived near where her team would be operating on the border of the Kruger Park. It was a particularly poor part of South Africa and her mother had confided to her once that her grandfather had often snuck into the Mkhuze Game Reserve to snare buck and hunt with his dogs. He was long dead, but Tumi had never forgotten her grandfather's fondness for his dogs; she wondered if she had inherited it, but she wasn't going to tell her new work colleagues she was descended from a poacher.

'It's been a while since I lived in the city. I was studying at varsity for a while, living away from home, but I deferred. I wanted to get some work experience and save some money, and I'm mad about animals, so I worked as a field guide at Madikwe Game Reserve for a while, but then I decided I wanted to do something to help stop poaching.'

Craig coughed. 'Sorry to interrupt, but Tumi, I need a full report from you in my email inbox by Monday morning, please. So, welcome and enjoy the *braai*, but go easy on the booze.'

She was grateful for the interruption. She didn't want to explain why she'd had to quit university. 'Yes, sir. I have to be careful in any case because I'm on painkillers. And I'll bring the report to you in person. I'm not taking any time off.'

'You take as much time off as you need. You're no good to me with one side of your body peppered with debris. And you can call me Craig.'

'Gemma, and the tree she wrapped her leash around, took most of the blast. I might not be able to work, sir, but I can still help out with the dogs, and I can still learn.'

Craig regarded her for a few moments and she wondered if she had said something wrong.

'Very well. But take it easy. When you're ready we'll pair you with your new dog, Shikar, another Weimaraner.'

'Shikar?'

'It's an Indian word,' Craig said. 'It means to hunt. She was Musa's, the guy you replaced. She's a good dog.'

'Thanks.' Tumi smiled. Zali excused herself and Sean shepherded Tumi through the backyard. The smell of sizzling *boerewors*, which Craig had returned to tending, made her stomach grumble.

Sean brought Tumi back to the other team members, Oliver and Charles. Both men had taken seats on green canvas camping chairs and they now stood.

Oliver turned away from them. 'I'm going to the bathroom.'

'Don't mind him,' Charles said when he'd left. 'Oliver used to be a sergeant in the army. He trained recruits, so he takes pleasure in being rude to people. He's a very fair person; he doesn't discriminate on the basis of race or tribe or gender – he hates everyone.'

Tumi laughed along with Charles, but she was still uneasy about Oliver. The senior ranger had said virtually nothing to her the night before, when they had met for the first time, and now he seemed to be deliberately shunning her. She would try to reach out to him.

The fact was that she had screwed up her first patrol. She would need to work hard to earn the trust of these men, even the ones who were being nice to her. Tumi felt even worse, if that was possible, because her training had been part-funded by a foreign non-government organisation called Canines for Africa that raised money to provide dogs and handlers for the fight against poaching. Despite Sean's gracious welcome to the team, she was terrified of failing at this job because she would not only have let herself down, but also the people who had invested in her training.

'Sean?' Tumi looked around, as did Sean. It was Zali. 'Please can you come and help me lay the table?' Zali called.

'I can help you, if you like,' Tumi said.

'No,' Sean said, smiling, 'you stay here and talk to Charles, and try to get to know Oliver, if he'll let you.'

Chapter 3

'Refill?' Sean said to Craig as he walked past the *braai*.

Craig checked his beer. 'I'm good, thanks. You go inside and do the woman's work.'

Sean laughed and went in. The house was pleasantly cool. Zali was in the kitchen. He couldn't help but admire the way the fabric of her dress clung to her bottom, nor notice the pale glimpse of thigh above her tan line as she got up on her toes to reach some wineglasses on a high shelf.

She looked over her shoulder and smiled. 'My knight in shining armour.'

'Housemaid, according to my best friend. Can I help?'

'Please. I need your extra inches, even in these heels.' Zali giggled. 'Sorry, I've had too much wine already.'

He came to her and she moved aside, just a little, as he took two glasses down for her. 'How many?'

'I need four of those, please. Now, tell me again where the plates are.'

He took down another two glasses. 'Bottom cupboards, the one on the far right.'

Zali must have seen the momentary pang of sadness in his eyes or heard it in his voice. 'Sorry. I guess this must be tough for you, coming to a party in the house where you used to live.'

'I'm fine.' He went to the lower cupboard and got the plates out for her.

'I hope you don't mind me inviting myself to your little get-together,' she said.

'Not at all, like I told you, I think it's great.' Sean hoped he sounded convincing. He liked Zali and what had started as a friendship, with her popping around to the anti-poaching camp to hang out in the afternoons, had blossomed into what she called a friends-with-benefits relationship. At thirty-five Sean was ten years Zali's senior, and had never had a 'FWB', but it seemed to suit both of them. He did wonder, though, if Zali wanted something more – while they tried to coordinate their days off, he felt that she put more effort into aligning their schedules than he did.

'Here, let me take those from you,' Zali said, and when she took them her fingers overlapped his and she held them there. 'How are you doing, after last night?'

He extricated his fingers. 'I'm OK. It was rough, but I'm pleased Tumi's OK.'

'Shame about Gemma.'

'Yes.' He looked away. He felt the lump rise in his throat, then Zali's hand on his shoulder. He looked at her. 'I'm OK.'

'So you say. Do you want to talk about it?'

He shook his head. 'Maybe later. But thanks for offering.'

'That's what friends are for, right?' She looked at him, into him. 'And other stuff.'

They stood there in the kitchen, she holding the plates, the wineglasses on the benchtop, neither of them knowing what to say next. Sean wondered if Zali was thinking the same thing he was.

Sean looked out the kitchen window and saw Christine standing beside Craig, who was tending the *braai*. Her hand was on his shoulder, and while she may have just been making a point, it was odd that Craig then covered her hand with his.

'Look at me,' Zali said.

He did, and her eyes were the most vivid blue he'd ever seen. He took in her full lips, the same colour as her glossy nails. It almost felt like cheating, but Christine was out there, laughing with his best friend. The thought made him feel queasy.

Then Zali kissed him and her mouth tasted sweet, like she'd been sneaking a chocolate from the bowl Christine had already filled for dessert. With her figure Zali could afford to be bad.

They moved out of sight of the window and he backed her against the kitchen counter. She felt so damned good pressed into the length of his body.

'Where can we go?' she whispered in his ear when they momentarily broke.

Sean peeked out the window again. Christine was laughing at something Craig was saying. Sean frowned. 'Follow me.'

As he led Zali by the hand down the corridor, they passed the master bedroom, where he'd slept every night with Christine. He slowed, legs suddenly heavy, and he was thinking that this was a very bad idea and not worth the risk. Despite himself he glanced inside the room.

Craig's camouflage fatigues were strewn on a chair and the floor, and his shirt was on the bed. The bed was unmade, which was very unlike Christine. She had always insisted on making it every morning as soon as she got up; she said a messy bed offended her sensibilities. Not now, obviously. Maybe she and Craig had been surprised by him honking his horn as he drove up the access road. He looked to the bureau and couldn't help but notice that the picture of Craig and him was face down.

Zali squeezed his hand. 'What's the problem?'

Sean clenched his teeth and fists, his fingernails digging into the palms of his hands. He had to tell himself to breathe.

He closed his eyes; the flash of anger was washed away by a wave of hurt. 'Absolutely nothing.'

On unsteady legs he hurried Zali on, past the guest bedrooms to the bathroom visitors used when they stayed. Sean ushered Zali in, checked up the hallway, then closed and locked the door behind them.

Zali mistook his rushing for lust, not the running away that it was. She kissed him hard as she reached down and undid his belt and the button on his shorts. This was all happening fast, but he didn't care. He unzipped the front of her dress.

'All the way,' she breathed into his ear. He did as ordered and the front fell open.

Zali reached down and wriggled out of her G-string. She was bare down there. Christine never waxed. He actually preferred the hair, but Zali's passion had inflamed him and he wanted to try to force his ex-wife from his mind right now.

'Sit up on the vanity,' he said.

'Too cold.' She turned and arched her back, bending at the waist.

He needed no encouragement. Zali's eyes met his in the mirror above the basin and she winked at him. She looked over her shoulder and he kissed her as he lifted up her dress and touched her. In her heels Zali was just right and he entered her from behind.

'Yes,' Zali said, loud enough to be heard in the kitchen along the hallway.

'Shush,' he said.

She pushed back against him and he forgot about trying to silence her as their bodies slapped together. Sean dug his fingers into her hips and Zali nodded in the mirror. He wasn't trying to hurt her, just to forget.

'Fuck, yes.' Zali touched herself as Sean moved in and out of her, savouring the vision of her mounting pleasure in the bathroom mirror.

Sean reached around and put a finger to her lips and she sucked it in, at first, then bit down on it as her body started to shake. He barely registered the pain as he erupted.

They hurriedly zipped up and kissed again. Sean looked in the mirror and wiped lipstick from his mouth as Zali brushed her hair away from her face. 'We need to get back to the party,' he said.

'Thank you, as well,' she said.

'Sorry. That was great.'

Zali grinned. 'It's OK, isn't it?'

He nodded.

'OK, you're right, let's get back out there.' Unlocking the door, she led him up the hallway towards the kitchen.

Tumi opened the back door and walked into the kitchen just as they reached it. 'Oh, hi, Zali, Christine was wondering how you were doing. Can I help?'

'Sure,' Zali said, 'if you insist. Shall we set the table?'

Sean went to the refrigerator, glancing out the window as he did so. 'Craig looks like he needs a beer.'

As he opened the fridge door and reached in to get two bottles, Sean felt Zali's hand on the small of his back. He looked over his shoulder. Tumi was busy, not watching them. Sean reached around and put his hand on Zali's. The small touch was comforting. Then he let go and went outside with the beers.

*

Later in the afternoon, after lunch, Sean sat outside in the garden with Craig, Charles and Oliver. Zali was in the house helping Christine stack dishes, as it was her domestic's day off.

Tumi had gone home.

'She was pretty beat up from the blast. I'm surprised she came,' Sean said.

Oliver drained his beer and reached into the cooler box beside his chair for another. 'I'm surprised she dared show her face.'

'That's a little hard, man,' Craig said. He had switched to brandy and Coke.

Oliver narrowed his eyes. 'She screwed up everything from the moment she got off the helicopter. I tell you, this is not a job for a woman.'

'Chill, brother,' Charles said.

'I am not your brother, Charles. I'm your supervisor.'

Sean decided he would stay out of this discussion. The more he drank, the angrier Oliver got, and Sean was having trouble keeping his own emotions in check, too. He kept thinking of Craig and Christine in his bed. *Her* bed, he reminded himself, but it didn't make it any easier to swallow. He lowered his eyelids and concentrated on his breathing.

'Sean,' Oliver said, and he looked up. 'You saw her. Tell Craig. She fucked up on the helicopter, couldn't even get off; she ignored your command to stop and she blundered into that bomb. The only thing that saved her life was that she screwed up again by getting her dog's leash wrapped around a tree that shielded her from the blast.'

Sean took a sip of beer. 'Like I told her, we all make mistakes.'

'And,' Craig said, 'let's not forget she had the courage to come here, with her wounds, to face the likes of you, Oliver.'

Oliver shook his head at the others' chuckles. 'It's not a joke. I know we're under pressure to employ more females, but she's going to put all of us at risk.'

'Well, for now,' Craig said, 'she's on light duties for a couple of days until her wounds heal, and she has to get used to working with another dog. I want you to work with her, Sean.'

'Me?'

'Yes.'

'I'm not a trainer.' He didn't want to be taken off patrol duties if there was some evil bastard setting IEDs to kill dogs and handlers. He drained his beer and tossed the empty aside, into a pile of others on the grass. 'I need to be in the field. We need to be out in the bush looking for whoever did this, not sitting here drinking and talking shit.'

Craig nodded, but smiled. 'Time for you to chill, as well, *boet*, but I hear you. Right now you've got more experience than any of the other handlers. You need to teach her how to survive this new threat. Work with her and Shikar, get her confidence up, and we'll both give Shikar some explosives detection training.'

'And keep doing your day job.' Charles laughed.

'Sheesh, Craig, that could take months, time we don't have. Stick a broom up my arse and I'll sweep the floor as well,' Sean said. Normally he wouldn't have questioned Craig's orders or judgement, but the sight of Craig's dirty shirt on Christine's rumpled sheets kept coming back into his mind.

Craig clapped him on the shoulder. 'If I didn't think you'd like it so much, *boet*, I surely would.'

Oliver finished his beer in just his third swallow. 'I say Tumi gets one more chance only. That is how I would manage her.'

Craig said nothing. Oliver was bordering on insolent, Sean thought – it was not up to him to say how Tumi should be dealt with, it was Craig's call. However, Sean could see that Craig was letting Oliver vent, rather than bringing on a confrontation. Craig had a good way with people and was a natural leader; he had to give him that. After recovering from the wounds he'd sustained in the contact where Sean had saved him from the Taliban gunman, Craig had moved to Kabul to a senior role in the company they'd worked for, overseeing the in-country training of new handlers and their dogs. Sean, on the other hand, had turned down offers of promotion to managerial positions in Afghanistan, preferring to be in the mountains and rocky deserts with Benny.

Charles stood up. 'Guys, I've had too much to drink. On that I think we can all agree.'

'This is the earliest I've ever seen you leave a *braai*, Charles,' Craig said.

Charles tossed his empty beer bottle in the bin. 'I thought I might look in on Tumi, to make sure she's OK.'

'You sly dog,' Craig said.

Charles gave an exaggerated shrug. 'What can I say? I'm all heart.'

'All something else. Be careful, man,' Craig said, his tone turning serious, 'she's had a rough time, and despite what Oliver says about her she is one of us, for now at least.'

Charles gave a salute. 'Affirmative.'

After Charles had left, followed by Oliver, it was just the two of them, Sean and Craig. Sean opened another beer, perhaps, he thought, to give himself some Dutch courage; he was longing to ask Craig what was going on with Christine, and at the same time dreading the answer. 'This is going to be my last.'

'ABF,' Craig said. 'Absolute bloody final. I'll believe that when I see it, China. Hey, you and Zali seemed to be spending a lot of time together today.'

'What about it?' Sean said, too quickly, too defensively.

Craig held up both hands in a peace gesture. 'Hey, I don't want to interfere, and you're both single and over twenty-one.'

Sean was quietly seething. What angered him, as well as Craig being with Christine, was that they were apparently intent on hiding their relationship from him, and he didn't have the balls to confront Craig about it. Sean needed to change the subject. 'What's going to happen next, about the bomb?'

Craig shrugged. 'You know how slow the cops are here, *boet*. They're calling in a forensics expert who specialises in explosives, but they have to come down from Joburg, and they're going over the scene again with a fine-tooth comb. The game has changed for us, for the dog handlers.'

'You think whoever set the booby trap was deliberately trying to get one of us, or a dog?'

'Ja. We know the poachers have been trying various counter-measures – cayenne pepper and chilli to put the dogs off the scent, even baits. We're a victim of our own success. The bad guys know that we've been a game changer and now they could be targeting us. We've got to be careful.'

Sean nodded. It had been the same in Afghanistan. There the Taliban had developed tactics to confuse sniffer dogs, planting food treats or tennis balls near hidden IEDs to distract dogs from the real thing. Taliban snipers had also been known to target dogs and handlers ahead of other soldiers.

Sean rubbed his chin. 'Since when did poachers start manu-facturing IEDs?'

'Since now, I guess. I'm hoping this bomb specialist can give us a clue as to how the device was made.'

'It's their strategy, as well as their tactics that worry me,' Sean said. 'Whoever did this killed a rhino and took its horn just to leave it as bait for us and our dogs, and then they tried to kill Gemma and Tumi. It's like they want to start the war all over again, to take out Lion Plains's rhinos, but first they have to remove us as a threat.'

'Whatever they're up to we have to be prepared for more of this shit,' Craig said. 'If they're targeting us in the bush with booby traps, they may look for us and our people outside of work too, in the townships and when we're on leave, when we least expect it.'

'It's like Afghanistan all over again,' Sean said.

Chapter 4

What Zohair Mohammed liked about Mozambique was that it bore no similarity to Afghanistan, or Iraq, or Syria, or even Pakistan.

He opened the sliding doors of his apartment and breathed in the tangy salty air. Zohair loved this view out over the sparkling blue Indian Ocean. Maputo's chaotic traffic was far enough below and behind him to register only as a backing track of horn honks and the duff-duff of car speakers with the bass turned up. The scent of peri-peri chicken sputtering on hot coals wafted up to him and made his stomach rumble pleasantly.

Lunch would have to wait. He went back into the flat. There was more work to be done.

He had been born in Africa, in the Kenyan port city of Mombasa. His parents had owned a general dealers store there, but when he was sixteen they had moved the family back to their homeland on Pakistan's north-western frontier.

Zohair's parents were devout Muslims and he had completed his education in a madrasa. After school he had gone to university in Lahore and studied electrical engineering. He had always been fascinated by electronics and even while studying he had run a small business repairing electrical appliances, radios, televisions and, as they became more widespread, mobile phones.

When the Americans invaded neighbouring Afghanistan, after the 9/11 attacks, there had been no shortage of sympathy for al-Qaeda and the Taliban mujahideen in the mountainous province where Zohair lived. The insurgents from Afghanistan crossed the border, seeking refuge, and as the war ebbed and flowed its tide washed over Zohair.

During a period of military service, he had been allocated to the signals corps, and there he had fast gained a reputation as an IT expert, with the added benefit of being able to fix various pieces of ageing equipment.

One day a man from Islamabad came to his village. He was well dressed, educated and urbane. He sought out Zohair, on the pretext of needing to get his mobile phone fixed. The man stayed in the village for a few days and made repeated visits to Zohair's shop. In time, he revealed himself as a member of Pakistan's Inter-Services Intelligence Directorate, the ISID.

While Pakistan was officially taking no part in the war in Afghanistan, and the country's leadership was ostensibly pro-American, Pakistan's secret intelligence service was quietly furthering the country's interests by providing support to the Taliban. Pakistan was wary of Iran, which was also supporting the anti-American and coalition effort, and in order to contain Iran's influence in Afghanistan the ISID was supporting pro-Pakistani Pashtun insurgents who were killing Americans. It was complicated, to say the least, but Zohair's role would be simple. His expertise in all things electronic and digital was needed, the ISID man had said, to make bombs for Pakistan's friends across the border.

He had been stupid, he now realised. He had been offered money and the recruiter had preyed on his as-then untested love of God – for this was to be jihad that he was taking part in – and his vanity.

Zohair's second problem, after his naive stupidity, was the fact that he was very, very good at what he did. He had learned, from the ISID and military officers trained in demolitions and bomb disposal, how to make improvised explosive devices – IEDs – and how to design them so that they might defeat the increasingly sophisticated countermeasures the Americans and their allies were frantically developing.

As he sat back down at the dining room table in the two-bedroom apartment and got to work soldering a circuit board, he reflected on how his skill had almost cost him his life, on several occasions.

Zohair had done so well as a bombmaker, and his devices had killed and maimed so many of the infidel soldiers, that the Americans had put a price on his head. Zohair had done most of his work in Pakistan. He and his colleagues supporting the struggle would receive notice via the ISID of military raids – token efforts designed by the Pakistani Army to placate their American allies – and have time to make themselves scarce before the soldiers arrived. However, as the war progressed, the Americans took to more unilateral actions.

They were looking, always, for the Sheik, Osama bin Laden, and the Great Satan's network of corrupt informers also survived on tip-offs about arms dealers and, especially, bombmakers.

What particularly drew the ire of the American military was not just the number of men that Zohair's devices had killed or wounded, but also the number of explosive detection dogs.

Dogs had proved early on to be one of Zohair's greatest enemies. He had studied the enemy's tactics and training and worked out ways to counter the canine threat to his handiwork.

Sometimes the simplest solution was the best. He would construct a small IED, nothing too complex, and instruct the

Taliban fighters to place it somewhere obvious, by a pathway, not buried too deeply. The idea was that the device would be detected by a dog. Then, when the explosive ordnance disposal people moved in to destroy or try to disarm the device, a much bigger, more sophisticated device, perhaps concealed in a dry-stone or mud wall near the decoy, would be command-detonated, using a signal from a mobile phone or an automatic garage door remote control. This would have the effect of killing the dog, its handler and whoever had come forward to investigate the first IED.

Tactics changed over time, though, and when the Americans and their lackeys had developed jamming devices, Zohair began switching from making bombs that were detonated by remote control devices to command wire detonation and old-fashioned pressure plates, requiring the man, or dog, to step on a switch.

Components changed, as well. His earlier devices had been packed with homemade shrapnel – nuts, bolts, screws, nails, even old kitchen forks – but as the coalition forces became more adept at using metal detectors and these became more widespread he'd had to rethink the best way to inflict harm.

This was where the natural environment came into play. The walls along farmers' fields were often made of rocks, and by planting explosives and a detonator inside a wall, then the building material itself, when flung outwards, was almost as good at killing and injuring as introduced shrapnel was.

And even if an IED did not kill, it still served its purpose. The Americans and others were scared. Their operations were slowed and hampered by the need to search for IEDs and when detonation occurred, even if a man was simply injured, then it still took time and resources to evacuate him and gave the mujahideen in the area time to escape, or an opportunity to target those experts who came to assess the blast.

His phone rang.

'Yes?'

'It is ready, the product we spoke of?' asked the man on the other end of the call.

'Almost.'

'Almost? You said it would be done by now.'

Zohair sighed. 'This is not, I am sure you understand, work that can be rushed. You will be able to collect it in half an hour, no less.'

'All right. I will be there in thirty minutes.'

'Fine.' He ended the call.

The man was Chinese, an ex–People's Liberation Army officer. He was rude. Zohair liked the African way of interacting, which was similar to his own countrymen's. A person did not come straight to the point of a conversation or business deal, one spent time greeting, asking after the other, taking time, perhaps sipping tea. The Chinese man barked like a dog.

Zohair hated dogs.

As quickly as he or his comrades changed the makeup of explosives the dogs would be trained to detect the new compounds. It was a game, where each side had to continually adapt and learn. His new enemies would learn soon, and they would be studying hard in the wake of the IED blast.

He had read about it, online, on the South African news sites and on Facebook, which he monitored. The dog's name was Gemma. He saw the picture of her, and her female handler, whose face had been pixelated out, to protect her identity. All the same he could not help but notice the swell of the woman's breasts and narrowness of her hips.

That was what Zohair had missed most about Africa, more than the sea and the sunshine and the beer (his family never knew that he drank, but he had done as a youth and had started again on his return to Africa) – more than all that, he had missed the women. He had just been discovering them when his parents had taken him back to Pakistan, where their religion had been more of a jailer than a guide. He had been a willing prisoner during the Afghan war, telling himself he had been supporting a noble cause. He wondered, now, if it was the respect and praise of the men who used him that had kept him making bombs, rather than his love of God. These days it was neither, it was money.

Zohair finished soldering, but left his rubber gloves on. He did not expect the Mozambican police, nor even the South Africans, to be as sophisticated in their forensic sciences as the Americans had been in Afghanistan, but he was not taking any chances. His DNA, despite his best efforts, was on various databases in the western world and he did not want to leave any trace on this device that might be used to track him down again. He was still on a wanted list.

He stood, stretched his aching back and went to the refrigerator. He opened the door and took out a Dois M beer, Mozambique's finest. He took the cap off this first – and definitely not the last – beer for the day and went out onto the balcony.

There was music, salsa maybe, something Latino, something undeniably sexy, wafting up on the spicy current. That was something else he had missed, especially during his brief time in Syria, where the madness of the Caliphate was all-pervasive. He was away from all that now, Allah be praised.

There was a knock at the door. He went back inside.

'Yes?' he said, one ear cocked.

'It is me.'

Zohair looked through the peephole. The Chinaman was alone; Zohair opened the door. 'Come in.'

The man wore a suit, despite the heat outside. His shoes were polished. Once a soldier, always a soldier. Zohair fancied the man might goosestep as much as walk to the dining table.

'You are finished?'

'I told you I would be. Would you like a beer?'

'No time. Business to do.'

Zohair set down his drink and went to the table. He carefully placed the device into a daypack, padded with foam. He picked up a garage door remote control.

'Command-detonated, with radio waves, as briefed,' he said.

'Good,' said the Chinaman.

'You press the red button. Red is dead, got it?'

The man nodded. 'I understand.'

'Range is about a hundred metres.'

'That will be fine,' the man said. He reached into the inside breast pocket of his suit and took out a brown envelope, which he handed over.

Zohair opened it and flicked through the wad of cash. There should be five thousand US dollars in there; not bad for a day's work, but less than ten per cent of the retail value of a kilogram of rhino horn.

'You will make ten more IEDs, yes?'

Zohair nodded. 'That was the deal, yes. I will have them ready by the allotted times.'

'We may need more.'

'Then we may need to renegotiate my fee,' Zohair said.

The Chinaman smiled. 'You think you can out-negotiate a Chinese?'

'I think you need my skills, and there is probably no one else in this part of Africa who can do what I do.'

The man wagged a finger at him. 'You are being well paid. Also, it would only take one phone call to the American embassy and you would find it would be Navy SEALS in black masks knocking on your door next time, and not someone as friendly as me.'

Zohair didn't return the smile. He had been threatened by far more dangerous men than this pumped-up little neo-colonialist functionary. There was nothing wrong with this man that a couple of kilograms of fertiliser and diesel fuel mixed up and hidden in his car wouldn't fix.

'You need me.'

'For now,' the man said.

Zohair spread his hands wide in a placatory gesture. 'Then let us not fight. Take some tea with me, if not a beer.'

'I must go. In China we value punctuality; none of this "Africa time".'

Zohair nodded and saw the man out.

He went back outside and looked at the clear blue sky.

It had been like that, the day they had come for him, in Pakistan. It had been, of all things, a bad meal of goat that had saved him. He had been collected, in a car, to be taken to provide training for some fighters who had chosen to become martyrs. He would teach them how to work the suicide vests he had prepared for them to wear, which they would detonate at checkpoints manned by the Americans and their dogs, the Afghan National Army and police.

He had gone downstairs and got into the Peugeot, but as the driver had begun to leave the curb Zohair had put his hand on the man's shoulder.

'Wait, I need to go back inside, to use the toilet.'

It had been like that all night. He got out of the car and was at the entrance to the apartment block where he lived, when a streak of smoke stained the clear blue winter's sky and a burning light descended upon the little car. Zohair had been picked off his feet and thrown inside, through the mercifully open door.

Part of the building had collapsed, blocking him inside, and his arm had been fractured and he had suffered a concussion. But the driver and the car, and four innocent bystanders on the street, had been obliterated by the Hellfire missile that had been fired from a Global Hawk Unmanned Aerial Vehicle, a UAV, or 'drone' as it was subsequently referred to in the media coverage.

The commanders had moved him after that, not just to another city or town or compound in Pakistan, as they had done previously when there had been threats; they had taken him to another country and another battlefield in the struggle.

Syria.

He had hated it there. His nerves had been on edge more or less constantly, so much so that he risked his own life every time his shaking hands picked up a soldering iron or he tried to mix the chemicals needed to make explosives. There had been rocket fire and bombing, from the Syrian government, the Americans, the Russians, the Australians, the Jordanians. As the city of Raqqa disintegrated around him so did any semblance of order that the rulers of the self-styled Caliphate might once have had. Those wide-eyed radicals did not praise or respect him, they threatened him with death if he ever so much as questioned an order.

At their direction, he had perfected the use of small drones to deliver grenades and IEDs. Ironic, since he had been nearly taken out by a UAV himself, but he had taught the Syrians and the foreign fighters how to turn small, commercially available hobby drones into frightening weapons of destruction.

Perhaps some commander with half a brain had sensed his growing disenchantment, because he had been given a wife, Yasmin, a pretty thing of Somali descent, presumably to keep him happy and committed. She had come to the Caliphate willingly, although when they were alone and she realised her new husband was kinder than most of the other fighters, and not likely to inform on her, she had confessed that Syria terrified her. It wasn't just the bombing and shelling, but it was the cruelty of the men, themselves traumatised by war and brainwashed into behaving like beasts of the jungle.

Zohair fell in love with her and Yasmin opened up to him, telling him that she wanted to go home. She took a huge risk by revealing this, and perhaps it was that she reminded him of Africa, or because he had been at such a low ebb, but he considered the unthinkable. In the moments they laid together, in between making bombs and suicide vests and modifying drones to carry hand grenades, before the fatigue overtook him, they would make whispered plans to escape.

They had been ready to leave, bags packed, but Yasmin had confided in a friend, an English-born Muslim girl, who had betrayed them. The hard men had come for him and Yasmin with dogs, in the middle of the night. What they and their dogs had done to her, in front of him . . .

Realising that he was clenching the balcony railing so tightly that his knuckles had gone white, Zohair forced himself to relax, concentrating on the whine and honk of the traffic and the beautiful, swaying music that Yasmin would have loved. It was true, he needed money to live the life he craved, to properly escape from the terrors of the past, but when the Chinaman had come to him saying he was specifically looking for IEDs that would target tracker dogs and their handlers, Zohair had been almost tempted to believe in God again. He didn't though, not any more. He believed in money, and part of him still lusted for revenge, if not against the men who had defiled and killed Yasmin, then at least their animals.

In Pashto, to call someone a dog was the most terrible insult, and Zohair had particular reason to hate these animals after he had watched the woman he loved . . . He swallowed the memories that threatened to unleash a tide of emotions. It would have been harrowing enough to have simply watched her be killed by the dogs, but there had been more. Daesh had given some sick men the opportunity to live out their most vile fantasies in the name of a cruel and sadistic deity.

Zohair spoke aloud, perhaps to a vengeful God, who might guide his hand and help him eliminate more of the loathsome creatures. 'I hate dogs.'

Chapter 5

The Sabi River Sun resort and golf course was busy on a Saturday morning so Tumi had to park her BMW 4 Series convertible on the grass just off the access road to the car park.

The long dry South African lowveld winter was coming to a close, and while the day was shaping up to be sunny and warm there was still a chill in the air in Hazyview just before eight in the morning. When Tumi got out she decided to leave her long-sleeved running shirt on over her singlet top.

It had been a week since the bomb blast and the cuts and scratches she had suffered were healing well, but like the rest of the team she still felt on edge in the wake of the violent, deliberate ambush. Gemma, the dog she had barely had time to get to know, was still in the veterinary surgery's version of intensive care.

Charles, whom she was learning was the most upbeat and optimistic guy in the unit – not to mention the cutest – thought the bomb was a one-off, but Oliver was urging caution and pushing for more patrols of the Lion Plains perimeter roads, concentrating

56

on looking for the tracks of poachers coming into or out of the reserve. The roads doubled as firebreaks, their verges cleared on either side, and Oliver maintained it would be easier there to spot places where a bomb might be placed.

Tumi was learning a lot about military tactics in these debates. Sean, who was a good teacher, if moody and quiet, said the way to defeat an enemy was to continue aggressive patrolling, deep into the bush, even if that increased their risk. Sean and Benny, as the best explosive detection team, were working long shifts and would sometimes go off by themselves for hours on end. Tumi wondered if Sean might be looking for time alone to think, but each day he also took her and Shikar on a light training patrol. In between, he was getting Shikar up to speed with detecting explosives, when Craig wasn't training the dog to track human scents selectively. The schedule was hectic and their Sunday afternoon *braai* the week before seemed more like a year ago. Today, Sean had warned her, was physical training and she was half excited about and half dreading what he had in store for her.

'Nice car, Lefty.'

She turned and saw Sean. He looked lean and wiry in running shorts and a T-shirt, legs thin and muscled, arms toned.

'Hah, hah. It's a hand-me-down from my dad,' she said.

Sean gave a low whistle. 'Sure. I'd like to see what he upgraded to.'

'I'm looking forward to some exercise,' Tumi said, wanting to change the subject. The car had been a birthday gift from her father, when they were on better terms. She didn't want Sean thinking she was a spoiled kid doing this job for fun, but nor did she want to explain how her domineering father had cut her off financially because she wouldn't follow the career path he had mapped out for her. At least he hadn't taken the car back.

Sean seemed content to drop it. 'We've only walked on patrol this week. You're sure you're fit to run?'

'I'm fine and I feel good.' She told herself she was ready for whatever he wanted to throw at her. Tumi was still embarrassed by the mess she had made of her first patrol the previous week, but she had been encouraged by Sean's friendliness at the *braai* and the walks in the bush they had undertaken since, even if it did feel like she still had her training wheels on. As Sean had told her, what they had done over the past few days really should have happened before that night insertion by helicopter where everything had gone wrong.

'Good.'

'But Parkrun?' She raised her eyebrows. 'It hardly seems like hardcore training.'

'You've never chased a man for real.'

'No,' she said. 'Only in my basic training.'

'And that was what, a kilometre, maybe?'

She shrugged. 'I can't remember.'

'If you get a hot pursuit, if we pick up the scent of a poacher, your dog is going to run as fast as it can. A man on the run, fearing for his life, is fuelled up on adrenaline. You'll have to run faster than you did in training; none of your instructors thought he was about to get a bullet in his back.'

'I understand.'

'Do you run?' he asked her.

'Sometimes.' They had exercised during training, and it was true that when she was studying she had occasionally gone for a jog. She never checked the distances or timed herself, but she ran until she was struggling for breath and had worked up a sweat. She ate well, rarely drank to excess, and liked to think she had a good figure. She could do this.

A crowd of about sixty people was coalescing for the weekly five-kilometre run.

'Why here?' Tumi asked.

'It's hard to find places to run where we work. We can't run in the game reserve because of lions, leopards and other dangerous game. Also, Hazyview's higher in altitude than Lion Plains so running will be harder here.'

Tumi grimaced. 'What have I let myself in for?'

He looked her in the eye. 'Training. We train hard . . .'

'And fight easy,' Tumi said, repeating the sentence he'd said more than once this week. 'Is that what you learned in the war, in Afghanistan?'

'You'll see.'

The blonde woman coordinating the event called the crowd together and briefed them on the run, which basically followed the perimeter of the property.

'Watch out for flying golf balls,' she said. 'And hippos and crocs in the water features.'

A few people laughed. Tumi wondered if the woman was serious. The runners moved towards the start point on the road and then the coordinator gave them the command to go.

Sean and Tumi took off, not in the lead, but among the first dozen or so runners. Tumi felt adrenaline coursing through her. She wanted to do well, to show Sean that she was fit enough for the job, and up for any challenge he decided to put in her way, and maybe even show her father that she could succeed at whatever *she* wanted to do with her life, even if it wasn't what he thought was fit for his baby girl.

Sean had a running watch, which he checked as they ran down the gentle slope and over a bridge past a water feature. Tumi saw that the woman had not been joking. There was a sign reading, 'Beware of crocodiles, hippos and bilharzia'. She had heard of the disease, borne by tiny snails.

'Keep up with me, Lefty,' Sean said.

The lead runners moved further ahead. Sean was either pacing himself or running slowly for her benefit. Tumi picked up her pace and edged ahead of him.

'You want to conserve your energy if you can, but your dog will be excited once she gets on a hot pursuit,' he said from behind her.

Tumi sucked lungsful of air. A hot pursuit was when rangers caught a lucky break or poachers were detected by one of the many means of electronic and visual monitoring used in the game reserves. If they were lucky enough to arrive just after a rhino had been killed – or better yet, when the poachers had been spotted before doing their evil business – the dogs would have fresh scent to work with.

'Shikar will run faster than she ever did in training. They know what's real and what's not.'

Tumi was breathing hard now, but Sean, still just behind her, was talking as if he was out for a stroll.

The run had started downhill, on the road, but a volunteer directed them onto the grass and up a mild gradient to the perimeter fence. Golfers waved from their buggies and called out encouragement as Sean and Tumi and the other runners raced past.

'If you let her off-lead to follow a poacher she won't slow down for you, and nor will the guy you're chasing. You want to try and keep your dog in sight.'

'Yes,' Tumi gasped. She had heard all of this in basic training.

Sean drew abreast of her. 'Don't slow down. Your dog won't and nor will the poacher; it's a matter of life or death for him. You have to be fit, Tumi. These are hard men we're up against; they're young and fearless, and they'll walk a hundred kilometres to bag a rhino and then another hundred back with the horn.'

'I know.' She couldn't keep the annoyance from her voice.

In a water feature Tumi saw the nostrils and wiggling ears of a hippopotamus. It submerged as they ran by.

'In the bush you'll have lions to think about,' Sean said. 'If they see you or Shikar running, they're going to overcome their natural urge to run away from humans and think you're prey. They might come for you.'

Tumi was finding it harder to breathe. 'Maybe just a quick break?'

'No.'

'But –'

'Don't stop, Lefty. A poacher won't slow down because you're getting tired. He'll be fired up. If you're not there when your dog catches him there's nothing to stop him drilling Shikar with his AK-47.'

'OK. And stop calling me "Lefty".' She was getting angry, but she drew on that to keep moving. She would *not* fail again. A Parkrun sign told her they had done three kilometres. Any relief she felt, however, was soon banished by the steep slope that confronted them. This was the hardest stretch of the course so far, but after the four-kilometre mark she could tell it was mostly downhill to where they had begun. Tumi sucked in deep breaths as they moved back onto a road, in between timeshare holiday houses, and ran towards the finish line.

'Pour it on, Tumi. Faster. Imagine you're catching him.'

'Yes,' she puffed.

The course had a final cruel trick, with the last couple of hundred metres uphill back to the car park. They had their times recorded and Tumi headed for a water dispenser.

'Not too much of that,' Sean said.

'Why not?'

'Come with me.'

She followed him – he didn't even stop for water – to his battered little car. He opened the hatch, reached in and pulled out a tracking lead.

'What is . . . what's that for?' she said between gulps of water. She was actually quite pleased with her time and the fact that she hadn't stopped running, even though she had wanted to. If Sean thought she had made a good effort, he didn't say.

'I'm your dog.' He unfurled the ten-metre-long lead.

'What do you mean?'

'We're going around again.'

'Around the whole course? Are you serious? Another five kilometres?'

'Poachers aren't on a Parkrun, they're running for their lives, and if you can only run for twenty-five to thirty minutes they'll easily outdistance you. Come.'

'I'm not a dog.' She wiped her mouth. 'Do *not* talk to me like that.'

He smiled. 'No, like I said, *I'm* the dog now.' He wrapped the end of the lead that would be attached to a dog's harness around his right hand and wrist and handed her the looped end. 'Woof woof.'

'You're not serious.'

He took off, running, and Tumi felt like her arm was going to be yanked from its socket. The empty plastic cup fell from her hand and she reluctantly ran after him, not letting go of the leash.

Sean looked back over his shoulder. 'If you let go of the lead you add another kilometre to the run.'

'We're not on duty,' she said as she ran after him. 'You can't order me around.'

'No, but you said you wanted this, to become a better handler. Do you think Oliver would be nicer to you?'

Tumi was furious now, but she channelled her anger into every footstep. Other runners, those who had been following them, laughed and waved as Sean ran past them, Tumi in tow.

'Sean, enough.'

He ignored her pleas, instead increasing his pace. The water Tumi had drunk was giving her a stitch in her side. She was fighting a rising feeling of panic. 'Sean!'

Sean carried on uphill, skirting a green. Golfers paused, mid-putt, to whistle and jeer at them. Tumi wanted to swear at them and tell Sean to stop this stupid game, but she didn't have the breath to speak. If she slowed she felt him tugging on the lead, pulling harder, running faster.

'You need . . .' He took a breath. Even Superman was finding this hard. 'You need a lead if you work at night. Then the lions . . . are out for sure . . . and you could get lost . . . if you lose your dog . . . or one of you will get eaten.'

Tumi glanced at the Sabie River as they ran alongside it and saw a splash. The danger of their job was sinking in. 'Sean . . . I . . . get the . . . point.'

She could definitely talk no more and wondered when this torture would end.

Sean was puffing hard now, but he was relentless. Tumi's legs were turning to jelly and she stumbled. For three long, crazy steps she thought she was going to fall, but she held on to the loop of the lead.

'Do *not* let go.'

'Won't . . .'

Tumi was sure she was going to die on this run, and now that Sean had stopped talking he seemed indefatigable. She gagged. The breakfast of a banana and a smoothie she'd had was coming up.

'Sean . . .'

'Don't stop.'

Tumi tripped and fell headlong. Luckily they were on grass. She rolled and when she got up onto her knees she threw up. She looked up through watery eyes and saw Sean staring down at her.

'Get up.'

'Fuck you!'

'What?'

'I said, fuck you.'

'Quitting, Tumi?'

'This is . . . this is . . . cruel.' She gagged again. 'And unnecessary.'

He had his hands on his hips and was breathing deeply. 'This is *nothing* compared to chasing a poacher through the thornveld in forty-degree heat for a couple of hours until you and your dog are nearly dead, and then having to face the prospect of gunfire. Do you want this or not?'

Tumi wiped her eyes. He was getting at her; Mister Nice Guy was gone. She wanted to be sick again. She wanted to lie down and die. She wanted to go home. Tumi breathed deep, trying to stop the panic from overtaking her.

'Up to you.'

She hated this man right then and there.

'What do you say, Tumi? Want to call it quits?'

Tumi got up. She spat. 'No.'

'Then pick up the bloody lead.'

She glared at him for a few moments then bent over and took up the loop.

Sean set off. Tumi followed him and she ran as hard as she could, harder than she ever had in her life. Despite her age and lithe build, and what she'd thought was a reasonable level of fitness, she wondered if she was going to have a heart attack.

Fuck him, she thought. Tumi put on a burst of speed and drew level with Sean.

'Do you want this?' he huffed.

'Yes.'

'How much?'

They were on a downhill, which helped, but even so her vision was swimming and blood was pounding in her brain as she overtook him, until she could feel tension in the lead and she was pulling on him. Immediately, she felt the lead go slack. Tumi looked back and saw Sean was slowing to a walk.

She stopped, bent at the torso, hands on her knees. 'Why, what?'

'Enough running for one morning,' he said.

'Then why do this if you didn't intend on going around again, and what happened to the extra kilometre?'

He smiled. 'I just wanted to see if you had it in you; if you'd get up again after you fell.'

*

Later, in the afternoon, Sean and Benny walked along the bank of the Sabie River. He liked this stretch because it was not choked by papyrus or long grass where a sleeping buffalo might lie, unseen, until the moment they disturbed it and accidentally whipped the seemingly indolent creature into a malevolent rage.

Walking on the sand, Sean could also keep an eye out for the telltale marks in the sand where a crocodile might have dragged its tail before entering the water.

A fish eagle cast a fleeting shadow, preceded by its lilting, sorrowful call. Sean shielded his eyes and looked up. The bird caught sight of some prey and dived, talons out, and rippled the surface of the river. With wings beating furiously it carried on, its glistening silver trophy, a young bream, wriggling in its grasp.

It was an aptly named river – Sabie was derived from the word for fear in the local language – and there was danger lurking everywhere along this beautiful yet treacherous waterway.

Sean loved it.

He had dreamed of it, when he was in Afghanistan. When times were tough, as they often were, Craig had cheered him up with a simple, 'We'll be back in the bush soon, *boet*,' and it worked every time.

Benny loved it as well. He ranged ahead of Sean, not working, but at the same time doing what he liked best, searching and sniffing and just being a dog.

Sean carried a fishing rod; he would be hunting tiger today – the hard-fighting tigerfish. He and Tumi nominally had the afternoon off, with Craig on standby if a dog and handler were needed, but as Sean had told Tumi, they were always on patrol when they were in the bush, even in their downtime, and always needed to keep their wits about them. Game reserve staff were allowed to fish at a few designated spots, out of sight of paying guests on safari.

'Find me a fish if you're such a clever dog, Benny.'

Benny looked back at the sound of his name, grinning, tongue lolling. He snapped at a fly that buzzed around his head. Sean laughed.

Benny trotted on. Sean paused and undid the buckles on his Rocky sandals. The sand was getting into them so he shook them, clipped them together, and threaded them over his webbing belt. The coarse river sand was warm on top and cooler below.

He had no idea what to do about Zali. Well, that wasn't completely true. Sex with her was fun, but he didn't think he was ready for a new relationship. He'd had a few girlfriends before Christine, but apart from a couple of casual encounters he had never been into one-night stands. The thought of Christine, and of Christine with Craig . . . He forced his mind to veer away.

He had always focused on his job, which had probably saved his life – he just needed to make sure that it now didn't kill him or Benny. With work in Afghanistan and other conflict zones drying up, he'd had to find something to do back home in South Africa, and he'd known that most of his options, if he couldn't get into anti-poaching work, would be in cities. That was a problem, as just about every South African city of a reasonable size had a casino.

People who lived and worked in the Sabi Sand Game Reserve, where Lion Plains was situated, generally left the game reserve when they had time off, but not Sean. If they didn't go home they flocked to the city, even if it was only nearby Nelspruit, to find bright lights and bars, company of the opposite sex, films, live music – anything that wasn't the bush.

There were a few die-hard guides who went into the Kruger Park, camping, or to other reserves, but Sean didn't have the money to pay for even a single night in a national parks rondavel in Punda Maria or Shingwedzi rest camp in the north of the park. Off-duty rangers always headed to the top end of the Kruger, to escape the crowds of tourists that thronged the southern roads and camps.

So Sean stayed in camp with Benny, when they had leave, and they made the most of the perfect dry season days. Sean fished, or read, or walked and Benny played, which was the same as work. Sean hoped that one day he would be free of his debts and he could start saving, for himself. He had never sailed, but fancied he would like to learn, and, in his dream, he would buy a boat and he and Benny would sail around the world, just the two of them.

Sean heard another fish eagle cry, or maybe it was the same one. He scanned the sky. Benny barked.

Sean looked down. Benny had doubled back and was now hunched down, indicating. Sean froze when he saw the snake.

'*Mfezi*. Benny, come, back away, boy,' he said quietly.

The Mozambican spitting cobra, *mfezi* in Zulu, reared up, its hood flaring. It swayed in front of the dog.

'Benny!'

Sean knew Benny was just protecting him, keeping himself between Sean and the serpent, but he also knew what was about to come next. 'Come!'

Sean dropped his fishing rod and reached for the nine-millimetre Glock pistol in his holster, but he was too slow. The cobra opened its mouth, fangs shining white, and spat a jet of poison straight into Benny's eyes. The dog yelped and barked and backed away.

Pistol drawn, Sean reached down and grabbed Benny's collar and yanked him out of the way of the next spray. The snake found a new target, leaning back and aiming at Sean's eyes. Sean felt the fluid sting his cheeks, but his sunglasses spared him the same damage that had been inflicted on the whimpering Benny. With the lenses clouded he couldn't take good aim, but he fired two rounds in the snake's general direction and the startled creature slithered away into the grass.

'You dumb, brave boy.' He unclipped his gun belt and let it fall to the sand, then scooped up Benny. The canine wriggled in his arms, trying to escape the pain that would blind him unless Sean acted fast.

Sean ran to the river and strode into the cool, fast-flowing water. He plunged protesting Benny's head into the water, clawing at the dog's eyelids to try and keep them open.

'I'm sorry, *bru*, but this is for your own good.'

Benny came up spluttering and barking, clearly unhappy at this enforced bath, and still whining from the pain of the acidic venom. Sean dunked him again and Benny fought harder still. Sean was drenched.

'Hey!'

He looked around and, to his surprise, saw Tumi, dressed in shorts and a T-shirt, running through the thick sand. At her heels was Shikar.

'Are you *crazy*?' Tumi called.

'Benny's just been sprayed in the face with *mfezi* spit.'

'*Eish*,' Tumi said. 'I'll be back. Come, Shikar.'

Woman and dog turned and went back the way they'd come. Sean pushed Benny under again and the growl that came from his dog when he surfaced was nastier than anything he had ever directed at him.

'Come out of the water before you get eaten by a crocodile.' Tumi and Shikar returned and Tumi was carrying a thermos flask. 'Set him down on the sand, by the water. Hold Benny down and keep his eyelids open.'

It was easier said than done, but when Sean had restrained

Benny as best as he could, and managed to pull back his eyelids, Tumi knelt next to them, at the river's edge. She used the cup from the top of her thermos to scoop fresh water and pour it directly onto Benny's eyes.

Benny tried to blink it away, but over and over again Tumi washed each eye.

'That's a little better,' Sean said. 'I hope we got it in time.'

'Keep holding him.' Tumi set down the cup and unscrewed the lid of the thermos. She held it above Benny's eyes.

'What's in that?'

'Rooibos tea,' she said. 'It's not too hot.'

'Tea?'

'Yes.' She poured the aromatic liquid carefully into each eye. 'It's got a soothing and mild antiseptic property. I learned about it in veterinary school and my mom once used it on my little brother when he was playing around a euphorbia tree and got some of that terrible white sap in his eye.'

'Wow,' Sean said. The bright green, spiky *Euphorbia candelabra* tree, common in the Kruger Park and its surrounds, was well known for its potentially deadly sap, which locals used to poison waterholes to kill fish, and, in days gone by, to coat the tips of arrows for hunting game. Sean had brushed against a branch while chasing a poacher once and the milky fluid had left his skin burned and blistered. 'Vet school?'

Tumi nodded as she continued rinsing Benny's eyes. 'I did a Bachelor of Science and a year at the vet school at Onderstepoort. I was going to be a veterinarian.'

'It's a tough course, I've heard,' Sean said. 'Stop wriggling, Benny.'

'It is. But I didn't fail.'

'Then why did you quit?'

'I didn't quit. Well, I kind of did. My father was putting enormous pressure on me to switch to a different course.'

'It's soothing him,' Sean said. Benny was still whimpering, but he was not protesting as violently as he had been. Tumi kept dripping the tea into Benny's eyes. 'Why did your dad want you to change? That's a prestigious place to study.'

'It is, but my dad thought there was a stigma attached to people becoming veterinarians.'

'How come?'

'It's about working with animals. My dad sees them as, I don't know, unclean or something like that. My dad said he would be embarrassed to tell people what I did if I became a vet. He'd rather me be a people doctor, or even a dentist or a radiographer than a vet. Good boy, Benny, you'll be fine.'

Sean nodded. The way Benny was responding to Tumi's gentle touch made him think that the animal world was the poorer without a vet like Tumi might have been. He had been born in Durban and learned to speak Zulu before he spoke English, thanks to his African nanny. He knew how important family was to Zulu people, and how difficult it would be for any child, but especially a girl, to defy her father. Still, Tumi did not strike him as the shy, demure type.

'I tried to study vet science anyway, even when my father stopped paying my university fees and my allowance. I applied for a bursary but didn't get it as my folks earn too much money; my father is a senior partner in an accounting firm.'

'Hence your car. You quit instead?'

'I got a job instead. I wanted to work with animals, with wildlife somehow, so I applied for a job as a trainee ranger in Madikwe Game Reserve. I got my FGASA qualifications and worked for them for a couple of years.'

Sean was impressed, and glad his instinct had been right. Tumi had guts and was not afraid to stand up for what she wanted.

Tumi ran out of rooibos tea, but went to the river and filled her flask with more water.

'I'm sorry, Benny, treatment isn't finished yet,' Tumi said.

'You didn't want to stay working as a guide?'

'I liked the work and learned a lot.' She shrugged. 'But, you know, the longer I spent in the bush the more depressed I got about the problems with poaching. I saw a rhino that had basically had its whole face removed, the bone of its skull was showing, but it was still alive. The poachers hadn't even bothered to finish it off, and it died in front of me. I cried all that night and I decided I had to do something to help stop all this senseless slaughter. I thought that by educating the well-off tourists who came to the lodge I could get them passionate about conservation and hopefully they might be inspired to donate money or whatever, but it wasn't enough.'

'You wanted to do more?' Sean felt like a fraud.

'Yes. If I couldn't complete my studies and help heal animals as a veterinarian, then I figured that if I took on something like this, I could at least help *protect* wildlife, and do something good. You know the feeling, right?'

'Yes,' he lied. He nodded. She was educated, black and female. She ticked all the boxes for advancement in virtually any job in South Africa and Sean did not, for a moment, resent that. If he had been born twenty years earlier he would have been guaranteed a job simply because he was a white male. He wouldn't even have needed an education.

'It must have been the same for you?' Tumi said.

Benny had settled. The tea and the continual dousing with water had flushed the venom from his eyes. Sean eased his hold on him and Benny didn't whimper. Instead he shook himself, covering them all in droplets of water. He wandered over to Shikar and sniffed her bottom.

'Dogs, hey?' he said.

'How did you end up here in the middle of nowhere?' Tumi asked, pressing him. 'I heard you and Craig worked in Afghanistan. That must have been hectic.'

'It had its moments.'

'And I've heard some of the other handlers say the money is *amazing* in places like that.'

He nodded.

Tumi's shoulders sagged. 'I'm worried now that I don't have the military experience that you and Craig and Oliver have. I guess what you really want is people who have been in the army or police.'

Sean shook his head. 'Not at all. That's a common misconception. Christine and Craig turn away ex-military dog handlers quite often, and they get foreign veterans offering to help all the time. Craig and I actually worked as field guides, like you, for a couple of years after we left school, that's how we met, on a training course. We both left in search of more action – me to the police and Craig to the army for a while – but we stayed in touch and we both ended up in Afghanistan working as dog handlers.'

'Did you join the American or British army or something like that?'

'We worked as civilian contractors,' Sean said, 'employed by the US Army. We worked with their special forces. The point is, Tumi, that despite what we did overseas, in our hearts Craig and I are bush people. That's what we want here. You're actually an ideal candidate for this job, because you know the bush and how to work around dangerous game. What you'll learn – I hope sooner rather than later – is that what happened to you and Gemma is usually way out of the ordinary around here. For the last few months we've had very little action. We don't need Rambos in this job, we need people who are happy to just walk in the bush with their dog on a nine-hour patrol or sit in an OP, an observation post, and be happy if all they see is birds. Sure, we need to be alert for new and changing threats, like the IED you and Gemma came across, but don't let your lack of military experience worry you.'

'Thanks. I'm sorry if I talk too much, ask too many questions, but I know I've got so much to learn and I'm so grateful to you for agreeing to mentor me.'

Is that what it was, Sean wondered, mentoring? It was more like he was her last chance. Tumi had the makings of a good dog handler and she was very smart, but she needed to trust her instincts and her dog's a little more rather than try and remember everything from the training manual.

'I read a book about dog handlers in Afghanistan,' Tumi continued. 'I think I'd be too scared to go to a war zone.'

He had to laugh.

'What's so funny?'

'You were almost killed by an IED.'

It was Tumi's turn to shrug. 'Part of the job.'

'In Afghanistan, maybe, but not here. You have to be careful, have to learn fast and work with your dog. It's not just an animal on the end of a lead; you need to have a bond with Shikar, and for the two of you to understand each other, intuitively.'

'I hear you. I think. But the pay here can't be as good as in Afghanistan. I'm not nosey, I'm just wondering what brought you to this war instead of a better paying one. I mean, I'm not trying to insinuate that you're a mercenary or whatever, I'm just curious.'

She wanted him to be an idealist, like her, but Sean's story was different, not so high-minded.

'We all have our own reasons for doing this job, any job, I guess.' Too late he realised he'd probably been too evasive.

Tumi put her hand on her mouth. 'Oh my goodness. I'm so sorry. I didn't think that maybe you don't want to talk about some of the stuff that happened to you over there.'

That was part of it, but not all of it. He couldn't put his hand on his heart and tell her he was hiding out here in the bush because of what he had seen in Afghanistan. He didn't deserve to play the part of the troubled veteran, the brave soldier hiding the unseen wounds who turned to the solace of the African bush to help heal himself.

Sean was a thief.

He looked her in the eye and her naivety, her enthusiasm, her honesty and her innocence touched him. But she was right, she asked too many questions.

'Thank you for looking after Benny.' *He's all I've got*, he almost said. But that would invite her pity, and simply open the flood-gates to more interrogation. Sean was hiding. No one other than Craig and Christine, and now maybe Zali, needed to know why.

'Want to come fish?' Tumi flashed him a big smile.

He did. It was what he had come out for. He liked Tumi, but he could not bear the thought of having to deflect, let alone answer, more of her questions.

'I think maybe I'll take Benny to the vet, just to check those eyes.'

'OK.'

He saw the look on her face. She held the smile, but he suspected he had just wounded her. 'It's not that I don't think you did a great job, Tumi. Far from it. For all I know you probably saved Benny's eyesight, and his job.'

'It's no problem,' she said too quickly, 'I was going to suggest you take him to the vet in any case.'

Sean stood. He felt awkward, not knowing how or if he'd hurt her and, if he had, how he could make it right. 'You're going to be a great handler, Tumi.'

She glanced up and gave him a small smile. 'Thanks,' she said quietly. 'I would have liked to have been a great vet.'

'Maybe you still will be, one day,' he said.

She bit her bottom lip. He turned away and called to Benny.

Chapter 6

Christine Glover's phone beeped as she and Zali walked the fence line of her property near Hazyview, forty kilometres west of the Sabi Sand Game Reserve where her canine anti-poaching unit was based.

The lowveld winter morning was cool and crisp, the grass the colour of gold. After the *braai*, Zali had called Christine, taking her up on her offer of a tour of the farm. They had scheduled it for the weekend. Christine didn't dislike Zali, and as a senior member of the Lion Plains management team it was important for her to get on with the younger woman, but they were very different people. Zali's job was all about keeping up appearances, not least of all her own, and pandering to wealthy tourists, whereas Christine was more at home on her farm, with her beloved animals.

'Excuse me,' Christine said to Zali as she took out her phone.

Christine checked the screen. It was an email telling her that her bank account had received a payment from Sean. It was for ten thousand rand.

She sighed. The money came in, every month, but it wasn't part of any divorce settlement. It was Sean trying to make up for the crime he had committed. He hadn't been charged by the police or convicted by a court, but Sean had stolen from her and he was doing his best to pay her back.

The trouble was that at this rate it would take Sean about ten years to repay his debt to her. She had overcome her anger and forgiven him, mostly; however, she would not tell him to stop. He'd said he wanted to make amends and she did not want him to relapse. She knew what he would do with that ten grand if he was not sending it to her. As bitter as things had become between them, she did not want to see him destroy himself.

Sean was a good man.

'Bad news?' Zali asked, no doubt seeing the look on her face.

'Good and bad. Nothing to worry about.'

A lioness made the soft, low two-part grunt that was as close to a roar as the female felines got. Christine and Zali went to the fence and peered in. Meg, the lioness, was calling to her cubs.

'Shame!' Zali couldn't contain her excitement. 'They're too cute.'

Christine gave an indulgent smile. The four tiny, squeaking bundles appeared one after another from the long grass where they had been playing. As much as she loved seeing them, she knew that these would be the last lions born on the farm she had bought, Hunde und Katzen. The name meant dogs and cats, in German. The former owners had bred lions, commercially, but Christine had vowed to make not a cent out of these cats or any of the other hundred that remained. These lions had been bred with one end-purpose in mind: to be killed. The less sinister part of the farm was the dog-breeding kennels at the far end of the two-hundred-hectare game farm. The former owners had bred Belgian Malinois like Benny, many of which were supplied to canine detection companies operating in Middle Eastern conflict zones, especially Iraq and Afghanistan.

However, foreign military interventions were winding down in those countries and the dog-breeding business had become less and less profitable. Christine had bought the farm knowing it would probably not turn a profit in the short term, but she had bigger plans for her tract of bushland and the animals that had come with it. Dogs were proving to be a game changer in the war on poaching and it was this domestic market for trained dogs and handlers that Christine wanted to develop. While police, military and national parks service dog units were employed in government-run national parks, private game reserves also needed canines to help with anti-poaching, and these had to be supplied by commercial operators.

The lioness lay down and her cubs came to her and began suckling. Christine smiled as she watched the hungry little ones climbing and falling over each other in their eagerness. As delighted as she was to see this simple, natural scene, she knew it was wrong.

'The fact is,' Christine said, 'these cubs were an accident. I was doing my best to keep the lionesses separate from the males, but one of my lions, Casper, a randy bugger, managed to get into the females' enclosure after one of my staff left a gate open.'

'Oh, dear. What will happen to these little guys?' Zali asked.

'The previous owners of the farm ran a tourist business for people who wanted to come and pat a lion cub. Animals such as these would have been quickly weaned from their mothers and then raised on bottled milk, more often than not fed to them by gleeful tourists and paying volunteers.'

'Can I feed one?' Zali asked.

'No. There's not going to be any more cub petting here, or breeding, for that matter.'

'How come?'

'As cute as they are, Zali, if we start handfeeding these cubs we're robbing them of anything like a normal existence for the rest of their lives. As it is they're going to die in captivity. If we get them habituated to humans now they'll rely on us all the time.'

'But they do, anyway.'

'True,' Christine said, 'but if we can at least let them live together like normal siblings and grow together they'll have a better quality of life. At least they're not destined to be shot by hunters, which would have been their fate before we took over this place.'

'Even though I've worked in lodges I'm a Joburg girl,' Zali said, 'so this might be a silly question, but tell me why you can't release your lions into the wild?'

'Lions are social animals; the pride structure is the bedrock of their lives. As big and as strong as my males look, they've never had to fend for themselves, and if I let them out into the wild then the resident males would kill them straight away, to stop them trying to mate with their pride females. My females would never be allowed into an existing pride and, besides, they would have needed to be trained from birth by their mothers to hunt.'

'So what will happen to these cubs and the other lions?' Zali asked.

'In the past, some of them were raised as *wild* lions, which means that instead of the cubs being weaned they were left with their moms in larger enclosures, though they still had to be fed. Basically, it was an easier way for the owners to raise them. When the males got to the age that they would have been kicked out of the pride in their natural habitat they were taken away, to separate enclosures, and kept until their manes were big enough for them to make a suitable trophy animal. After that, they were set free in B Plot, a larger enclosure, allowed to supposedly roam free for a bit, then shot.'

Zali gave a shiver. 'That's barbaric.'

'Yes, and it was business. The female cubs, in time, would become breeders, perpetuating the whole industry.'

'So that's what people mean when they talk about a *canned* hunt?' Zali asked.

'Yes, basically the lion has no chance. It's like shooting fish in a barrel, as the Americans would say.'

'That sounds ridiculous.'

'Yes, and it was. The reality is that if you have an animal that has spent its life in a cage, being fed regularly, and then you release it in a hundred hectares, it is going to be confused, disorientated, and hungry. The other thing that was undeniable was that even if it took an extra few hours or a day or two more, it would inevitably be found by the hunters and shot.'

'I don't get it,' Zali said. 'I mean, I've met hunters, at the lodge, and a cousin of mine shoots springbok on a farm in the Karoo, but I don't understand how anyone could shoot any animal.'

'My father hunted,' Christine said.

'Really?'

'Yes, but he only ever shot for the pot, that is, he made sure that any animal they killed was for food. Mostly he hunted kudus and impalas. My dad only hunted on foot; he taught me to track. I know he and Mom wanted more kids, including at least one boy, but she couldn't have any after me. So I was both son and daughter to my dad, and he asked me if I wanted to hunt, but I said no. Quite often he would come back from a three-day safari with nothing to show for it, other than the fact that he'd enjoyed being out in the bush.'

'I kind of get that,' Zali said, 'and I guess my cousin is the same.'

'Everyone has a line they won't cross,' Christine said. 'You have yours, about what you would and wouldn't do, and I have mine. Some people are vegans, refusing to have any animal killed for their benefit. My father's line was that he wouldn't kill an animal solely for a trophy.'

The lioness was tired of feeding the hungry little mouths so she stood. One tenacious cub refused to let go of the teat and clamped down with its sharp little teeth. Christine and Zali both physically winced at the sight of the cub being dragged along for a few steps before the mother shook it off.

'Now that has to hurt,' Zali said. 'What will happen to all these lions now?'

'Well, this is definitely the last litter to be born here. All of my lionesses have now been darted with contraceptive drugs.'

'It all seems so . . . I don't know, artificial?'

Christine nodded. 'You're right. Humans have created this mess and these poor animals will have to live out their days in captivity. The challenge for me, for us, is to make sure that the time they have left alive is as stimulating and rewarding for them as it can be. Also, I want everyone who passes through this place to learn about canned hunting and lion cub petting and how one is related to the other.'

There was silence for a moment and Christine could see Zali chewing over everything she'd said, a slight frown on her face.

'Let's go see the boys,' Christine said.

'Yes!'

Inwardly, Christine gave a little groan. She knew that for all her earnestness, Zali, like the well-meaning volunteers Christine sometimes allowed to stay on the farm, was secretly only here to see her interact with her two favourite lions, Felix and Casper.

Christine had a public profile as the female lion whisperer. There was already a male one, Kevin Richardson, and when a friend had taken a video of Christine rolling about in the grass with the two fully grown male lions, she had posted it on YouTube. It had gone viral. Christine had no desire to compete with Kevin on the world stage and she admired the work he did as a global ambassador for the plight of wild lions, but nevertheless she had found herself a theatrical agent and occasionally took on a filming job to help cover the costs of keeping the lions. She hoped an added benefit of any publicity she gained would be drawing attention to the problems big cats were facing around the world. Felix and Casper had appeared in everything from television commercials for cat food and cars, to roles in feature films. The lions also brought in the paying volunteers and Christine needed their money.

Zali got her phone's camera ready while Christine opened the first of the two security gates on her beautiful boys' enclosure.

Just the sound of metal on metal must have roused them from their snoozing because Christine soon saw movement through the trees ahead on their lovely bushy plot of land. The first shaggy mane came into sight, and from its blond hue she knew immediately that it was Felix. She would never admit it publicly, but he was her favourite. He needed the most love and affection. While Casper sometimes barely deigned to let her touch him, eventually he would become jealous of Felix and would push or bite his way through to her.

'Hello, my beautiful boy,' Christine said to Felix as he bounded up to her.

Christine was a little over five foot seven, but she still stood only eye to eye with Felix. She braced herself for the impact of the big shaggy head that bumped into hers and she rubbed herself against him. He didn't smell cat-like, as people usually imagined; it was more of a rich, dry smell, earthy and warm. She scratched him behind the ears. At the fence Zali was madly clicking and videoing away, but Christine allowed herself to just relax in the company of her big friend.

Felix and Casper were like brothers to her. She had raised them from cubs when her father had rescued them from a hunting farm near where they lived and transferred them to Hunde und Katzen when she'd bought it.

'That's amazing,' Zali said. 'I mean, I've seen you on TV once, but in real life it's even more incredible.'

Christine stood and heard Zali gasp as Felix reared up on his back legs and she caught him in an embrace that looked like a clumsy dance step. Christine staggered a little, but Felix knew to ease off before she fell over. His two-hundred-kilogram bulk seemed to get heavier all the time, even though he was fully grown.

Casper wandered up to them, trying not to look like he cared about all the affection Felix and Christine were sharing.

'I haven't forgotten about you, don't worry,' Christine said soothingly.

Felix and Casper bumped heads, with Casper emitting a low growl to let his brother know it was time for his share of the love.

Christine sat down in the grass and the two lions plonked their ageing bones down next to her, with Casper making sure his head was in her lap first. As he rubbed against her she was pushed backwards so that she was looking up into the clear blue sky. It was tempting to just forget about Zali and her day's work-load and to fall asleep here with her feline big brothers.

She did, however, have to be careful. Christine was often asked if she worried that one day Felix and Casper might suddenly snap and kill her, as had happened to more than one owner of captive-bred big cats. She was only half joking when she answered that the biggest risk she faced was one of her lions falling asleep on top of her and squashing her. It had nearly happened once. Casper had been off somewhere pretending not to be jealous and a particularly tired Felix had lain across her breasts and fallen asleep. Christine had found herself being suffocated. Every time she had taken a breath his weight had compressed her lungs a little more until she realised she couldn't get enough air in. She had yelled, poked and prodded him, but it wasn't until she managed to get a finger into one of his eyes that he woke, rather startled and unhappy.

'Up you get, Casper,' she said now, and the lion reluctantly rolled over onto his back, soaking up the sun.

Christine used the opportunity to stand and brush herself

down. A stray claw had ripped her shirt, but not touched her skin.

'I buy all my clothes from Mr Price,' she told Zali as she walked to the gate, indicating the tear. 'I go through a shirt a week.'

'That was awesome,' Zali said.

Christine smiled. She had performed her trick, but if she was honest, she never minded spending time with her boys. She closed and locked the gates to Felix and Casper's enclosure and came back over to Zali. 'Continue the tour?'

'For sure.'

They went to the short wheelbase open-top Land Rover that Christine used as a runabout on the farm and got in. Christine drove out of the lion sector, pausing while Zali jumped down and opened a gate in the fence that quarantined the various lion enclosures from the wilder part of the game farm, where plains game roamed free. Zali closed the gate after Christine drove through and hopped back in.

Christine knew that Zali spent her working days living among big game in the Sabi Sand Game Reserve, and while seeing a woman wrestle with a lion was something different, she assumed Zali would not need her to stop at this part of the farm. She was wrong, and had to admit she was touched when Zali asked for her to stop when they saw a giraffe.

Zali took out her phone. 'Sorry, I can't go past one of these, I love them so much.'

'Me as well,' Christine said as Zali snapped a picture. 'My mom always said if I grew up with eyelashes like a giraffe's I'd never need mascara and I'd always have a man.'

'You do have those, kind of,' Zali said.

Christine laughed, but with little mirth.

Zali put her phone away as they drove on through the bush. 'Do you? Have a man?' she asked tentatively.

Christine looked over at her. 'Why do you ask?'

'Oh, I don't mean to pry, but I was wondering if there might be something between you and Craig. I mean, you live out here together and he's a good-looking, single guy.'

'We live in separate houses.'

'Sorry, Christine, it's your private life. You probably don't need a stranger you've known five minutes butting into it.'

'Thanks.' Christine slowed to let half-a-dozen wildebeest amble across the road.

'Did you always live out here in the lowveld?' Zali asked.

She was chatty, Christine thought, and she felt bad for cutting her off so abruptly, even though she could see Zali was fishing. She didn't know how much Sean had told her of their past, but she would be bound to learn some of it sooner or later. At the *braai*, and a couple of other social occasions, Christine couldn't help but notice that Zali always seemed to gravitate to Sean and hang on the few words the man spoke. Zali had asked Sean to help her set the table at her place and she'd thought at the time that they were inside for quite a long time alone. She wondered if there was something going on between them.

'No, I'm from near Rustenburg originally,' Christine said. 'I was breeding dogs, just a few, on my family's farm, Malinois mostly – like Benny. Our dogs were being bought by a private military working dog company that was using them in Afghanistan and Iraq. I met Sean when he came home on leave from the war and he decided to come visit the farm on behalf of Craig, who had by then become his boss in Afghanistan. When we met it was a hard time for me. My mom had died a few years earlier and my dad passed away a month before Sean arrived on the scene.'

'Sorry to hear.'

'Thanks. He was lovely. The truth was that Dad had left a mountain of debts. The conflict was winding down in the Middle East and our income wasn't keeping up with Dad's expenditure.

He'd borrowed heavily from the bank. I met Sean and I didn't tell him of my financial problems, but we fell for each other.'

'He's a good-looking guy.'

Christine raised her eyebrows and immediately noticed Zali's cheeks colouring. 'Yes. Yes, he is. Anyway, when I told him about my troubles Sean asked if he could invest in the dog-breeding side of the farm. He'd had enough of Afghanistan and wanted to come back to South Africa, somewhere quiet and remote.'

'And?'

They drove on. Christine mulled over how much she should tell Zali about Sean's troubles and their past. If he hadn't confided in her about his addiction, then Christine didn't think she should be the one to tell Zali. On the other hand, if there was something between the two of them then Zali probably should be made aware that Sean was a man deeply affected by his past.

'So, Sean and I became business partners and lovers. We sold my parents' farm and with the money I made I was able to clear all of Dad's debts. I had enough money left over, along with Sean's stake, to buy this place, which was closer to the game reserves we wanted to supply dogs to, and had more natural bush, which we both loved.'

'Cool.'

'Yes. It was also about us stopping this place from continuing as a canned hunting farm. It seemed like Sean couldn't wait to invest. It all happened so quickly. He was still coming and going to and from Afghanistan for a couple of months at a time, but he couldn't wait to get back to the farm and when he did, he was content to just stay in the farmhouse.'

'Was Sean . . . troubled, by what he saw in Afghanistan?'

Christine gripped the steering wheel and kept her eyes on the road. 'I don't think anyone who was there came away completely unscathed. I worked in Afghanistan as well, managing a canine company, but Sean was on the front line; he saw men and dogs killed and injured, including Craig and Benny. Yes, he was troubled, probably still is.'

There was a long pause as Zali took this in. *Time to change the subject*, thought Christine. 'The dog kennels are up ahead. Probably not as interesting to you as the lions.'

'Oh no,' Zali said quickly. 'I love dogs.'

'Well, you've come to the right place.' Christine parked the Land Rover and they got out and walked towards the first fence and line of kennels. As they approached, the Malinois in the nearest enclosure gambolled up to them, tongue lolling.

'They look in great shape, and you keep the kennels beautifully,' said Zali.

'Thanks. I've got great staff.' Christine wondered if, having asked the question, Zali didn't want to hear anything more that might put her off Sean.

Zali walked slowly past the other dogs, then stopped and looked back at her. 'Why did you and Sean break up?'

Again, Christine hesitated over how much she should tell Zali. If Sean was getting himself straightened out, then it would be cruel of her to talk at length about his addiction. But at the same time she thought that if he *was* getting on top of his problems, why couldn't he have done so while they were still married? It wasn't as if she hadn't tried to help him. She knew she'd been patient and supportive.

'Money problems,' she said at last.

'Oh.'

Christine became annoyed. She was trying to protect Sean, and Zali had just formed the impression that they had split over something trivial. 'It was bad.'

'I'm sure,' Zali said. 'You really don't have to explain.'

'Sean was . . . he made some decisions that were irresponsible, to say the least, and he almost cost me this farm.'

'Well, I guess these things happen when you're running a

business – sometimes gambles pay off and at other times they don't.'

Interesting word choice, Christine thought darkly. 'It's not that simple, Zali. If Craig hadn't bailed me out and come to my rescue I would have been bankrupt.'

Both women turned at the sound of a car horn. This part of the farm was more open than the rest, and over the short-grass veld, near the farmhouse in the distance, they saw Craig's Land Cruiser coming towards them along the rutted dirt track.

'Speaking of Craig, it looks like you've got company,' Zali said. 'And I need to be getting back to Lion Plains. Thanks so much for the tour, Christine, it's been wonderful.'

'Sure. How about you take my Land Rover back to the farmhouse. I'll get a lift back with Craig.'

'No problem.' Zali took the keys from her and they walked back to the Land Rover.

Christine closed the door on Zali as she started the engine, then said through the open window, 'Sean's a nice guy, Zali, but just take one word of advice from me, please.'

Zali put her sunglasses on. 'What's that?'

'Think twice before trusting him with any money.'

Zali's expression was inscrutable behind her sunglasses. She turned back to the wheel as Christine stepped away from the car, then drove off. A minute later Craig pulled up beside Christine. He leaned an elbow out of the driver's side. 'Playing tour guide?'

'Yes,' Christine said, 'and fending off questions about Sean. Can you give me a lift back to the house?'

'Sure.' Craig got out of the truck and opened his arms. 'Hug first.'

Christine gladly went to him and they embraced, then she went around to the passenger side. 'Thanks, I needed that.'

'Stressful time for us all,' Craig said as they headed back towards the farmhouse. Zali had already parked Christine's Land Rover and they could see her Golf winding its way down the driveway. 'Is there something going on between her and Sean?'

'Judging by her interest in my marriage breakup, yes, I think so.'

Craig looked across at her. 'Did you tell her about the gambling?'

'Not in so many words. I thought I would protect Sean's privacy, but now Zali thinks we broke up because Sean made a bad investment and I'm some evil greedy witch who couldn't forgive him for one little mistake. I should have told her about Lusaka.'

'Yeah,' Craig said. 'That cost you a contract.'

Christine nodded. It was a painful memory. Soon after she and Sean had married she had done a deal to train and supply tracker dogs to an NGO in Zambia which was funding an anti-poaching unit in South Luangwa National Park. Christine had asked Sean to fly to Zambia to oversee the dogs' introductions to their new handlers and she should have picked up the warning signs from his reluctance to go.

'It was partly my fault, forcing Sean to fly to Zambia. I should have asked more questions about why he didn't want to do the job. I had no idea he was going to hit the first casino he found in Lusaka and go on a three-day gambling bender with the money he took for expenses.'

Craig gave a weary nod. 'In hindsight I should have warned *you*, when I found out you two were first seeing each other. I saw him blow his pay a few times at the tables, though sometimes he could hold it together. He's a rubbish drinker and he told me once that he'd been gambling since he was a teenager. Did he ever tell you about his childhood?'

Christine nodded. Sean had told her after he had returned from Zambia, after she had re-booked his flights on credit because he had emptied their cheque account, that he and his sister had been beaten incessantly by their alcoholic father when they were children. 'He said gambling was a way for him to forget, that it was an addiction and it produced a high, via some chemical in the brain. The only time he could truly live in the moment and not think about all the terrible things he'd been through, as a child and in Afghanistan, was when he was playing cards, or roulette, or the slots.'

Craig sighed. 'I've heard it all before, Christine. Him talking to therapists and to us is good, but in the long run he doesn't change. You and I both know that's why he spends all his down-time with Benny out in the bush at Lion Plains – it's because he doesn't trust himself to go into town.'

Christine hated to admit that Craig was right, that Sean would never be fully over his addiction, but hearing his friend talk like that made her want to defend her ex-husband. 'Well, he can't go into town because he's still sending me most of what he can spare from his pay. I got another payment from him today.'

Craig thumped the wheel and Christine gave a start. 'Sorry, Chris, but, *jislaaik*, the guy has himself banned from casinos across South Africa – they have his picture in all their offices ready to stop him if he tries to enter – and then he goes and does a flip-ping online course in theatrical makeup so he can disguise himself and slip past the security people at the casino in Nelspruit!'

'I know, I know.' It would have been mildly funny, Christine thought, if it hadn't almost destroyed her business and cost her the farm. She had been sick, and Sean had gone to Hazyview with Oliver to fetch a prescription for her. While there, he had snapped. He'd left Oliver, taken her *bakkie*, sold it at a fly-by-night car dealership and used the cash to stake himself at the casino. He had taken the time to disguise himself before entering. By the time she found him, penniless and begging for small change in the Riverside Mall car park, he had gambled away his share of Christine's farm. She'd had to buy it back from the hard-hearted entrepreneur Sean had lost to.

'Sean's a good man, as long as we take care of him,' Craig said, 'and he keeps himself away from temptation. But that pittance he's sending you is never going to pay off his debt. Meanwhile *I* am here, Chris, trying to help you make this business work and take care of you as a man should.'

Christine frowned, but reached across the console and touched his arm. 'I know. And please don't think I'm not grateful. You saved me, Craig, and I'll never forget that.'

He stared straight ahead, through the windscreen. 'Good.'

Male egos, she thought to herself. Craig had bailed her out, and he had been with her when she had cried her way through the divorce. There had been much more to the breakup – couples counselling, her paying for Sean's therapy, him trying to lock himself away in isolation on the farm. They couldn't even go on holiday, in case Sean slipped away from her and found a black-jack table.

Unable to deal with their marriage disintegration because of her lack of trust in him, Sean had run off once more, but he had come back and asked for one last chance, for a job in the bush with Benny, whom Christine had cared for every time Sean had gone off the rails. They had split, but she'd given him the job, and Sean and his dog had retreated to the African bush.

Craig pulled up at the farmhouse and stared at her, sitting in the passenger seat. 'Well?'

Christine looked back at him. He was, in many ways, her saviour, and she had taken comfort in his arms and with his body. He was handsome and good and he had rescued her and she could not blame him for being jealous because he could see that she had not totally exorcised Sean from her life.

'Come inside,' she said.

Chapter 7

Tumi lay on her back, panting, her green uniform mottled black from sweat. Shikar looked almost as exhausted, tongue lolling and chest heaving.

A gunshot rang out and Tumi sat upright. 'What the fuck?'

'Someone's trying to kill you, Tumi!' Sean was standing behind her, and had just fired at a target fifty metres away on their makeshift bush shooting range in a remote corner of the Lion Plains property.

'At the sound of gunfire, you run,' he barked. 'You drop down out of sight and you crawl a few metres. If someone is watching you they'll be trying to draw a bead on you, so you don't want to pop your head up at the same place where you went to ground. Then, when you've found a place with cover and/or concealment, you observe, you aim and you fire.'

'Got it. Run, down, crawl, observe, aim, fire.'

'Yes, Tumi.' Sean pointed his rifle down range again and fired at another target. 'Go!'

He ran with her and Shikar. 'Run, Tumi, keep your safety catch on.' There were trees around the range and he ushered her towards one. 'Down!'

Tumi dropped to the ground and crawled, her rifle in the crook of her arms. Shikar seemed to know what to do and she lowered her body as well. It was not an easy drill to do with a dog attached to one's body by a lead. It looked like Shikar was trying to drag Tumi through the dirt at one point. 'Keep control of your dog; she'll be worried by the gunfire as well.'

'OK,' she said. Tumi was panting, but adrenaline was coursing through her now.

Once she made it to the tree Tumi got behind it and tried to rise to one knee, but Shikar's lead had become wrapped around her forearm. 'Damn.'

'Stay calm, Tumi. You need to have a sense of urgency, but don't rush. You've got a loaded weapon in your hands. Drop down and untangle yourself and then try again.'

Shikar was a good dog, patient and not flighty. She sat while Tumi unthreaded her arm and composed herself.

'Observe!'

Tumi raised her head and peered around the tree.

'Target, sixty metres, half left. Lone poacher, he's aiming at you, firing.'

'Seen,' she said.

'Aim.'

Tumi brought her rifle up and peered through the sights. She flicked the safety catch to fire.

'Two rounds, fire!'

Sean watched her as she pulled the trigger. Tumi made the rookie shooter's error of flinching as she fired, causing the rifle's barrel to jerk up a little with each shot. 'Safety catch to safe. Stand up. Leave Shikar there.'

They both stood and Sean walked beside her to the wooden target, which they inspected.

'I missed completely with one shot.' She sounded dejected.

'Yes, but the other wasn't bad.' He pointed to it. 'You just need more practice and I can show you how to correct your breathing.'

'I feel wasted.'

He was tempted to go easy on her, but he knew that training had to be as realistic as possible and as intense as she could handle. He sensed she had more in her. However, as they turned to head back to Shikai, Tumi wasn't concentrating, and swung the rifle around until it was pointing at Sean.

'Don't point that weapon at me!'

'Sorry.' Tumi lowered the barrel and took a step backwards, almost cowering. As she did so the gun went off and a puff of dust erupted from the ground between Sean's legs.

'Bloody hell.' He reached out, grabbed the weapon and took it from her.

Tumi raised her hands to her face. 'Oh my, I'm so sorry, Sean.'

'What the fuck is going on here?' said a voice from behind him.

Sean looked over his shoulder and saw Craig and Oliver striding towards them.

'Nothing,' Sean said.

'We knew you were training so we decided to come take a look,' Craig said. 'I know I told you to make Tumi's training tough and realistic, but I didn't expect you to reduce her to tears, Sean.'

'It's . . . it's not Sean's fault,' Tumi said. 'I almost killed him.'

'Shush, Tumi,' Sean hissed.

'What do you mean?' Oliver said.

'It's nothing,' Sean said. 'Tumi's had a hard morning and she's worked well.'

Oliver ignored him and directed his questions at Tumi, who was still crying. 'What did you do? Where is your weapon?'

'I accidentally fired my rifle. The shot hit the ground, between Sean's legs. That's my rifle he's holding; he took it off me.'

Oliver poked a finger at her. 'I'm writing a report on you. With your failure on the patrol that almost cost the life of your dog, and now an ND – negligent discharge – of your weapon, you can now consider yourself on two warnings. One more failure and you will be out. If this was the army you would be on a charge now, and punished.'

'It's not the army, Oliver,' Craig said.

Sean shook his head. Tumi should have kept her mouth shut. She sniffled, wiped her eyes and lifted her head to look Oliver in the eye. 'I am sorry.'

'I don't care if you're sorry,' Oliver said. 'You put a fellow operator's life at risk.'

'Let's all take a deep breath,' Craig said.

Oliver was a bully, but what he had said was one hundred per cent true; Tumi's actions would have been dealt with harshly in any army. Sean had intended on giving her a stern reprimand, but he would have explained to her that as long as she learned her lesson, and could prove so after some more training with firearms, that would be the end of the matter. Oliver, on the other hand, seemed to be looking for an excuse to remove Tumi from the team altogether.

'Tumi,' Craig said. She looked to him. 'We'll talk later in my office.'

'Yes, Craig.' She nodded.

Sean handed her the rifle. Tumi checked the safety catch and deftly removed the magazine of ammunition. With the rifle pointed away from the three men she pulled back the cocking handle, ejecting the round that had entered the breech after her accidental firing. She picked up the round, put it back in the magazine and put the mag back in its pouch. Tumi presented the rifle to Sean for inspection.

Sean put a finger into the breech and confirmed it was empty. 'Clear. You did good drills just then, Tumi. That's what we want and expect.'

She nodded, taking the weapon back, then eased the working parts of the rifle forward and fired on the empty chamber.

Tumi slung her rifle, then turned and walked away from them with Shikar towards Sean's *bakkie*, parked a few hundred metres to the rear, out of sight.

Craig turned to Sean. 'You're lucky you weren't hurt, *boet*. This girl seems clumsy and that's what got her into trouble during the hot pursuit the other night.'

'A booby trap got her into trouble,' Sean said. 'Shit like negligent discharges happens, even among highly trained soldiers. We all know that. I was about to give her a bollocking.'

'Pah,' Oliver said. 'We don't need her kind in the unit.'

Sean squared up to him. 'Her kind? A woman?'

Oliver met his stare. 'A recruit who can't handle a rifle, or a dog, and who endangers the lives of the people around her. She should be back in varsity or in her privileged life in Joburg. This is work for . . . for people who know what they are doing.'

Sean was sure Oliver had been about to say it was work for 'men', but he had cut himself short.

'It's dangerous work we do,' Sean said, putting his case to Craig. 'Tumi needs to be given a chance to learn from what happened today and I have a feeling she won't make the same mistake twice.'

'The point is that she shouldn't have made the mistake the first time,' Oliver interrupted. 'She needs to go back to where she came from.'

'How's she doing, otherwise, Sean?' Craig asked.

'She's working on her fitness, and her knowledge of the theory of tracking, detection and dog handling is good. She just needs more practice. Also, we were working on some exercises to improve her confidence. Full credit to her, as well, for telling you the truth about what just happened. She's carrying some baggage that's stopping her from achieving her full potential, but she has the makings of an excellent handler.'

'That sounds like soft western bullshit to me,' Oliver said. 'If she cannot do her job properly she is a risk to herself and to the rest of us.'

Sean nodded. 'I'm not disagreeing with you, Oliver. However, I think Tumi does have the potential to do well and it's up to us to train her and support her.'

Craig folded his arms and looked from man to man. 'I can have her reassigned to doing perimeter security on the reserve, checking vehicles and stamping gate passes, or we can give her another chance to cut it as a fully-fledged dog handler. What do you say, guys?'

'No second chance,' Oliver said.

'I say yes.' Sean grinned. 'It was me she tried to kill.'

'And it could be me next time we're jumping off a chopper and she accidentally lets a round off,' Oliver added.

Craig raised a hand. 'It's not up to you, Oliver, and nor is it up to you, Sean. The buck stops with me. Sean, give Tumi that bollocking, and, if you want to, keep working with her. Let's see how she goes when she's back on duty tomorrow and I'll assess her performance in the field next time we get called out. I expect I'll have the chance sooner rather than later.'

'*Yebo*,' Sean said.

Oliver paused a few seconds, seemed to bite back a retort, then nodded. 'Very well.'

'Have you got a minute?' Sean asked Craig.

Craig checked his watch. 'Sorry, *boet*, I've got a meeting with the police in half an hour to see if they've learned anything new about who planted the IED. There are also going to be some army guys there – the military has deployed a bomb disposal unit to Skukuza in case we find any more IEDs. Maybe we can find some time tomorrow?'

'Sure.' Sean watched Craig's back as he and Oliver left. With their conflicting schedules – Sean training Tumi and Craig teaching the dogs to differentiate between human scents – this was the longest Sean and Craig had spent together since the *braai* where Sean had noticed Craig's uniform on Christine's bed. Sean had been mulling over the pros and cons of confronting Craig with what he had seen, as perhaps there was an innocent explanation for it. However, the business with Tumi had dominated their conversation. Now that Craig was gone Sean relaxed his breathing; he had been gearing up for a possible confrontation that he was not looking forward to.

He shook his head. *Reality check*, he told himself. *No matter how hard you try or how much you want her, Christine doesn't want you any more.*

Chapter 8

The next day Sean asked Tumi to go with him to Hazyview. Craig had told him to take the *bakkie* in for a service and Sean didn't trust himself to go to town alone.

She had taken the dressing-down well and asked, later in the day, if Sean would supervise her in some more firearms training. He had been impressed with the way she'd handled the criticism and then picked herself up again.

They had slept late, as they were both rostered on duty that night. While Sean had been taking Tumi on patrols during the days since the *braai* as part of her ongoing training, this would be the first time since the explosion that she would be out after dark, and as Craig had said, the moon was getting bigger, which meant rhino poachers would potentially be at their most active.

They left Sean's Hilux at the NTT Toyota dealership and a mechanic gave them a lift to the Hazyview Junction shopping mall.

'Lunch?' she asked.

'Sure,' he said.

They went to the Meat & Coffee Co, a combined cafe and butchery, and ordered burgers and Cokes. As they were working that evening they stayed away from alcohol.

'Are you nervous about tonight?' Sean asked Tumi while they waited for their food to come.

Tumi stirred the ice in her glass with a straw. 'A little. A lot.'

'Trust your training. There's an old saying among paratroopers that knowledge dispels fear, except on night-time jumps, when fear dispels knowledge.'

She laughed. 'Do you still get nervous?'

He shrugged. 'We do a dangerous job, in dangerous country. Poachers aside, you and I both know there's plenty out there that could kill us or our dogs. Fear's only a bad thing if you give in to it, if it paralyses you. Otherwise, it sharpens your instincts and your focus. It's the same in a war. The job is ninety-nine per cent boredom and one per cent pure terror, but it's the one per cent you remember, the bit that counts.'

She nodded. 'I hope I don't let you or the others down.'

'Like I said, trust yourself and your training, and trust your dog.'

Sean had begun the process of training Shikar in explosives detection, along with Tumi. There was more work to be done, for both of them, and Sean would somehow have to get hold of more and different types of explosive substances to try and anticipate the gamut of what they might expect in the future. 'You know what to do if Shikar indicates on explosives.'

'Yes,' Tumi said. 'It will be a passive indication, as we've trained her for. She'll sit and look at the threat, but she won't bark, like she's been trained to do for human scents, or rhino horn or ivory.'

'That's right. And you stay well back. That's the most important thing. We'll call the bomb squad.'

Sean was not the only handler in the lowveld who had seen military service in the Middle East, and throughout the dog units in the South African National Parks service and private companies, such as Christine's, training had begun for explosive detection. No one knew if the booby trap that had injured Gemma was a one-off or a sign of things to come, but nobody was taking any chances.

'This whole idea of bombs, IEDs, is terrifying. I hate the thought of not knowing what we or the dog might turn up when we're out in the bush,' said Tumi.

'That's part of the reason IEDs have been such a successful weapon – fear. We have to take time out of our normal operations and training cycle to train for a new threat, and handlers are going to be more cautious, maybe slower, in following up the scent of poachers from now on. The bombmaker has already achieved part of his mission: to disrupt our operations and put a brake on us.'

'Evil bastard.'

Sean wondered if she talked that way around her father. 'Yes, but it also shows they're trying to stay a step ahead of us. The bad guys know we're a major threat to them and they're trying to counter us. It's been the same throughout history. Every major war has found a use for dogs, in attack and detection roles, and in every war the enemy has to work harder and harder to defeat man's best friend.'

Sean's phone rang. 'Hello?'

It was Zali. 'Howzit, Sean, are you in Hazyview?'

He told her where they were.

'Cool. I'm in Checkers, I'll see you just now.'

'Zali,' he said to Tumi as he put the phone away.

Their burgers arrived and Sean was halfway through his when Zali walked in and took her sunglasses off. She had once more swapped her khaki bush uniform for something very feminine. A couple of heads turned. He stood and kissed her on the cheek.

'You remember Tumi?'

'Howzit,' Zali said. 'How are you doing? All recovered?'

'Much better, thanks.'

'You've been a hard man to contact lately,' Zali said to Sean. 'Did you get my messages?'

'Yes, sorry,' he said. 'I was going to call today. Tumi and I have been busy with training and the schedule's been hectic since the *braai*.'

'I can vouch for that,' Tumi interrupted, 'Sean's been doing his best to destroy me over the last few days.'

'Join us for lunch?' Sean asked. He felt guilty for ignoring Zali's messages. He had been feeling down and, although he wouldn't admit it in front of Tumi, the extra training was tiring for him as well. Plus Sean felt like he had used Zali, especially at the party, to vent his anger over Craig and Christine, whereas she, it seemed, was genuinely interested in pursuing a relationship with him.

'I can't. I'm in a hurry and I just got off the phone to Julianne Clyde-Smith.' Zali turned to Tumi, 'You remember, the owner of Lion Plains?'

Tumi nodded.

'What is it?' Sean asked.

'Well, apart from her being very upset and angry at the upswing in poaching I have to go to Nelspruit to pick up a new car for the lodge to do guest transfers, a Discovery, and it's arrived a few days early. Can you believe it, here in the slowveld, something happening ahead of schedule?'

They laughed. 'No. And a new Discovery. Nice.'

'*Ja*,' said Zali, 'I called Craig just now and he said you could maybe come with and drive the Discovery back to the lodge for me. I'm not game to drive it yet until I have a chance to get used to it.'

Sean looked to Tumi, who shrugged. 'Cool with me. I can take your *bakkie* home when the Toyota guys are finished with it. I'll see you back at camp this evening.'

Sean's heart started beating faster and his palms were sweaty. He disliked changes to the routine. Nelspruit, more lately known by its new name of Mbombela, was the capital of Mpumalanga Province. It boasted several shopping malls and a casino.

'It'll just be a quick trip, Sean,' Zali said.

'And Craig's fine with it?'

'Yes, yes,' Zali assured him. 'You'll be back at work in time for the night shift.'

Sean looked to Tumi again.

'I'll be fine,' she assured him.

'OK then, let's go,' Zali said. 'Maybe get a doggy bag for your burger.'

Sean did and paid the bill, and they both said goodbye to Tumi.

He and Zali left the cafe and got into Zali's little Golf GTI, an older model, with a few dents. They left the Hazyview Junction mall and turned onto the R40. Soon they were in the hills above the town, passing banana farms on each side of the road. Sean's anxiety was ratcheting up a notch with every passing kilometre.

'So are you going to break the silence, or must I?' Zali asked.

Sean turned and met her eyes.

'I've called you three times since the *braai*,' she continued, 'and that was me playing it cool.'

'Yes, and I really have been busy with Tumi's training and also helping to train the other tracker dogs on the reserve in explosive detection.'

She frowned. 'If you don't like me, you can just tell me.'

He felt bad. 'No, it's nothing like that. You're beautiful, Zali.'

'Then tell me what you want.'

He exhaled. 'Sorry. I don't know how to handle this.'

'Well, neither do I.'

Sean looked out the window again. He didn't want to hurt her feelings, but nor could he explain how angry he had been at discovering that Craig and Christine were probably together.

He had no right to be pissed off and Zali would just think him a jealous loser. Perhaps that would be for the best.

They drove on in silence through the hills above White River, both keeping their thoughts to themselves. As they entered the outskirts of Nelspruit, Zali indicated left just as they came to the end of the Riverside Mall shopping complex.

'The Land Rover dealership's further down the road,' Sean said, his pulse quickening.

'I know.' Zali made the turn and then went right, into the entrance of the Stayeasy hotel, which was next to the Emnotweni Casino.

'What are you doing?'

'I need to go to the hotel.'

'OK. Can I come with you, inside?'

She raised her eyebrows. 'Of course.'

'I can't be seen around here.'

Zali paused for a moment. 'Why not? Did you rob the mall or something?'

'Long story.' Sean put on his baseball cap and pulled the visor down low over his eyes. He figured that as long as he didn't try to enter the casino he would be OK. If he had been driving his *bakkie*, someone from security would have been walking towards them now.

Zali pulled the car into a parking spot and turned off the engine. Turning to him, she put a hand on his arm. 'Sean, what's wrong? What do you mean, you can't be seen here? Seriously, are you in some kind of trouble? Christine said –'

'What did she say?' he asked, too quickly.

'Nothing bad, just that you had some financial troubles. Did you?'

'I'm not a bank robber, Zali.' Taking his cap off again, he ran a hand through his hair and his fingers came out damp. 'It's nothing. Forget it.'

'Sean,' she squeezed his arm with urgent tenderness, 'you can tell me if you're worried about something, if you're troubled.'

The mix of excitement and anxiety was almost intoxicating. He gripped the doorframe to steady himself as he got out of the car. 'I'm OK.'

'OK.' Zali got out, took a few steps then looked back over her shoulder. She beckoned him with a finger to follow. Her high heels accentuated her calves and the clack on the pavement reminded him of the slap of poker chips in his hands. He was torn. He imagined the digital tinkle of the slot machines, the low light, the cool of the air conditioning. Inside that place was a haven for him, a place where he could forget. He couldn't let go of the car door.

Zali stopped and turned around. 'A guest who was staying at Lion Plains the other day said she wanted to leave me this book she was reading, but she hadn't finished it by the time she left. She said she was coming here to the Stayeasy and she'd leave it for me. You said you wanted to come in, so are you coming?'

The temptation to go inside the casino was becoming unbearable.

He remembered the therapist's mantra. *In for five, hold for five, out for five.* He tried, but struggled to focus. Sean locked and closed the door, concentrating on the simple action of keeping the handle up so the lock wouldn't pop.

Money.

He needed it. The standing payment to Christine had just come out of his bank account, so that left just nine hundred rand, give or take, for him to live on for the next three weeks until payday. It was a pittance.

What the hell difference would it make? he asked himself. He received food and lodging as part of his job and he had nowhere to go, nothing on which to spend the little money in his account. *If,* the non-logical part of his brain said, *if I took that cash and played it at the tables I could make enough to pay Christine back and start a new life.*

. Sean lifted his feet, one step at a time, to the door of the hotel. A porter opened it.

'Coming in, sir?'

'No. Yes. I don't know.'

The man smiled indulgently.

He could almost hear the slots. It would be so easy. He started to walk towards the casino.

'Where are you going, Sean?'

He stopped, not wanting to look back.

'Sean?'

Sean took another three steps towards escape, then heard the heels, felt the small hand on his forearm.

'Sean, I can't play this game any more. Where are you going, anyway? The bloody casino?'

'I don't know.'

He turned around. She had her hands on her hips. 'Do you really not want to be with me that much? I just thought we could spend some time together, but clearly you don't want to.'

Sean took a long, ragged breath. He realised, now, the story about the guest leaving the book at the hotel must be a ruse. Zali had booked a room in the hotel for the two of them. 'It's not that, Zali. I like you, I really do.' He glanced back to the casino entrance then took a step towards it.

'Look at me. I booked a room for us, Sean, just for the afternoon.'

Sean stopped.

She sighed. 'I know you've had problems, Sean. I'd like to help you, if you let me reach out to you.'

He could see it, in her eyes; this was not just about a tumble in a hotel room for Zali. She clearly didn't know about his gambling problem but she really did want to help him, and he had no idea what he had done to deserve that. Sean weighed up his options. He could ignore her and go to the casino and possibly never come out, or he could go with Zali and make her think they shared the same feelings about each other.

He knew he would hate himself whatever he did.

'Sean? Please?'

God help me, he thought. He took Zali's proffered hand and followed her into the hotel.

Chapter 9

'I told you, Sean had to go to Nelspruit. It's not my fault he's not here,' Tumi said to Oliver, who was riding in the back of the *bakkie* with her, Shikar and Charles. Craig drove, as fast as he dared through the Sabi Sand Game Reserve at night.

Clyde, the team's old bloodhound, named in honour of Julianne Clyde-Smith, was in the front with Craig. Tumi gripped Shikar's lead so tightly that the cord dug into the palm of her hand, hurting her. She was sitting; Oliver and Charles were standing over her, rifles leaning on the padded bar that ran along the top of the Hilux's cab. It was rigged out like a hunters' truck, with a shaded area in the back for the dogs.

They were hunting. People.

They had all heard the gunshots at the anti-poaching unit camp, and were getting their gear on even before the radio call came through.

Oliver might have been a chauvinistic pig, but he knew guns and gunfire and had an intimate knowledge of the Lion Plains property. He was talking to the Sabi Sand's warden via his handheld radio while Craig concentrated on driving. 'Shots came from the west, by Ngwenya Pool. Proceeding there now, over.'

Oliver and Charles scanned not only the bush, but also the dirt road in front as Craig drove. Charles rapped on the roof of the cab and Craig braked.

Charles jumped down, ran back and checked some tracks. 'Reverse!'

Craig changed gear and backed the vehicle up.

'Bamba.' Charles pointed to a drag mark half a metre wide that crossed the road.

'Leopard kill?' Craig's voice was annoyed rather than impressed that Charles had pointed out a leopard had caught something.

Charles broke off a long stem of grass and pointed to the furrows. 'No, it is someone covering their tracks, using a branch to make it look like a leopard dragging its prey.' He raised his eyes to Tumi to explain. 'See, leaves from the branch they used to cover their footprints have fallen off, here; they missed two. They must be rushing.'

'Good work, Charles,' Craig said. 'Tumi, you and Shikar follow these tracks. I'll keep Clyde in reserve in case you lose the trail.'

'You mean for *when* she loses it,' Oliver said as he climbed down.

'She won't,' said Charles.

Tumi vaulted over the side wall of the *bakkie* and Shikar followed her. She had been practising getting in and out of vehicles, and also exiting from a wooden frame Sean had nailed together in the same dimensions as a helicopter cargo door.

'You'd better pick up the pace, Oliver, or she might outrun you,' Craig said from the driver's seat. 'Stay in touch by radio. I'll drive around to the far side of Ngwenya Pool, meet you there unless you make contact.'

'Affirmative,' Tumi said as she fitted Shikar's tracking harness with practised ease. Sean had told her that if she acted professional then the men would treat her with respect. She was worried about Sean, though. 'Any word from Sean?'

'*Ja*,' Craig said. 'I got an SMS from Zali. When they got to the Land Rover place they said the new car for Lion Plains hadn't, in fact, arrived, and would only be coming next week. They were driving back and Zali's Golf blew a tyre. Her bloody spare was flat so Sean had to hitchhike back to Nelspruit to get it fixed. He'll be back just now, but let's get on with it.'

Craig accelerated away, his rear wheels spinning on the gravel. Oliver and Charles cocked their rifles and when Tumi did the same Shikar lifted her nose and strained at her lead in anticipation. Tumi took her to the drag mark.

'Shikar, *soek*.'

Shikar responded to the universal command used by dog handlers and began sniffing around the tracks. Then the dog headed into the bush and Tumi had to fight to maintain her balance.

The bush was fairly open in this part of the reserve. It was the end of the dry season and passing elephant herds and the warming winds had denuded the trees of their leaves. Oliver and Charles moved out to the flanks, left and right of Tumi and Shikar, and just behind them. If Craig or Sean had been with them they would have been behind them, depending on what sort of tracks they were following.

Shikar barked, indicating something fresh. Tumi dropped to a knee. Shikar was focusing on a patch of dust darker than the surrounding ground. Tumi touched it.

'Blood,' she said as Charles arrived by her side.

He touched her shoulder. 'Good work.'

'Thank Shikar. Look, Charles, part of a footprint.'

Tumi pressed her fingers together. 'Still sticky. They're not far ahead of us.'

'*Ha famba*,' he said, xiTsonga for 'we go'.

'Affirmative.' She felt the rush of adrenaline make her heart pound harder, energising her body all the way out to her fingertips. 'Shikar, *soek*!'

Shikar kept her nose close to the ground and Tumi concentrated on reading the dog while still keeping watch around and in front of her. The African night held dangers aplenty in addition to the armed poachers somewhere ahead of them. There was the threat of lions and leopards, which would love to kill a dog, or of running into an angry old buffalo bull or a herd of elephants. A hyena called in the distance.

Branches whipped Tumi's face and arms and barbed thorns hooked her camouflage uniform and scored her exposed skin. It was cold in the middle of the night, the temperature not far above zero, but the thrill of the chase and Shikar's speed kept her warm. Tumi remembered her first disastrous night on patrol and tried to keep the fear and the terrible memories of Gemma's shattered, bleeding body at bay. In the days afterwards she had caught herself shaking, wondering how it was she had survived. But she knew she had a purpose: to protect her country's wildlife and to catch the men who would seek to profit from the deaths of innocent creatures.

Shikar led her downhill, on a hippo path, towards a stream. Then the dog stopped and raised her head.

Tumi remembered the refresher training Sean had delivered. The footprints she had seen had indicated that there were probably two poachers – Charles would know for sure – and that they were running. At some point they had stopped trying to cover their tracks. But now when she looked around, even with the aid of the bright moon, she could see no more tracks on the other side of the stream.

The poachers would have gone into the stream and run along it, one way or the other, to put them off the scent. Tumi lengthened Shikar's lead to about six metres, splashed through the water and began casting the dog along the far side of the stream.

Charles and Oliver caught up with them. She kept her inward smile of satisfaction to herself as she noticed how Oliver, the biggest of all of them, was breathing the hardest. She felt like she'd hardly worked up a sweat.

'They would have gone through the stream to try and lose us,' Charles said.

Tumi nodded, but kept quiet and did her job. She didn't need to tell Charles that she had already worked that out.

'They are two,' Charles added.

I already worked that out, too. Tumi watched Shikar. The dog was as eager as she was to pick up the trail again, but was having no luck. Tumi directed her to try the other direction, downstream, instead.

'Shikar, *soek.*'

Shikar wagged her tail and sniffed around. She came to a rocky drift, where the shallow water gurgled around smooth-worn stone and indicated with a bark.

'Here!'

Oliver and Charles came to her.

'Yes,' Charles said, 'they would have used this stony ground to try and throw us off their trail. It's harder to track here.'

'Not for her. Shikar, *soek*, girl!'

*

The poachers' names were Luiz and Armando. Luiz was the elder of the two, much older, and a veteran of Mozambique's protracted civil war.

He worked for the Chinaman now; he had killed his former boss, Fidel, who had once fancied himself the king of rhino poachers in the town of Massingir.

The Lion Plains property, where he was hiding behind a lead-wood tree at this very moment, had gained a reputation as *the* place to see rhino in the Sabi Sand Game Reserve. The camp's tough-talking owner, Julianne Clyde-Smith, had trumpeted the success of sniffer dogs as one of the key factors in her strategy to keep poachers out of the reserve.

Luiz liked a challenge.

'Armando, take the horn, keep going.'

'The dogs?'

'Let me take care of them. I have been wanting to try out the Chinaman's new gadget. Give me one of the ears.'

Armando opened the canvas military rucksack he was carrying. Inside was the horn of the rhino they had killed, as well as its tail and ears. The buyers from Vietnam increasingly wanted evidence that the horns they were being sold had come from a wild, free-ranging rhino, and not from a stockpile of humanely removed horn.

Some of the horn on the market, Luiz knew, had come from old stockpiles that had been stolen from various national parks authorities, and a criminal few of the people who bred rhinos in South Africa circumvented the laws against international trade in rhino horn and managed to get some out of the country. The middlemen Luiz dealt with had convinced the high-net-worth individuals in Vietnam who made up their customer base that it was far more prestigious to have the horn of a wild animal than a farmed one. Taking a free-ranging rhino meant that the hunter had captured its spirit and power, making the horn that much more potent.

It was all nonsense, of course, Luiz knew. The horn was not used as an aphrodisiac, as many people still believed, but as a cure for hangovers or fever. In fact, the value of the horn was in its cost and rarity; a wealthy Vietnamese businessman might display it to show his peers how well off he was, or give the horn as a gift as part of a lucrative business deal.

For Luiz, however, it was about the money, and the hunt. Next year it could be elephant ivory, or pangolin scales, or vulture heads.

It didn't matter to him. Wildlife was a commodity, something to be hunted and traded, it was as simple as that. He came from a background of war and poverty and he never wanted to be poor again.

War, however, was different. He could not, hand on heart, say to someone like young Armando, less than half his age, that he missed the war, because he did not. The people following him, with their dogs and their drones and their helicopters and night vision sights and thermal imaging cameras, were hunting him, but Luiz was as wily a prey as he was skilled as a predator.

Armando handed him the ear and a couple of drops of fresh blood squeezed from the tough skin. Good, he thought, the dog would go wild.

'Keep running, Armando. Get the horn to safety. You won't be bothered by the dog or the rangers.'

'*Sim,*' the young man said.

Luiz opened his own satchel and took out the device. He had handled explosives in the war and set his own share of booby traps – grenades, mostly, with a trip-wire strung between the pin and a tree to catch an inexperienced RENAMO soldier. This was something different altogether.

Luiz scraped a shallow hole in the dry earth, set the device, and covered it with dirt and leaves. He tossed the ear a few metres away, broke off a branch, and swept the ground around his trap with the leaves before retreating into the bush. He moved a hundred yards off, and when he found a large jackalberry tree behind which to hide he took the garage door remote control from the satchel and settled down to wait.

*

Tumi fought to control Shikar.

It was a balancing act, literally sometimes, as the dog took her over fallen trees, across slippery granite rocks, and through thickets of thorny acacias. She also had to judge whether to give Shikar her head or keep tighter control of the dog.

If it had been daylight she would have unclipped the lead and let Shikar run free in a hot pursuit. The threat of big cats and the added complication of darkness, however, meant Tumi couldn't release Shikar.

There was so much to remember, so much to process. Shikar moved faster, pulled harder, straining at the lead. The blood and scent of the horn she was picking up was fresh, which sent her into a single-minded frenzy. All Shikar would get at the end of the chase was a chance to play with her ball, but that was enough for her. For Tumi, reward would be the capture of a poacher and the satisfaction of having done her job properly. Compliments could come later; for now she just wanted to be accepted as a member of this team – by all its members.

Shikar stopped and barked.

Tumi paused and held up a hand so the men behind and to each side of her would also stop and let the dog do her work.

'What is it, girl?'

Shikar sniffed around, barked again.

Tumi knew she was indicating, that maybe she had found some more blood, but the dog seemed unsure. She looked back at Tumi. *I don't know either.*

Tumi couldn't see exactly what had piqued Shikar's interest.

Then Shikar sat and looked straight ahead.

Tumi's blood went cold.

'What is it? Why has the dog stopped?' Oliver said, now beside her.

'She's indicating.'

'I can see that. So what? More blood?'

'I don't know,' Tumi said.

'It's your job to know.'

'Oliver, be cool,' Charles said. 'Let her work.'

Oliver shook his head. 'She doesn't –'

'Shush,' Tumi said. 'Shikar is giving a passive indication, as well as just barking.'

'So?' Oliver said.

'Do you have binoculars?' Tumi asked Oliver.

'It's night-time, you have no need of them.'

Charles came to her side. 'I've got a pair.'

'Thanks, Charles.' Tumi took the compact field glasses and raised them to her eyes. It was only a short distance and despite what Oliver had said, she knew from her time as a safari guide that binoculars helped in the ambient light from the sliver of moon and the stars. She could see what Shikar was looking at, what had made her bark. 'An ear.'

'Rhino ear?' Charles asked.

'Yes.'

'Then get your dog working again,' Oliver said.

'No.'

'Listen to me, woman, I give the orders.'

'Sean's started training me in explosive detection. When one of the dogs picks up a trace of explosives we've trained them to give a passive reaction, just like Benny did when he found the bomb that injured Gemma. That's what Shikar's doing now.'

Oliver licked his lips and looked from her to Charles, probably for support. 'Your dog's inexperienced, as are you, and this explosive detection training has only just begun. It is too soon; Shikar is confused. Proceed, girl.'

Eish, Tumi thought, bridling. This man was so arrogant he would risk their lives and that of Shikar rather than admit he might be wrong. She knelt down.

'We're wasting time,' Oliver said. 'Let's just go around the ear, then. We can take a GPS reading and pick it up later for evidence purposes. Take the lead, Tumi, do as you're told.'

Tumi tried to remember everything Sean had told her about

IEDs, based on his experience in Afghanistan. The rhino's body part might be attached to a trip-wire, or there might be a pressure plate on the ground near it, so that if a dog or a human stepped on the plate, or picked up the ear, it would activate a switch. Or Shikar could be confused, or it could be none of those. Tumi was feeling less confident by the second.

'What do you think, Tumi?' Charles asked her quietly.

What she thought was that she wished Sean was there. 'I don't know.'

'See what I mean?' Oliver said. 'Let's go. Bring your *confused* dog, Tumi.'

Charles moved forward, towards the rhino's ear. 'This is interesting. There is no spoor or sign that tracks have been covered up.'

'So?' Oliver asked.

'Maybe it was tossed there, from a distance, rather than dropped by mistake,' Tumi said.

Charles cast about, looking for tracks. 'Good thinking, Tumi.'

Shikar barked again, while looking at the ear, then got up, walked a few steps and sat down once more, passively indicating towards a spot a couple of metres in front of Charles, away from the rhino ear. Tumi could read Shikar better after training with her, but this behaviour was still unusual.

'Charles, come back!' Tumi said.

'What?' Charles asked. He was focused on the ground in front of him.

'Come back. Shikar's definitely found something!'

'No, Tumi,' Charles said, 'I've picked up some spoor here over here. Let's go.'

'Yes, come, Tumi,' Oliver commanded.

Oliver was away from them, on the left flank. Tumi saw the mound of grass and leaves now. Charles was heading towards it. 'Charles!'

'It's OK, it's nowhere near the ear.'

Tumi stood and started towards Charles, but she knew her dog would get to him quicker and she had to stop him. 'Shikar, rim hom!'

'What the hell?' Charles had taken part in enough dog training, sometimes wearing a bulky padded bite-protection sleeve or suit, to know that the unusual combination of words 'rim hom', unlikely to be used accidentally in any normal conversation around working dogs, was the command for a dog to attack a human.

Shikar got up and ran to Charles and put her jaws around his arm.

'Get this bloody dog off me!'

'Come, Shikar, bring him!'

Shikar worried at Charles's arm and emitted a low growl. Charles had fear in his eyes as he backed away from the disturbed ground. 'OK, OK, I'm coming.'

'Shikar, *ous*!' Tumi called as Charles came a few paces closer to her. Shikar responded to the command and immediately released Charles, who was shocked, but not badly hurt. Depending on their training, most working dogs were taught to deliver a full-jaw bite, holding on to an arm or leg, with their rearmost teeth, not their sharp canines.

'This is the end for you, Tumi,' Oliver hissed. 'Using your dog to attack one of your comrades. You'll never work in this job again and –'

The mound of twigs and dirt erupted and the shock wave knocked Charles over and sent Shikar skidding and running back to Tumi.

Oliver had dropped to his belly, the soldier's response to shell-fire, perhaps. Tumi wondered, but had no time to dwell on it.

Tumi ran to Charles and knelt beside him. 'Charles? Charles?'

Her hands roamed over his uniform and equipment, looking for signs of injury. 'Charles, talk to me, please.'

*

Luiz was impressed.

Technology had come a long way. The bomb was light, portable, easy to lay and had almost done its job.

Almost.

His orders had been to kill a dog. To kill a handler, as had almost happened to the woman last time, would be to invite the wrath of God down on all their heads. As it was, the social media, according to the Chinaman, was going crazy with outpourings of sympathy for the 'hero' dog, Gemma. Luiz cared nothing for animals.

While the dog had initially been distracted by the rhino's ear, it had also detected the explosives, which had forced Luiz's hand. Luiz wondered if he had killed the man. It would be a problem, long term, if he had, but for now it possibly created an opportunity; his enemies would be focused on treating the man rather than following him and Armando.

Luiz pocketed the garage door remote, still marvelling at how something so simple, so ordinary in South Africa, could be turned into a weapon of destruction. The forensic examination would show, regardless of whether the man was dead or seriously injured, that the improvised explosive device had been designed to kill or maim something small, like a dog.

What concerned Luiz, as he jogged along, nimble-footed, instinctively avoiding tree roots and rocks, was that the dog had acted differently from how he'd expected. Dogs barked when they found blood or the scent of a human, or a cartridge case or a weapon. Luiz had studied the tactics of his opposition. This dog had barked at first, when it had first seen the rhino ear, as Luiz had hoped it would, but it had then sat down and quietly stared at the spot where he had laid the IED.

Interesting.

His enemies were adapting already, and the dogs, or this one at least, had been trained to indicate explosives. Luiz and the

Chinaman had hoped that the introduction of explosives would paralyse the tracking dog effort in the Sabi Sand Game Reserve, and possibly the Kruger Park. Instead, the anti-poaching jackals were responding, and quickly.

Luiz had not survived the civil war by being tied to ridiculous Eastern European military doctrine. He was, first and foremost, a Shangaan hunter. He had been trained in the arts of war, but he knew how to read the bush and his prey and to learn from them both.

The remote-detonated IED would give the jackals something to think about and Luiz would need to learn from what had happened tonight. For now, Armando was ahead of him, signalling with a fair to middling imitation of a Mozambican fiery-necked nightjar.

Good Lord, deliver us, Armando whistled.

'You have stopped,' Luiz said.

Armando smiled. 'Yes. I decided to wait for you.'

'Why?'

Armando put a finger to his lips and pointed ahead. Luiz saw the silhouette of a big white rhinoceros bull. He clapped Armando on the arm. 'Good man.'

Chapter 10

Sean drove Zali's little Golf through the bush like a rally car. Benny was in the passenger seat, head out the window, tongue lolling. At least one of them was grinning.

He felt sick with dread. When he and Zali had arrived back at the Shaw's Gate entrance to the Sabi Sand Game Reserve, the security officer on duty had told him his team had been called out to track rhino poachers after an animal had been killed.

Sean had asked to use the radio at the gate office and had made contact with Craig. Sean had told Craig he would take Zali home after stopping by the anti-poaching camp to pick up his rifle, and then join him in the bush. Craig told him he was heading to the far side of Ngwenya Pool.

Sean knew the waterhole well. Ngwenya meant 'crocodile' in xiTsonga, and the pan was well named as there was a four-metre monster in residence. He had taken Zali to the lodge, kissed her on the cheek and squeezed her hand.

'Be careful, please, I need you alive,' she had said to him.

Sean felt a mixture of shame, confusion and anger in equal parts as he drove. In his defence, he told himself, Zali's little car really had suffered a blowout on the R40 and her spare tyre had been flat. He had wasted time hitching back to the Tiger Wheel & Tyre at Nelspruit, but that was where the truth of their story had begun and ended.

Zali had received an SMS that morning from the Land Rover dealership telling her the Discovery's delivery would be delayed. She had chosen not to tell her boss Julianne or Craig about the change in plans and had made the hotel booking with the intention of taking Sean there.

He remembered the pull of the casino, and even though he had not been able to hear the chimes, or see the flashing lights, or smell the booze and cigarette smoke on the die-hards, he had imagined it all. Just the anticipation of those familiar sights, sounds and smells, not all of them pleasant, had been enough to create a physiological response. He'd felt his heart tighten, the sweat prick his palms, his breath shorten.

It was almost like what he'd felt with Zali. He knew he could no more bury his feelings and memories in sex than he could in gambling, no matter how attractive either option seemed. Right now he wanted nothing more than to lose himself, but he knew he could do that in a marginally more constructive way, through work.

Sean had worked with guys in Afghanistan who had been model soldiers and contractors, throwing themselves into their work and pushing themselves and those around them to be the best operators they could be. But some of these over-achievers were suffering from post-traumatic stress disorder. It was an insidious condition that manifested itself in many ways, none of them good. Some sufferers fell apart crying and howling; others drank or smoked or injected themselves to death; some committed suicide; and still others worked so hard and expected so much of themselves that they burned themselves out.

Sean gambled.

And he worked. Sean drove with the window open, the chilly night air helping him banish the unwanted thoughts from his mind and get back to the job at hand. Craig was waiting at Ngwenya Pool and Tumi, Oliver and Charles were heading towards them. Sean's phone rang. He looked at the screen and answered, driving one-handed.

'Craig?'

'There's been another IED. Charles is hurt.'

'Fuck.' Sean heard an accusatory tone in the statement, as though he were to blame. It tallied with his feeling of guilt.

'I've called the chopper,' Craig said. 'Tumi and Oliver are waiting with him.'

'Of course.'

'They were following a trail westward, towards the perimeter fence. Get these bastards, Sean.'

'Will do.'

'Take over from Tumi and call me if you find spoor. I'll be your backup.'

'Affirmative.'

Sean pictured the map of Lion Plains as he drove. If the poachers kept moving west they would pass the airstrip where well-heeled guests landed in charter aircraft for their safaris. He calculated the speed at which men could run through the bush against the time the first rhino had been shot. Sean sped towards the airstrip.

Once there he stopped the Golf by the small open-sided building that served as a terminal but was really just a shady place to wait. He opened the doors and Benny bounded out. Sean took the LM5 semiautomatic assault rifle he'd picked up from his room and cocked it. Benny was instantly alert.

Sean had picked the airstrip because it was elevated, set on a long, ridge-like hill, with a view over a large swathe of Lion Plains. If the poachers had kept on their westward course from

Ngwenya Pool they would be moving from right to left through the bushy valley below him.

'Still, Benny.' Sean fitted the dog's collar. Both of them stood still, heads raised, Sean listening and Benny air-scenting.

Somewhere off to his right an elephant trumpeted noisily, disturbed by something. It could have been a lion or a leopard – elephants detested big cats almost as much as Benny did – or it might have been fleeing humans.

There was no mistaking the next sounds. Gunshots.

Sean turned towards the sound of the first and fixed the location as best as he could just as the second bullet was fired. Birds, insects, even frogs in a near-dry stream somewhere all stopped making their noises. Sean surveyed the land. There were no roads into the block from where he was sure the noise had come.

It was dangerous, and as dawn was approaching the moon was setting, making it even darker, but time was of the essence. Sean unclipped Benny's lead. 'Benny, *soek*!'

Benny bounded away and Sean ran as fast as he could, trying to keep up with the dog. He had none of his normal field gear, having only stopped to pick up his rifle, so he was relatively unencumbered. Even so, as soon as he moved off the grassy airstrip into the bush below he started falling foul of branches and vines and had to watch his step on the uneven ground. Benny, however, moved below and over the obstacles with ease. Sean could see just why African wild dogs were such consummate hunters; nothing seemed to slow a dog in the bush.

Sean would lose Benny, but then a short sharp bark would tell him where he was and Sean would draw a ragged breath and carry on. He came to a small clearing where Benny had stopped. The dog lifted his head from the ground proudly and barked.

'Good boy. Benny, *soek*.'

Benny bounded ahead and Sean redoubled his efforts and charged after him. They ran downhill, splashed through a shallow stream and Sean scrambled up the opposite bank. Benny stopped at the top and looked back at him.

Sean sensed Benny had seen something. 'Come, Benny.'

The dog seemed reluctant to give up the chase, but turned and came to him. Sean clipped the lead to Benny's collar and quietly told him to heel. They moved slowly to the top of the bank and Sean brought his LM5 up into his shoulder.

'Shush, Benny.'

Sean heard the rasp of a saw, and when he peered over the lip of the bank he saw two men bent over the carcass of a sizeable rhino. One kept watch with a heavy-calibre hunting rifle while the other attacked the animal's horn with a bowsaw.

Rage boiled inside Sean. He unclipped Benny's lead.

Sean took out his phone and sent an SMS to Craig, giving him his approximate location in relation to the airstrip and the fact that he and Benny had just crossed the stream, the Amanzini Spruit.

Sean knew the ideal thing would be to wait for backup, but he could also see that the man with the saw was nearly done. Soon these two would be on their way. He put his phone away and brought his rifle up to his shoulder.

'Drop your guns, you're surrounded,' he called. It was corny, but the men instinctively looked up and around.

The man with the hunting rifle, the elder judging by his tight grey curls, whipped around, fired a shot in Sean's direction and then dived and rolled on the ground so that the rhino's bulk shielded him from sight and shot.

The other man dropped his saw and snatched up an AK-47 that had been lying on the dead beast's flank.

'Hey, drop it, man!' Sean shouted.

The man ignored him and raised the assault rifle. Sean had no choice: he took aim and squeezed the trigger. The man dropped.

The other man called out. 'Don't shoot. I'm coming out.'

'Toss your rifle away, where I can see it,' Sean called.

A second later Sean saw two hands appear from behind the rhino.

'Don't shoot.'

Sean kept his sights trained on the man as he stood, slowly. 'Where's the rifle?'

'I do not know,' the man called back. His voice was gravelly, his English accented.

'I just saw you holding it.'

'No, not me, sir. I am just a poor bearer.'

Sean thought the man's mother tongue was Portuguese, the national language of Mozambique. The man was lying, but he appeared to be unarmed. 'Come out from behind the rhino.'

'Yes, sir.'

Sean stood and as he did so, momentarily lowering his LM5, the man turned and ran.

'Shit. Stop, or I will release my dog!'

The man disappeared.

Sean unclipped Benny's lead. 'Have it your way,' he said to the poacher. 'Benny, rim hom!'

Benny shot away like an arrow from a bow and Sean ran after him. Sean paused by the rhino carcass to briefly confirm that the other man was dead. Sean picked up the man's AK-47.

Ahead of him he heard barking, then growling. Sean dropped the AK and brought his LM5 up to his shoulder. Benny had the man on the ground. Sean lowered his rifle again; there was no way he could shoot without risking the shot hitting Benny, and besides, the man was down. He was about to give the command for Benny to release when a gunshot rang out.

Benny yelped.

The poacher rolled out from under Benny, raised a pistol and opened up on Sean, who dropped to the ground as bullets whizzed around him. He felt something tug at his sleeve. Sean crawled to a fallen tree, but by the time he was able to peek around the end of the trunk to look for his target, the man had gone.

Benny whined.

'Benny!'

Sean felt the rage rise up inside him. The bastard had shot his dog. He was torn between the desire to hunt this man down and kill him, or to stay and care for Benny.

'Fuck.'

Sean dropped to his knees. Benny writhed under his touch, trying to escape the pain. He ran his hands over Benny's fur and his fingers came away wet and sticky with blood. Benny whined again.

'It's OK, boy,' Sean said, praying he was telling the truth. He cursed himself for not taking the extra couple of minutes he would have needed to grab his field pack with its first aid kit. Instead he quickly unbuttoned his uniform shirt and used his Leatherman to cut strips off it. He found the wound on Benny's right front leg. 'What has this bastard done to you?'

Sean tried to wipe off the blood, but more welled to the surface. He felt around some more and Benny yelped and tried to cower away, but Sean held him tight. He found an exit wound on the other side of the leg.

'Thank God,' he said.

From what Sean could see the bullet had gone cleanly in and out of the dog's body, and while the blood welled it was not pumping out hard so no arteries had been severed. The important thing now was to staunch the blood and get Benny to the vet as soon as possible. Sean balled strips of material and pressed them against each of the bullet holes then tied them off.

If the poacher was smart he would be long gone. If he came back to inspect his handiwork Sean was sure, in the state he was in now, that he would shoot the man in cold blood.

Sean took his phone out and called Craig. He reported what had happened.

'I'm close,' Craig said. 'Coming along Bushbuck Road. You should hear my engine soon.'

'Affirmative.' Sean ended the call. Craig would be at least a few minutes away.

Sean kept pressure on the bandage as he sat with Benny, but when he held up his other hand he could see that it was shaking. He pulled out his phone again and dialled Christine.

As their boss, she needed an update, but he was calling her for another reason. He had played it cool and calm for Craig on the phone, but Sean was terrified of what might happen to him if Benny died. He needed to hear a familiar, reassuring voice, even if it belonged to the ex-wife he had wronged.

When Christine answered he recapped what had happened. Craig had already called her with the news about Charles. Sean told her that he'd killed one poacher but that the other had wounded Benny and escaped.

'Benny will be OK, Sean,' Christine reassured him. 'He's a fighter; you and I both know he went through worse in Afghanistan. You'll be OK as well. You're strong, more than you know.'

Sean sniffed back his emotions. 'Thanks.'

'Sean, listen to me, I need you to do something for me.'

'OK.' He swallowed as his fingers clung to Benny's fur.

'I can't just sit back and hope the police come up with something, Sean. We need to seize the initiative here, and try to get a lead on who is doing this to us and why. I'd ask Craig but he has his hands full and he'll be dealing with the police as well, so I don't want to compromise him, or for the police to later accuse him of withholding evidence.'

'So you want me to be the fall guy?' Sean said.

'No, it's . . .'

'It's fine, Christine,' he said, and he meant it. 'I'm happy to do this for you, for the team. I want to get these bastards and

I'll do whatever it takes.' He had almost said, 'You can trust me, Christine,' but he knew that would be wishful thinking. 'I'll look around, see what I can find before the cops get here.'

'Thank you. I feel guilty asking you to do this. I don't want you to hold stuff back from the police or slow their investigation in any way, but I want in on this, Sean. I want us to do what we do best: sniff out the enemy and neutralise him.'

'Same here,' he said. God, he admired her strength. Sean paused on the line, not ready to hang up, but worried about speaking his mind. As hard as he tried, he could not get the image of Craig's clothing on Christine's bed out of his mind. As much as he told himself that she was single and free and could do whatever she wanted, he could not help feeling betrayed. He drew a deep breath. 'About Craig.'

'Yes? You can tell him I've asked you to look for evidence for our use if it makes you feel better,' she said quickly.

'That's not it.'

It was her turn to pause. 'What then?'

'You know,' he said, leaving the words hanging.

He could hear her breathing on the other end of the call. 'I don't want to hurt you, Sean, please believe me, that's the last thing I want,' she said quietly.

Too late, he thought. 'It's fine.'

'Sean . . .'

'I've got to go.' It was true; Sean heard a vehicle engine and knew Craig was arriving. He ended the call.

Sean flashed the LED torch he always wore on his belt and heard the sound of the vehicle crunching over small trees as it drove off-road towards him. When Craig arrived he saw that Oliver, Tumi and Shikar were in the back. Shikar whined as they pulled up, sensing Benny's distress.

Sean carried Benny to the vehicle. 'How's Charles?'

'We got him on the chopper,' Craig said. 'Looks like he took some frags, and he may have concussion and some hearing loss, but he's alive.'

Tumi jumped down out of the back of the *bakkie* and called Shikar to follow. The Weimaraner bounded out and sniffed Benny as Sean carried his dog past them.

'What are you doing?' Craig asked Tumi.

'Looking for evidence.'

'We have to get Benny to the vet,' Craig said.

'I know,' Tumi said. 'Check, Shikar.'

'Get in the truck, Tumi.'

'I'll be OK,' she said. 'We still have a job to do and I can find my way back to the camp. It's not far from here. It'll be daylight soon so Shikar and I will be fine.'

Craig looked to Oliver.

'I'm going on leave today. I'm going back with Craig,' Oliver said.

'Craig?' Sean said.

'Yes, *boet*?'

'Look after Benny for me, OK? Get him to Graham Baird.'

'Will do, though Benny will probably try and *moer* me when he realises we're going to the vet. Sure you don't want to come with?' Craig asked.

Despite the seriousness of the situation and the shock of seeing Benny injured, Sean almost smiled – Benny hated Graham the vet. 'I do, but I'll stay with Tumi. We're going to get him.'

Craig shook his head. 'I wish I shared your optimism. Right now I'm one man and one dog down, and with Oliver due for leave we're almost finished as a fighting force.'

*

Tumi retched and threw up. Far from becoming used to the sight of dead men and animals the reality of the job was taking a toll on her.

As the tears streamed from her eyes and she blew her nose to clear out the vomit she could hear Oliver laughing.

'Drop it, Oliver,' Craig said. 'Tumi probably just saved Charles's life.'

It didn't matter. As far as Oliver was concerned she would only ever be *just* a woman, no good for anything other than cooking and making babies. To hell with him. She wiped her eyes and nose and spat.

'Shikar.' She coughed and cleared her throat and took another look at the dead man. He could not hurt her, but still his eyes stared at her accusingly. '*Soek!*'

The dog left the body alone and she used the lead to guide her, to cast about in a circle around the rhino carcass. There was so much blood. She swallowed hard to stop herself being sick again.

Shikar was in her element, nose to the ground.

The *bakkie* drove off and relative silence returned to the bush. Sean stood nearby, but did not come to her, did not offer advice or tell her what to do.

'Don't you want to be with him, with Benny?' she asked without looking back from what Shikar was doing.

'Yes.'

'Then why didn't you go? Do you think I can't survive out here in the bush, alone, because I'm a woman?'

'No. I have to be here for when the cops come, like I said, and I have to be here with you.'

Tumi looked over her shoulder. 'You don't trust me.'

He met her eyes. 'No, it's because you're my partner, and we don't let each other down. We are going to get whoever injured Gemma, and hurt Charles and Benny.'

She blinked, then wiped her eyes with her free hand. 'Why are they doing this to us?'

'We're the enemy, and this guy,' he pointed to the dead rhino with the top of the barrel of his LM5, 'is worth nothing but a quick buck to the people who shot him and the bastards who make a fortune off his horn.'

Tumi nodded wearily. 'Shikar, *soek*,' she said again.

Shikar stopped and barked. Tumi came to her. 'Good girl, Shikar. Sean?'

'Yes?'

'Have a look. Blood. Did you shoot him?'

'No, but Benny had hold of him and put him on the ground.'

'*Soek*.' Shikar picked up the scent and barked again. 'Bullet casings, Sean.'

Sean broke a twig from a tree and stuck it in the ground next to the spent cartridges. 'Copper, probably Russian, maybe a Makarov. Ex–military issue in Mozambique. This is where the bastard shot Benny and fired at me.'

Tumi noticed a hole in his shirt. 'What happened?'

Sean plucked at the camouflage clothing. 'Oh, yeah. I remember now. The bullet went through one side and out the other.'

Shikar sniffed along the poacher's trail and barked again. There was plenty to keep her interested.

'There's some fabric here; looks like Benny took a chunk out of him and his clothes. And something else.'

'What have you got?'

Tumi dropped to one knee. She took a handkerchief from her pocket and used it to pick up a small black plastic box. She held it up for Sean to see. The sun was struggling up and the bush was turning pale grey around them.

'Tumi, this is fantastic. It's a garage door remote, our first piece of real evidence.'

'I tried to tell Charles,' Tumi said, passing it to him, 'that what looked like the bomb didn't have to be located near the rhino's ear that Shikar had found. I was trying to remember everything you told me about bombs, I mean, IEDs.'

Sean inspected the remote. 'This one was command-detonated and the cops can hopefully learn something from this.'

'Yes,' Tumi said. 'I couldn't remember the term, but it was like you said; a decoy object had been placed to get the dog's attention, and then when we all started to come closer the guy detonated the explosives by remote, somewhere we weren't expecting it.'

'Yes,' said Sean. 'The bastard was watching you all when he pressed the button.'

It was cool in the pre-dawn gloom, but even so, Tumi felt like she'd just fallen into ice-cold water.

Chapter 11

Christine used a wheelbarrow to move the fifty-kilogram bag of Superwoof dog food from the storeroom to the dogs' runs on her farm. She had called the hospital to get a progress report on Charles; he would be laid up for a while but his injuries would not result in any permanent disability, for which she thanked God.

Christine needed to keep busy, to stop herself from climbing the walls, so she threw herself into her daily chores. To save money, she did as much of the labouring around the farm as she could. She also found it therapeutic and good, if monotonous, exercise.

She had already raked around the runs. The dogs' night homes were enclosed with wire fencing, and mesh was also placed around the lower thirty centimetres of the fence to keep out mice, which would try to get to the dogs' food, and snakes, which would go for the mice and the dogs both. As an extra precaution, raking the soil around the entire circumference of the enclosure allowed Christine to spot the crescent-shaped slither marks of snakes that might have been moving about in the night.

Christine had just got off the phone to Craig again and, shortly after him, Julianne Clyde-Smith, who was in her office in London. Christine sighed. In the last ten days or so Lion Plains had gone from being a model of how to fight rhino poaching to losing three of the precious animals, making it the hardest-hit part of the greater Kruger Park.

Julianne was an incredibly wealthy businesswoman who had made her fortune in IT and diversified into travel and tourism. She owned several safari lodges and concessions in southern and east Africa. She affected a casual, friendly style in her public persona, which endeared her to the media, but she was almost fanatical in her quest to fight poaching. Also, as Christine had just learned, she had zero tolerance for what she perceived as failure.

'What do you need?' Julianne had asked her.

'I could just say money,' Christine said, 'but what I really need is time, to train our handlers and dogs in detecting all types of explosives, detonators and other IED components, and we need more people qualified in disarming or destroying these things. The South African Police simply don't have enough resources.'

'Then we will develop those skills,' Julianne had said. 'Or, rather, you will. What do we know about who planted these devices?'

'Nothing, yet, but I'm working on that. I'll get back to you.'

Christine dropped off food to each of the half-a-dozen dogs and, when they had finished eating and she had topped up the water for all of them, she opened their runs. The dogs bounded out and her favourite and the closest she had to a pet, Anubis, named after an Egyptian god, pushed the others aside to nuzzle her. Anubis was a jet-black German Shepherd from champion stock. 'Hello, my boy.'

Normally patting Anubis soothed Christine, but not today. She was unsettled as she and the dogs walked to her farmhouse. While her entourage arrayed themselves, by pecking order, on couches or floor space, Christine sat down at her computer.

With Anubis curled at her feet, she logged on to the internet and opened Facebook. She entered the name *Ruth Boustead* in the search field. A match came up.

It had been a long time since she and Ruth had been in contact. Christine saw from the new profile picture that Ruth still had that fresh-faced California beach girl look and there were some images on her home page of her in a white bikini, paddleboarding. She was still fit by the look of it. Ruth listed her job as 'wage slave for Uncle Sam', but Christine knew that Ruth was no run-of-the-mill public servant. She had degrees in computer science, electrical engineering and chemistry.

Ruth was one of the smartest women Christine had ever met. And she worked for the FBI. They had met in Afghanistan when Ruth was working there as an analyst and Christine was running the in-country operations for a canine company that supplied dogs for security at the embassy.

Christine opened a new message box and typed, *Hi Ruth, long time no talk. How are you?* Christine busied herself with some emails and then a few minutes later went back to Facebook. She was pleasantly surprised to find that Ruth had replied and was showing as being online.

They exchanged a few messages, each asking how the other had been since they'd seen each other two years earlier, and then Christine asked Ruth if she had time to chat using video. *Sure*, Ruth replied.

'Howzit? That's what you South Africans say, isn't it?' Ruth asked when they both turned on the camera function.

Christine waved. Ruth hadn't changed a bit, and Christine wondered how different she looked and if the stresses she had been through with Sean had taken a toll. 'Yes, that's right, and a howdy to you.'

'Well, no one actually says "howdy" where I live, but it's nice to see you again.'

They both laughed.

'Ruth, I have a problem,' Christine said.

'Shoot. We do actually say "shoot", which can be dangerous in a country where so many people are armed.'

'Same here,' said Christine with a chuckle. 'Ruth, there's someone targeting my dogs and their handlers over here in South Africa with IEDs. They're small devices, but so far they've injured two of my people and two of my dogs, one of whom may not make it.'

'Oh, that's you?' Ruth raised her eyebrows. 'At TEDAC we get news updates every day from around the world and I read about those incidents. I didn't realise it was your people. Sorry to hear that.'

'*Ja*, me as well. You guys have a database of terrorist bomb-makers, right?'

'Yes, that's correct. That's where I work now, TEDAC, here in beautiful downtown Huntsville, Alabama.'

'TEDAC?'

Ruth nodded. 'It stands for the Terrorist Explosive Device Analytical Center. The Bureau – the FBI – is an acronym-rich environment. We analyse data on IEDs from around the world and use it to try to defeat terrorist bombmakers.'

'Yes, I remember in Afghanistan you were analysing IEDs to find the guys who made them.'

'Yep. TEDAC is where all the data I gathered in Afghanistan went. We have databases of fingerprints and DNA left by bombmakers and these guys – engineers they sometimes call themselves – are like many people doing a job, they do things slightly differently from each other and have patterns and routines in their work. That's often how we catch them.'

'Fascinating. Would TEDAC be interested in investigating what's going on here?'

'Hmm, I'd like to say yes, Christine, but the truth is our remit is to disrupt terrorists who pose a threat to America and our interests, so I don't think any of our technical or scientific people will be catching an airplane to Johannesburg any time soon. Sorry.'

'I understand. I'm worried, though, that this problem is too big for the South African Police and their forensic or bomb squad people. My guy who's dealing with the local cops keeps getting stonewalled by them. According to him, they don't know how to deal with this kind of IED and their labs are so overworked with other criminal cases that it doesn't seem like we'll get a lead on what the devices were made of or where they were made any time soon.'

'That sounds pretty typical of a lot of cops, although here in the US we've learned some lessons since 9/11 and we're much better these days at getting our various law enforcement agencies together. Having said that, there is still what I call the penis factor, please excuse my French.'

Christine gave a small laugh. 'Boys will still be boys and want to protect their little fiefdoms.'

'I hear you,' Ruth said.

'So what can I do?'

'Well,' Ruth tapped a finger to her lips, 'if the Bureau got a request for help from the South African Police Service we would have to process that through official channels. But it could take a lot of time and, like I said, unless we were convinced that the threat in South Africa posed some danger to our interests, it's not guaranteed that we could help.'

'Time is something I don't have, Ruth.'

'I wish I could help you, Christine, but I'm just a cog in the machine.'

'You're more than that.'

'Still . . .'

'Still, do you remember that vehicle checkpoint in Kabul?' Christine asked.

Ruth said nothing for a few seconds and Christine wondered at first if the screen had frozen, or if Ruth was about to terminate the connection. Christine felt bad, but said nothing. She hadn't wanted to play this card, but her whole livelihood was at stake, so she'd do what she had to do.

'That's a little unfair, Christine,' Ruth said at last.

'You told me one of my dogs had saved your life. Didn't you mean it?'

Ruth had been stopped in her vehicle at a security checkpoint near the US embassy in Kabul when one of Christine's handlers and his dog had been searching the car ahead of them. Christine was there, conducting quality assurance checks on the handler and his Malinois. The dog, Fifty, named after the rapper Fifty Cent, had given a passive indication of explosives. Christine had waved to Ruth to back up.

The driver of the car had got out and the Afghan soldiers manning the checkpoint had hesitated, because she was a woman. She had started to run and the handler had sent Fifty after her. It turned out the woman was a Taliban recruit who was wearing a suicide vest. She detonated the bomb, killing herself and Fifty and injuring the handler. A later search of her vehicle showed that it was packed with explosives.

'Are you playing hardball with me, Christine?'

'Yes. I'm sorry, Ruth, but I'm desperate. One of my dogs and handlers saved your life and now someone is deliberately trying to kill my people. All I'm asking for is some help in trying to find out who's behind this.'

'I've got a soft spot for dogs, and you're right, Christine, Fifty did save my life.' Ruth shrugged and lifted her hands, palms up. 'But what do you want me to do?'

'How can you help us identify one of these bombmakers? Could you run some sort of database search?'

Ruth drew a breath, then exhaled. 'I guess. I could look for engineers who are African or have a connection to southern Africa. Also, if you can find out what sort of explosives the bomb-maker used, that's something, though not a lot. We also have fingerprint and DNA databases. If you had a component that had traces of the bombmaker himself on it we could try and run a match, but that would involve getting evidence to the States, agency to agency, and then my bosses would have to decide to proceed with offering assistance.'

Christine knew how bureaucracy worked – or didn't; she was African born. It was nonetheless infuriating. 'Sean thinks both IEDs were command-detonated by someone close by using a garage door remote. One of my handlers, a smart young woman, found one of the remotes, but we've had to give that to the local police.'

'Hmm,' Ruth said, touching her lips again, 'that gives us a little more, knowing what type of remote was used. It's not unusual for terrorist bombmakers to use different types of triggers, depending on the tactical situation and the target, but the sloppy ones fall into patterns and use the same methods and components over and over.'

'Oh, and Ruth, the bombs were small, Sean says. He thinks they were deliberately made and set to take out my dogs or to wound rather than kill. Is it enough for you to at least start a search?'

Ruth shrugged again. 'It's not a lot, but if Sean is right we might have something on bombmakers who make it their business to take out dog teams.'

'So you'll help me?' Christine said.

'I guess it wouldn't hurt if I carried out a preliminary search for you,' Ruth said. 'I mean, you're a citizen with information about a possible *terrorist*.'

'And there are American guests staying at the safari lodge that pays for my team, so you could say they are potentially at risk, just as my handlers and dogs are. Even though they're not; you could say the guests are cutting their stay short by two days and flying out tomorrow. The lodge, Lion Plains, is virtually empty since the news about the bombs made it into the newspapers – courtesy of the same cops who don't seem to want to even ask you for help.'

Ruth nodded. 'I can see how this would be bad for business for you all; I guess the lodge relies on foreign tourists.'

'Yes, and any perceived threat, like Ebola, crime or terrorism, can be enough to make a well-heeled tourist choose a different African country for their once-in-a-lifetime safari. However, it's my people and my dogs I'm most worried about, more than my client's business.'

'Yes, I get that. OK, Christine, I do owe you, so let me do a search with what you've given me.'

Christine took a deep breath. 'Ruth, I hate to say this, but I think you owe me more.'

Ruth frowned. 'You're right, but remember I have to play by the rules here. If you were to, say, hypothetically, get me some components from an IED made by your guy, then I could maybe kick this up the chain. However, if you choose to go off the reservation you may be denying the South African Police of some leads they could use to catch the perpetrator, Christine. You're playing with fire.'

'No, I'm playing with people's lives. Thanks, Ruth. I'm sorry I came across like I did, like I was trying to blackmail you or something.'

Ruth held up her hands. 'No, it's fine. I'm also a big girl. I know that sometimes we need to navigate our way around the rules, if not actually break them, to catch the bad guys in this world. They don't play fair. Any other information you can find out about the IEDs – what type of explosives were used, detonators, timers, shrapnel or accelerants – would all be useful as it might help me narrow the search. I've also got a contact in your part of the world I can reach out to via a back channel.'

'Who's that?'

'Well, I shouldn't use his full name, but if you hear from a guy called Jed, just be aware that he works for a big American *company* that has an interest in terrorism, if you get my drift.'

Christine nodded. She had met a few men and women from the Company, the CIA, in Afghanistan in the course of her work. 'Do you think he might be able to help?'

'Jed makes it his business to keep track of the bad guys in southern Africa; if there's been any chatter about bombmakers, there's a chance he might have picked up on it.'

'Thanks, Ruth, I'll be in touch if I learn anything new.'

'Same here, Christine. Take care.'

Christine closed down her computer. She rolled her shoulders. She was tense and sore and she knew it was to do with the stress of the situation. She checked her emails and found one from Charles, sent from his hospital bed via his phone. Thankfully, he was doing OK and would be released from hospital soon. He had a partially damaged eardrum, but the doctor expected he would recover. She typed a reply, wishing him a speedy recovery, but telling him he should not feel under pressure to return to work too soon.

'Why us?' she asked aloud.

*

David Li pulled up at the gate with the words *Hunde und Katzen* in wrought iron above it. He leaned out of his car window and pressed the talk button on the intercom mounted on a pole.

'Hello?' said a female voice.

'I am looking for Miss Christine Glover, please,' he said.

'That's me. Who is this?'

'My name is David Li, Miss Glover. We spoke on the phone a couple of weeks ago.'

There was a pause, no doubt while she searched her memory. 'Oh, yes, I remember. Sorry, Mr Li, as I told you, lion hunting safaris are no longer offered on this farm.'

'Yes, Miss Glover, you made that quite clear. However, I find myself in this part of the country on business and I would very much like to say hello and discuss a business proposition with you. It will not take long, but could be worth your consideration. Trust me, it has nothing to do with hunting.'

David was a patient man. He knew that he would not get another opportunity to talk to the woman on the telephone, but he hoped that she would have enough innate politeness not to turn away a stranger who wanted to talk business. He also knew how parlous her financial situation was.

'All right, Mr Li, follow the road a kilometre, straight on and bear right when you come to the fork.'

'Thank you.' He smiled and put the Mercedes into gear.

David followed her directions, and as he approached the stone-clad farmhouse with the thatch roof the woman emerged with a pack of dogs at her heels. He opened his window halfway. 'Miss Glover.'

'Mr Li.'

'Is it safe for me to get out?' There were hounds close enough to fog the outside of his windows.

Christine put her hands on her hips. 'Heel, Anubis. Come on out, Anubis won't kill you unless I tell him to.'

David got out of his car. He kept his hands up high, slightly concerned that one of the dogs might bite off a finger. He wore tan chinos with loafers, a pink polo shirt and Ray-Ban sunglasses; he did not want some dog standing up on its hind legs and pawing him.

'What can I do for you, Mr Li?'

'Please call me David.'

'OK. Come inside, the dogs won't hurt you.'

'I must confess, I have something of a fear of dogs. I was attacked as a child.' It was true, the animals unnerved him, and Li thought that by revealing his fear he might put the woman more at ease around him, and perhaps make her take pity on him.

'I'm sorry to hear that.'

'Thank you for your understanding.' They walked side by side, but David made sure he kept his distance from the big black German Shepherd. 'I know what people say, that there is no such thing as a bad dog, only a bad owner, and it's true that the people who owned the dog that attacked me were less than desirable, but I always felt the dog had a particular hatred of me. I don't know if maybe the owners had trained it to attack non-white people.'

'That's terrible if what you say is true.' Christine led him into her home. It was a simple but comfortable affair, stone walls and polished concrete floors, but too much dog hair on the chairs and couch for his liking. He sneezed. 'Bless you. I'll put the kettle on. Coffee?'

'Tea, if you have it, rooibos if possible.'

'Sure. Now what can I do for you? Take a seat.' She gestured to a lounge chair.

He sat, doing his best to hide his distaste at the hair. 'I'd like to discuss a business proposition with you, Christine.'

'Not hunting, not even plains game.'

'No, of course not, you made it quite clear when we spoke on the phone that there would be no more safaris. You're not alone in this, many other hunting properties are being progressively converted to lodges offering photographic safaris or other environmentally acceptable activities.'

'You sound disappointed.'

'Not for me, so much, but for some of my clients.'

'What sort of business are you in, David?' she asked. 'Are you a safari outfitter? Travel agent?'

He rocked his head from side to side. 'Yes and no, a bit of both.

I'm more what you might call a facilitator. I deal in some imports and exports and I network a good deal. I see myself as something of a conduit between Africa and the Far East.'

Christine raised her eyebrows.

David put his hands up, feigning horror. 'I can assure you, I do not deal in anything illegal. Contrary to what you might think, not all people of Asian descent are rhino horn and ivory poachers or smugglers.'

'I wouldn't suggest such a thing.'

'No, but I could tell that you, like some other people, mistake "import–export" as a euphemism for smuggling.'

'I apologise if I caused any offence.'

He smiled inwardly; he had her correctly pegged as an English-speaking South African liberal, nursing a guilt hangover from having been brought up during the apartheid era. Such people loathed being branded as racists. 'Not at all. It is I who should be sorry for arriving unannounced. It is impolite, especially in my culture.'

The kettle whistled and Christine poured coffee for her and tea for him. 'Well, now we've got the apologies out of the way, what can I help you with?'

'I'd like to invest in your business, specifically your lions,' he said.

'My lions are not for sale.' Christine sipped her coffee.

David held up his hand. 'Please, at least hear me out. You are very well known, as is your work to promote the cause of wild lions. I, too, am a fan of big cats, and I think it is terrible what is happening to lions in the wild. I would also like to see wild lions protected.'

'I'm listening, but I'm not selling.'

'Please.' Christine did not reply, so he continued. 'I represent some people who would like to invest in your facility here, to help with the upkeep of your lions and to help you to better promote the plight of wild lions by attracting visitors here who could see your lions and learn more about them and their wild relatives.'

'I've had plenty of people suggest that to me, David, but I don't have the money or the inclination to act on that suggestion. If people come here they're going to want to see me rolling around on the ground with Felix and Casper, and I don't want to become a circus act.'

'I understand completely, and you have your other business, training dogs and handlers for anti-poaching work, I believe. You must be busy.'

'Yes, very.' She sipped some more coffee and sat back in her lounge chair.

'But it must cost you a good deal of money to keep all the lions that came with this property, not to mention your own big cats. I don't mean to sound nosey or rude, but I have done a bit of research on your situation.'

She raised her eyebrows again. 'So what is my "situation"?'

'You had to borrow heavily to keep this farm after your ex-husband gambled away his stake in it. I have contacts in the casino industry. Sean Bourke is well known to them, for the wrong reasons. Also, I read in the media that your dogs and handlers have recently been targeted by particularly heinous weaponry.'

She set down her cup. He could see that her hackles were rising. 'What do you want?'

'To help you.'

'By turning my farm into a zoo.'

'Not at all. You have an excellent location here. There is a shortage of accommodation in this part of South Africa. The Kruger Park is full to bursting; more South Africans than ever are holidaying at home given the state of the rand, and the rest of the world has discovered Kruger. My investors think that a lodge on this farm would be well patronised. The presence of your lions, and even your dog training, would be an added attraction for tourists, and if you wished to make yourself available then I am sure some of your tens of thousands of Facebook fans would pay a good deal to see the "female lion whisperer" at play with Felix and Casper.'

She said nothing, but he detected from slight movements that she was biting the inside of her lip. He believed that he had guessed correctly, that the thought of setting up some form of accommodation on the farm had crossed her mind at some point. Tourism had boomed in the Hazyview area in the past ten years, and there was no sign of a slowing of demand for places to stay near the Kruger Park. Probably the only thing that had stopped her was money.

'The people I represent would provide the money for building a lodge, perhaps twelve permanent safari tents with en suite bathrooms and a communal lounge and dining area with a pool, and funding for staff and leases on game-viewing vehicles. There would be no outlay by you, and the consortium would pay you an annual lease of, say, one million rand, plus twenty per cent of net profits.'

She picked up her coffee again, affecting an air of casual disinterest, but he knew he had her attention. 'What would your investors expect in return?'

'A twenty-year lease with an option to extend, your guaranteed appearance at a number of shows with your lions, perhaps ten or twelve a year, and ownership of half of your population of lions – excluding Felix and Casper of course.'

Christine finished her coffee and set down the cup. 'Why do your people want my lions?'

'The income from the lodge will provide the lions with food and a safe place to live for the term of their natural lives. It's only fair that the operators of the lodge would have a moral right to call some of the lions their own. The people I represent are fanatical about big cats.'

'And what would they do with the lions?'

'Do? Well, they would take care of them. There might be scope, if the lodge does well, to replicate the model in other parts of Africa – not close enough to be in competition with you, but perhaps in Botswana, Zimbabwe, Zambia?'

'I've made a commitment not to breed my lions, David, so I cannot be a party to someone setting up a petting zoo, breeding lions to be handled by tourists and then, as often happens, shot by trophy hunters when they get older.'

'Rest assured,' David said, 'the people I represent know about you and your views on lions and canned hunting. I swear to you they have no intention of setting up a petting zoo or of organising for your lions to be hunted. They will all live full and enriched lives.'

'I would want something like that in writing.'

'Naturally.'

'When we spoke last time you said you had clients who wanted to hunt. Are these the same people?'

David shook his head. 'Most assuredly not. Different people. The people I represent now are solely interested in developing a photographic camp on your property, Christine.'

'And they want to use my lions as zoo attractions.'

'They want to educate tourists about the problems faced by wild lions, and one of the best ways to do that is to give visitors the chance to see big cats up close.'

'That's an argument that's been used by zoos for centuries. I don't necessarily buy it, but I do believe zoos have a conservation role to play. I'm just not sure I want my lions exploited.'

'They wouldn't be exploited,' David said. 'They would be kept in the manner that you intend, supervised by you, and they would be helping the cause. Also, it would relieve much of the financial burden you currently face, generate income for use in whichever way you see fit, and ensure the lions see out their days in a happy, healthy, productive manner.'

He could see she was considering the idea or, at least, not dismissing it out of hand. 'These investors, where are they from?' she asked.

'China. With mainland China's economy expanding so rapidly, Chinese people have more disposable income than at any time in history and are travelling further and wider across the globe than ever before. Younger Chinese are becoming more aware of wildlife and the need to conserve it.'

'All well and good,' Christine said, 'but what about the hunters you wanted to bring here, when you first contacted me. Where are they from?'

'Also China.'

'I didn't know the Chinese were into big game hunting, if you could classify canned hunting as that.'

'It's not only Americans who like the idea of mounting a lion's head on their wall. Personally, I have never hunted and nor would I wish to.' That was the truth. He found the idea of blood sports abhorrent, but he did want those lions, at almost any cost.

'Tell me, David, what happened to the bones of the lions that were shot on this farm in the past, once the trophy hunters – whatever their nationality – had taken away the skin and the heads?'

She was not stupid. 'You would have to ask the previous owners of your property.'

'I did,' Christine said. 'They were as evasive as you are being right now.'

'There are no restrictions on the export of lion bones, and while some airlines are refusing to ship big game trophies out of Africa, there are enough that still do to allow this *legal* industry to continue.'

'That's pretty much what the previous owners told me as well. Is that the corporate line for you people?'

'By *you people*, I hope that you are not casting aspersions on my ethnicity?' David said, playing the race card again.

She slapped the arm of her chair. 'No, by *you people*, I mean morally repugnant criminals.'

David paused, composed himself, took a sip of tea then set his cup down. 'I am not a criminal, and I resent any implication to that effect. And please, let's not raise our voices.'

Christine took a deep breath. 'The export of lion bones is a loophole in legislation that will be closed soon.'

'But it hasn't been closed yet. When your lions die, of natural causes, I can act as a broker and offer you, legally, a handsome payment for their skeletons.'

Christine stood and glared down at him. 'Over my dead body.'

'You know, Christine, the bones of big cats have been used in traditional Chinese medicine for centuries.'

'Yes, tigers originally, and now that they've virtually been wiped out in the wild you're substituting them with lion bones. That's why there has been this insidious trade in bones flying under the radar for years.'

'It is not illegal.'

She put her hands on her hips. 'No, it's just disgusting.'

'Look at it this way –'

'There is no way to look at it.'

'Please,' he said, 'let us discuss this rationally.'

'No!' She stabbed a finger at him. 'You're going to tell me that canned hunting, breeding lions to be petted as cubs and shot as adults, has supplied the de facto market in lion bones for years.'

He folded his hands in his lap. 'Yes, Christine, that is exactly what I am telling you. Also, as the South African government has pointed out in past reports, lion farming is a major industry in this country. It provides employment, directly and indirectly, from the people who work in the hunting camps as professional hunters, guides, skinners, hospitality staff, right through to small-scale farmers who sell donkeys to the farms for food for the lions. In South Africa, as you know, big game hunters can only hunt lions on private land, and lion farms fill this role, meaning the population of wild lions in South Africa is sacrosanct, unlike many other African countries where wild, free-ranging lions are hunted on land bordering national parks.'

He could see she was seething now. 'I know the situation with lions as well as or better than you, and I can see through your proposals, Mr Li.'

'What do you mean? My investors are serious about wanting to set up a photographic safari camp.'

'Yes, I'm sure they are, the greedy bastards, and they want to buy half of my stock of lions to breed future generations for the slaughter.' Her voice was shrill, raised again. 'For their bloody bones! Now get up, Mr Li, and get out of my house before I have my dogs chase you out.'

David stood. He had tried the straightforward business approach, and while her response was predictably angry, it was disappointing. 'Thank you for your time. I'm sorry you do not wish to hear more of our proposal. I hope you don't come to regret your decision.'

She squared up to him and pointed at him again, a gesture he found exceptionally rude. 'If you try and buy into any other game reserve or lion farm in South Africa I'll make sure the world knows on social media that you're a filthy trader in death and helpless animals. You're no businessman, you're a common smuggler. Now get the hell off my property.'

He turned and walked out of the house. Anubis gave a low growl, and David looked over his shoulder at the dog. He shivered, but he was able to still his fear with the knowledge that he had access to weapons that would not only potentially destroy Christine's dogs, but also her business. There would come a time, and soon, when she would be begging to sell to him, or, if that failed, perhaps begging for her life.

Chapter 12

Sean came to visit me in hospital, which was good, because the place was freaking me out, know what I mean?

'Benny, stop licking yourself,' that bastard Graham said to me.

You're just envious, Doc.

Graham held up his bandaged finger to my face. 'You've got a funny way of thanking me, Benny.'

Bite me, Graham. As if.

'Stop barking. There are other animals trying to sleep.'

Whatever. It was good seeing Sean and Tumi, and Shikar of course. Shikar had a sniff of my wound and I whimpered a little, which made her lick my chops. I could get used to getting shot.

Seriously, it wasn't as bad as getting blown up. I've had bites from other dogs that needed more stitches than Graham put in me. There was this female Afghan hound . . . but that's another story.

Sean looked worried, and I picked up on that. Right now, all I want to do is get back out in the bush and back to work. I don't even care about Vin, the leopard; things are bad, and the humans need my help.

'Benny, I said stop that.'
Come a little bit closer, Graham . . .
He did, but he had a syringe in his sore fingers and . . .

*

After they had finished visiting Benny at the veterinary surgery, Sean drove Tumi back to camp. Benny was sedated from the injection Graham had given him, but the vet assured them Benny would survive.

Sean had told Tumi to grab some sleep and when he awoke in the early afternoon, there was no sound from her tent. Sean had quietly let Clyde, the old bloodhound, out of his run.

Sean did not doubt Tumi's capabilities, but he felt she needed a good rest after seeing the events of last night. Also, after what had happened to Benny he did not fully trust himself with what he might do if he found the man who had shot his dog. It might be something best not witnessed by someone he had come to regard as a friend in a very short time.

When they came to the place where the rhino had been killed, the midday sun was scorching. Sean held the small fragment of green cloth to Clyde's nose and the old dog breathed it in with the appreciation of a sommelier getting his first noseful of a Château Lafite Rothschild.

The poacher's body was gone, to be delivered by the South African Police to the Mozambican border for claiming by his relatives, if there were any. A flock of white-backed vultures took off as Sean approached.

Shikar had found the bullet casings at the crime scene and a police forensics officer with a metal detector, axe and knife had hacked into the rhino's body and found the slugs inside. All had been taken for evidence, along with the garage door remote that Tumi had found.

Sean could hardly withhold the remote control from the police, however before the forensic team had descended on the crime scene, Sean had done as Christine had suggested and got a head start on the investigation by finding something they might be able to use. He had discreetly torn off a scrap of fabric from the patch Benny had ripped out of the man's clothes. He was now glad he had illegally souvenired this small piece of evidence.

People were deceitful, not least of all himself, Sean thought as he fitted Clyde's tracking harness. Dogs were honest. 'Clyde, *soek*.'

Head turning, ears flapping, Clyde ambled off. He was getting old and at Clyde's last check-up Graham Baird had discovered a lump that was cancerous. According to Graham, Clyde, who was already an old dog, was not long for this world, but he still seemed to like getting out and working. Benny was good at attacking, and tracking humans and explosives, and Shikar was proving a real keeper when it came to following animal scent and bullet casings, but Clyde's nose put both of theirs to shame; he could pick up a trail that was three days old, so this was almost like a hot pursuit for him.

They left the stinking carcass and Clyde's nose vacuumed the ground for minute particles of the man they were after. At times he would lose the trail and Sean would cast him in a circle until he picked up another trace.

Sean's phone, set to silent, vibrated in his pocket. 'Here, Clyde, sit, boy.'

The old hound panted, probably glad of the rest, while Sean took out his phone. It was Christine.

'Howzit?'

'Fine, sort of,' she said. 'Where are you?'

'In the bush. I just left the rhino carcass, with Clyde. He's on the scent of the poacher who shot Benny. I kept a bit of the DNA on a piece of shirt Benny tore off.'

Christine exhaled audibly. 'I really don't want to get you in trouble, Sean.'

'Relax,' he said. 'I haven't kept anything that the cops don't also have a sample of. The poacher will be long gone, but I'm hoping to at least find out where and how he got out of the Sabi Sand.'

'Cool,' she said. Christine then told him about a conversation she'd had with Ruth Boustead from the FBI in America. 'We need to find out everything we can about these IEDs. That piece of shirt might also help us. If we can find that poacher, the cops might be able to get a lead on the bombmaker from him.'

'OK,' Sean said. He knew Christine well enough to detect a note of worry in her voice. 'What's wrong?'

'I just had a visit from a Chinese guy called David Li. He's a businessman, of sorts. He wanted to buy into the farm, specifically the lion side of things. Seems like he wants a lifetime's supply of lion bones. I told him to go fuck himself.'

Sean didn't laugh. 'Flashy guy, well dressed, receding hairline, new Merc?'

'Sounds like him,' Christine said.

'I know Li, by name and sight, not personally but from, well, from my previous life. He's a high roller at the tables in Joburg, talks big, doesn't care how much he wins or loses. Are you OK?'

Christine sighed. 'A bit shaken, to tell you the truth. And I felt bad.'

'About what?' he asked.

'About earlier this morning, when we talked. You asked about Craig, and, I guess, me.'

'You don't have to tell me anything,' he said. He had tried to ask the question, about what was going on between them, but now he did not want to hear the answer. It was easier not knowing.

'I owe it to you, Sean. Craig's your friend, as am I, I hope.'

'You are,' he said.

'Craig's been good to me, Sean. He helped me out.'

After I failed you, Sean said to himself, but stayed silent.

'I like you, Sean,' she carried on, 'I really do. I also like Craig. We've become –'

'It's OK, really,' Sean said quickly. He didn't need to hear more.

'Damn it, Sean, just let me finish.'

Sean covered the mouthpiece of the phone and spoke softly but firmly to Clyde. 'Watch him!'

Clyde followed the command and started barking on cue, at nothing.

'Sean?'

'I've got to go, Christine, Clyde's on to something.'

'Sean, don't fob me off like this. You hurt me, but I never stopped –'

Sean ended the call. It was best for both of them, he told himself, if it stopped there. Besides, he and Clyde had work to do.

'Clyde, *soek*.' Sean had a compass on his watch and a hand-held GPS on his webbing vest. They headed west, towards the outer perimeter fence of the Sabi Sand Game Reserve, away from Mozambique, which was across the adjoining Kruger Park to the east.

That didn't mean the poacher was not Mozambican. The Tsonga people who lived on the border of the Kruger Park were related to the Shangaan, and both their traditional homelands straddled the line on the map drawn hundreds of years earlier by Europeans to separate the former Portuguese colony of Mozambique and South Africa. Local people moved, legally and illegally, across the international border for work, for school, for weddings and funerals, and for crime.

The poacher had spoken with a Portuguese accent. Again, that didn't mean he lived in Mozambique, and the trail seemed to indicate otherwise, but Sean kept an open mind. Christine had said the garage door remote could possibly have given the FBI some leads on who might have made the IEDs, but that the South

African Police were showing no interest in seeking overseas help. If Sean could find something else that provided a possible link to the bombmaker, then they might be able to pass the evidence on to the Americans directly. Quite how they would get it there, Sean had no idea.

Sean heard a vehicle engine somewhere ahead of him, and when Clyde led him through some thick bush at a dry creek crossing he saw that the land opened up. A couple of hundred yards further on was the perimeter of the game reserve. He could see a work truck, and labourers in blue overalls with picks and shovels milling about. A security company *bakkie* had just pulled up. Clyde picked up the pace towards the workers.

'Sean, howzit?' called a man in camouflage. It was Conraad, one of the senior managers in the reserve's security company.

'Good. Clyde's telling me to come this way.'

'*Ja*, well, I'm not surprised. Some *skelm*'s been crawling under the fence here.'

'It's the guy who killed the rhino yesterday.'

'You're sure?' Conraad asked.

'Clyde's on his trail.'

'He must have dug himself out.'

'He's good,' Sean said. 'An old *toppie*, short grey hair. We got his young offsider.'

'*Ja*. I heard you drilled one. Good job.'

Sean closed his eyes, briefly, pushing the image of the dead young man out of his mind. He opened them. 'I need to follow this guy.'

'Want backup?'

Sean nodded. 'Oliver's on leave and Charles is in the hospital. Tumi was nearly killed and saw her first dead body yesterday, so she's taking a mental health day.'

'So much for Lion Plains's ace dog unit, hey?'

'You offering backup?'

'Sean, you know you should let the local police know if you're conducting a pursuit outside the game reserve as you're out of your jurisdiction. I could call them for you if you want to get moving.'

Sean knew Conraad was right, but if he did find some evidence linking someone to the bombs he didn't want to have to hand it over to the police. 'I don't want to waste time waiting for some cops, Conraad, and this trail will probably lead nowhere. I understand if you need to make the call, but don't feel like you need to hurry.'

Conraad winked. 'Understood. But I'm still happy to come and back you up. If we do find something we can call the police then. I'll leave these guys to plug the hole and drive back to the exit gate. I'll look for you on the other side.'

'Cheers, Conraad.' Sean felt himself being backed into a corner, but Conraad was doing the right thing. If he did find something he would do his best to keep it to himself.

Sean let Clyde off his lead and told him to go under the fence. The labourers moved aside, giving the big dog a wide berth, and Clyde got down on his haunches and scrambled under the wire. Sean had to get down on his belly and leopard-crawl while one of the workers, who was wearing protective gloves, held the coiled razor wire up for him to get under. Clyde, tongue lolling, ears flapping, was ready to get back to work.

'*Soek!*'

As they were out of the game reserve and there was little chance of encountering dangerous animals, save perhaps the odd leopard, Sean let Clyde off the lead. The dog ranged ahead. Out here there was much to potentially confuse him, as people and cattle used the road they were crossing. Clyde followed his nose up the road then back again until he finally crossed, some hundred metres from the hole in the fence.

'He's clever, boy. He was trying to throw us.' Sean checked the ground and saw not a sign of a footprint. The old poacher had covered his tracks. Once outside of the Sabi Sand he would have felt a measure of comfort, and with no one in pursuit he had painstakingly obliterated any visible sign of his presence. But not his smell.

Reinvigorated, Clyde set off. They moved through land owned by the local community that served as a buffer zone between the areas where most people lived and the game reserve. There was remnant natural vegetation, mostly stunted acacias, but much of it had been cleared for firewood, or by the grazing of cattle.

Clyde moved at a steady pace, and although Sean was armed, he kept his rifle slung over his shoulder so as not to alarm any herdsmen or other locals they might come across. All the same, he did not drop his guard.

'*Sean, Sean, Conraad, come in,*' said the voice on his radio.

'Copy, Conraad,' Sean replied.

'*I'm out of the gate now, heading along the perimeter fence. Can you give me an idea where you are now?*'

'I'm in the trust land, over. The guy headed a couple hundred metres south and then cut out due west.'

'*Copy that.*'

After a few minutes Sean heard a vehicle engine behind him and the whoosh of traffic on tar road off to his left. He realised Clyde had been leading him southwest, towards the R536, the main road that led from Hazyview to the Paul Kruger Gate entrance of the Kruger Park, via Mkhuhlu.

'Conraad, Sean.'

'*Go ahead, Sean.*'

'I can hear you, I think. I'm about four hundred metres in, getting close to the R536. Wait a minute.'

'*Roger, over.*'

Sean looked at Clyde. The dog had raised his head to look around and then set off at a faster pace. Sean could see what had his attention.

'Conraad, there's a couple of huts up ahead through the bush. Clyde's making a beeline for them. I think they must belong to herdsmen or something.'

'*Roger, Sean, I think I know the buildings you're talking about. There should be a rough road to them coming up from the tar.*'

Sean glanced around and saw that Conraad was right. 'Affirmative. I see the track.'

'*All right, I'm coming just now. I'll hit the tar and turn in on the gravel track.*'

'Copy,' Sean said.

Sean and Clyde went to the huts. They were simple affairs of mud brick with grass thatch, not kept well enough for people to live in them permanently. They were either old, or only used seasonally. There was a place between the huts where a fire had been made, a circle of stones with ash in the middle. Sean went to it and held his hand over it. There was no heat emanating from it, but when he dug his fingers into the ash he felt warmth.

Clyde busied himself around the huts, but he seemed to have lost the scent of the man he was following.

'What happened, Clyde?' Sean asked. The dog stopped, raised his big head and barked.

Sean looked up at the sound of Clyde's barks and saw Conraad's *bakkie* approaching.

'Typical dog, you heard the truck even before I did.' He reattached Clyde's lead.

As Conraad drove up, Sean looked about. He noticed tyre tracks. That in itself may or may not have been significant. While it looked as though the huts were not permanently occupied, someone had driven into this fairly remote part of the buffer lands recently.

Conraad stopped and got out. 'What are you looking at?'

'Tread patterns.'

Conraad shrugged. 'There's no control over people coming and going from this area. Could have been anyone, any time.'

'Why bother coming out here?'

Conraad shrugged. 'Looked in the huts yet?'

'No. Do we need a warrant or something?'

Conraad winked, then said, 'What's that?'

'What's what?' Sean asked.

'I just thought I heard a woman call for help from inside one of those huts, but I'm not sure which. I think we need to look in there.'

Sean grinned. 'You've been watching too many American cop shows.'

Conraad laughed and went to the first hut. He pushed open the rickety door, which was barely upright on one hinge, and went in. Sean and Clyde followed him. Inside were the remains of a broken slat bed and a thin, stained foam mattress. There were half-a-dozen empty Carling Black Label beer bottles on the floor, cigarette butts and a battered old pot minus a handle.

Sean looked up and saw daylight through the thatch roof. Clyde sniffed around. There was no shortage of interesting odours, but he gave no indication that the man whose scent he had been following had been in there.

'Try the next one?' Conraad said.

'Sure.'

They went out and Clyde began vacuuming. He wagged his tail and when Conraad opened the door of the next hut, Clyde strained at his lead. 'Move aside, please, Conraad. Maybe let Clyde go in first.'

'Ja, sure.'

Sean closed one eye before he went in after the dog. It was a bright sunny day outside and inside it would be dark and gloomy. If he had gone in with both eyes open it would have taken his eyes seconds to adjust. Closing one eye meant that one was already accustomed to the dark. It was a trick he had learned in Afghanistan and it had saved him once. He had seen a Taliban shooter lying under the bed in the room of a compound he and Benny had been searching and had been able to dive and roll out of the line of fire as the man opened up. The US Army Special Forces operators behind him had taken care of the bad guy.

Clyde barked.

'Room's clear,' Sean said over his shoulder, 'but the oke's been in here. Clyde's going crazy.'

Conraad came in and took an LED Lenser torch from a pouch on his belt. He scanned the inside of the hut.

Sean went to a window and opened the curtain. 'This place is in much better condition.'

'Ja.' Conraad played the narrow beam of light over the interior of the roof's beams. 'That looks waterproof.'

As in the other hut, Sean found a bed, but this one had all its legs intact. There was also a chair. The walls had been whitewashed at some stage but there were a few unsavoury-looking stains on them now. There were straws of long, dry, yellow thatching grass on the floor and small animal droppings, probably from a mouse that lived in the roof, Sean thought. Thatch roofs were beautiful and provided excellent insulation, but they also provided a home to a variety of reptiles and small mammals.

Clyde walked around the inside of the hut and sniffed the walls.

'So your poacher was here?' Conraad said.

'Seems so, though obviously he's not hiding here now.'

'No, he's not.' Sean took Clyde outside and cast him about the yard between the huts. They walked around the back of the one they had just searched and found an old desk pushed against the outside wall. Clyde sniffed around underneath it. Sean took out his handkerchief and, holding it so as not to leave fingerprints, he slid open the single drawer. He pulled it all the way out and checked underneath it.

'Nothing?' Conraad said. He went back to looking at the car treads.

'No,' said Sean.

'So it looks like he came here and was maybe collected by his buddies.'

'Could be,' Sean said.

'Any other ideas?'

Sean wasn't sure. 'Clyde did a great job picking up the old trail to get us here, but he seems confused now. He keeps wanting to go back into the hut. I guess that's because that's where the guy was last, and his scent is strongest there. Maybe he spent a night here.'

'Maybe,' Conraad said. 'As good a place as any to hide out.'

Sean rubbed his chin. 'Sit, Clyde.'

Conraad checked his watch. 'Sean, I'd love to stay and shoot the breeze, man, but I've got to check on those guys plugging the hole in the perimeter fence and then I've got a security committee meeting to get to. Bloody meetings; I spend too much time in offices and not enough in the bush.'

'No problem,' Sean said. 'I'll call the cops and tell them what we found here. I can get one of our people to come and collect me and Clyde.'

'You sure? I can give you a lift and we can call from the car if you like?'

'Thanks, but I'm happy to wait.'

Conraad shrugged. 'Suit yourself, *boet*. You might find some warm Black Labels stashed somewhere.'

Sean smiled and waved Conraad off. He took out his phone and dialled Tumi. They exchanged greetings.

'Tumi, where are you now?'

'I could ask you the same question, Sean. Where's Clyde? I noticed he wasn't in his run when I left camp earlier.'

'I took him out for another look around the rhino carcass.'

'I wish you'd woken me.' Tumi sounded miffed. 'I'm driving. I've been to see Charles in hospital. He's doing OK, but one of his wounds is infected from all the rubbish that was blown into it. The doctor wants to keep him in a couple more days as he might have to undo some stitches and see if there's any more shrapnel or tiny stone fragments in him.'

'OK. Have you got Shikar with you, by any chance?'

'Yes, I have,' she said. 'The nurses let Charles come outside to see her. It really brightened him up.'

Shikar probably hadn't been the only one Charles was happy to see, Sean thought, but he didn't say anything. 'Can you come help me, please, and bring Shikar? I know I told you to take the day off, but this is really important.'

'Sure. I don't want to be left out of stuff, Sean.'

'I'm sorry. We're partners, Tumi. I just thought you needed the rest.'

'Maybe ask me next time if I need a rest. I can look after myself.'

'After the way you handled last night, I have no doubt about that, partner.'

'Thanks,' she said. 'Do you want me to call Craig for you?'

'Not for now,' Sean said. 'What I'm doing is not strictly legal, pursuing a suspect outside of the reserve. Are you OK with that?'

'We're partners, right? You just said so. I've got your back.'

'OK. Thanks. Craig's got his hands full dealing with the police and if we turn up something solid I can always pass it on to the proper authorities.'

'I'm good with that,' Tumi said.

Sean gave Tumi directions then ended the call. Clyde had wandered away and Sean called him back. There was another reason, two in fact, why he didn't call Craig. One, because he wanted to do what Christine had asked him and prove himself worthy of her trust, and two, he couldn't trust himself not to say something he might later regret now that he was sure his friend had been sleeping with his ex-wife.

Chapter 13

When Tumi took the turnoff to the Shaw's Gate entrance to the Sabi Sand Game Reserve she called Sean, as they had arranged, and he talked her in the rest of the way to the huts.

Sean and Clyde met them at the start of the rough dirt track that led off the access road. Tumi switched off her engine and opened the door for Shikar.

'Shikar, find,' Tumi said, using the command for Shikar to locate any one of the substances she had been trained to detect.

'I haven't even told you what we're looking for yet,' Sean said. 'In fact, I don't know.'

'No, but you're following the poacher who maybe set the bomb for us and Shikar now knows how to detect explosives, as well as other sorts of ammunition and weapons. Who knows what the guy might have hidden around here? We're close to public roads so he wouldn't have wanted to be roaming the street carrying incriminating evidence.'

'Exactly. Well done.'

Tumi smiled. 'Have I passed some sort of test?'

He shook his head, but grinned. 'School's out, Tumi. This is real life. Christine wants to catch the guy who's been trying to get us and the dogs, and we're going to have to do the police's job for them. Craig says their bomb squad hasn't come up with any leads on the origin of the devices. He says the cops want us to butt out, but that's not how we're going to roll. Are you on board with this?'

'Affirmative.'

She was not exactly dressed for the bush, wearing skinny jeans, sandals and a white T-shirt. Sean, however, was in uniform. She wondered if he even owned civilian clothes. He looked like there was too much stuff on his mind for such niceties, and it was getting him down, but then again, Sean had worn that same expression since she'd first met him. He was nice, and a good mentor, but he didn't say much.

Shikar roamed ahead, along with Clyde, whom Sean had also let off the lead.

'Can I ask you a question?' she said.

'Sure. I may not answer, but give it a try.'

'Christine's your ex-wife, right?'

'That's a matter of public record. Yes.'

'Are you still in love with her?'

He stopped and turned to look at her. 'Where did that come from?'

Tumi shrugged. 'Well, to tell you the truth, the only time I ever see you smile or look remotely animated is when you mention her name, like just now. She's given you a job to do and you look as excited as Benny or Shikar are when we tell them to *soek*.'

He shook his head. 'I'm nobody's dog, Tumi.'

She felt bad. 'Sorry, no, I didn't mean to suggest that. It's just that . . . I don't know, call it a girl thing.'

He ran a hand through his hair and started walking again, this time not looking at her. 'We're still friends,' he said eventually.

'I don't know. I guess I never stopped loving her, even though I hurt her. I did some stuff – not cheating on her – but some stuff she couldn't forgive me for. I think I'm going to spend the rest of my life trying to make it up to her, and I don't think it's going to do any good.'

'I see.'

'Phew,' he said.

He looked to her again as they walked and she thought she detected a half-smile. 'I don't think I've ever talked to anyone so much about me and Christine and what's gone on between us.'

'You are a man of few words, then.'

They came to the two huts that Sean had described over the phone to her.

'The hut on the left, here,' Sean said, 'was where Clyde picked up the strongest scent of the man. I'm wondering if he stayed here for a night, because Clyde seemed to be more animated here than when he was on the trail.'

'Let's see what Shikar has to say,' Tumi said.

She caught up with her dog, who was wandering around the huts. Shikar came to an old desk behind the hut Sean had pointed to.

'I wonder what that's doing here?' she asked.

Sean shrugged. 'This hut's more liveable than the other.'

Shikar barked.

'Good girl, Shikar.' Tumi took the rubber ball she had brought with her and threw it. Shikar bounded away with joy, skidded to a halt in the dust, and retrieved the ball and ran back. 'Good dog.'

Tumi went to the desk and Shikar joined her and barked again. Shikar rested her chin on the top of the desk and sniffed.

'There's some sort of stain on here, on the top, Sean.'

Sean and Clyde joined Tumi. Clyde looked up. He was lower to the ground than Shikar and couldn't see or smell what the other dog and the humans could.

'I didn't notice that,' Sean said. 'Dirt? Blood maybe? The legs of the desk are dusty and dirty, but it looks like someone's wiped the top, which is odd if it's been sitting outside for a while.'

'Maybe someone moved it outside,' Tumi said. This was more like a mystery, like being a detective than a dog handler. Tumi felt a jolt of adrenaline energise her limbs. 'Can we go inside?'

'Sure,' Sean said.

'Come, Shikar.' Tumi went to the door and opened it. 'Shikar, *soek*.'

The dog went in and began searching and sniffing, under and on top of the bed. She moved to a spot on the wall and began sniffing up and down the whitewashed paintwork.

'What have you found, girl?'

Sean was behind her. He said nothing, which Tumi appreciated. He trusted her and Shikar to do their job without feeling the need to offer advice or guidance. The silence encouraged her. Tumi went to Shikar and looked up and down the wall from the floor to where it met the thatch roof.

Shikar had her head up and was sniffing the wall above Tumi's waist height. Shikar barked.

'She's indicating,' Tumi said, as much to herself as to Sean, 'but at what?'

Tumi made a fist and began knocking on the wall where Shikar had been sniffing, trying to feel if there was a hollow, or perhaps a plastered-over compartment. It felt solid and all she ended up with was a sore hand. Tumi bent forward and inspected the wall up close. 'Can you open the curtain, please, Sean, give me a bit more light?'

'Sure,' he said.

Tumi looked at the wall and then around the hut. 'It's cleaner here than the rest of the wall space. Someone's wiped it.'

'Like the desk.'

Shikar whined.

'Yes.' Tumi knelt and tried to spot where the cleaning had stopped and started. 'But there's a patch here, down low, that's dirtier than the rest. It's about the same dimensions as the desk. I think the table was here, someone wiped it and the wall above it, and . . .'

Tumi gave a small shriek as Shikar reared up on her hind legs and put her forepaws on Tumi's shoulder. The dog, now able to raise herself up, was sniffing higher up the wall than she could previously reach. Shikar barked.

'She's getting excited,' Sean said.

Tumi didn't need to be told. She eased herself out from under Shikar. 'Help me get that desk, please, Sean. I've got an idea.'

They left the dogs, went outside, and carried the table back in. Tumi lined it up against the wall where the marks were.

'Good work,' Sean said. 'I didn't see those stains when I first checked.'

Tumi held the desk steady. 'Up, Shikar!'

Although not a small dog, Shikar leapt up. She barely fitted on the tabletop but she scrabbled even higher against the wall, reaching up as far as she could, almost touching the thatch. Shikar barked.

'Yes, I thought so! There must be something in the roof. Good girl, Shikar.'

'Let's have a look,' Sean said.

'Down, Shikar,' Tumi commanded.

'Hold the desk for me, please Tumi.'

Sean wore a custom-made Penga Ndlovu hunting knife on his belt. He took it out, climbed up on the rickety piece of furniture and started prodding the thatch. 'Maybe you want to take the dogs outside now.'

'Shikar, Clyde, go outside.' Tumi threw Shikar's ball out for good measure and both dogs chased it. Tumi closed the door behind the dogs. 'I'm not going out. Do you think there might be a bomb up there?'

Sean shook his head. 'The poacher covered his trail well and it was damned hard to follow in places. If he wanted to get one of us he would have led us to this spot and set the IED somewhere we could have tripped it. If there's something up here it's well hidden. I was more worried I might disturb a black mamba.'

'*Eish*, I think I might be more afraid of snakes than I am of bombs.'

Sean continued to probe the bundled dry grass that made up the roof. 'Shikar could have smelled blood that the poacher might have had on his shoe.'

'Or rhino horn?'

'Maybe,' Sean said, 'though I doubt the guy would have stashed something so valuable here, unless he was planning on returning to get it.'

'Do you think he might be around here, waiting, watching us?' Tumi felt a shiver crawl up her spine.

Sean shook his head. 'No. If he was close by, Clyde would have gone crazy with his scent. I think he met someone here and then drove off. There are tyre tracks outside that look to be about a day old. That's not to say he won't come back. This might be a place where he caches stuff, stores what he needs.'

'I understand,' Tumi said. She guessed Sean had experienced the same tactics in Afghanistan where, as she understood it, the Taliban had blended in among the local population, hiding their bombs and weapons until they were needed.

'Aha,' Sean said. He stopped probing. 'There's something metallic up here.'

'Let me help,' Tumi said. It was her dog who had led them to the roof, and she wanted to be part of the find.

'See if you can find something else outside to stand on, Tumi.'

She dashed out and looked around the little encampment. Off in the grass, at the edge of the clearing, she found a rusted two-hundred-litre fuel or oil drum. She tapped it and found it was empty. Tumi rolled the drum to the hut, upended it, and walked it along the floor to where Sean was pulling grass out of the roof. Tumi stood the drum up again and jumped on top of it.

'Careful,' Sean cautioned her as she swayed, arms out, trying to get her balance. 'I don't want you breaking a leg.'

Tumi laughed then steadied herself. 'This is exciting.'

'And dangerous. These people play for keeps, Tumi, as you know.'

She nodded and reached up. 'Let me help.'

'OK, but carefully.' Sean continued pulling away stems of thatching grass.

Tumi felt the cool metal of the object he had found. It was long and cylindrical. 'A rifle?'

'Seems like it.' Sean pulled away some more grass.

Tumi could see most of the weapon now.

'It's a Mauser, heavy calibre,' Sean said. 'This is what's known as a takedown rifle – it can be easily disassembled into two pieces so it's easier to transport, perfect for a poacher to stuff in a small pack or bag.'

Tumi took her phone out of the pocket of her jeans and passed it up to him. 'Take a picture of it.'

'Good thinking.' He snapped a shot and handed the phone back to her.

'Are you going to take it out?' she asked.

Sean lowered his arms and Tumi did the same. He looked at her. 'I'm not sure.'

'Are you thinking what I'm thinking?' she asked.

Sean rubbed his chin. 'Maybe. Are you thinking that whoever stashed this rifle here is going to come back for it?'

'That's exactly what crossed my mind,' Tumi said. 'We could stake this place out, like they do in the movies, wait for the guy and then call the cops and nab him.'

'Or maybe follow him.'

'Yes,' she said. 'And find out who's making the IEDs.'

Sean looked her in the eyes. 'You know we should just call the cops, Tumi. That's the right thing to do.'

She nodded. 'Yes, I was just thinking the same thing, but from what Craig's told you we know that the police are overstretched. I want this guy, Sean, whoever is doing this to us.'

'He nearly killed Benny.'

'Exactly.'

Sean grinned. 'Then let's do this.'

Chapter 14

Sean and Tumi lay in the bush, in the shade of a marula tree, watching the two huts where they had discovered the hidden rifle.

Tumi shivered. Sean had told her the hour before dawn was the coldest, and he could see now that she believed him.

After they had discovered the weapon, Sean had sent her to their base camp with a list of supplies and equipment to bring back with her. He had stayed with Clyde and kept watch on the huts. Tumi had returned with both their field packs. She was now wearing civilian clothes that would not give away their position: black jeans, a dark blue shirt and hiking boots. Sean kept his gear packed and ready to go at a moment's notice; his large pack contained all he needed for an overnight or extended patrol, including food for him and his dog, and extra water and sleeping gear.

Sean had set up sleeping shelters for both of them, green waterproof sheets strung between trees, and concealed them with branches. They had a line of sight, through the foliage, to the two round huts. During the afternoon and into the night Sean had instructed Tumi on the art of surveillance. They spoke in whispers and tied the two dogs to trees a hundred metres behind them, leaving them with water. Every few hours one of them went and checked on Clyde and Shikar.

Sean would have felt more comfortable with Benny in the bush; the two of them had spent many nights out in the hills and the *dasht* – the rocky desert – of Afghanistan and Sean could trust Benny not to bark and give away their position. Clyde was good at what he did best, following cold trails, but if the shit went down Sean wanted Benny's aggressive attack-dog instincts by his side.

He watched Tumi studying the huts through the binoculars she had brought with her. She was impressing him. Tumi responded well to instructions and had a thirst for knowledge.

'If we see someone come, what do we do? Grab him?' she whispered.

Sean shook his head. 'We wait, we watch. If he comes in a vehicle we radio it in to Craig. If it's someone on foot we get the dogs and we track him, from a distance. You get pictures, first.'

Tumi nodded. She was a keen amateur wildlife photographer and she had brought her Canon camera with its 100–400 milli-metre zoom lens. Tumi already had the hefty piece of equipment out and ready, the open case on the ground next to her.

'And we can give the picture to the cops if we lose him – or her.'

'Yes,' Sean said. In reality, they would be in trouble from the police for mounting this unauthorised surveillance operation, especially if they lost whoever came to collect the rifle. He liked the way Tumi thought, outside of the box, open to the idea that the gun could be collected by a woman or a girl, as well as a man. It might make more sense for a poacher to distance themselves from the crime by sending a female.

'You know,' Sean said, 'some of the poachers who enter the

Kruger Park bribe a woman to travel with them, so they arouse less suspicion when they enter through the gate.'

'Even better if the woman has a small child with her.'

He smiled. 'I was just about to say that.'

'I'd make a good poacher. In fact, my grandfather used to hunt bush meat, I'm ashamed to say.'

'Nothing to be ashamed of,' he said. 'My father went to prison for embezzling the bank he worked for.'

'Wow.'

Sean shrugged. 'We all have our skeletons in the closet, Tumi.'

'I learned a lot from him, though,' she said.

'I'm sure you –'

Tumi held up a hand. 'Sorry. Sean, listen.'

He cocked his head. 'Francolin.'

'Yes,' she said. 'Though the new name for them is spurfowl.'

'I stand corrected,' Sean whispered.

The bird was squawking and it wasn't the normal early morning or late afternoon time for it to call.

'Something, or someone, has disturbed that bird,' Tumi said. She peered through her binoculars. 'There.'

Sean looked where Tumi was pointing. She had good eyes. He took the binoculars that she offered him. He could see movement through the trees on the other side of the huts. Whoever it was stopped. Sean had to look hard to see the person there. They were being cautious.

The figure gradually emerged from the shadowy cover of the trees. 'It's just a boy.'

Tumi had whispered, but Sean still put his finger to his lips and she nodded in acknowledgement. She was right, the youngster was possibly no older than fifteen or sixteen, but he was moving with the exaggerated caution of someone who knew full well that what he was doing was not right. He carried a backpack. If the boy was caught with an unlicensed weapon he would be charged and fined; if it could be proved from ballistics testing that the hunting rifle had been used to kill a rhino, the boy could be looking at jail time. Hunting rifles of a calibre large enough to bring down a rhino – or an elephant, which was increasingly becoming the target of choice in Mozambique and the far north of the Kruger Park – were not easy to come by. Robberies, often violently executed, were carried out on farms where poachers were reasonably assured of finding the weapons they needed. Who knew, perhaps a farmer or his wife had been brutalised or even killed to get hold of this rifle.

Sean could sense that Tumi was itching for action, so he placed a gentle hand on her forearm and she nodded again. They stayed perfectly still, hardly breathing, as they watched the boy. He, too, was watchful, checking all around him as he moved straight towards the hut with the rifle in it.

Tumi grinned and Sean winked at her when they saw the youth head not to the front door, but to the old wooden desk, which Sean and Tumi had moved back outside. When he reached it he took off his backpack, set it down on the tabletop, unzipped it and reached inside. He fiddled with something for a few seconds, then slung the rucksack back over one shoulder. He picked up the desk and then pushed open the door of the hut with his back. He knew exactly what he was doing and where he would find the rifle.

Sean put his mouth close to Tumi's ear. 'Go back and get the *bakkie* and the dogs. Stay with them until I SMS you, OK?'

She gave a little frown at the prospect of potentially missing out on some action, and he couldn't blame her, but she eased herself up and, while the boy was still inside out of view, crept back to where Clyde and Shikar were tethered.

The boy emerged after a few minutes, again carrying the desk. Sean focused on him with the binoculars. He wondered if he had left the rifle where it was – perhaps his job had simply been to check if the weapon had been disturbed. However, when the boy turned, Sean could see that something bigger had been crammed into his backpack and now it had angular protrusions. Sean guessed the lad had broken the rifle down into its two pieces; he knew what he was doing, all right.

It saddened Sean, but didn't surprise him. Craig had passed on intelligence gathered from his sources in the villages near the Sabi Sand Game Reserve that teenagers in the local schools were sometimes targeted by poachers, who offered them what seemed like a fortune to try their luck burrowing under the security fence and trying to shoot a rhino. These amateurish poachers were invariably caught before they could kill an animal, but that didn't stop others from trying.

The boy checked around him, then went to the closest tree to the huts, broke off a branch and returned. He started sweeping the dirt where he had walked, backing away from the scene.

Clever, Sean thought, but it wouldn't stop the dogs from tracking him. As long as he didn't have a car waiting nearby, or a bicycle, they would be able to keep pace with him. Sean wondered what the plan was for the boy, who now took a last look at his handiwork and then moved back into the bush.

Sean sent a message to Tumi, telling her to bring the dogs and the *bakkie* forward. A few minutes later he heard the vehicle's engine and Tumi pulled up.

'You take Shikar, follow the boy's trail, and the rifle.'

'Me? Alone?'

'Yes,' Sean said. 'He's a long way from the nearest community. My hunch is that he's going to be picked up by someone. We need to be able to follow in a vehicle. Also, with the civilian clothes you're wearing you won't spook them.'

'OK.' Tumi smiled. 'Shikar, *soek*!'

'Tumi?'

She looked over her shoulder, holding back Shikar, who was already vacuuming the ground for scent of the boy and the rifle.

'Be careful. Don't get too close to him, just keep him in sight.'

Tumi patted the nine-millimetre Glock pistol in the concealed holster clipped to her belt and tucked inside her jeans, and further hidden by her shirt. 'Will do.'

Sean had some time to spare. He needed to wait to hear from Tumi which direction the boy had gone in, and he didn't want to crowd her or their target. He walked over to the hut and stood in front of it, hands on hips.

While he waited Sean mentally tallied everything the boy had done, from the time he had appeared. He looked again at the desk and opened its single drawer. There was nothing in it. The teenager, he recalled, had set his backpack down on the desk and reached into it, before re-shouldering the bag and carrying the desk inside.

'Why?' Sean asked out loud.

There was no one to answer the question. The kid, Sean told himself, had had to do something before he had his hands full, and it was something he needed to do with light – the sun was only just up and it would still be dark inside the hut, which had no electric light inside.

Sean went to the door and opened it. He took out his torch and played the beam around the floor, walls and the thatch roof. There were a few stalks of yellowed grass on the floor where the boy had removed the rifle, which was to be expected, and scuff marks in the dust.

'What did you do?' Sean murmured.

He left the hut again, picked up the desk and carried it inside, just as the boy had done. Just as he put it down his phone rang, and he looked at the screen.

'Tumi, howzit.' He held the phone in the crook of his shoulder and used the marks in the dust on the floor to place the desk where the pick-up guy would have put it.

'Good. I can see the boy. Shikar and I tracked him through

the bush. He's on the tar road, the R536, sitting there. I think he's waiting for a pick-up.'

'Good job. I'm coming just now.'

'Do you want me to grab him if you're not here in time?'

Sean put his phone on speaker then set it down on the desk, which he climbed up on. 'Don't put yourself in danger, Tumi.'

'We've been through this. My job is dangerous, Sean.'

He heard the exasperation, maybe even resentment, in her voice. 'He's our best lead to the guy who's been killing our rhinos and trying to blow up our people and dogs. If we take him he might clam up and we'll have no way of getting to his superiors.'

'Well, if we lose him, then we'll have no rifle, no lead, and – wait . . .'

Sean was carefully probing the thatch with his knife, the same way he had done when he'd found the rifle. The boy had not simply ripped out the rifle and then gapped it; he had gone to the trouble of replacing most of the dislodged thatch – some of it had fallen on the floor – but Sean wondered if he had left something else behind, the thing that he had checked inside his backpack when he had first gone to the desk.

'What is it, Tumi?'

'Damn, there's a taxi coming. It's slowing down for him. The kid didn't even put his hand out to signal him.'

'Pre-arranged pick-up?' He continued searching. 'Tumi, get the registration number and we'll pass it on to the cops. They can stop the van, and get the rifle.'

'Sean, the registration number is HGB106MP. Do you copy?'

He had a good memory. 'Got it. But you call the cops.'

'I've got to go. I'll call you when I can.'

'Tumi, wait.'

But she had ended the call. The tip of Sean's knife hit something solid.

*

'Wait!' Tumi yelled. 'Is this a taxi?'

She and Shikar emerged from the trees near the youth, and Shikar, excited to be so near her quarry, was pressing her nose up against the young man's leg.

'Get that damn dog away from me. Of course this is a taxi, *sisi*, are you blind?'

'As a matter of fact, yes, I am.' Tumi had put on her sunglasses and was looking past the boy. 'I heard the bass coming from this thing's speakers and guessed.'

'Get in,' growled the driver of the taxi.

'There's this girl,' the boy said, 'she wants a ride.'

'Hurry up, boy,' said the driver.

Tumi was facing away from the driver, but she looked at him out of the corner of her eyes. He looked like a tough guy, scarred knuckles gripping the steering wheel, chunky gold chain, bald head and enormous shoulders. She had already committed the younger man's looks and clothes to memory. There was no one else in the taxi.

'She's blind, baba.'

He had called the man 'father', but that was just a term of respect, probably, Tumi thought. Unless the gangster wannabe behind the wheel really was his parent.

The driver raised his voice: 'What are you doing out here all alone in the bush, blind girl?'

'There's no need to shout. I'm staying not far from here, with my aunt, and I went for a walk to exercise but my guide dog got distracted by some animal or bird or something and wandered off the main road. I'm guessing that's where I am now. Where are you going?'

'To Mkhuhlu.'

'Please take me. If you can drop me at the Shoprite I can find my way to my aunt's from there.'

'You're a long way from the Shoprite.'

'I'm blind, not crippled. I like to exercise and so does my dog.'

The driver laughed. 'Your tongue's as sharp as your body, girl. Get in. What's your name, beautiful?'

'Tovhi.'

'Bandile, help Tovhi get in.'

Tumi kept up her act, not looking directly at either man, but watching them nonetheless. The boy took her elbow and Shikar gave a low growl.

'It's OK, girl, he's not going to hurt me,' she said to the dog.

'Keep that thing away from me. It looks like it wants to hump me, or kill me or something,' the teenager said.

Tumi forced a laugh and felt about for the seat. 'She won't hurt you. Sit, girl.'

It was hot inside the taxi, and it smelled of cigarettes, spilled booze and sweat. Tumi noticed a couple of empty Black Label bottles rolling around in the footwell of the front passenger seat. She caught the scent of beer on the driver's breath when he looked over his shoulder. He waved a meaty hand close in front of her face and she forced herself not to flinch.

Tumi saw the older man mouth two words at the boy. *'She's fine.'*

Tumi swallowed. These men were both criminals. Maybe she should have done what Sean had told her. Still, if they tried something she had Shikar, and she had her Glock under her shirt. Maybe they would be armed, but they wouldn't be expecting her to have a gun. The boy had the poacher's hunting rifle in his backpack, but that was broken down into two pieces. Sean had stripped and checked the weapon as well, but he hadn't taken the ammunition out of it; he didn't want to give away the fact that they had discovered the rifle. Her mind was reeling, going over what might happen next and what she should or should not have done. The fear was rising inside her, but she told herself to stay calm.

'You all right? You look worried,' the boy said.

'Bandile, right?'

She saw how the kid rolled his eyes and looked to the back of the driver's head. He was obviously not happy that the man had used his name but did not have the temerity to chastise him.

'Whatever,' he said. 'Tovhi, right?'

'Yes.'

'So, are you scared?'

'I was lost in the bush, what do you think?'

'You've got a smart mouth, sister.'

'Don't like smart girls, Bandile?'

'I like all girls, pretty ones, that is,' he said.

'How old are you?'

'Seventeen, nearly eighteen.'

'Hmm.' She smiled, still looking ahead. 'How come you're not in school today?'

He shrugged. 'I got more important things to do than mathematics or science.'

'What's more important than an education?'

'Money.'

The driver turned up the volume. Rap bounced around the walls of the minibus. 'You got that right. You want a beer, Tovhi?'

She wanted to keep her wits about her, but the driver had been suspicious enough of her to try and check if she was blind. He was relaxing now and she wanted to keep him at ease.

'Sure, but I'd prefer a Vodka Cruiser.'

The driver reached over to a small plastic cooler box sitting on the front seat, fished a Black Label out of the slurry and handed it back to Bandile.

The boy opened the bottle and put it in her hand, wrapping her fingers around the cold wet glass, then reached for another.

The driver's hand struck with the speed of a mamba, slapping the side of the boy's head. 'No beer for you.'

The boy rubbed his cheek, but placed the bottle back in the cooler box.

Father and son, I was right, Tumi thought. Neither of them seemed to be a criminal mastermind, but she had no doubt they were dangerous. Rival taxi companies went to war sometimes and settled their disputes over routes and monopolies with AK-47s; the father looked like a battle-scarred veteran and the son, who wore a surly frown after his rebuke, seemed mean. He was staring at her breasts now. Tumi suppressed a shiver.

'So what were you doing out in the bush away from anything?' she asked vaguely in the direction of the boy.

'I had work to do. Important stuff.'

'In the middle of nowhere?'

'How do you even know where you were?'

She giggled. 'You're right about that, I was lost. I figured I'd get as far as the entrance to the Kruger Park and then turn around and head home.'

'Long walk for a blind girl,' the father said from the front.

'About twenty kilometres. Not far if you like to keep your figure.'

The driver took out a beer and steered with his knees while he levered the top off with his teeth. He glanced over his shoulder at his son. 'You get what you were sent for?'

'*Yebo*,' said the boy.

'Good. Boss'll be pleased.'

'I want to do more,' the boy said, the pair of them ignoring her while she sat quietly, sipping her Black Label. 'I want to get out, do some *business* myself, not just run errands.'

'Ha. There will be time for that. You just keep your nose clean and do as he tells you, and don't upset him. My cousin is not forgiving of fools, boy, remember that.'

Tumi filed away the new piece of intelligence about the family relationship.

'What's your next job?' Tumi asked.

'I have to go to Mozambique.'

Through her sunglasses Tumi obliquely saw the father look back and scowl.

'You need to talk less, boy.'

'Hey, don't mind me,' Tumi said.

The boy shifted across the seat of the taxi, closer to her. Shikar, between them, gave a low growl.

'Take care of that dog,' the boy said.

'She takes care of me.'

'She got you lost.' The boy laughed. He reached over and put his hand on her knee.

Tumi squealed and Shikar barked.

'Get your hand off me.'

The father looked back again. 'Keep the noise down back there. You, girl, you might be blind, but you look and sound like the kind to party. Don't talk back at my son like that. He's just being friendly.'

Tumi felt her blood start to boil. Violence against women, sexual and otherwise, was a big problem in South Africa. She wanted to teach these two fools a lesson, but she also needed to keep them happy and unsuspicious. She bit her tongue. 'I'm sorry, baba, it's just that Bandile gave me a fright when he touched me and my dog is very protective. She might bite someone if she thinks they're a threat.'

'I'm not a threat,' Bandile said.

The father's phone rang. He put his beer between his legs, drove with one hand and answered the phone with his other, talking loudly.

Tumi lowered her voice. 'I know that, Bandile. So, tell me about this business you're in. It sounds mysterious, all this lurking around in the bush and crossing the border to Mozambique. Are you moving something illegal, like drugs? Maybe you can help me score.'

She saw his grin out of the corner of her eye. Tumi felt like the boy was the kind of would-be player who enjoyed bragging to a girl and talking himself up, and now that she'd hinted that she used drugs he would be less likely to see her as the innocent little blind girl she had first appeared to be.

Bandile reached over to the seat behind them, where he had laid his backpack. He glanced forward to make sure his father was still busy, then unzipped the pack. He hunched over it first, shielding the contents from Tumi's view, but then seemed to remember she couldn't see.

Tumi was careful to keep looking straight ahead, but using her peripheral vision she saw the barrel of the disassembled rifle. Bandile reached in and pulled out a tin, then zipped up the bag. He opened the metal box and took out a joint. He held it under her nose.

'Smell this.'

She took a deep breath. 'Now we're talking,' she whispered.

Shikar's ears went up and she barked.

'Tell that dog to shut up,' the father called from the front, then returned to his call.

'What's wrong with her?' Bandile asked, tucking the tin into the pocket of his jacket.

'Nothing, she's just overly protective.' Tumi cursed silently. She should have realised Shikar would indicate when she smelled the marijuana. The dogs were also trained to detect drugs as part of their security duties at the game reserve. Julianne Clyde-Smith was almost as fanatical about drugs as she was about poaching and Tumi had heard that more than one staff member had been suspended or fired for using or, more seriously, dealing to others. 'Maybe we can light up later.'

'Maybe,' said Bandile.

'So tell me,' she said, leaning closer to him over Shikar, 'what do you do, is it drugs you're moving?'

He hesitated, but then she put her hand on his thigh and he smiled. 'All I can tell you is it involves big money.'

'Does it involve stolen stuff?'

'Important stuff. The boss trusts me as he knows I'm smart and I know the bush as well as I know the town. I pick up important equipment for his business and today I made a drop-off as well.'

'Really?'

'Yes.'

'How important was the drop-off? Was it cash?'

He looked towards his father, yet again. 'Can't say.'

'That's not very impressive.' She leaned even closer. 'Do you have to get the boss's approval to even talk to a girl?'

Tumi thought she might have pushed him too far. He clenched his fists tight and scowled at her.

'No!'

The father was laughing and joking with someone now.

'What were you doing?'

'I had to collect some stuff, I told you. Dangerous stuff.'

'Dangerous stuff?' she asked. 'I like dangerous guys. Was it drugs?'

Emboldened, he relaxed his fists. 'No.'

'What, then, tell me.' She gave his thigh a little squeeze. 'Nice muscles.'

'A gun.'

'Oh.'

'What do you mean, "oh"?'

'Well,' she said, still looking ahead, 'this is South Africa, you can get a gun pretty much anywhere.'

'Not this kind of rifle.'

'Rifle? Like an AK, you mean? How gangster are you, Bandile?' She gave a teasing little laugh.

'Big calibre, hunting rifle.'

'Oh,' she said, eyes suitably wide. 'Like for taking out a cash-in-transit van or something big like that?'

He shook his head. 'Maybe even more dangerous. People shoot you on sight if you get caught with a gun like this.'

'Sounds hectic,' she said. 'Hey, want to give me your phone number?'

'Sure,' he said, not cool enough to hide his eagerness.

Sticking to her cover, Tumi used the voice recognition feature of her phone and asked Siri to enter Bandile's number, which he recited to her, as a new contact.

'So, you picked up the rifle today?' she asked, picking up their conversation.

'Like I said, it wasn't just a pick-up I did today. I left something behind, something that would blow you away if you know what it was.'

Tumi swallowed. 'Blow . . . blow me away? I don't understand. You mean, like, I would be totally impressed by what you left behind?'

'I'm not talking about blowing you away like that, *sisi*, I'm talking more about setting someone's world on fire, if you know what I mean.'

'Huh?'

Bandile's father was winding up his conversation, saying his goodbyes. 'Just picked up a blind girl with a dog,' Tumi heard him say.

The boy eyed the older man nervously, and Tumi zeroed in on the driver's conversation.

'Don't know what type of dog, but not a Labrador. What's special about them?'

Tumi cursed silently. This oaf and his son obviously did not know that most guide dogs were Labradors, but whomever he was talking to did, and had planted a seed of suspicion.

She also needed to keep Bandile talking. 'Sorry, I don't follow what you mean, Bandile.'

'I've probably said too much.'

The father looked back at them. 'What have you two been whispering about? Hey? Tell me, boy.'

'Nothing.'

The driver tossed his empty bottle on the floor, where it clinked against the others. He looked up and swerved as a cow ambled out from the overgrown verge. This guy would kill them with his driving, Tumi thought.

'What breed of dog is that you have there?' the driver asked.

'She's a Weimaraner. They haven't traditionally been used as guide dogs, but people are experimenting with them overseas and now here. She's great.'

He looked to her, away from the road again. 'You were eavesdropping on my conversation, girl. What are you playing at?'

'Nothing, I just heard you mention me and my dog.'

'Damn cows.' The father honked his horn.

'Did you mean you planted a bomb, Bandile?' she whispered to the boy.

He stared at her, not confirming but not denying it, as an innocent person would. Tumi needed to call Sean, but there was no way to do that with these two criminals listening in.

'Dad,' the boy said, urgency plain in his tone.

'Watch him,' Tumi said. Shikar started barking loudly.

'Tell it to shut up,' the driver said. 'I can't hear my son.'

Sean had shown Tumi how to train Shikar to bark on command. It was a useful trick that could be employed on routine patrols. Much of their work was keeping poachers out of the Lion Plains Game Reserve property. If a poacher approaching the property heard a dog barking, then he would think twice about entering, Sean had explained.

'Shut up, dog!' Bandile said. He reached for his backpack.

'Shikar.' Tumi was worried Bandile might have a pistol in the bag, or a knife. Though her voice was low her dog's head snapped around. 'Rim hom!'

Shikar sat up and bit down on Bandile's arm. The boy screamed.

'What's going on?' The minivan veered crazily.

'Get it off me,' Bandile yelled.

'Sorry,' Tumi said, 'I don't know what's got into her. Stop it, baby, stop it. Leave him alone.'

Shikar recognised none of Tumi's pretend commands and shook and worried at Bandile's arm while climbing up onto the seat.

'Get that dog off him or I'll shoot it.'

Tumi put herself between the driver and Shikar and Bandile. She had no doubt he meant what he said.

'Let us out of the van,' she said. 'I'm worried Shikar's going to hurt him.'

'I'm already hurt! This thing is trying to kill me. Help me!' Bandile shouted.

'Control that dog!' the driver growled, but nonetheless he pulled the van over to the side of the road.

'Shikar, *ous*!' Tumi said. Shikar responded immediately to the command she had been taught to release the person she was attacking.

Bandile's right arm was bloodied but he reached over with his left and opened the sliding door of the taxi. Tears welled in his eyes. 'Get out!'

Shikar bounded out of the van and Tumi followed, hanging on to the lead. The driver eyed her, making no move to leave, but then changed his mind when he saw a police *bakkie* coming towards them. He put the van in gear and accelerated away.

Tumi took out her phone and called Sean. 'Hurry up, answer.'

'Tumi?'

She allowed herself the briefest sigh of relief. 'There's a bomb, where you are.'

'I know, I've just found it.'

Chapter 15

Christine broke the speed limit. Even by South African standards her driving was maniacal.

She had been on her way to the Sabi Sand Game Reserve, to meet with Craig at Lion Plains, when Tumi had called. Tumi gave her directions to the huts they had been staking out. Craig was also en route, although he was coming from deep within the Lion Plains property where he and a forensics team had been investigating the death of yet another rhino.

Christine had asked Craig not to tell the police about the bomb Sean had just found, and while he had been initially hesitant he had eventually agreed to her wishes.

Christine gripped the wheel hard to stop herself from falling apart. She could not shake the feeling that if something terrible happened to Sean it would be all her fault. Why, she asked herself, had she been irresponsible enough to tell him to start acting like some amateur sleuth? Sean and his dog Benny had been trained to detect IEDs in Afghanistan, and while Sean had said that what he'd found was a 'simple' IED, she was already starting to regret not calling for the South African

National Defence Force bomb squad that was temporarily based at Skukuza.

She raced past the turnoffs to the settlements of Belfast and Huntington, and the back of her *bakkie* went into a drift as she took the turnoff to Shaw's Gate at a dangerous speed. She was thrown against the door as she fought to regain control of the vehicle, then geared down, planted the accelerator and tore up the dirt road that Tumi had described to her.

'Please, God,' she said aloud as she bumped along the track.

Tumi was standing about fifty metres from the pair of huts, Shikar and Clyde sitting obediently on either side of her. Christine drove up as close as she could and got out.

'He's still in there,' Tumi said.

Christine did not know Tumi well, though she thought she detected a slight tone of resentment, which made Christine feel even guiltier. 'I told him he didn't need to try and disarm it if he didn't want to.'

'*I* said the same thing to him.' Tumi put her hands on her hips. 'He told me you wanted us to do our own investigating. I know I'm the junior on the team and it's not my place to say anything, but I hope to God you know what you're doing.'

'Me as well.' Christine started towards the huts, but Tumi grabbed her arm.

Christine shook off Tumi's hand and glared at her. 'What do you think you're doing?'

'Sean gave me strict instructions that no one – not even you – was to disturb him.'

Christine took a deep breath. 'All right. Sean told me on the phone that you'd been tailing a suspect, possibly the person who planted this bomb.'

She nodded. 'I've got his name and phone number.'

'Good work.'

'I'm sorry for speaking harshly just then, Christine,' Tumi

said. 'Sean told me before that we're partners, him and me, and it's tearing me up thinking of him inside with that thing.'

The truth was that Christine was one hundred per cent sure she felt far worse than Tumi did. This was the man she had loved, and her reckless decision to pursue a rogue investigation could cost Sean his life, or result in him being seriously wounded and disabled. *What have I done?*

Tumi laid a hand on her arm, gently this time. 'You're doing the right thing. Sean told me you know people in America who can help us. I'm not sure we can trust our own cops to get to the bottom of this and if it turns out, as Sean thinks, that we're dealing with poachers based in Mozambique, the South African Police will have a hard time getting to them. The guy I was following told me he's on his way to Mozambique, so that's almost proof enough.'

'I . . .' Christine didn't finish what she was about to say because Sean emerged from the hut carrying what looked like a plastic water bottle with wires and other components taped to it. She ran to him.

He smiled. 'Fancy seeing you here.'

Christine started to cry.

He reached out with his free hand and took hers. 'It's OK.'

'I was so worried about you,' Christine sniffed.

'I'm fine. As far as IEDs goes it wasn't particularly smart or overly dangerous.' He held up the bottle and she saw pink liquid sloshing about inside. 'Petrol. It's an incendiary device, a fire-bomb. There's just enough explosive to set off the fuel and burn the place down by igniting the thatch roof, where we found it.'

'Why?'

Sean shrugged. 'There's a timer, it's set for an hour from now, so we only got it just in time. My guess is it was designed to obliterate any trace of whoever was here.'

'Put that thing down,' she said to him.

Sean looked at her, not comprehending, but did as she asked, setting the IED down in the grass. She came to him, wrapped her arms around him and said into his ear, 'Thank you.'

Tentatively, he put his hands on her back.

Christine heard a vehicle approaching and looked over her shoulder to see Craig's *bakkie*. He pulled up and got out and ran to them. Christine broke from the hug and took a step back.

'Sean, *boet*, are you all right?'

Christine's eyes flicked from man to man. Craig's words of concern weren't echoed in his curt tone.

Sean's face was unsmiling. 'I'm fine.'

Craig put his hands on his hips. 'Good. Now explain to me what the hell you were playing at? You're not a bomb disposal guy! Sheesh, you could have been killed. Why didn't you call me, or call the cops?'

Christine stepped between the two men and looked at Craig. 'It was my call. I told Sean to keep a lookout for evidence that we could use to try and get a handle on the bombmakers.'

'What are you doing going behind my back, Christine?'

'I was going to tell you,' she said to Craig. 'But you've been busy with the police. I've got a friend, from my days in Afghanistan, who works for the FBI in their terrorist bomb research centre. She said if I can get her something our bomber has touched or a sample of his work she can run it through their databases.'

Craig took a deep breath and nodded. '*Ja*, OK. Makes sense, but we can do both – maybe send this person in the States some pictures and schematics, and also hand this device over to the local police. You can't go off reservation like this, Christine.'

She glared at him. He was right, and that was what frustrated her. She had been reckless because she was desperate. The thought made her realise that what had just happened illustrated a key difference between Sean and Craig. Sean, despite his quiet and almost gentle persona, was also a risk-taker – it was no wonder he was addicted to gambling. Craig, on the other hand, was straight down the line, a good leader who followed the rules and expected those around and under him to do the same. On the day Sean and Craig's patrol had been ambushed in Afghanistan, Sean had run forward to rescue his friend, even though Benny had indicated the presence of a second IED.

Christine swallowed her anger. 'All right.'

'Who's running this company?' Sean said.

Both Craig and Christine looked at him and Christine noticed that Tumi had moved closer, her curiosity clear in her expression. Christine felt her cheeks start to burn. 'I own this company, Sean, as you very well know, and Craig is our operations manager. I should have consulted him before I sent you looking for evidence.'

'It's all right, Chris,' Craig said. 'I have no doubt you would have told me.'

'*Ja*, a bit of pillow talk,' Sean said.

Christine rolled her eyes, and saw Tumi put her hand over her mouth.

Craig took a menacing step towards Sean. 'Do we have a problem, *boet*?'

Christine saw Sean's hands turn into fists. He stuck his jaw forward. 'You're both free, single and over twenty-one, *boet*. I don't see why you thought you needed to sneak around like some cheating bastard.'

Craig's nostrils flared. 'Maybe we were thinking of your feelings.'

'Please, do we have to do this now?' Christine asked.

Tumi stepped into the ring that had formed between the other three. 'Sean, how about we go and check on Benny. Also, I'd be really interested to learn how the firebomb was going to work. Maybe you could show me the different components while you photograph it, before we take it to the police? What do you say?'

Christine closed her eyes and said a silent prayer of thanks that she had employed Tumi.

Sean shot Christine a look that could have penetrated a flak jacket. 'Please look after Clyde for me.'

He picked up the bomb and walked away, with Tumi and Shikar on his heels.

*

Tumi drove to Hazyview and Sean sat in the front of the car, brooding. Shikar was in the back.

'What went on back there is none of my business, Sean, but are you OK?'

He looked across at her. She was pretty and smart and she should have been a veterinarian, like old Graham who they were going to see now. Tumi was turning into a good dog handler despite her unfortunate start, but she was also changing in other ways. She was getting tougher, more street-smart, less academic, though she had a good mind. 'No. But you're right, it's none of your business.'

Tumi said nothing more until she stopped the car outside the veterinary surgery and they got out. She told Shikar to stay.

'What you did today was very brave,' Tumi said to Sean.

'It was borderline stupid.' He stopped. 'You, however, showed courage coming to that *braai* to face Oliver and then going straight back to work after you got blown up. Christine's instincts were right; we have to have the guts to go after these people ourselves because even if the police do get off their arses and find out who's been making and planting these IEDs, it's highly likely they'll find out the bastards are in Mozambique and they won't be able to do anything about them.'

Tumi frowned. 'She cares about you.'

'Who, Christine?'

'Duh,' Tumi said. 'Men are so stupid. Zali might be your girl-friend, but Christine's still got a thing for you.'

194

'We're divorced,' Sean said.

'Yes, but she still loves you.'

'She left me,' Sean said.

'That doesn't mean she stopped loving you.'

He sighed. 'I'm a gambler, Tumi. I sent her bankrupt – stole from my own wife. She was right to leave me.' He turned away sharply. 'I have to get my dog.'

'OK.'

They went into the surgery. Graham Baird was handing a cat over to a blonde woman.

'Miaow Miaow will be good as new, Patricia,' Dr Baird said to the cat's owner, 'just try and keep her away from the hyenas.'

'Sure thing, Doc, thanks. Bye.'

Sean held the door open for the woman, who left.

'Howzit, Graham,' Sean said.

'Fine, and you?' the vet said. 'And hello, Tumi.'

'Hi, Doc. How's Gemma doing?' Tumi asked.

Graham shrugged. 'She's sedated, again, and I'm treating her for an infection from all the muck and bits of shrapnel that entered her wounds. If she pulls through, and I have to tell you it's a big "if", Tumi, she should be able to walk on three legs, but with only one eye she's going to need some looking after.'

'I've already decided I'll take her if she makes it.'

Sean looked at her. He swallowed hard. Seeing or hearing about injured animals always brought him close to losing it. 'That looked like an African wildcat that woman had just now, Graham.'

'It was,' Graham said. 'Patricia and her husband manage a game lodge. Miaow Miaow is something of a pet; she comes and goes but the resident hyenas are always gunning for her. She was lucky to escape her last tussle with them. Benny's out the back, he seems keen to get away.'

Sean smiled. 'No offence, Graham, but he hates you.'

'He joins a long and esteemed list of many people and a few animals, then.'

Benny began barking at the sound of Sean's voice. 'How is he, Doc?'

'Benny's almost as good as new – for a dog who's taken a bullet, of course. The damage wasn't as bad as it would have looked, and I've stitched him up. To be honest it's not much worse than another dog might have inflicted on him. He's almost given up trying to rip the sutures out with his teeth.'

'He wants to get back to work.'

'No doubt.'

'Thanks, Doc, give me the bill and I'll do a bank transfer.'

'No problem.'

They went through to the back of the surgery where an assortment of dogs, cats, birds and even a baby duiker were in scrupulously clean pens. Benny jumped up on his hind legs and barked even louder.

'Hello, boy.'

Tumi went to Gemma, knelt down beside her and stroked her coat. She seemed barely aware of anything.

Sean couldn't watch too much of that. He picked Benny up in a bear hug, moved him out of the pen and set him down. He ruffled his fur under his neck.

'Yes, yes, I know you want to be gone, Benny. No need to thank me,' Graham said.

'Doc, what paperwork do I need to take Benny into Mozambique?' asked Sean.

'Nothing too onerous. You need a certificate of vaccination against rabies – I gave Benny his shot within the required twelve months so I can do you one of those; tick and tapeworm treatment within ten days of travel; and a veterinary health certificate, which I can download and complete for you when you need it. When were you thinking of travelling?'

'Now.'

'Sean?' Tumi looked up from her spot on the floor next to Gemma.

He ignored her. 'Can you do all the paperwork now, please, Doc?'

'I don't see why not. Oh, there's one more thing. You also need an import certificate. You're supposed to apply for that in advance, but you know what the border's like – cash is king.'

'Sean, we can't go to Mozambique,' Tumi said. She gave Gemma a final pat then stood up.

Graham looked to Tumi, then back at Sean.

'Just do the paperwork, or as much as you can, please, Doc,' Sean said.

Tumi stamped her foot. 'Sean.'

'Yes?'

She lowered her voice. 'You're going to follow the boy with the gun to Mozambique, aren't you?'

He nodded. 'You said you got his phone number; well done. Give it to me, please.'

'No.'

'What do you mean, no?'

'No, I'm not giving you the number.'

He exhaled. 'Yes, you are.'

'No, I'm not, unless Shikar and I go with you.'

'Tumi . . .'

She looked to Graham. 'Please do the same paperwork for my dog, as well, Dr Baird. She's outside. I'll go get her.'

Chapter 16

Zohair looked up from the circuit board, put down the soldering iron and reached for the ceiling, stretching his arms.

Up the road from the apartment block a muezzin was calling the faithful to prayer. It was faint, a gentle reminder, barely audible, rather than the insistent demand in the Caliphate that pierced even the thickest walls and closed windows that hadn't been shattered by airstrikes. He scratched his chin, where the beard had once been. He much preferred this new look and would shave again before he went out later. Zohair looked over his shoulder and saw the pink sky. Maputo was waking from its afternoon siesta, getting ready to salsa.

He stood up, went to the fridge and got himself a Dois M. The beer was like showering under a waterfall in a jungle, not that he had ever done that. He wanted to travel. He needed money.

Zohair went through the small lounge room, slid open the balcony door then checked his watch, and his wallet. As much as he hated dogs and saw this particular assignment as a means of serendipitous retribution, he wanted to wind up this work, and soon. However, the Chinaman paid well and his bank balance was growing. He could afford to spend a little more, get better girls, do different things with them.

The sea breeze coming in over the balcony was languid, its scent reminding him too much of Mombasa and the life he had left behind. He would go back there if he didn't think the Americans would find him, and kill him. He was still wanted; they had long memories, those infidels, just like their enemies in ISIS. Too many people from both sides wanted him dead, which was why Maputo was a good place to hide.

Zohair's phone rang and he checked the number.

'Yes?'

'I'm coming to see you,' David Li said.

'Now?'

'Half an hour.'

Damn, Zohair thought. He had hoped to be finished and strolling the street looking for company – or, better yet, going to the bar on the platform at the old railway station, the one Gustave Eiffel, he of the Parisian tower fame, had designed. The platform bar was the hangout of hipsters, university intellectuals, the arty and literati – and particularly fine women.

'Can we meet somewhere else?' Zohair asked.

'No. Your place. It doesn't do for us to meet in public.'

Zohair went back to his chair at the table. 'Very well.'

The line went dead.

He did some more work on the device then unplugged the soldering iron. He would assemble the components tomorrow. The work of bombmaking was, for him, boring and repetitive, but it was still best done with a clear head and a steady hand. Zohair was tired; he held up his hands, doing his best to still them, but they shook nonetheless.

Zohair had read of the success of his work online. He was pleased he was defeating the dogs but even more pleased about the financial reward he received for his work. In Afghanistan and the Caliphate, the hard men had told him his reward was a place in heaven and, if the Americans eventually got him, then he would enjoy the company of virgins. Zohair smiled to himself – working girls were much more fun. Li had not given him an indication that anything was wrong, so he was assuming the incendiary device, or firebomb, as he'd described it to the uneducated, had also been deployed successfully.

Li's poachers were as canny as any mujahideen warrior Zohair had served with. They wanted to cover their tracks, disrupt the enemy, and maximise their chances of success. They were shrewd and well resourced and, another thing in their favour, they did not have the might of the Great Satan's military and intelligence services bearing down on them. He was very grateful America cared next to nothing about Africa. He went to the balcony and looked at the passing parade of glittery tops and stretched lycra below. There was treasure aplenty down there. He looked at his watch, then went to the fridge for another beer.

Zohair had turned on the TV but the DSTV yielded nothing new. The Caliphate was finished in Iraq, and Raqqa in Syria, where he had once lived, had long since fallen, but Zohair knew the ISIS reptiles would be back sometime soon; the Americans and their lap dogs could cut the head off the snake, as they liked to say, but the body would keep wriggling and the eggs it had laid would continue to hatch.

There was a knock at the door.

Zohair opened it and the Chinaman walked in.

'You are well?' Li asked.

Zohair nodded. He did not offer the man a beer. 'I was expecting you tomorrow, to pick up the package.'

'And I will be here for it, but I wanted to talk to you about another job, something bigger.'

'A bigger dog?'

'No, much bigger. This is something right up your alley, something that you would have had more experience with.'

Zohair smiled. 'What do you want me to destroy, a Humvee or a tank?'

'Yes. May I have a seat?' Li asked.

'Of course.' Zohair gestured towards the sofa.

Li took a seat and Zohair sat down with his beer. 'You want to blow up a tank?'

'More like an armoured personnel carrier,' Li replied. 'The South African National Parks service has an ex-military vehicle in the Kruger Park that it uses to transport cash and other valuable goods from time to time. It's a modified truck, called a Casspir. I don't know what the name means.'

'It's an anagram,' Zohair said, 'a hybrid of the initials of the organisation that designed it, the Council for Scientific and Industrial Research, and their customer at the time of production, the South African Police. It was designed to carry a crew of two plus twelve soldiers.'

'I'm impressed,' Li said. 'You know your armoured vehicles, old and new.'

Zohair actually knew a lot more about the Casspir, but he didn't especially want to give Li the satisfaction of hearing it. The Casspir was revolutionary for its time; it was designed to withstand landmine blasts. It was raised high on its suspension and, most importantly, it had a v-shaped hull so that when a mine exploded underneath it, the force of the blast was directed to the sides of the vehicle's body.

Zohair sipped his beer. 'The South Africans put a lot of effort into researching this stuff during their wars in Angola and Namibia; much of what the Americans and their coalition allies know about making vehicles resistant to explosive devices came from Africa. I studied the development of armoured vehicles; I needed to know how they were protected in order to destroy them.'

Li fixed him with a stare for a few seconds. 'I knew you were the right man for this job.'

'You want to blow up a vehicle carrying the national parks payroll?'

Li shook his head. 'No, something much more valuable than that. There is a stockpile of rhino horn at the Kruger Park's headquarters, Skukuza Camp. This is horn that has been taken from rhinos that have died from natural causes, and also horns that have been confiscated from poachers caught inside the national park. On board the vehicle, shipments will also be a number of complete lion skeletons, as the park authorities know that these are becoming increasingly valuable and harder for traders to source.'

'Shipments, plural?' Zohair said.

Li nodded. 'This collection has been growing for many years and the authorities fear that the storage facility at Skukuza is not safe enough for such a pricey cargo. It is to be moved in four vehicle runs from the Kruger Park to a bank vault in Pretoria soon. My plan is to let the first two shipments go through, for the people on board to become complacent, and then hit the third, next week.'

Zohair set down his beer and rubbed his chin. 'Tell me exactly what you want.'

'Can you devise and build a device capable of immobilising and breaching an armoured vehicle, without inflicting too much damage on what's inside?'

'What you are asking for are two different things. I can destroy the vehicle easily enough, but that will also possibly start a fire that will burn the horn. You want to immobilise it. But stopping it will not necessarily breach the armour to allow access to the horn inside. For that you then need another charge, possibly a limpet mine, to get inside.'

'A limpet mine?'

Zohair nodded. 'Old-school technology, but still useful. It's a charge with either a magnet or even glue on it that is stuck on the exterior of a vehicle, or ship, or whatever, and when it blows it creates a hole in the armour.'

Li smiled broadly. 'I knew you could help me with this.'

'I haven't said anything about helping you yet. This may very well cost lives, human lives, not those of animals.'

'You took many lives during your time in the wars in the Middle East. Have you suddenly become squeamish, Zohair?'

The bombmaker finished his beer. 'No. Pragmatic. Destroying a vehicle will make world news – in fact the injury to the dog, Gemma, generated almost as much sentimental news coverage as the killing of that lion in Zimbabwe, Cecil, by a hunter. If you start taking out armoured vehicles with IEDs then the Americans will sit up and take note. My name is on a watch list; they still want me dead, and an attack like this may very well lead them to this part of the world.'

'What you are saying,' Li leaned back on the sofa, 'if I read you correctly, is that I need to make this job worth your while.'

'How much horn and bone are they transporting?'

Li gave a slight shrug and a noncommittal tilt of his head.

'Come on, David, you must know otherwise you wouldn't be bothering to court me. You have good sources within the park, clearly, so you will have a dollar value in mind.'

'I know the when and the where of the shipments, not exactly the how much.'

'All right,' Zohair said, 'I'll do some guesswork for the both of us. The South African courts recently granted an appeal by a private rhino farmer to sell off five hundred kilograms of his stockpiled horn, in a domestic trade auction. At about four or five kilograms per horn that means the consignment came from around a hundred rhinos, give or take. I'm wagering the Kruger Park stockpile is easily that size, if not bigger.'

'I don't know,' Li said, hiding his subterfuge poorly with a small smile.

Zohair's brain was geared towards science, engineering and calculating. 'At today's price of around sixty-five thousand US dollars per kilo, we are talking millions of dollars here.'

Li shrugged.

'I'll need to leave here, resettle somewhere else so the Americans don't find me, and I need enough money to retire on,' Zohair said. 'I want a million US dollars.'

'Ridiculous.'

Zohair stood. 'David, I'll escort you to the door. I'll see you tomorrow, when you may pick up the *final* device that I am making for you. After that, unless you agree to my terms, there will be no more business between us.'

Li waited a few moments to see if he was bluffing. 'Three hundred thousand dollars.'

'You are hiding something from me, David.'

The businessman raised his eyebrows.

'Yes. You could hire a band of thugs from Johannesburg to hijack this armoured car in a ram raid. Yet you come to me and ask me to make a specialised bomb. When it goes up, this attack will attract every policeman in a hundred-kilometre radius, not to mention the military bomb squad that I see online has now been deployed to the Kruger Park.'

Li smiled. 'You are a clever man, Zohair.'

Zohair nodded, not at the compliment, but because he was correct. 'This is as much a diversion as a hijacking. What else are you after?'

'A lion farm.'

'Aha. So the prize is much bigger, and therefore more lucrative. My price is one million, David.'

Li stood. 'I need to discuss this with some other . . . investors.'

'You have my fee.'

'If we cannot agree a realistic figure,' Li walked to the door, 'then I can no longer guarantee your safety here in Mozambique. I have had men watching you, Zohair, for your own safety, to make sure you are not being followed or watched by your enemies.'

'That is kind of you, David, but I am more than capable of looking after myself.'

'Hmm,' Li said. 'I wonder. You never know what might happen to a man who is wanted by the mighty United States. Someone, not me, of course, but someone who might know of you or your expertise might decide to simply "drop a dime" as the Americans say, and call the US embassy in Maputo.'

Zohair put his hand on the door handle before looking back at David. 'Are you in the habit of checking under your car, David? I was, for many years, and still do.'

Li squared up to him, but was a head shorter. 'Are you threatening to put a bomb in my car, Zohair?'

'Oh no, goodness gracious, no, David. A car would be far too obvious a place to put a bomb.'

'We can and we will negotiate, in good faith, Zohair. Let me look at the projected revenues for this job. You are, of course, basing your estimate of the value of the horn on the street price, on what it will be sold for in Hanoi and Ho Chi Minh City – Saigon. The people I deal with are humble traders, middlemen, if you like, and their margins are small.'

'Look at us,' Zohair gave a small laugh, 'a Chinese and a Pakistani haggling. You know how much your target is worth, David. You will pay me commensurately, or we cannot do business.'

'Five hundred thousand.'

Zohair spread his hands. 'You have been a good customer, David, I will lower my price to eight hundred thousand.'

'Six.'

'Seven hundred and fifty thousand,' Zohair smiled, 'or you go find another bombmaker.'

'Hmm. Very well. I will put that to my colleagues. I'm sure I can make them see the value of your particular skills. Will you start work on the device now, Zohair?'

'Devices, plural. Yes, I will accept your deal in good faith, David, and make it tonight.'

'Good night, David.'

Li paused. 'One more thing.'

'Yes?'

'Zohair, I really am the middleman for the syndicate that wants to take out the Casspir full of rhino horn and lion bones, but I have another problem I think you might be able to help me with.'

'Go on.'

'Your veiled threat to me before, about a car bomb; can you make me one of them? Something small but effective?'

Zohair nodded. 'Of course.'

'If I can get you what you ask from the syndicate, will you make me such a device?'

'For that much money, yes, I am sure I can help you. Is it another armoured vehicle, though?'

Li shook his head. 'No, not at all. It is a very old Land Rover, on the lion farm I mentioned.'

'Diesel?'

Li thought for a moment. 'I suppose so, though I'm not sure. I can find out. Is it important?'

'Yes,' Zohair said. 'Petrol is, of course, highly combustible, so a small charge will turn the vehicle into an inferno. Diesel burns more slowly, so you will need a bomb that will cause more of a blast, assuming you wish to kill someone.'

'Yes, I do.'

'I pity him.'

Li smiled. 'Her. Good night, Zohair.'

He waited until the door closed behind Li. Zohair didn't like or trust the gangster, but he had so far proved honest when it came to payments. Zohair wondered if he would really come through with that much money or, once the Casspir had been immobilised and breached, if there would be a bullet and a shallow grave in the bush waiting for him.

He wondered who the car bomb was meant for; a woman, Li had intimated. Zohair didn't care who the targets were or how many people were killed or injured. All he cared about now was money. These jobs might be his way to finally have enough to drop out of sight for good and start his life again, the way it should have continued from his boyhood, on a palm-fringed African beach with a full-figured woman or two in his bed.

Chapter 17

C hristine answered her phone; it was late in the day. 'Howzit, Craig?'

'I've been better,' the leader of her dwindling dog team said. 'We've had another poaching incident. I'm at the scene now.'

'God, not another rhino.'

'No. Worse, in a different way.'

'How can it be worse?' she asked.

'Lion.'

Christine shuddered. 'Hell.'

'Looks like it. They've left the head and skin, but taken the paws and opened it up. The leg bones are gone, Christine.'

She felt her insides turn. 'Can you follow up?'

'Sheesh, Christine,' Craig said, 'Sean and Tumi have been AWOL since yesterday – I don't know where they are – and Oliver's still on leave.'

Christine put a hand to her forehead. Her business was collapsing around her and her Lion Plains anti-poaching unit had gone from being a showcase for the effectiveness of dog patrols to the losing side in a war zone. On top of that, the two men in her life she depended upon most had fallen into a state of undeclared war, apparently over her. 'All right, I'm coming. Where are you?'

'It's getting dark, Christine. Let's meet at the lodge.'

'All right.'

Christine ended the call and went to her Land Rover. 'Stay, boy,' she said to Anubis. The German Shepherd looked sad to be left behind. Christine drove the old Land Rover as hard as she could and made it to the Shaw's Gate entry to the Sabi Sand Game Reserve in a little over forty minutes. Once inside she sat on the speed limit until she bounced her way up the hill to Lion Plains.

Craig and Zali, who was on duty as the lodge manager, were there to meet her.

'Can I get you something, a cool drink maybe?' Zali asked.

'No, I'm fine. What more can you tell me, Craig?'

'One of the game-viewing vehicles on the afternoon drive saw vultures gathering on a kill, and then noticed that some of the birds were not well. They were choking and screeching; a few collapsed on the ground. The ranger radioed it in and I responded.'

'Two-step?'

Craig nodded.

'What's two-step?' Zali asked.

'Carbofuran,' Christine answered. 'It's an agricultural pesticide that's very effective against birds and animals. The name comes from the distance you can supposedly walk before keeling over.'

'I found a kudu,' Craig said. 'It had been snared and the carcass cut open and laced with poison, and the lion then ate the buck, as did the vultures. There are two dead hyena at the site as well. We've known this could happen for some time.'

'Doesn't make it any easier to deal with,' Christine said. They all knew that poison was becoming the silent, deadly weapon of

choice of poachers across the border from South Africa in neighbouring Mozambique and Zimbabwe. There had been incidents
of mass killings in Hwange National Park in Zimbabwe, where
poachers dumped cyanide in waterholes to kill elephants and
take their ivory. The spin-off was that scavengers such as lions,
hyenas and vultures were also killed after feeding on the dead
elephants. In Mozambique, oranges laced with two-step were
staked out on sticks, to kill elephant and rhino and, increasingly,
there was evidence that buck were being killed and baited with
poison to kill lions. 'They're after the bones.'

'Yes,' Craig said.

'I read about that,' Zali said. 'The Chinese use tiger bones for
traditional medicine, but as they become rarer and harder to
source the market has been supplemented with lion bones.'

'Exactly,' Christine said. 'I had David Li the other day wanting
to invest in my farm and develop it as a tourist trap. There was no
doubt about what they really wanted: a guaranteed future supply
of bones.'

'The way things are looking we could use another source of
income for the business,' Craig said.

'Not if it's a back door way to get hold of lion bones,' Christine
said vehemently.

'Understood,' Craig said.

A guest in matching khaki safari pants and shirt walked into
the lounge area where they were sitting and caught Zali's eye.

'Duty calls,' Zali said, and excused herself.

'I can't believe the poachers had the time to remove the lion's
bones on the spot,' Christine said.

'We're stretched thin and not running our regular patrols,'
Craig said. 'With Charles out of action, Oliver on leave and Sean
and Tumi away there's only so much we can do. These guys were
pros with the skinning knife, by the look of it; it didn't take
them long.'

Christine clenched her fists. 'I *told* Sean to come back here, to camp, after he picked up Benny.'

The fact was, Christine felt responsible for all of this. She had put the idea of going off reservation and trying to find clues that would lead them to the bomber into Sean's head. He was like Benny with a bone or, more accurately, like a fanatical retriever when he was on the scent of something.

Craig looked over at Zali, who was locked in conversation with her guest. 'Do you regret that Sean found out about us?'

'No,' she said, fairly sure she was telling the truth. 'Though I would have preferred to have told him on our terms, when the time was right.'

'When would that have been?'

She heard the resentment in his voice and couldn't blame him. 'Not in the middle of this war.'

'Maybe not ever?' Craig held her eye.

'No. He was bound to find out eventually.'

'I don't want to feel like I'm having an affair with you, Christine. Am I?'

'No.' She needed to change the subject back to the issue at hand. 'I asked him, rightly or wrongly, to look for leads so we could conduct our own investigation into who's behind the bombings, but I'm annoyed that he might have taken Tumi away on some goose chase.'

'He's a grown man, Christine,' Craig said. 'He knows what he's doing.'

'Taking the law into his own hands, and putting Tumi at risk in the process, is what he's doing.'

'From what I've seen of that girl so far she's like a mini version of him, tough, determined and stubborn.'

Craig had either moved on from or was covering up his feelings about Sean finding out about their relationship, which was a relief. 'What do you know about the lion bone trade, Craig?'

'Well, I know that the previous owners of Hunde und Katzen were definitely trading in bones. After they sold off one of their lions to be hunted, if you could call what they did hunting, they would sell the bones to some Chinese guy, or so I heard.'

'I wouldn't be surprised if that was David Li. He said he was some kind of middleman, working for a consortium, but he was too smarmy for his own good.'

'I don't know any names, although when I used to source my dogs from them for Afghanistan I do remember seeing a Chinese guy a couple of times. Mid-thirties, brand labels, latest model Merc.'

'Sounds like Li,' Christine said.

'People are worried,' Craig said, 'that if the South African government bans lion hunting altogether the quasi-legal trade in bones will become completely illegal, and then poachers will start targeting wild lions to fill the gap in the market. There's some evidence that this is what happened when rhino hunts were banned in South Africa.'

'Well, whatever the reason, it's terrible that a lion has been killed here,' Christine said, 'not to mention that Julianne Clyde-Smith will go ballistic.'

Craig reached out and put his hand on Christine's shoulder. 'I want you to know I'm here for you, Chris, and I'll support you all the way, and not just as your business partner.'

She put her hand over his. 'Thank you.'

He nodded. 'And I worry about Sean, as well, as a friend, even if he hates me now. Him finding out about us has obviously upset him, but trust me, Chris, you made the right decision ending it with him. You gave him plenty of chances and he kept letting you down. If he can sort himself out then I wish him well, but I want what's best for *you*, and, yes, for us.'

She squeezed his hand. 'I know you do. I'm sorry, I should have told you about all this earlier – Li's offer, the evidence I asked Sean to find. I just haven't had a moment to think. But you have a right to know.'

He looked into her eyes. 'I also need to know it's me you want, not him.'

Zali, having sorted her guest's problem, came back to them. 'Are you guys all right? Can I get you anything?'

Craig turned away from Christine, perhaps, she thought, not wanting to press her for an answer to his question.

'Thanks, Zali,' he said, 'but I'm going back out on patrol. I want to see if I can pick up the spoor of whoever killed the lion, maybe on the fence line if they came from the South African side of the reserve. I might get lucky with poor old Clyde. I've alerted the Kruger guys, in case the poachers are heading through the park towards Mozambique.'

'It's just so awful, what happened to that lion,' Zali said.

'The small mercy in all of this is that the lion they killed was very old,' Craig said. 'His name was One Eye; he lived a good long life despite losing half his sight a few years ago, but he recently lost his pride to a couple of younger males. They *donner*ed him big time and he was probably close to death. One Eye was just skin and bone, no pun intended.'

'I can't say it's for the best,' Christine said, 'but it's some consolation at least.'

'This is terrible,' Zali said. 'I feel so helpless. Can I do something?'

'Maybe just try and keep the boss off our backs for a little while longer, Zali, until we can figure out what we're going to do about this mess,' Christine said. 'We've lost the advantage in this fight, but I'm not going to give up.'

Craig stood. 'Me either. I'm going back out into the bush.'

'I want to help, Craig,' Christine said. 'I'm going to drive the perimeter road, see what I can see.'

Zali looked at her watch. 'I'm about to go off shift. I was

going to go back to the staff quarters, but can I come with you, Christine?'

'Sure.' She looked to Craig.

He came to Christine and hugged her. 'Go safe, my love.'

'You too,' she said. They kissed. It felt odd, Craig using the term of endearment towards her, even though they were sleeping together regularly. There was too much else to think about. She turned to Zali. 'OK, let's go.'

Zali fetched her walkie-talkie from her office so she could stay in touch with the lodge and the two women went to Christine's vehicle. Craig's *bakkie*, painted in camouflage colours, left with dirt spurting from the rear wheels. Clyde was in the back flapping his big ears around.

'We'll go in the opposite direction,' Christine said to Zali, 'and track around the property anti-clockwise. Like Craig says, it's a slim chance, but we might pick up some spoor that he and Clyde can follow up on.'

'OK,' Zali said.

Christine drove through the back-of-house area of the lodge, past the staff accommodation, which was decidedly humble compared to the luxurious units where the guests stayed, and onto the game-viewing road that followed the edge of the Sabie River. 'How's work?'

'Been better,' Zali said. 'We've had several cancellations since the news got out about the bombs. On Facebook people seemed far more concerned about Gemma the dog than Tumi or Charles being injured.'

'That's social media for you,' Christine said. She scanned the riverbank on both sides. At this time of year the Sabie was low and it would have been easy for a poacher to find a place shallow enough to wade across.

'Bookings are down as well.'

'Yes, well, Julianne's not happy, as we know.'

'She's flying in from London tomorrow,' Zali said.

Christine sighed. 'Great. I'll borrow a bulletproof vest from one of my guys. How are things going with you otherwise?'

'How do you mean?' Zali asked.

'You know, life in general. I know that all of this stuff has taken a toll on us all, including Sean. I've seen the look in his eyes, and I know the pressure he's been under.'

'He's only human, you know.'

'Trust me, I know.' Christine couldn't miss the defensiveness in Zali's tone. She slowed as the dark bulk of a buffalo loomed ahead. The animal, an old male, looked at her through nasty bloodshot eyes. Christine waited for him to cross. 'I'm not talking as his boss, Zali. I'm concerned for him, as a friend.'

'We're all under stress. This has shaken him up, and Craig and the others. You know better than most what they went through in Afghanistan, dealing with the constant threat of IEDs and being blown up.'

'Of course,' Christine said. 'The other way of looking at it is that if anyone can outsmart or catch whoever's doing this, it's Sean and Craig.'

Zali looked at her. 'Do you think the anti-poaching unit might be targeted because of what Sean and Craig did in the war?'

Christine shrugged. 'The thought did cross my mind, but if this was a revenge attack by someone who one or both of them wronged in Afghanistan, then surely the bomber would have been out to kill them? It seems like he's just targeting the dogs, as the devices have been relatively small from what I can gather. Whoever he is and whatever the reason he's doing it, he's shaken us up, and every other dog unit in the Sabi Sand and Kruger, too.'

'Maybe he just hates dogs,' Zali said.

'Maybe. More likely it's all about money. Tracker dogs have been highly successful in the Kruger Park and that's helped shift the poaching problem to other reserves.' She was thinking aloud.

'I think our unit is a victim of its own success. We've done such a good job of ridding our part of the Sabi Sand of poachers that it's become something of a haven for rhino, and that's made all of us a target again. Take out the dogs and you open up a way for the poachers to get back in and wreak havoc. And now the bad guys are after bloody lions as well, and there are no dogs to protect the cats – ironic.'

'Makes sense, though,' Zali said.

Christine kept her eyes on the bumpy road and the bush on either side. As well as the uneven surface she had to be constantly aware of the risk of running into animals, literally. Night was falling and predators such as lion, leopard and hyena would be more active, and buffalo and elephant harder to spot. There was something else on her mind. 'Do you like Sean?' she ventured.

'Yes.' Zali drew the word out a little, as though giving a cautious response. 'I like him a lot, in fact. Are you OK with that?'

Christine forced a laugh. 'Of course I am. I'm not carrying a torch for him.'

'That's good to know. Did you find him . . . distant sometimes?'

Christine kept her eyes on the road. 'Sometimes, yes. He's been through a lot, in Afghanistan, and he had a rough childhood.'

'Sure,' Zali said, 'but all the same I'm starting to wonder if he's just not into me.'

Christine wondered how long they had been seeing each other, as more than just friends, and how often they'd had sex.

Zali broke the short silence. 'Hey, can I ask you something else?'

'Go ahead.'

'Does Sean have a problem with casinos, with gambling?'

Christine felt a jolt in her chest. *What has he done?* Sean had hurt her to her very core and she would not wish what she had gone through on anyone else. She did her best to sound only mildly interested: 'Why do you ask?'

'It's just . . . we were in Nelspruit the other day, near the casino at Riverside, and he was acting strange, like he was being drawn into the place. I know you told me to watch him around money, so I was a bit worried.'

Christine flicked her head around. 'Did he go inside?'

'No.'

She exhaled.

'You seem relieved.'

'No, no. It's just that, well, Sean's my employee, and I recall you two were going to Nelspruit to pick up a car, not hang out in a casino, that's all.'

Zali's cheeks had turned red. 'Like I said, he didn't go in, and neither did I, and neither of us was rostered on for work at that time of the day. We went to the mall.'

In fact, Zali was right, Christine was relieved Sean had apparently resisted temptation. She knew he did his best to keep himself away from such places and she was quietly proud of him. On the basis of that she decided it was best to protect Sean's privacy and not tell Zali of his past. If he wanted to tell her, at some point in the future, then that was his business. All the same, her curiosity was also aroused.

'The mall's not exactly next to the casino, Zali.'

'We stopped for some lunch. He did *not* go into the casino, I promise you.'

'The eateries are also not close to the hotel or the casino.'

'We went for a walk,' Zali said.

Christine glanced across at her and saw that Zali was looking away from her, out the window. She told herself to be cool and that whatever was going on between Zali and Sean was none of her business. But her curiosity got the better of her. 'I met that marketing manager from the hotel group, when she stayed at Lion Plains. She said if my anti-poaching guys or I needed a room in Nelspruit she could sort us out a complimentary stay, just as she'd offered the Lion Plains staff.'

'Who said anything about the hotel?' Zali blurted.

Christine held up a hand. 'Hey, it's fine. Please believe me that if there's something going on between you and Sean it's none of my business any more and, in fact, I think the two of you would make a great couple.'

'That's really nice of you to say, Christine, but I'm finding it hard to keep whatever it is he and I have going. He's been really busy with training Tumi and doing extra patrols, but even when he does get downtime he seems to find excuses to be alone.'

'Just tired?'

Zali shrugged, 'Maybe. I'm not sure.'

'*Lodge One, Lodge One, this is Raptor One,*' said a voice on Zali's radio.

'Copy, Craig,' Zali said. Raptor One was his call-sign, and as the lodge manager, Zali's was Lodge One.

'*In contact with poachers,*' he was huffing, as if running. '*On Impala Road, by the Mini Serengeti. Call the warden and the MAJOC, Zali.*'

'Roger. Be careful, Craig.' She turned to Christine. 'Oh my God!'

'Call the head warden, Zali, and ask for backup,' Christine said. There was the unmistakable sound of gunshots as Craig ended his transmission. Christine stood on the brake and threw the *bakkie* into a U-turn. 'I know where he means.'

'Oh my God,' Zali said again, 'did you hear that? There's shooting. Have you got a gun?'

Christine nodded. 'Pistol, yes, in the glove compartment. Do as he says, Zali, call the warden and the JOC now!'

'OK.'

Zali contacted the Sabi Sand's warden on the radio then used her mobile phone to contact the MAJOC – the Mission Area Joint Operations Command, JOC for short, the headquarters of the war against poaching in the greater Kruger Park, located adjacent to the Skukuza Airport inside the reserve.

'He's on his own with no backup,' Christine said, the realisation hitting her that this was her man and that because of a series of failures there was no reaction force left to help him.

Christine drove as fast as she dared, her headlights sweeping the bush as she rounded a bend. A herd of startled zebra galloped away. 'Mini Serengeti's the big open area, right?'

'Yes,' Zali said.

Christine could see through the trees an area that resembled an open rolling field. She wound down the window.

'Gunfire,' Zali said. 'Hurry, Christine.'

Christine turned right and accelerated faster along the edge of the clearing; there was less risk of her being surprised by an animal here. 'There's a spotlight under the seat.'

Zali reached underneath her, found the high-powered hand-held light and plugged its cord into the cigarette lighter. She put her arm out the window and played the beam around.

'There!' Christine pointed through the windscreen with one hand.

Zali held the light on a running man. 'It's Craig!'

'Turn the light out!' Christine braked. 'You're making him a target, Zali!'

Zali turned off the light. They heard more gunshots. After a few seconds there was silence.

'Let's go,' Christine said. She put the truck in gear again and pulled out of the safety of the trees. 'Get my pistol out. You know how to use it?'

Zali nodded. 'Craig showed me on the rifle range, when the anti-poaching guys and the lodge rangers were doing firearms training.'

'Then be ready to use it.'

Zali took out the pistol, turned it over in her hands a couple of times and then pulled back the slide on top, racking it and chambering a round.

Christine drove down the gravel road towards where they had last seen Craig, then up and over a mound on the verge where a grader had last levelled the road. They bounced along the open grassland known as the Mini Serengeti. Christine switched on the headlights.

Zali shrieked. 'There, on the ground. It's Craig!'

Christine accelerated, gripping the wheel hard. She pulled up next to the prone form and both women jumped out.

'Craig!' Christine started to run to him, but in her panic she wasn't thinking straight. She looked over her shoulder. 'Zali, bring the first aid kit.'

'OK.'

Christine dropped to her knees. Craig moaned. She cradled his head and ran her free hand over him. 'Where does it hurt?'

'My side, but only when I laugh.'

He wasn't smiling, but she took his grim humour as a good sign.

Zali arrived and had the presence of mind to bring a torch. She gave them light and Christine felt the wetness on Craig's shirt. She took a breath to brace herself then gently laid his head in the grass and started unbuttoning his uniform.

'Hurts like hell, actually,' Craig said. 'Winded me.'

'More light, please, Zali.' Christine leaned closer. 'It looks like the bullet grazed your ribcage. I can't see any bone.'

Zali knelt as well, unzipped the first aid kit and pulled out a wound dressing with a bandage attached.

'Clyde?' Craig said, then coughed.

Christine ignored Craig until she and Zali had managed to wrap the bandage around him and tie it securely. When she was certain the pad on the dressing was absorbing the blood and slowing the flow, and that Zali was radioing an update to the reserve's warden, Christine picked up the torch, stood and shone it around until it fell on the bloodhound.

'He's not moving.'

Craig rolled over and winced.

'Stay still,' Christine ordered. She got up and walked to where Clyde lay.

'I . . . I think he took a bullet. How is he, Chris?' Craig asked.

Christine knelt down next to the big bloodhound. Clyde lay motionless on his side. She laid a hand on his big, still heart, then started to cry.

Chapter 18

As they drove through Mozambique on the EN4, the Estrada Nacional 4, the usual chaos of the Komatipoort–Ressano Garcia border crossing behind them, Tumi used Sean's phone to Google pet-friendly hotels in Maputo. They decided that it might be easier to stay on Bandile's trail in a city environment, and not attract attention to themselves, if they could kennel the dogs somewhere.

Tumi continued to impress Sean. She had called Bandile and apologised for the way in which Shikar had attacked him, saying that Bandile's father had made the dog – and her – nervous. Bandile's tone had softened, and he had admitted that his father could be intimidating. Then, with the phone on speaker, Tumi had picked up the conversation she had begun with him in his father's minibus taxi, flirting with him while getting a fix on exactly where he was. Bandile had revealed that he was in a taxi and let Tumi know what time he expected to cross the border. They were ahead of him, and once they were through customs and immigration on the Mozambican side they had found a place to park, watch and wait for Bandile and his fellow passengers to appear from the arrivals hall and reboard their ride.

Sean closed the gap with the minibus taxi, known as a *chapa* on this side of the border, as they entered the chaotic traffic of the Mozambican capital, so that he wouldn't lose their quarry. The taxi pulled over, ahead of them, outside the city's imposing Cathedral of Our Lady of the Immaculate Conception. The old church was an impressive concrete and cement confection, painted a bright white.

'He's getting out,' Tumi said. 'That's Bandile, there.'

He could see she was right. Sean drove past the parked *chapa* and pulled over a hundred metres further on. 'Quick, Tumi, get in the driver's seat. Take the dogs to the hotel and wait for word from me.'

'But –'

'Do as I say, please, Tumi. If Bandile sees you and recognises you, he'll know straight away something's up. He never saw me. Go!'

'OK, OK.'

Sean slid out of the *bakkie*. 'Stay,' he said to Benny. 'See you soon, boy.'

Sean put on sunglasses and a green baseball cap and joined the people thronging the sidewalk. He walked quickly, but not so fast as to attract attention, until at last he spotted the youth with the backpack. It looked like he was carrying the same pack, with the protruding bulges indicating the rifle was still inside.

Bandile was a tall young man, who stood out in the crowd, so Sean was able to hang back. He was not the only white man on the street, but there were so few of them around that he needed to keep his distance. If Bandile was being remotely cautious he might notice an equally tall, fair-skinned man following him.

Sean tracked him through an open-air street market selling shoes that looked second-hand, possibly charitable donations.

Bandile slowed to look over his shoulder, which told Sean that he was being careful. Sean dropped back further. It was weird, being in such a big, busy city after months living in the bush. There was the noise of music and people chatting in Portuguese, and the smell of peri-peri chicken sizzling over hot coals from restaurants that left their windows open to entice would-be diners. Maputo was a little bit of southern Europe, cosmopolitan and slightly chaotic, flourishing in a steamy hothouse climate on the edge of the Indian Ocean. It was a world away from South Africa.

Sean's phone rang. He checked the screen. 'Tumi.'

'Howzit, Sean. I'm at the hotel. It's close by. I've dropped off the dogs and I'm heading back to where I left you.'

'OK. Check the GPS and head for the Polana Hotel. We seem to be moving that way and it will be in the satnav for sure. You can base yourself there if we move past it. I've still got the target in sight.'

'Roger,' she said, and ended the call.

Sean stayed in the crowd, his eyes on Bandile's jauntily bobbing head. The boy had put in earbuds, connected to his phone, no doubt, and seemed to have dropped his guard. *Good*, Sean thought.

As he walked Sean recalled his last visit to the city. It had been with Christine, on a weekend getaway, yet another attempt to start over after she had learned about his addiction the hard way. They'd had lunch at the Costa do Sol. The iconic art-deco building was as old as some of its waiters, who added to the timeless feel of the place as they sat on the covered balcony at the front eating peri-peri prawns and drinking Vinho Verde.

Sean had left Christine in their hotel room that evening, ostensibly to go outside to get his phone, which he had left in their *bakkie*. He had ended up in the Polana's casino.

Christine had been tired after their long lunch and an afternoon of lovemaking and had fallen asleep. Sean had been wired, unable to sleep, and half drunk. She had nodded off and awoken at nine that night to an empty bed.

He remembered the fight as he weaved along the crowded sidewalk. Christine had been frantic, searching the entire hotel for him. She had tried calling him, but his phone battery had gone flat in the *bakkie*. As he had entered the gloomy but welcomingly air-conditioned gambling rooms he had lost all thought of his pretty wife, of the simple pleasures they had shared.

Instead he'd unsuccessfully fought off images screening in his mind – a limbless GI; a child lying dead on a dusty Afghan roadside; a compound that had been hit by a five-hundred-kilogram JDAM bomb, the human abattoir inside; his father beating his sister.

The slap of the cards, the clack of the chips and the hum of the air con had soothed all that away.

'I came out ahead,' he had said to her, bleary eyed, at dawn, standing otherwise mute in the face of her deserved tirade.

'You. Came. Out. Ahead? For fuck's sake, I thought you were dead, Sean!'

He had thought, at the time, that she was overreacting, that he was still a free man, that he could come and go as he pleased, that he wasn't crazy. He was wrong. No, not crazy, he told himself, just addicted. He shook his head to clear it as he saw Bandile turn off.

He was in luck. The boy walked up the driveway to the front door of the Polana Hotel. Sean took out his mobile.

'Sean?' Tumi said.

'Where are you?'

'I can see the Polana. Actually, I can see you.'

'Park somewhere. I'm going in.'

'Want me to stay in the car?'

'Can you disguise yourself?'

'Hat and big sunglasses?'

'That'll do. Come inside and wait in the lobby if you can't see me.'

'OK.'

Sean crossed the road and paused beside a parked tour minibus. Bandile was being questioned by a doorman. The doorman nodded at something the young man said, then let him in. Sean went up to the same man, who held the door open wide for him and smiled. *Double standards*, Sean thought to himself.

Inside Sean saw that Bandile had stopped in the centre of the lobby and removed the earbuds from his ears. He took out his phone, checked the scene and then headed towards the hotel coffee shop.

Sean gave him time to get inside then followed him in.

'Table for one, sir?' the maître d' asked him.

'No, for two, please,' he said, in case Tumi joined him.

'This way please, sir,' the man said.

'I'd like to go over by the window, if you don't mind.' From the table he had in mind he could watch Tumi approach as well as be closer to Bandile and the person he had just joined.

Sean took out his phone and tapped an SMS. *I'm by the window. Come closer if you can.*

Roger, Tumi texted back a few seconds later.

Bandile's height shielded the face of the man he was meeting but when the boy pivoted to wave for a waiter to come to their table, Sean got his first good look at his contact.

It was David Li.

Shit, Sean thought to himself. Li knew him. When he'd spoken to Christine after Li had visited her farm he had said that he knew Li by reputation and sight, but what he hadn't confessed was that they had played in the same poker game once and Sean had lost heavily to him, probably badly enough for Li to recognise him. Sean put a hand to his forehead and looked down as though he was studying the menu which the head waiter had laid down in front of him.

Sean thought about what he was witnessing – the man who wanted to buy Christine's farm was meeting with a kid who had

planted a firebomb and had connections to the poachers who
had laid at least one of the IEDs. He sent her another message. *At
risk of being identified. Keep watch from outside.*

*

OK, Tumi typed on the screen of her phone. She was half
obscured by a potted palm whose narrow trunk was surrounded
by cigarette butts.

'Excuse me, do you have a light?'

Tumi looked around. A brown-skinned man, maybe Indian, in
a crisp white cotton shirt, jeans and a Panama hat was smiling at
her, holding up a cigarette between two fingers. 'Sorry, no.'

He held out a cigarette packet to her. 'Would you like one?'

Tumi shook her head and tried to keep an eye on what was
going on inside the coffee shop at the same time. 'Um, no thanks,
I don't smoke.'

'I just thought, as you are standing where the smokers congre-
gate, that you might be one of us.'

She looked back at him. He was staring at her, looking her up
and down. 'No.'

'Then what are you doing here, hiding behind a palm tree? Are
you waiting for someone?'

'Yes, that's right. I'm waiting for someone. A man.'

'Oh.' He raised his eyebrows and his smile grew broader. 'Any
man? I wonder if you might like my company.'

'Why would I . . .?' It dawned on her what the man was
suggesting. She was a single girl loitering outside a fancy hotel.
This creep must think she was a prostitute. Tumi didn't try to
hide her annoyance. 'No, I am *not* the sort of woman you think
I am, sorry.'

'Then what sort of woman are you? A spy? Are you watching
those people inside the coffee shop over there? Are you a pick-
pocket or some other sort of miscreant, young lady?'

Tumi started to freak out. Who *was* this creep? 'I don't know what you're talking about.'

'Zohair?'

They both turned at the follow-up sound of a girlish shriek.

'OMG, it is you!' The voice belonged to a young woman who tottered towards them on almost impossibly high red patent-leather platform shoes. Her miniskirt, stretched precariously across an ample bottom, was the same vivid scarlet. She wore a skimpy top of sparkling lime-green sequins.

The man, who had been smarmy and intimidating until this point, now looked scared.

'No, you have mistaken me for someone else.'

'Oh no, you bad boy, I know who you are. And what are you doing with this dowdy-looking specimen?'

Tumi frowned at the newcomer, who looked exactly like the sort of girl she thought the man, whose name must be Zohair, was looking for.

'Back off, girl,' the woman said to Tumi, 'this one's mine.'

Zohair took the woman by the arm. 'Shush. Stop your nonsense, please, you are embarrassing me.'

This situation, Tumi thought, had gone from scary to comedic in a flash. She tried to keep her attention on what was happening inside the coffee shop, and caught a blur of movement in her peripheral vision. The Chinese man and young Bandile were getting up and moving. Her phone beeped.

Zohair had taken the gaudily dressed hooker a short distance away from the hotel. Tumi glanced at him, mainly to make sure he was not going to bother her any more, and saw him produce a wallet from his trousers. *Simple business transaction*, she thought.

Tumi checked the screen of her phone. There was a message from Sean. *You tail them. I'll get the bakkie. Leave keys in pot plant.*

She took the keys out of her pocket and, looking around to

make sure no opportunistic car thief might spot her, dropped them in the pot with the cigarette butts.

Tumi pulled her hat down lower and, after Bandile and the Chinese man had got a lead on her, stepped out from behind the potted palm. Zohair, she noticed, was alone now, and standing on the footpath. She felt a shiver down her back as she noticed how his eyes lingered on her. However, she had to concentrate on her targets, the man and the youth in front of her.

As she walked, Tumi took out her phone and tapped a message back to Sean. *Have them in sight, but some creep is following me. Maybe Indian. Jeans, white shirt, Panama hat, name of Zohair.*

Roger, Sean messaged back a few seconds later.

Tumi noticed that Bandile was still carrying his rucksack. He and the Chinese man turned off the Avenida Julius Nyerere and down an alleyway. Tumi hung back, worried that with fewer people in the laneway she would be easily spotted if she moved in too quickly. She slowed her pace, and when she reached the spot where they had turned off, she stopped and peered around the building on the corner. The smell of urine assaulted her.

About fifty metres on, the Chinese man had stopped by a parked late model black Mercedes sedan. He was paying a boy in what looked like cast-off clothes some meticais cash; presumably the youngster had been guarding the car. The Mercedes had blue and white number plates ending in GP, South Africa's Gauteng Province, Pretoria or Johannesburg. Tumi opened the Notes function on her phone and tapped in the registration number. She called Sean.

'Tumi?' It sounded like he was driving.

'Sean, they've turned into an alleyway; there's a cafe on the corner with a big Laurentina beer billboard above it. Can you see it?'

'Affirmative.'

'They're by a car, a late model black Mercedes. The Chinese guy is getting something out of the boot.'

'OK, I'm stuck in traffic about two hundred metres back towards the Polana, barely moving. Oh, and I can see the Indian guy you mentioned. He's behind you, but he's stopped. I'll keep an eye on him. The Chinese dude is David Li, a shady businessman from Joburg. He tried to buy Christine's farm and she thinks he's a trader in lion bones. Now it looks like he's connected with the poaching on Lion Plains and the IEDs so be careful. Call me when they start to move.'

Tumi looked over her shoulder but she couldn't see the creepy guy who had accosted her.

When she turned back around she saw an African man, older, with a cap of tight grey curls walking past her and down the alley. The man wore a leather bomber jacket despite the heat of the day and there was something oddly familiar about him, as if she'd seen him somewhere before.

There was no one else in the laneway now, and the man headed straight towards Bandile and the Chinese guy, Li.

Tumi tried to work out what was happening. Li closed the boot of the Mercedes, and when they came around to the front of the car Tumi could see that Bandile was still shouldering a rucksack, but it was a different colour and make to the one he'd been carrying before.

Li waved to the man with the grey hair, who came to them.

On the right-hand side of the car, away from the three men, the boy in the raggedy clothes who had been guarding the car was still hanging around, possibly hoping for another paid job or a bigger tip.

Li and Bandile got in the back of the sedan and the grey-haired man climbed in behind the wheel.

Tumi redialled Sean. 'Looks like they're moving now. Three of them. Another guy, older with curly grey hair, just joined them. He's driving. Bandile's picked up something and dropped the rifle in the boot of the car.'

'Are they coming back out to the main road?'

'*Yebo*, it's a one-way alley, nowhere else for them to go. Wait a minute . . .'

'What is it?'

The street kid who had been hovering near the car suddenly reached inside the Merc through the front passenger window. Tumi guessed the driver had opened the windows to let in some air while the air conditioner kicked in, because of the sweltering heat.

The boy grabbed a briefcase and ran down the alley.

The right-hand side back door opened and Li got out, pulling a pistol out of a shoulder holster under his sports jacket as he did so.

'Stop! I'll shoot!' Li ran after the boy.

'Tumi?' Sean said.

'Something's going down, Sean,' she said into the phone. 'Some kid just stole something from the car and Li's chasing him.'

The man behind the wheel put the car in reverse and, with Bandile still inside, started to back the car down the narrow alley.

Li paused, wrapped his left hand around his right and fired. Tumi flinched at the sound of shots as Li's gun hand bucked twice. The youth was almost at the end of the alleyway and Tumi saw him stagger and fall to his knees, but then he got up again. The man reversing the car had to stop as a truck turned into the lane from the other end. The fleeing boy used the bigger vehicle as cover and broke left as he left the alley.

'What's happening?' Sean said.

'Li just shot the kid and –'

Chapter 19

The narrowness of the alley channelled the explosion's orange fireball into a jet of flame, which shot out over the traffic that stood at a standstill on the main road.

Sean, still a hundred metres down the road, pulled over and mounted the sidewalk. Pedestrians, already screaming and running from the blast, dived out of his way. Sean switched off the engine, took the keys and jumped out. He ran towards the alley.

'Tumi!' She had been at the dragon's mouth and his heart pounded in fear as he dodged oncoming men, women and children and fought his way towards where the bomb had gone off.

He checked his phone as he ran. The call had ended. He tried not to think of the bodies he had seen obliterated and quartered by IEDs, the men screaming, the stumps of limbs gushing blood.

Ahead of him he saw a woman walking, dazed, her forehead gashed and blood staining her shirt. A man was on the pavement, lying still. A car was blocking the main road, its side windows shattered by shrapnel or flying debris. Horns and car alarms set off by the shock wave were blaring, and the first ambulance siren was audible, though still some way off. How they would get through the worsening traffic jam he had no idea.

Too late, Sean remembered he had a first aid kit in the *bakkie*, but he had to get to Tumi.

'*Ajude-me, ajude-me, meu pai!*' a young woman screamed, asking for help for an old man she was gesturing to, on the ground. The old man's face was bloodied, but he was groaning, so at least he was conscious. 'My father!'

Sean grabbed her by the upper arms and moved her to one side. 'I'll help you just now. I need to find someone.'

He felt the heat as he approached the entrance to the alley. There was a woman lying on the roadway. He ran to her and rolled her over, drawing a deep breath. She was dead, but she was not Tumi.

'Sean . . . Sean.'

He got up and spun around. Tumi was on one knee, trying to stand. He went to her, hugged her and drew her to her feet. 'Tumi. Are you hurt?'

She shook her head. 'I can't . . . what did you say?'

Sean knew from experience that the blast might have temporarily robbed her of her hearing. He held her face in his hands and spoke slowly and loudly so she could read his lips. 'Are you OK?'

She nodded. Tumi patted her body and Sean checked her at the same time. There was a graze on her temple, where it looked like she had fallen, but otherwise he could see no blood on her. Thankfully, Tumi had been hiding just around the corner of the building.

'Stay here.'

Sean took another deep breath, steeling himself for what he knew he was about to see, and smell.

What was left of the Mercedes was still ablaze and the oily, chemical odours of burning paint and rubber and plastic couldn't hide the worse proof of death, cooking flesh.

Sean held his right forearm up in front of his face. It seemed no one else had dared walk down here, into this canyon of death. Blazing like candles in the front and back seats were two bodies, one in the driver's seat. What had Tumi said? The man with the grey hair had been driving, Bandile had been in the back and Li had got out to chase some kid.

He put his hand over his nose and mouth as he passed the funereal pyre. He swallowed hard as his stomach heaved. Through the smoke he looked for David Li. There was no sign of him.

Sean carried on to the end of the lane. While he relied on Benny's sense of smell, Sean was an accomplished tracker himself and he couldn't miss the signs on the ground. On the road were two spent shell casings, from pistol bullets by the look of it. A little further on he saw some fresh, wet spots on the potholed tarmac. He knelt again and dipped his finger. Blood. But whose?

At the end of the laneway he saw people starting to cluster around the entrance. Some had their phones out, taking pictures, others were making calls. A woman was crying. Sean looked around. There was no sign of David Li or the boy it seemed he had wounded. Sean turned and went back to the other end of the thoroughfare, averting his eyes as he passed the burning car. There was nothing anyone could do for the man and the boy inside.

Tumi was coming towards him, still unsteady on her feet. He jogged to her and put an arm around her waist.

'The Indian guy,' she said, loudly. 'I can't hear myself.'

'It's OK, Tumi. What about him?'

She leaned so her mouth was closer to his ear. 'The man who was following me, he's behind you.' She pointed over his shoulder.

Sean turned around and saw the man in the Panama hat crouching down near the burning car, as if he was taking a close look at the damage or how it had been caused. Sean thought the man must have preceded him into the alley and had maybe hidden behind one of the other cars while Sean was checking the scene. He must have reappeared, thinking Sean was gone. Sean took out his phone and selected the camera function. The guy was taking way more interest in the car wreck than the average ghoul and it wasn't as if he was overly concerned about the burning bodies inside.

As Sean was zooming in on him, the man looked over his shoulder and saw Sean was staring at him. The man stood quickly, then ran away.

Sean reached into his pocket, took out the keys to his *bakkie*, pressed them into Tumi's hand, then set off in pursuit of the man.

A few brave or curious souls were edging into the alleyway from the far end and Sean had to dodge them as he sprinted. 'Out of my way.'

He reached the mouth of the lane and looked left, saw nothing, then right. The man had melted deeper into the crowd but their eyes locked for a split second.

'You,' Sean called. 'Stop.'

The man turned and sprinted. Sean had to fight his way through the throng, which was at its thickest here. Sweaty bodies impeded him and people swore at him in Portuguese as he shoved and cursed back. The only consolation he drew was that the man he was after was similarly slowed. It happened like this in Africa – a car accident, a public tiff, anything out of the ordinary was enough to draw an instant crowd. The explosion was pulling an auditorium-sized audience.

His quarry was on the main road now, which was still blocked solid because of gawkers and people who had simply given up, abandoned their cars and run from the blast and ensuing fire on foot. Horns blared unendingly and drivers abused each other and gesticulated wildly. The sirens were getting close, but they might have been in another country for the good that they could do now.

TONY PARK

The Indian jumped up on the bonnet of a car and Sean realised he, too, needed to rise above this crowd. He stepped on the rear bumper of a Toyota Fortuner and then clambered up and over the roof then onto the bonnet.

The other man leapt from a Corolla onto a Defender and tiptoed along a roof rack packed with camping gear. Drivers shook their fists at him and Sean as they pounded along metal roofs and slid down windscreens. Sean reckoned he and the man were evenly matched in age, but he believed he would be the fitter of the two. The target looked weedy, not used to a life in the outdoors.

Sean was gaining on the Indian. 'Stop,' he cried again.

The man was on the road now, knocking over an elderly woman and palming a man in the chest to get past him. The crowd closed around him and Sean had to fight back the tide. His chest was heaving, but he was used to chasing men through the bush. If only he had Benny, he thought; his Malinois would bring this bastard down in a flash. Benny would actually enjoy it. Sean was just getting mad. This guy was connected to Li in some way, Sean was sure of it. Or was he the bomber, checking on who had been killed in the blast and why someone had got away? Either way, Sean was going to catch him and find out.

*

Tumi's ears were ringing but her hearing was returning.

She looked around, collecting herself as she walked down the alley. On the ground she saw a Panama hat. She stooped to pick it up. It had to be the one the Indian had been wearing; when she had seen him run off he had been bareheaded.

Tumi ran to where the young street boy had fallen, hit by David Li's gunshots. In her dazed state she had watched Sean check the blood spots on the ground, and with a bit of searching she found them herself. She knelt and rubbed the brim of the hat in the nearly dry blood.

As she returned past the destroyed car she realised she had been lucky not to have been seriously injured. Turning out of the alleyway, she fought her way up the road in the opposite direction to which Sean had run off.

She found Sean's truck, parked crazily on the footpath, but it was shaping up to be a morning of traffic madness. Fortunately, not many cars had banked up behind Sean, who had stopped before entering the worst of the gridlock. Tumi got into the *bakkie*, started the engine and reversed into the road. With some honking of her own she was eventually able to turn around and drive away from the blast zone.

Tumi drove as fast as the traffic allowed, back to the B&B where she had left the dogs. Exchanging a few words with the owner, she soon had Shikar and Benny loaded in the back.

'Now, be good, you two. We're going to work.'

Both barked and wagged their tails. They seemed to get along well together, very well, in fact. Benny was sniffing Shikar.

Tumi wagged a finger at Benny. 'Not now. I just told you, there's work to be done.'

Before she set off Tumi turned on Sean's GPS and changed the settings so that she had a bigger view of Maputo. She worked out where the laneway was and decided that if she skirted around the other end of it she would miss the traffic jam that was probably still near the site of the explosion. She entered a new destination and set off.

When Tumi got close enough to see the smoke rising from the alley she saw that both ends of the laneway were now crawling with Mozambican police, fire and ambulance officers. Red and blue lights strobed the buildings from afar and it seemed that even more onlookers had gathered. Tumi found a place to park, got out, locked the car and unloaded the dogs.

'Come, Shikar, come, Benny, and no biting any civilians.'

The presence of the two enthusiastic hounds ensured that

Tumi had a relatively easy passage through the army of spectators. She must have looked an odd sight, but no one stopped her and the police were too busy interviewing bystanders, taking pictures and talking on mobile phones to pay her more than a passing glance.

Tumi realised, however, that she would not be able to get to where the bloodstains were as the alleyway was now sealed off at both ends with police tape, belatedly quarantining the scene of the crime. She was pleased she'd had the foresight to grab the Indian guy's Panama and impregnate it with the street kid's blood. She didn't know what the dogs would make of it, but there was one way to find out.

Tumi held the hat to both their noses. Shikar and Benny were instantly alert, straining at their leads. It was tough enough, sometimes, for Tumi to keep up with Shikar on a hot pursuit, but now she had two eager canines tugging her along. They were at the end of the alley where the bloodstains were and Shikar strained as she tried to head towards where the blood was.

'Good girl, Shikar, but we can't go up there.'

Tumi tugged on the lead and all but dragged Shikar away from where the boy had been shot. She remembered that he had run left, with David Li in pursuit, so Tumi cast about in that direction.

'Shikar, *soek*.'

Benny nuzzled the Panama as well. He looked up at her, seeming confused, which was understandable, as she had presented him with the blood of one person and the sweat-stained hat of another. It would be a challenge for all of them.

Shikar moved on, nose to the ground, then stopped and sat, tail wagging. Tumi moved up, dropped to her knee and saw, in front of Shikar, more tiny spots of blood on the footpath.

'Good girl!' Tumi pulled the squeaky toy she habitually carried with her from her pocket and Shikar barked with joy and bit down on the rubber ball. 'Let's go. *Soek*!'

They set off. A little boy shrieked in fear and tripped over backwards trying to get away from the dog on her mission. 'Sorry,' Tumi called to the mother, who scooped her child up and out of the way. Benny barked, causing more consternation.

'Shush, Benny.'

The dogs were in a completely different environment from their usual workplace and Shikar at times seemed distracted by other scents. Benny kept wanting to stop and pee on lampposts, and judging by the smell of them, Maputo's human population used them as much as did the city's dogs. 'Benny, come.'

Shikar sorted through her confusing surrounds and picked up more blood spots. When Tumi stopped to check them she found they were still wet. Benny got a good whiff this time and joined Shikar on the hunt in earnest. They were getting closer. Tumi felt nervous – David Li was armed and had been prepared to shoot the boy who stole his briefcase. Tumi was unarmed, but she did not want to turn back now.

'*Soek!*'

*

The Indian turned down a narrow alley similar to the one where the bomb had gone off, and Sean redoubled his efforts to catch him. The man was fitter than he looked.

Sean had his Glock pistol in a pancake holster but he knew he could not draw it and simply shoot this guy. He didn't know how or if the man was related to the bomb or the poachers or David Li, but he had been hanging around both the meeting place at the Polana and the alley where Li's accomplices had been killed. Maybe, Sean thought, he was one of Li's men and had been working counter-surveillance – looking for people who were tailing his boss – and that was how Tumi had come to his attention.

And where the hell was Li?

'Hey, stop!' Sean tried again. 'I just want to talk.'

He was in luck, he thought. It looked like the man had turned up a cul-de-sac, a dead end.

Seeing his predicament, the man looked around and, spying an open door, ran inside a building. Sean followed him. It appeared to be a run-down block of apartments. The smell inside and unidentifiable but suspect-looking stains on the walls told him he was definitely not in the good part of town.

Sean ran up the stairs, calves and thighs protesting – stairs were one thing he did not encounter patrolling the Sabi Sand Game Reserve. He looked up as he ran and saw the man's face. The next thing his mind registered was a hand appearing over the stair rail and the sight of a pistol. The firearm boomed in the confines of the building and there was a clang and sparks as a bullet ricocheted off the metal banister. Sean paused and flattened himself against the grimy wall.

'Hell.'

He took out his pistol, racked it, and drew a deep breath. The shit, as the Americans he had served with in Afghanistan liked to say, was about to get real. Sean took his phone out and dialled Tumi.

'Sean?' She sounded as puffed as he was.

'Tumi, the dude's shooting at me.'

'Hectic,' Tumi said.

'An understatement, but yes. What have you got?'

'Shikar and Benny are hot on the trail of the young guy that David Li shot. I'm getting closer.'

'You're not armed.'

'Right.'

'Then don't get too close, Tumi. These guys mean business. If you see some cops, get them in on the chase.'

'OK, will do. What about you?'

'Wish me luck. I don't appreciate being shot at. I'm going to SMS you a picture of the Indian guy. Email it to Christine for me.

If this guy was involved with the bombing somehow then maybe someone can ID him.'

'Will do, and good luck. Be careful, Sean.'

Sean ended the call, quickly sent the message and put the phone back in his pocket. He continued up the stairs, cautiously, Glock up and ready. 'Where are you, you bastard?'

*

Zohair could see light above, from an old-fashioned leadlight skylight, some of whose panes were broken. He stopped and heard soft footsteps below. The man who was following him was close, but he was being cautious.

He fought a losing battle to calm his breathing; his deepest fears were catching up with him, but the chain of events was confusing. After their meeting, Zohair had followed Li, partly out of curiosity, but also because their conversation had aroused his suspicions. There was something Li wasn't telling him, he felt sure, and Zohair wondered if Li were not meeting someone else in Maputo. He had not come to collect an IED this time and their discussion could very well have been carried out by WhatsApp or one of the other online messaging systems that even the Americans had trouble cracking.

Americans. That was his first thought when he had seen Li's car explode in the alleyway. For an instant he had been transported back to the time when the Hellfire missile had screamed out of the sky and almost killed him. Professionally, however, he knew a fraction of a second later that Li's Mercedes had been destroyed by a car bomb, not a drone strike. But who had killed Li? Given his own history he had not discounted the possibility that it was the CIA, and that they had mistakenly presumed he would get into Li's car at some point.

He ducked his head over the staircase railing for a fraction of a second and glimpsed the white man's face and his gun. He was rewarded with two quick shots in his direction. Zohair stuck his hand over the banister, fired two blind shots from his own pistol, then powered on up the stairs.

Zohair reached the top of the stairs and barged into the door. It was locked. He kicked, but it refused to budge, so he shot through the lock. The door yielded and he ran out onto the sun-scorched flat rooftop.

From the streets below Zohair heard the unending cacophony of horns and sirens. Maputo was well and truly roused from its afternoon siesta and the area would be crawling with police by now.

That was of no help to him. Who was this man following him? Zohair presumed it was whoever had set the bomb and that the man knew of his association with Li. But who had been the prime target, him or the Chinese gangster? Was his pursuer from the CIA or some underworld rival of Li's?

Zohair ran to the low wall that divided the roof of this building from the high-rise Portuguese 1960s concrete apartment block adjoining it.

'Stop!' The man behind him fired.

Zohair vaulted the wall and landed hard, two metres below, and rolled. He saw a face appear over the wall and fired at it. The man ducked for cover. Zohair scrambled to his feet and charged towards a structure and door that led to this block's internal staircase. Thankfully he could see that it was ajar.

Glancing over his shoulder he saw the man jump and also lose his footing. Instead of turning to fire he pushed the door open, but his flight was checked when he stumbled into the first of two young boys who had apparently been coming up the stairs to investigate the noise coming from the roof.

The first boy screamed when Zohair grabbed him and, ignoring his frantic Portuguese, shoved him out through the door before entering the stairwell himself and slamming the door shut. From inside, he heard the boy scream again, no doubt from coming face to face with a second man carrying a gun.

Zohair levelled his pistol at the second boy, the smaller and younger of the two, who had remained in the stairwell. The boy raised his hands, his face frozen in terror.

'Stay down,' the man outside yelled to the first boy.

Zohair held the index finger of his free hand up to his mouth. The boy in front of him stayed silent, but his lower lip started trembling. Zohair lowered his pistol and he thought he saw a momentary look of relief in the boy's face. Instead of putting the gun away, however, he took aim and shot the boy in the foot. As he ran down the stairs he heard the younger boy's howl of pain. The door burst open above, but Zohair had reached the landing below and was gone.

*

The dogs led Tumi to an urban park, the Jardim dos Professores, by Maputo's Natural History Museum. They sniffed about, apparently at a loss. Tumi wondered if the boy they were following had got in a car or a taxi here, taking his scent and blood trail with him. But it was unlikely, she thought, that a taxi driver would pick up a person with a gunshot wound. Tumi cast the dogs in a circle and looked around herself. There was a çafe called Acácias on the far side of the park, where half-a-dozen patrons were seated at tables sipping coffee. Someone read a newspaper, but she couldn't see behind the pages if it was a man or a woman.

Then a red-haired middle-aged man carrying a bicycle helmet, muscles showing through stretched lycra, appeared in the cafe from inside the building. Tumi guessed he had been using the bathroom. He looked across at her then strode purposefully towards her and the dogs.

'Oh no,' he said aloud. He turned to Tumi. 'Did you see my bicycle?'

'Sorry?' she said. He sounded Australian. She wondered if he was a diplomat, maybe, or a businessman.

'My bicycle, it was resting against that tree, near where those dogs are.'

'No, sorry, I didn't see it. You say it was parked there? Was it locked, with a chain or something?'

He shook his head and held up his hands in frustration. 'I was two minutes. Isn't anything safe in this bloody town?'

Tumi gathered the dogs and took them further from the tree, casting about in a bigger circle. She figured that if the injured youth had stolen the Australian's bike then the next spots of blood from his wound would be further than the intervals the dogs had been tracking when he was running.

'*Soek!*'

Shikar moved ahead of Benny, nose to the ground. She stopped and sat down, indicating a spot on the side of the road.

'Good girl, Shikar!'

The man in lycra came to her side. 'They're your dogs?'

'Yes. Sorry, I have to go. I'm pretty sure the person who stole your bike is a guy I'm tracking.'

The man looked at her curiously. 'Then I'm coming with you.'

'OK, but we're going to have to run.'

'Let slip the dogs of war!'

Tumi told the dogs to chase and they bounded away, down-hill, around a bend towards the harbour. Tumi and the man, his riding shoes clattering on the pavement, sprinted after them.

Shikar and Benny loved the hot pursuit, tongues lolling as they ran. It was only due to the fact that Shikar had to stop occasionally to check the blood trail that Tumi and the man, who breathlessly told her his name was John Roberts, were able to keep the dogs in sight.

*

Sean pushed the startled boy on the rooftop out of the way and kicked open the door to the stairwell, pistol up and ready to shoot.

On the floor was another child, screaming and clutching his foot.

Sean took a quick look over the handrail but saw no sign of the Indian man. He dropped to his knee beside the boy, his friend or brother now standing behind them.

The boy needed emergency medical treatment. 'Shit.'

Sean told the other boy to take off his T-shirt and then he wrapped and tied it around the younger child's wound. Sean put his pistol in his belt and lifted the boy in his arms. It was a long walk to ground level and the child writhed, screamed and cried in his arms.

The second boy tagged along, holding on to Sean's shirt tail. Sean looked over his shoulder. 'Speak English? Doctor? Ambulance?'

The boy nodded and seemed to understand. He ran ahead of them, leaping several stairs at a time, and then out into the street. When Sean emerged from the building he could see that the boy was already mobilising people to help. A woman came to him and started roaming her hands over the child.

She spoke to the boy in Portuguese, then turned to Sean and said: 'I am nurse, I will take care of him.'

'OK,' Sean said. '*Obrigado.*' He looked up and down the busy streetscape. There was, predictably, no sign of the man he had been following.

Chapter 20

Benny was barking madly, which warned Tumi he had stopped running and had found something, or someone. Tumi and John sprinted around a bend and saw that the two dogs were standing over a boy in filthy clothes who lay sprawled on the edge of the road. A bicycle was next to him, on its side.

'That's my bloody bike,' John said. 'If he's pranged it I'll wring his neck.'

'That kid was shot,' Tumi said, as they covered the distance to him. 'Benny, Shikar, heel!'

'Shit, I didn't realise that,' John said. When they reached him it was clear the young man was seriously injured. 'Let me have a look at him.'

'I've done first aid training,' Tumi said.

'Me too,' Roberts said, 'and had to use it in Afghanistan.'

'OK, I'll let you lead,' Tumi said. 'You speak Portuguese?'

John nodded as he began carefully checking the youth. 'My wife's Mozambican. I came here on a UN mission to clear land-mines in the late nineties and never left.'

'Landmines? Explosives, like bomb disposal?'

'Sort of,' John said. 'He's taken a bullet in the side. Could have hit one of his organs. He's lucky he could even ride the bike, let alone make it this far. He must have been running on pure adrenaline.'

'He was being chased by the man who shot him.' Tumi looked around her. There was no sign of anyone else following them.

John pulled off his lycra T-shirt, balled it and pressed it against the bullet hole. The boy winced and yelped. 'Sorry, mate, this is hardly sterile, but I've got to slow the blood flow.'

Tumi's phone rang. She answered it while John worked on the injured youth. 'Sean, howzit?'

'*Kak.* I lost the Indian and he almost killed a couple of kids, but they're alive. How about you?'

'I've got the guy who David Li shot, but no sign of Li.'

'Keep your eyes peeled, Tumi. Have you got the *bakkie*?'

'No.' She described where she had left it, adding that she had hidden the keys in the exhaust pipe, and gave him the location of where they had found the boy and the stolen bike.

'Good thinking,' he said. 'I'll get the truck and see you soon.'

Tumi ended the call. She looked around them. Beyond the fallen bicycle was the leather briefcase the boy had stolen from the parked car. Tumi went to it and picked it up.

'What's that?' John asked.

'The kid stole it,' Tumi explained. 'Whatever's inside was worth the owner trying to kill him to get it back. It's heavy.'

'He needs a doctor,' John said. 'I'll call for an ambulance if you can keep your hand on his wound.'

'Sure.' Tumi knelt by them, one hand pressed on the Australian's blood-soaked T-shirt. She flicked the catches on the briefcase lid with her free hand.

John was standing, speaking rapid Portuguese into his own phone, which he'd been carrying in an armband.

As she lifted the rigid lid on the briefcase Tumi had a moment's panic, thinking back to the explosion she had witnessed. She closed her eyes to try and shut out the memory of the burning bodies.

Nothing happened.

Inside was a manila folder. She lifted it out and underneath were a dozen gold ingots. She drew a breath.

'What is it?' John was standing beside her, looking over her shoulder. 'Holy shit, it's gold.'

John dropped to his knees again and took over holding the shirt to the boy's wound. '*Quase seu dia de sorte.*'

'What did you just say to him?' Tumi asked, opening the folder.

'I told him it was almost his lucky day,' John said. 'Those ingots are worth a bloody fortune. Who owns them and why were you tracking down the thief?'

Tumi ignored the questions for now. She pulled a clear plastic envelope from the folder and opened it. Inside was a sheaf of photographs. She sifted through the prints.

'What are they of?' John was craning his neck again, as curious as she was about the contents of the briefcase. 'Lions, is it?'

'Yes, in an enclosure. And buildings; I know this farm – it's Hunde und Katzen near Hazyview. There's a map in here as well.'

'The gold I understand,' John said, 'but what's with the lion pics? Does this belong to some rich tourist?'

'No, a Chinese gangster from Joburg.'

Tumi shuffled the pictures, and when she came to the next print she gasped. She dropped the others back into the briefcase.

John looked over. 'What now? More wildlife shots?'

'No.'

They both looked up at the sound of a siren. An ambulance rounded the corner and pulled up next to them. Behind it was Sean driving his *bakkie*. He parked across the road, got out and strode across to them.

Tumi looked up at him, the last picture still clutched in her hand.

Sean looked around, taking in the scene. 'Tumi, are you OK?' She nodded.

A pair of paramedics arrived and took over the care of the wounded boy from John who, shirtless, stood and wiped his hands on his shorts. 'John Roberts,' he introduced himself to Sean.

'Sean Bourke. Tumi and I work together.'

'She's one hell of a gutsy lady, and her dogs are pretty good too. I'd shake your hand, mate, but I'm covered in blood.'

Sean nodded at John and then looked back to Tumi. 'What have you got there, Tumi? What's so valuable that Li would try and kill this guy to get it back? Rhino horn? Cash?'

She looked up at him. 'There's gold in the briefcase, some ingots. I've got no idea how much it's worth, but there's something else. Pictures . . . this one in particular. It was in the briefcase as well.'

Sean came to her and took the picture from her. She picked up the others again, from the case, fanning the images of lions and farm buildings so he could see all of them. He stared, however, at the portrait of the woman in his hands.

'Christine,' Sean said.

Tumi saw the look in his eyes, a mix of fear, panic and disbelief. She swallowed hard. There was another sheaf of papers in the case, stapled together. Tumi handed Sean the other pictures and retrieved the document.

Sean flicked through the other pictures. 'These are all shots of our – of Christine's – farm. All the buildings, all the lions. Li wanted to buy the farm. Maybe he just took some pictures to show his investors.'

Tumi skimmed the document. She didn't think there was any innocent explanation for what was in the briefcase. 'You'd better see this, as well.'

'What is it?'

'It's a diary, of sorts, of Christine's movements, her comings and goings over the past couple of weeks. It's timed down to the minute.'

Sean reached over and she handed the papers to him. He looked through them. 'They've been watching her, taking pictures, putting her under surveillance. And there's gold in there, you say?'

Tumi nodded, picking up the open briefcase, and though she turned away and tried to show Sean its contents in private, John Roberts craned his head to look over her shoulder.

'I buy a bit of gold. There's about fifty thousand US dollars' worth in there,' he said.

Sean took a deep breath. 'He's planning on killing Christine to get his hands on the farm and the lions.'

Sean took out his phone and called Christine.

'Sean, hi, I tried to call you, but couldn't get through. Craig was in a contact with poachers last night, he was wounded, but he's OK. The doctor's keeping him in overnight, but he should be fine. How are you?' she asked him as soon as she answered.

'I'm fine. It's you I'm worried about.'

'Me? How come?'

Sean gave her a quick rundown on the events of the afternoon, and then he told her about the contents of the briefcase. Christine was quiet for a few seconds. 'Do you really think Li would try to kill me?'

Sean ran a hand through his hair. 'It sure as hell looks like he's been paying more attention to you than a speculative buyer would. How bad did it get between you and him when he came to visit?'

'I told him to go to hell and that I would expose him as a lion bone trader if he tries to buy into any other reserve or lion farm . . .'

Not good, Sean thought. 'There's motive right there.'

'I'm worried, Sean. What if he sends some of his gangsters in here to kill the lions?'

'I'm much more concerned about you. Go to the lodge. I can be there by tomorrow. You can stay with me.'

'No!'

'No need to yell, Christine. I just want you safe.'

'No, Sean, I can't leave the lions unguarded. I'm worried about the staff here; what might happen to them if someone came here to try and get the lions?'

Sean sighed. 'All right. How about I come to you?'

There was another pause on the other end of the call. Sean could imagine the mixed feelings going through his ex-wife's mind.

'Sean . . .'

'Don't worry. I'm not coming to stay. But you agree with me that the stuff we found in Li's briefcase is worrying, don't you?'

'Yes.'

'Then let me come over with Benny and I'll provide some extra security for you.'

'I'll come as well,' Tumi said in the background.

Sean turned to Tumi. 'No, you need to go back to the lodge.'

'No, I need to come with you.'

'Sean?' Christine asked. 'Who's that talking? Is that Tumi?'

'Yes. I'll put you on speaker.'

'Howzit, Christine,' Tumi said.

Christine exhaled audibly, giving in. 'Hi, Tumi. All right. Sean, if you're coming to my place then bring Tumi and the dogs with you, and I'll tell Craig to come here when he gets out of hospital, and Zali to come as well. I'll try to get a message to Oliver, who's due back tomorrow. We all need to talk about where we go to from here. My business is on its knees.'

'OK.' He was far less concerned about her company's bottom line than he was about Christine's safety, but there was no point saying so. Sean then gave Christine more detail about their surveillance operation and how it had ended with the car being blown up and the Indian-looking man escaping from the scene and shooting a child to get Sean off his tail.

'So this random armed guy was watching Tumi while she spied on David Li and the boy you were chasing.'

'Yes, but I caught him later checking out the results of the car bomb. He's involved somehow. I got Tumi to email a picture of him to you.'

'I'll check my emails now,' Christine said.

'It's all starting to add up; only problem is we have no idea who this guy is or how to find him again, unless we can identify him from his picture.'

'I'll send it to TEDAC, the FBI bomb analysis people in the States. It's a long shot, but if he was that interested in the car then you never know. No other leads?' Christine asked.

'I have his hat,' Tumi said.

'You do?' Christine said. 'Great work!'

Tumi had dropped it on the ground when they had come to the thief on the bicycle, who was now being wheeled away on an ambulance gurney. Benny and Shikar were sniffing the Panama. Tumi ducked over, shooed the dogs away, and picked it up. 'Yes, I do, Christine, and I have his first name. It's Zohair.'

'Guard that hat with your life and bring it to me, Tumi,' Christine said. 'Now. As in right away. We need to get all this stuff to TEDAC. Get out of Mozambique before some efficient cop finds you and wants you to make a statement.'

'OK, we're coming home,' Sean said. He wished.

*

David Li was not a brave man; he left fisticuffs, standover tactics and killing to other people. That was why he had been ready to brief an assassin in Mozambique.

Killing Christine Glover needed to be done professionally and to be made to look like one of the many farm killings that were a regular occurrence in South Africa. The job needed to be done by someone with no ties to Li or his associates, which was why he could not trust Luiz with the job. If Luiz were caught during or after the murder he would probably roll over on him. It was all academic now, anyway – Luiz was dead.

From a clump of bushes David watched the African woman and Sean Bourke, Glover's estranged husband, and the dogs and the foreign cyclist, who had joined the hunt for the runaway thief. David stayed far enough away not to be observed. When the street kid thief had found the unattended bicycle David, already gasping for breath, had given up chasing him on foot. He had taken a table in the cafe to contemplate his next move when the girl with the dogs had arrived. He had thought his luck had changed, and had jogged down the road behind the cyclist and the woman, but he had been too cautious.

No, he told himself. One could not be too cautious in this game. If it had been just the woman, or perhaps only her and the man in lycra, David might have had the courage to go up to them and shoot them dead in the street. He had been trying to summon the will to do so and overcome his fear and revulsion at using his firearm for its intended purpose again when Bourke had arrived on the scene. The fact was the odds of success were too low.

It was time to pause, to wait, to regather his wits and his forces – now that he had lost Luiz and the boy Bandile. He would still get what he wanted and the prize at the end would more than cover the loss of the gold ingots. Of course, if things worked out exactly as his newly formulated plan dictated, he would also recover the gold.

That son of a whore Zohair had betrayed him. He thought about the bombmaker, and how he would deal with him. He, too, would keep. David had a good idea where and when he would catch Zohair or, better still, when someone else would catch him.

What annoyed David most about Zohair was that he appeared to have second-guessed him. David had always planned on killing Zohair, as soon as he delivered the roadside bomb capable of blowing up the South African National Parks armoured car. Someone else could detonate it. Somehow, Zohair must have worked out that his days were numbered – perhaps, David thought on reflection, he had agreed to the man's outrageous fee too easily, or Zohair had become unduly spooked by David's threat to reveal his location to the CIA.

For now, he needed to get out of Mozambique and back to South Africa, where he was safe. The closest people he had to bodyguards in this country had just been blown up.

David took out his phone and dialled the last number from his log of recent calls. He waited while it rang.

'Hello?' said the man, just before it would have rung out.

'Zohair?'

'Who is this?'

'You know exactly who it is,' David said. 'I won't ask why you tried to kill me.'

'I don't know what you're talking about,' Zohair protested.

'What, there are two bombmakers in Mozambique who want me and my men dead?' David allowed himself a small laugh.

There was a pause. 'I did not plant a bomb in your car, but I was following you today and I saw the explosion.'

'Why follow me? What is wrong?'

'What is wrong? You threaten to betray me to the Americans, and then I have a western man with a gun chasing me through Maputo! I've just seen your car blown up, and I'm thinking that perhaps the Americans were hoping that I was going to a meeting with you in your car in that alley, but somehow, the bomb was triggered prematurely.'

A police car, siren blaring, went past him, lights flashing, heading towards the scene of the bombing.

'Zohair, I understand,' David said.

'Understand what?' the bombmaker asked.

'I understand that you are worried about the Americans, but I swear to you I have told no one your location. You are being paranoid. Be honest with me, have you been making IEDs for anyone else?'

There was a pause.

'Your life may depend on this, Zohair,' Li persisted.

'Yes. A South African man, a big Zulu, wanted a device to destroy a cash-in-transit van.'

'I see.' That was a plausible cover, Li thought. Hold ups of armoured cars carrying cash were common across the border. 'And you recently sold him a bomb.'

'Yes, a car bomb with a mercury tilt switch. As soon as the vehicle starts to roll, the mercury moves and makes the electrical connection for the detonator.'

'Describe the man.'

'Big,' he said again. 'Bald headed, muscled, with the build, the bearing of an ex-soldier perhaps. He called himself Oscar, but I assume that was an alias.'

David thought about the description. He had many enemies in business, but this man sounded too familiar.

Zohair sighed. 'I am not the one trying to kill you, whatever you may think. I had a quick look at your car. I am certain it was my device that was used, and for that I am sorry. That doesn't change the fact, though, that someone was following me.'

'Zohair, I believe you now, but listen to me, it is not the CIA who are following you.'

'How do you know –'

'There are members of Christine Glover's canine squad, here in Maputo, now,' David said. 'It is them who were following you, and me for that matter. You must have aroused their suspicion while tailing me.'

'Dog squad – the people my devices were used against?'

'Yes. The black woman from the squad followed a street urchin who stole a briefcase from my car. I pursued him and that is the only thing that saved my life.'

'The man who followed me was well built, about six two, fair brown hair.'

'Sean Bourke, the senior dog handler,' David replied. 'They were here, watching us. They must have got a lead on the boy who was working for us as a courier and followed him here from South Africa. How, I don't know, but we have problems.'

'We?' Zohair said in a surprised tone. 'Trust me, I am about to leave. Maputo has become too hot for me.'

'For both of us,' Li said. He had a reasonably good idea who had tried to blow him up, though he was not exactly sure when and why the man had turned against him. He would find out, but first he needed to move his agenda forward, especially in the light of the fact that he had lost the gold and briefing notes he'd planned to hand over to a freelance assassin, to get rid of Christine Glover once and for all. 'Have you finished the devices I need for the vehicle, the one we discussed?'

'Yes.'

'Fetch them. Now. I will meet you at the old railway station in twenty minutes.'

Chapter 21

Sean and Tumi arrived at Christine's farm the following day around lunchtime. Christine had sandwiches and drinks ready for them.

She could smell him and it wasn't all unpleasant. It brought back memories that she pushed away. 'Do you guys want to freshen up?'

'God, yes,' Tumi said.

'I'll see to the dogs,' Sean said.

Tumi frowned. 'Now I feel bad.'

'Don't.' Sean touched her shoulder. 'You did a great job. Get yourself cleaned up.'

'And rest if you want,' Christine said. 'Feel free to lie down in one of the spare bedrooms.'

'I'll be fine after a shower.'

'Inside, third door on your right. There are towels and everything you need in there. I can sort you some spare clothes if you like.'

'I'm good, thanks.' Tumi retrieved her holdall from the *bakkie*.

Sean went to the back of the truck and opened the tailgate. 'Come, Shikar, Benny boy.'

Christine stood between the house and the vehicle, watching Sean's back. She remembered its breadth, the hours she'd spent mapping him. She knew every freckle and mole, the puckered scar from shrapnel from a rocket-propelled grenade that had nearly killed him in Afghanistan. The imperfections on his otherwise great body didn't bother her. Christine drew a breath; unfortunately he was *too* flawed a hero.

'You going to bring the dogs in?' she asked him.

He nodded without turning. 'Won't hurt. They can sleep with Tumi and me in our rooms.'

'Sure.'

Christine ran a hand through her hair. She could feel her cheeks beginning to flush. This was silly.

'Sean!' They both turned as Zali appeared at the doorway and ran to him. She wrapped her arms around him and kissed him. 'I was *so* worried about you. And Tumi, of course. We saw the bomb on BBC World on the TV.'

'I'm fine,' he said, putting his hands on her forearms and prising her gently away. 'All good.'

'You're so modest.'

Barf, Christine thought to herself. She turned on her heel to go inside and called out, 'Give me Benny and Shikar, Sean, you go help Zali with the rest of your gear.'

'You sure?'

She nodded. 'Yes.'

'Come, Benny, Shikar,' Christine said. Benny loved her and came straight to her side, nuzzling her. Shikar padded over behind him. Christine watched Sean go to Zali, who put down the bag she had taken from the back of the truck and hugged him again.

*

'Oh my God, I was so worried about you, Sean,' Zali said into the fabric of his shirt against his chest.

He touched her hair, conscious of the fact that Christine could still be watching them. 'I'm fine.'

'It's good to see you. You heard about Craig?'

'Yes,' Sean said.

'You're not going to ask how he is?' Zali asked.

Sean shrugged. 'He's alive. He's a tough bastard; I'll say that for him.'

'Craig phoned Chris this morning. He told her the doctor said he would have been killed if the bullet that hit him had been a millimetre closer to one of his arteries. Craig said the hospital was keeping him in for at least another day; he's hopping mad and wants to come join us here.'

'We can survive without him.'

'Yes, that's what Christine said, or rather she said she had faith in you.' Zali paused. 'Is she still sweet on you, Sean?'

Zali looked deep into his eyes and he felt uncomfortable, wondering if she was going to try to kiss him again. Instead, though, she moved back from him, patted his chest and suggested she help him with the rest of his gear. Sean hefted a dive bag bulging with extra weapons and ammunition. Zali took his backpack.

He followed her into the house. He had a feeling something had changed. While she had been concerned for him, she hadn't fallen all over him. Zali had been good to him and he knew he had been a less than ideal boyfriend to her, if, in fact, that was what he was.

Benny and Shikar were busy eating in the kitchen, from bowls that Christine had set out. Christine was talking on her phone.

Sean went down the hallway on autopilot towards the guest room. The door to the master bedroom was open and he saw her familiar clutter, a 'pending file' of clothes on a chair, a pile of books on the bedside table and shoes scattered about. Her scent was there as well. On the bureau was the picture of him and Craig and their dogs in Afghanistan.

Zali had gone on ahead of him and was already in the spare bedroom. She was staring out the window.

'You OK?' he asked.

'Not really.' She did not turn around.

He put his dive bag on the floor and went to her, placing his hands somewhat tentatively on her shoulders.

She placed her hands on his, held them there for a few seconds, then turned to face him. 'It's not working, is it, Sean?'

'What do you mean?'

'Us.'

He found it hard to meet her eye. 'You're lovely, Zali.'

She nodded. 'But it's not me you want, is it?'

'You're beautiful, inside and out.'

'I know.'

They both laughed, a little.

'I'm sorry,' he said.

'I know,' she said again. 'I see the way you look at Christine, still.'

He frowned. 'That's a lost cause.'

'Well, you have to deal with it, Sean. I'm sorry, but I deserve better than to be your fallback girl.'

He nodded. 'Yes, you do.'

'I have to end this, for my own good, Sean. Can I have a hug?'

He held her, and while he felt bad, in case he had led her on in some way, he knew this was for the best.

There was a creak; that door had squeaked ever since they'd first moved in and he had never got around to oiling it.

Sean looked over his shoulder. Christine was standing in the open doorway.

'Sorry to interrupt,' she said.

'Chris, I —'

'Craig wants to talk to you. You're not answering your phone.'

He reached into his pocket. 'Flat battery.'

'You need to work on your priorities.' Christine handed him the phone then slammed the door.

Sean grimaced. 'See what I mean?'

Zali was wide-eyed. 'You think *that* means you're a lost cause? She thinks we're still an item. Go to her, tell her we're not.'

Sean didn't have time to ponder her words. He excused himself, opened the door and went into the hallway. No matter what Christine felt for him, if anything, she was with Craig and they had plenty to worry about.

'Yeah?' Sean said into the phone.

'Howzit.' Craig coughed. 'I'm fine, thanks for asking, as long as I don't cough. Are you all there?'

'*Yes*. Me, Zali, Tumi, the dogs. I'm hoping Charles will be released soon. Oliver's due back from leave today, and Christine left word at the lodge for him to come here.'

'What do you make of him?'

'Oliver?' Sean asked.

'Yes.'

Sean thought about the question. 'Surly. Talks tough because of his time in the army, but he's always the first to put in for leave if he's not feeling well or scratched himself and used it as an excuse to get out of work.'

'Like now. He extended his leave because he said he hurt his back jumping out of the chopper; said Tumi was responsible for the injury when Gemma's leash got wrapped around his legs and he fell over.'

'Sounds like him,' Sean said. 'But right now, I'd take him in whatever state he's in, physically or mentally. I could use an extra gun here.'

'Because I'm not there, you mean?'

'It is what it is,' Sean said. He had no desire to tell Craig to put his feet up and take it easy, but nor did he want him around. Christine had described Craig's wound to him and no matter how close it had apparently come to some vital organ, Sean didn't think it was as serious as Zali had made out. He thought, rather, that Craig might be playing the sympathy card with Christine.

'I'm worried about Oliver, *boet*,' Craig said, ignoring Sean's surliness. 'He's been causing trouble since Tumi joined us, and before.'

Sean didn't know if he could call Craig '*boet*' or brother again, but he had to put his personal feelings aside for the moment. 'Before?'

There was a pause. 'Last time Oliver took leave for a supposed injury was the time before the bombings when we lost three rhino. You remember that?'

Sean thought back to the last significant attack. 'Yeah, I do.'

'It was like the poachers were able to zero straight in on that trio. The rhinos had been hanging around camp, remember? A cow and her grown calf and the big bull that stayed near the female for a week or more. They were pretty static. And when the poachers hit and we needed every man on deck, Oliver was gone.'

Sean processed the information. 'Oliver? You think he might have been tipping off the poachers?'

'Don't know, *boet*,' Craig said, 'but I've had time on my butt here in hospital to do some thinking. You remember that night, Tumi's first patrol, when she and Gemma were injured?'

'Of course.'

'Who was on duty?'

Sean thought back to the evening. 'Oliver and Charles were on a routine night patrol.'

'I spoke to Charles in the hospital,' Craig said, 'and I told him he'd better tell me what really happened that night or I'd put him through a polygraph.'

'And?' Sean asked. It was not unusual for staff at private game lodges involved in anti-poaching and security, and even hospitality, to undergo lie detector tests. While the suggestion that staff could be subjected to polygraphs might be abhorrent in some countries, it was accepted practice in South Africa.

'Turns out Oliver told Charles he had a girlfriend in Justicia. He was ordering Charles to cover for him some nights, so Charles would set up an OP and go to sleep while Oliver supposedly snuck out of the reserve for a couple of hours to have some fun. Charles is a good guy, but we both know what an intimidating *doos* Oliver can be. I think that he was maybe not off seeing his chick, if he even has one, but maybe spotting rhino or even shooting them himself. Maybe this time he killed the rhino, took the horn, and set the IED. Whatever the truth, he's finished as soon as we get through all this mess.'

Sean thought about the theory. 'It was Oliver who heard the shots that were fired that first night and told the pilot where he thought the attack had happened.'

'Don't you think it was a coincidence that whoever planted the bomb knew *exactly* where to set it?' Craig said. 'The rhino was killed nearby, but the dogs could have easily missed the booby-trapped horn.'

'I don't know,' Sean said. 'Maybe Gemma was just a really good dog.'

'Tumi was barely out of training, Sean, yet the pair of them vectored in on that horn in just a few minutes, even allowing for Tumi to nearly break her neck getting out of the chopper.'

'I see your point,' Sean said. Oliver would not have been the first anti-poaching operator, national parks ranger or cop who was turned by the lure of money from rhino horn. 'It's one thing if Oliver has been tipping off poachers, but do you really think he'd get in on a scheme designed to kill dogs and even humans?'

'I don't know,' Craig said. 'Whoever did it took the horn off that rhino, but instead of running off with it they used it to lure our people and our dogs close to a bomb. This is a strategic move.

The bad guys want to target our rhino for real, and they know that in order to do that they first have to disrupt our dog patrols. I want to talk to Oliver, maybe put him through a polygraph. It's been a while.'

'Yes, it has.'

'Sean, just keep an eye on him for me, OK?'

'*Ja*, all right.'

'We can talk more when I get out of hospital. Just be careful for now, *boet*.'

'Yeah.'

'Are you all right, Sean? I mean, can you handle all this?'

Sean ended the call without replying and Christine came to him. She looked like she had regained control of her temper. Although he and Zali had just broken up, he did not know what she had to be offended by, seeing them hug. He waited for her to say something.

'Craig was being cagey,' Christine said. 'What did he want?'

'He thinks Oliver might be a problem, maybe even selling us out.'

Christine raised her eyebrows. 'He's a pain in the arse, but a traitor?'

Sean shrugged. 'He should be here soon. I'll keep an eye on him, which is what Craig wants me to do for now.'

'Sean . . .'

He looked at her.

'Sean, Craig isn't here, and he's not going to get to the farm any time soon.'

He licked his lips. 'What are you saying?'

'I'm saying we need you, Sean.'

He knew what she meant. She wanted him to step up, to take charge of the preparations for the defence of the farm, if that was what it was coming to.

She continued, 'I know that whoever David Li was going to give all that information to won't get it now, because you intercepted it, but that doesn't mean he won't go ahead with organising the hit on me and the farm.'

She was right, and he knew it. 'He'll be in more of a hurry now, if anything, especially as he knows we're on to him, and there is no way you're going to sell the farm and the lions to him. You're not going to sell, are you, Chris?'

'If you have to ask that, then you know me even less well than I thought you did.'

'I know you,' he said. *Too well*, he thought. She would die rather than surrender the farm and her precious lions to someone like Li.

'Look,' she said with a sigh, 'whatever is going on between you and Zali –'

'It's over. What you saw earlier was her saying goodbye. She dumped me.'

'Oh,' Christine said, clearly taken aback. 'Um, I'm sorry.'

He shook his head. 'Don't be. She's a lovely girl, but she's got her whole life ahead of her. She needs someone more her own age, someone who's, well, got a fresh start on life.'

Christine reached out and put a hand on his arm. 'Don't put yourself down; you're doing well. She told me that you nearly went into the casino in Nelspruit, but didn't.'

He didn't like the idea of people talking about his problems behind his back, but he couldn't help but feel a little pride that he had managed to stay strong. It didn't matter, though, as Christine was with Craig. 'Thanks, I guess. I'm pleased you've got someone.'

Christine looked away.

They both turned at the sound of footsteps. Zali walked up the hallway from the spare bedroom. 'Sorry to interrupt.'

'It's fine,' Christine said.

'I've just been talking to Julianne Clyde-Smith. She called me as she knew I was coming out to the farm to meet you all and

Sean was just busy on your phone. She said Sean has brought some evidence of some kind from Mozambique that you need to get to the US?'

Christine nodded. 'Tumi's got a hat belonging to a guy who ran from the scene of the bombing in Maputo, the one Sean chased. He's tied to all this in some way.'

'Julianne thinks the best and quickest way to get the evidence to America is for someone – me, she suggested – to fly it there,' Zali said.

Sean looked to Christine. 'Good idea. Zali, you don't need to be here.'

Zali glanced at him. 'I'll try and take that the right way, Sean.'

'Sean's concerned for your safety, as am I,' Christine said. 'This is not your fight.'

'I don't want to leave you guys if I can help in any way,' Zali said.

'The best thing you can do, the most help you can be for us right now, is to help us find the bomber, and taking the hat to Alabama on the first flight out of Joburg might be the best chance we have of achieving that.'

Zali chewed on her lower lip for a few seconds. 'OK. I'll get going.'

Sean found Tumi, who had finished showering, and she gave him the hat, which he handed over to Zali. She gave him a kiss on the cheek, squeezed his hand and said her goodbyes to them all. Christine gave Zali Ruth Boustead's details in the States.

'Good luck, you two, in everything,' Zali said as she got into her car. 'I mean it.'

After she'd left, Sean told Tumi to lie down for an hour and that after that they would both go on a patrol around the farm to check its fences and security.

Tumi left them and Sean and Christine were alone in the sunshine, outside the farmhouse.

'What did Zali mean, "Good luck ... in everything"?' Christine asked.

Sean shrugged, then looked Christine in the eye. 'She thinks the reason things didn't work out between her and me was that I never stopped loving you.'

'Did you?' she asked quickly.

'No.'

Christine blinked a couple of times and her eyes glistened. 'Me neither.'

He exhaled. 'So what do we do now?'

She stood on her toes, put her hands behind his head and kissed him.

Sean felt himself dissolve into her arms as they held each other tight and continued the kiss. They moved, in circles, as if in a dance, in through the kitchen. The two dogs, Benny and Shikar, looked up from their bowls, but neither human noticed them.

Christine kicked the bedroom door shut behind them and broke from him to rip the sheets from the bed they had shared. Sean didn't care that Craig had been sleeping there; all that mattered was that he was here, now, with Christine. He brushed the hair from her face so he could better see her.

They tumbled together onto the bare mattress and tugged at each other's belts and zippers. Getting undressed gave them a moment to pause.

'You risked your life for us, in Mozambique,' she said.

'So did Tumi and ...'

'Yes, but you did it for me,' she said.

He nodded. He had wanted to win her back. 'Is this my reward?'

'No.' Her smile was crooked, but warm. 'But I'm sick of punishing you.'

He pushed himself off the bed and stood, ostensibly to get his shirt off. Christine looked up at him.

'Let me go, now, if this is wrong,' Sean said. 'I can't take losing you twice.'

She slid across the bed and wrapped her arms around his waist and laid her cheek against his hard belly. 'Just don't let me down again.'

He put his hands in her hair and he had never felt more afraid, nor stronger in his life. 'I won't.'

He shrugged out of his trousers and helped her out of hers. She giggled as he struggled a little to get her jeans over her feet. They were in danger, but he didn't want to die without having made love to the woman he truly loved. Christine took his hand and drew him down, until he was over her, between her, in her, where he belonged.

When he was as much a part of her as was possible he stopped and stared down at her.

'Don't hurt me, Sean, not again.'

'I won't. I promise.'

He didn't know what would happen next, or what, if anything, she would say to Craig. Even if she considered this a one-off, a mistake she might later regret, he would fight for her. When their marriage had been foundering, sex had been an effort, stilted attempts at reconciliation, or the handshake to seal a promise that he would change.

This was different. It was as though Sean was seeing Christine for the first time through clear eyes, like an alcoholic who was finally sober or the junkie who had come clean. He couldn't change the past, but nor could he put her, this, at risk again. He knew now where his demons came from and he was better equipped to fight them and keep them at bay. Benny had helped, as had getting back to the African bush, and even training Tumi had given him a renewed sense of purpose.

But this was what he could go on living for. Not the act, but the mix of love and desire he saw in the eyes of a good woman, and the healing power of two hearts.

They rolled over on the bed and it was Chris's turn to gaze at him. She threw back her head and dug her nails into his chest as he met her every movement. He was greedy for her, insatiable. He had to be a part of her.

Forever.

Christine slumped against him as their chests rose and fell in unison. It would be wonderful, he thought, to drift off to sleep with her, to hide in this room, this bed, forever, but there were other enemies out there to fight. They heard footsteps in the hallway. Tumi coughed.

Sean kissed Christine. 'I have to go to work.'

She reached up and touched his cheek as he rose. 'Be careful. I need you alive.'

*

Sean pulled on his clothes and went to the kitchen. Benny had finished his food and was lying on the linoleum floor, back legs splayed to maximise his contact with the cool surface.

'Come on.' Benny got up. Sean had brought the dive bag of firearms to the lounge room. He unzipped the bag and took out an LM5 semiautomatic assault rifle, three magazines and a couple of boxes of 5.56-millimetre ammunition.

Once outside he went to the old knob thorn tree and sat under it. There was no sign of Tumi or Shikar. He was quietly pleased; Tumi had turned into a good operator and did not need his direction to start a preliminary patrol of the farm. He would normally have felt bad for not joining her just yet, but he would not have forsaken his reunion with Christine – if that was what it was – for anything.

He ran a free hand down the bark of the tree and remembered once saying to Christine that if they ever had kids, it would be a good place to hang a swing. Benny sniffed around the trunk, urinated on the far side, then settled in the dry grass next to him.

Sean opened a box of bullets and started loading magazines. The repetitive work soothed him after a time. Benny crawled over and lay down against his thigh. Sean ruffled the hair under his chin and checked under Benny's bandage – the wound looked clean, with no sign of fresh bleeding. 'You've got the life, haven't you, boy?'

Benny stretched, then settled into a snooze. Sean fitted a full magazine to the rifle and when he cocked the weapon Benny instantly woke again, the noise, like the fitting of his collar, telling him there was work to do.

Sean stood, his own tiredness slipping away at the prospect of danger. He and Benny walked the farmhouse's familiar fenced perimeter. He passed the house kennels and the training grounds, and made his way to the gate. Sean opened it, reminding himself to lock the padlock on his way back in, and Benny trailed him along the track up the hill, towards the lion enclosures. He looked back over his shoulder, but there was no sign of Christine. In a way he was relieved; he didn't want her having second thoughts and coming out to tell him that what had just happened was a mistake that they would have to hide from Craig.

Sean and Benny walked up the open, grassy slope of the hill towards the lions and as they came closer to the big cats Benny's ears pricked up and he became more alert.

'Don't worry, Benny. These pussycats can't hurt you. It's them that are in trouble right now, my boy.'

Sean heard the low, sad call of one of the male lions before they came into sight. Perhaps they could smell them coming.

Benny barked.

'Quiet, boy. There's nothing to worry about.'

Benny hated the lions, always had, but he usually shut up after a word of warning. He continued barking.

'What is it?'

Sean slowed his pace. He could read Benny and he knew that

something was not right. Instinctively he brought the LM5 up, his right index finger resting just outside the trigger guard.

'Benny, *soek*.'

Benny stopped barking and moved forward. Sean let him get ahead a little then followed, the butt of his rifle snug in his shoulder. Benny sniffed the ground, then paused and sat, indicating. Sean wondered what he had picked up. The lion enclosures were in sight now and Sean could see one of the big males standing at the fence.

'What have you got, boy?'

Sean went to Benny and dropped to one knee. In front of Benny he caught the glint of light on brass. He looked about, found a twig and used it to skewer the open end of a rifle cartridge case. It looked like a 7.62-millimetre round, bright and shiny as though recently fired, not dull and tarnished by the weather and age. Sean held it to his nose and could still smell the cordite.

'Good boy.'

Benny looked up at him and Sean reached into his pocket for the spare chew toy he always carried with him. He held it out to Benny, who grabbed it in his jaw and shook it as Sean kept hold. Filled with unease, he looked around, but couldn't see anything untoward.

'We have to keep working, boy,' he said to Benny, extracting the toy from the dog's mouth with some difficulty. 'Benny, *soek*.'

Benny got up and ranged ahead, though his pace slowed notably as he came closer to Casper and Felix's enclosure.

'They won't hurt you, boy.' But Sean felt the hairs on the back of his neck rise.

He wondered who had been shooting near the lion enclosure. To the best of his knowledge Christine didn't own a military-style assault rifle. She had a .410 shotgun, in case of snakes in the house – though she said she hated the idea of killing a snake and would only use it in self-defence if she was bailed up by a deadly black mamba.

Sean moved up to the enclosure, his LM5 at the ready. As he got closer he recognised the slightly smaller of the two lion brothers, Felix, who was also distinguishable by a long scar down the left side of his face. The wound had been inflicted by Casper, but no more would the siblings fight.

Casper was dead.

Chapter 22

Christine lay on the ground sobbing into Casper's coat. Felix nudged her with his big head, trying to rouse her from her grief, but she could barely speak.

She heard barking and looked up. Sean was heading back to the enclosure, with Benny beside him, the dog's tongue lolling. They both looked hot and tired. Christine blinked away tears. She felt physically weak, drained of the strength she knew she needed, but seemed incapable of mustering.

Sean rested the butt of his rifle on the ground, holding the tip of the barrel by his side. 'No sign of the shooter. Benny couldn't pick him up.'

'Casper hasn't . . .' Christine sniffed, 'hasn't been dead long, maybe only a few hours.'

'You didn't hear anything?'

She shook her head. 'Not a thing.'

'Could have used a silencer,' Sean said.

Christine ruffled Felix's mane. 'Where's Tumi?'

'She's working the western perimeter fence,' Sean said, 'though that's a long way from here. I just called the police, to see if they could send some people, but there's been some sort of explosion on the road between here and the Kruger Park. The available guys from Hazyview are on the scene and the anti-poaching people from the park can't get through, even if they wanted to come help us.'

Christine looked up. 'Explosion?'

Sean nodded. 'All they could tell me was that it was a vehicle, not if it was an IED or something deliberate, or an accident.'

'Oliver's here,' Christine said. 'He arrived while you were out scouting with the dogs. I sent him back to the farmhouse.'

Sean reached into his pocket and pulled out the bullet casing he had found earlier. 'Did Oliver bring a rifle with him from the reserve?'

Christine nodded. 'The R1.'

Sean held up the spent cartridge. '7.62-millimetre.'

'The same as from Oliver's rifle?'

'Same type, yes,' Sean said. 'It's a heavier calibre than the LM5s Tumi and I use. Oliver packs a bigger rifle in case the team runs into trouble with buffalo or elephant. Did you see him drive up?'

Christine stood, pushed Felix aside and brushed herself down. The lion sniffed his brother, still confused by his lack of response. 'No, he just appeared. He told me he got a lift from the Sabi Sand with one of the other security guys who dropped him at the main road.'

Sean rubbed his chin.

'You think Oliver shot Casper?' Christine asked.

'I've got no reason to think that, but Craig's worried about him and wants him to take a polygraph. In fairness, we should all take the test.'

'I agree,' Christine said. 'I don't want to start accusing people on hunches, but Oliver has always been a difficult customer.'

Sean nodded. 'And he's been anti-Tumi since she started. However, you said you didn't hear a shot.'

Christine shrugged and wiped her eyes. 'There are plenty of

bangs and barking around this place so I guess it's possible I missed a shot. Sean, I –'

She felt so desolate, and she could see that he was worried about her, but after they had made love she had begun to worry about Craig and the fallout that was inevitable after what had happened. Sean came to her and put his arms around her. Christine wanted to melt into him, the way she once had when she was feeling down, when she'd believed she could count on him to look after her and be strong for both of them. That, her logical self reminded her as he held her tight, had been an illusion. Had he really changed? Was she crazy for even contemplating giving Sean another chance? Making love to him again had felt so natural, and so wonderful, but was she really ready to let him back into her life fulltime? His addiction had almost ruined her financially and probably would have if Craig hadn't helped her pick up the pieces of her life. As hard as she had tried to understand Sean's underlying problems he had wounded her terribly, and that hurt reminded her of a cut she'd suffered to her hand as a teenager – it was scarred over now, but some of the nerves had been damaged, and she'd lost some of the feeling there forever. Right now, however, her sadness over Casper dwarfed everything.

'They killed my lion, Sean,' she sniffed into his shirt. He stroked her hair. Christine pushed him away, firmly but not unkindly. 'You've got work to do. I don't want to lose any more people or any more animals.'

He sighed, then nodded in resignation. 'This place is too big, Chris, and there aren't enough of us to protect you. I tried telling the cops that we're expecting an attack here, but they said if the only casualty so far is a lion that they'll get someone out to investigate once they deal with this vehicle business on the road.'

'What do you suggest?'

'You need to protect the lions, as well as yourself,' Sean said.

'Yes.'

'We can't move the lions out of their enclosure and into the house, so I think we all need to relocate to here.'

'In with the lions?' Christine asked.

'As close as we can get to them, yes.'

She looked at him. 'You really think Li and his people are going to come for us?'

Sean shrugged. 'Killing Casper could be Li's warning shot, literally. We've got evidence that he was going to pay someone to take you out. That means he was making plans. Now that he knows that we're on to him, he'll either try and pretend like it was never going to happen and not proceed with the hit, or he'll do it sooner rather than later. I'm worried that this exploding vehicle the police are dealing with might have been some kind of deliberate diversion to keep the cops occupied. What do you think?'

She thought about it. 'I think Li's greedy and he knows what he wants. I think he'll want to get rid of you guys now as well as me.'

Sean nodded slowly. 'I'm afraid I agree. I'll take Benny for another sweep of the fence line.'

Was she doing the right thing, she wondered, putting Sean, Tumi and even Oliver's lives at risk to protect her farm and her animals?

'You're doing the right thing, Chris,' Sean said.

It was like that when they were married. It was as if he could read her mind sometimes. She wondered if he was also trying to reassure her that reconnecting with him was the 'right thing'.

'Am I? I'm not sure, Sean.'

'It's not just your livelihood, it's the proper thing to do. I wasn't sure what Craig and I were fighting for in Afghanistan. The government there was corrupt, the Americans and their allies had no real strategy, and most of the people there would have been happy to see us go. But this is different. We're fighting for the right thing here, Chris.'

'I hope so.' She looked into his green eyes and felt the lump rise in her throat again.

He came to her and put his arms around her.

She fought it, arms stiffly by her sides for as long as she could bear it. All of three seconds. Then she collapsed into him, sobbing, and let him take her weight. He held her and rocked her as her body shook against his.

When she had calmed she moved a hand up and wiped her eyes. 'What . . . what am I going to do with Casper?'

He mulled it over for a short time. 'Casper was known and loved by people all over the world. You have to tell his story.'

'What? Put a picture of his body on social media? Sean, I don't know if I can.'

He gripped her by the arms. 'It's hard, but you have to. You have to tell the world about the threat to lions and the trade in their bones. Casper won't have died in vain if you can help mobilise people to fight this war.'

Christine sniffed. 'Yes. You're right. Sean . . .'

'Yes?'

'About what happened before. I need time to think about things.'

'Was it just a moment of weakness?' he asked.

'I don't know.'

He held her gaze for a few moments then looked down. He turned away and called Benny.

*

Knowing that Oliver was back and on the property somewhere, Sean called him on his mobile phone.

'Oliver, please can you come to the lion enclosure, but see Christine first and ask for some *nyama* for Felix. And bring the spare keys to the enclosures.'

'Yes, *boss*.' Oliver's sarcasm was clear.

'Just do as I ask, please, Oliver.' He didn't think he needed to add 'because Craig's not here and I'm now in charge'. 'And ask Christine for a couple of twenty-litre jerry cans of water – I know she keeps some at the farmhouse in case the borehole pump breaks – and a couple of patrol tents.'

The fact that he was in command worried him. He didn't know if he was ready to lead the remaining members of the team. Sean had picked up enough knowledge about military tactics during his tours of Afghanistan to prepare a reasonable defence of the farm, but he did not know if he would be able to hold the others together if things got rougher than they already were. Oliver was insubordinate, Tumi was still raw, and he was so concerned for Christine's safety that he wished that she, not Zali, was about to fly to the United States. Li had been set to brief a hit man to kill Christine and now Sean and the other two were in the firing line.

While he waited for Oliver he walked Benny around the far side of Casper and Felix's enclosure, over to where the lionesses were kept. Benny was, as usual, curious about the mix of scents, but picked up nothing suspicious.

Sean saw Tumi coming over the rise of a grassy hill, Shikar by her side. He waved to her to come over.

By the time Tumi reached him, Oliver arrived in a farm *bakkie*. They all greeted one another, Oliver as cool to Tumi as usual.

'Shikar and I couldn't pick up anything on the other side of the fence,' Tumi said.

'Same on this side.'

'Are we here to feed lions,' Oliver asked, 'or to protect this place?'

'Could be one and the same thing,' Sean replied. 'Do you have the keys?'

Oliver took the keys to the enclosures from his pocket and handed them over. Sean had seen Christine and her staff go through the routine countless times, but it still took him some time to find the right keys for the multitude of locks. He opened a vacant area and had Oliver drive through the gate. The pair of them then dragged the leg of a dead horse from the back of the *bakkie* and let it fall with a thud into the grass. Local farmers donated livestock and other animals that had passed away to Christine's lion refuge.

Sean had Oliver move the vehicle back out, and then he unlocked a gate between the empty enclosure and the space where Felix was now pacing along the fence. Sean left, locked the exterior gate, and used a remote control on the key chain to open the battery-powered sliding gate between the two areas. Sean had been in with Christine when she interacted with Felix and Casper, but he was wary of doing so by himself. He was doubly cautious today as Felix seemed confused by the loss of his brother. Felix was roaring impatiently as he waited for the gate to roll open far enough for him to squeeze through.

Felix trotted into the vacant lot and began devouring the section of horse. Sean used the remote to shut the gate behind the lion. If Felix was worried about being locked in, or still concerned about the death of his brother, he wasn't showing it now as he chomped down on flesh and cartilage.

'What do we do now?' Oliver said. Tumi was with them again.

'We set up camp in the enclosure where Felix and Casper were. I want a camouflaged OP here, on that small *koppie*.' Sean pointed to a small rise studded with granite rocks. He knew the lions liked to sit and snooze up there as it gave them a good vantage point over the whole farm, and he wanted the spot for the same reason. 'Oliver?'

'Yes?'

'Take the water jerries and the patrol tents up to the rise, please.'

Oliver gestured to Tumi with a flick of his head. 'What about her?'

'She's going back on patrol.'

Oliver grunted and went to the *bakkie*, where he began unloading the water containers.

'You can leave your rifle in the vehicle,' Sean said.

'What do we do with the dead lion?' Tumi asked. 'It's spooky.'

'He won't hurt you. We'll leave him there for now and we'll burn him tomorrow, give him a Viking send-off. I don't want the bastards who are after us to get hold of his bones.'

'You make it sound like we won't get out of this alive,' Tumi said quietly.

Sean had no reply to that. 'You can leave if you want, Tumi. You didn't sign up for this.'

She glared at him. 'It's bad enough that Oliver treats me like a second-class citizen – now you're acting like I'm some sort of precious little flower that's going to bend in the wind.'

'Sorry,' he said. He walked to the *bakkie* and looked towards the rise. Oliver was plodding, slower than necessary, up the hill with the water cans. Sean leaned into the back of the truck and picked up Oliver's 7.62-millimetre R1 rifle.

'What are you doing?' Tumi asked.

He said nothing as he checked the safety catch, removed the magazine and set it down. He pulled back the cocking handle and a round was ejected from the breech.

Tumi bent and picked up the fallen round from the grass. 'He's been walking around with his rifle cocked, with a bullet in the chamber, like he's ready for action.'

'Yes,' Sean said. He locked the working parts of the rifle back by depressing a plunger under the weapon, then poked his little finger into the breech and barrel. When he pulled it back out, his finger was dark grey with cordite residue. 'This has been fired since it was last cleaned.'

'Maybe he doesn't clean his rifle that often,' Tumi said.

'Maybe, but it's unlikely. Oliver was in the army, and whatever we think of him I never heard anyone say he was anything other than professional when it came to his soldiering.' Sean laid the unloaded rifle down in the rear tray of the *bakkie* then took up the magazine. Deftly he unloaded the bullets from it. When they were laid out in the vehicle he counted them, twice. 'Nineteen.'

'The magazine holds twenty rounds, right?' Tumi said.

'Right.'

Chapter 23

Tumi took Shikar up the hill to where Oliver was laying out the first of two camouflage pup tents.

He straightened his back. 'Have you come to help me?'

'Yes,' she said.

'I thought he was sending you out on patrol.'

'Change of plan. Maybe Sean thought you needed help putting up a tent,' Tumi said.

Oliver scowled at her. If he saw her joke, he wasn't about to have a laugh at his own expense. 'Unroll the other one.'

She told Shikar to sit, then shook the second tent out of its bag. 'Why don't you like me, Oliver?'

He was on one knee, hammering in a peg with a rock. He stopped and turned to face her. 'It's not you I don't like.'

'No, just women.'

He went back to hammering. 'I like women. Ask anyone in Huntington and they'll tell you that women like me.'

Her skin crawled, but she wanted to understand him. Sean had told her to keep him busy, much to her chagrin, while he went to inspect Casper's body again. Tumi swallowed the insulting retort that had been forming in her mind. 'OK, so you're popular with the ladies. Why don't you like me?'

Oliver got up and moved to the next corner of the tent. Even the way he hefted the granite rock made Tumi feel nervous. He seemed to be in a state of barely contained anger. 'I told you, it's not you I dislike.'

'Then what?'

He set down the rock. 'It's women serving in a front-line role, in anti-poaching. It is not correct.'

'Ha. Listen to you. "*Not correct*". Don't you know what century this is?'

'You mock me, but I am concerned for your safety.'

Tumi was taken aback. 'Concerned?'

He shrugged and picked up his rock, like the caveman she thought him to be, and started pounding another tent peg into the hard earth. 'Yes. I had a sister . . .'

She waited for him to carry on, but he seemed to clam up. 'What about your sister, Oliver?'

He hit the peg harder, but it was thin and cheap and it bent under the onslaught. He cursed and pulled it out of the ground. 'She joined the police. Like you she wanted to do *good*.'

'Did something happen to her?'

Oliver had lain the tent peg on a flat rock and was hitting it with the rock in his hand, trying to straighten it. Sparks began to fly. 'She had just found out she was pregnant. I was going to be an uncle. Then she was shot, trying to stop a cash-in-transit robbery in Joburg. She and the baby died.'

'She must have been a very brave woman.'

He looked to her. 'She was stupid.'

'Oliver –'

'She should have been at home, or gone to university to be a schoolteacher like my mother wanted for her, but she wanted to *do* something for this country. I don't want to talk about it any more.'

She could see the pain in him now, and realised it had manifested as anger and a belief that women should be closeted at
home, cooking, cleaning and having babies. Tumi had no wish
to antagonise him on the subject of women in front-line roles.
She wondered if Craig and Sean knew about his family history.
As sad as his story was, he could still be working against them.

'It was terrible what happened to the lion, wasn't it?' she
said.

Having straightened the peg, Oliver was now trying to hammer
it back into the ground, in a different spot. 'This whole farm is a
waste of land and money. Christine should raise cattle or grow
crops to feed the people.'

'And what about the lions?'

Oliver finished hammering the peg and got up. 'They should
all be shot. She should do like the previous owners did – charge a
fortune for rich American hunters to shoot the lions and then sell
their skeletons to the Chinese. These lions are like cattle, bred
for the slaughter, and if the Chinese like Li get their lion bones
from farms like this then they wouldn't be killing wild lions, like
they've already started to.'

'A lot of people wouldn't agree with you, Oliver.'

He fitted a collapsible tent pole. 'It's the same with the rhinos.
When the Vietnamese and Chinese were allowed to come to
South Africa and legally hunt rhinos they took the trophies – the
horns – back home and this was enough to satisfy the market
for rhino horn. When the do-gooders overseas made the hunting
stop, the supply dried up, and that's when the poaching got bad.
If they just legalised the trade in rhino horn the killing would
end; same goes for lion bones.'

Tumi had heard the arguments for and against legalising the
trade in rhino horn, ivory and lion bones, and while she did not
agree with Oliver, Sean had wanted her to keep him occupied
and she was succeeding at that.

'In fact, our government has set a quota for the export of lion bones,' Tumi said.

'Yes, but they should just open it up and let the market sort itself out.' He clipped the nylon of the tent to the poles he had just erected then moved on to the next one. 'You can help me.'

She went over to him. Like most men, Oliver had a big ego, and it seemed if she agreed with him – or did not actively disagree – he could be less objectionable. Tumi unrolled and positioned the second pup tent on a flat piece of ground free of rocks and began assembling the poles while Oliver started hammering in the pegs. 'Why do you think someone shot just the one lion?'

He kept working, not making eye contact. 'I don't know. Probably to send Christine a warning. I heard that the Chinaman, Li, wants to buy the farm and the lions. She would be wise to sell and make some money. The way her company is going we will all be out of work soon.'

Tumi bit her tongue. 'Yes, things are pretty desperate.'

'The government should legalise the trade in rhino horn as well,' Oliver said.

She wondered if he was deliberately trying to change the subject, to deflect her questioning away from him and the dead lion, Casper. 'Do you really think that will save the wild rhinos?' she asked, to keep him talking, but he didn't reply.

He finished hammering in a peg, stood, and took off his shirt. 'It's getting hot.'

His bare chest glistened with sweat and he looked straight at her. He forced a smile and winked at her. 'Like what you see?'

'I wasn't looking at you. What were you saying about rhino horn, Oliver? I'm interested in this stuff, about poaching and what we can do to stop it.'

He grunted and knelt to resume his physical labour. 'The government and all the private landholders who farm rhinos should flood the market in Asia with rhino horn that's been humanely taken from the animals. It grows back, you know?'

Of course she knew that, but his argument was, in her opinion, simplistic and flawed. Tumi could have reminded Oliver that the last few dead rhinos they had found had been missing their ears and tails, proof that the market in Vietnam was demanding wild-killed rhinos.

But she said, 'Yes, I do know. You have a point, Oliver.'

He seemed satisfied with himself. He got up and stretched and looked her up and down. 'Do you have a man?'

She felt uncomfortable being asked such a question while being ogled. 'Yes,' she lied, 'I do.'

'Then you should be with him, married, producing children, rather than out here in the bush risking your life for a few mangy old lions.'

Tumi swallowed. Thinking on her feet, she continued, 'He . . . he's at university. We are waiting to get married when he finishes his degree. In the meantime I . . . I mean, he has given his blessings to me working.'

'Hmm.' Oliver dropped the rock he had been using as a hammer and took two steps closer to her. 'Your boyfriend is probably having sex with half the chicks at varsity.'

'Oliver!'

'Don't look so shocked. Men have needs. If you're not looking after your man then how can you expect him to be faithful to you, Tumi?'

His tone was calm, his voice smooth, devoid of its usual surliness, and the change made him seem all the more sinister. Tumi shivered. She had not expected this. She took a step back and nearly stumbled on a loose rock.

'Careful, we don't want to bruise that cute little booty of yours. In fact, it's a bit too small for my liking. Maybe we can get a nice meal together later? Get the boss lady to cook for us and fatten you up? But before dinner, let's have some fun, hey, girl?'

She held up a hand. 'Stop.'

'I know what's good for you, Tumi, what you really need.'

Tumi looked around. She had left her rifle in the truck. Shikar was over by the lion enclosure, watching Felix eat. 'Shikar!'

The dog pricked up her ears and came running.

Oliver had a nine-millimetre pistol in a holster on his belt. He drew it and cocked it. 'If you tell that useless dog of yours to attack me I will kill it before it gets within twenty metres of me.'

'Shikar, stop!' The dog slowed to a walk, looking at Tumi. She knew something was wrong. 'Sit, Shikar. Good girl.' Her heart pounding, Tumi turned back to Oliver. 'What are you going to do now, Oliver, shoot me if I don't have sex with you?'

'You're going to do as I tell you.'

Tumi backed away from him and drew a deep breath. 'Sean!'

Oliver scowled at her as she screamed the name again. He unloaded his pistol, pulled back the slide to eject the round that he just chambered, then picked up the fallen bullet and put it back in the magazine again. 'Bitch.'

*

Sean's hands and forearms were covered in blood. He had looked skywards and said a quick prayer before he'd taken the hunting knife from the sheath at his belt and cut into Casper's body.

The blade was razor sharp, but even so it was hard work cutting through Casper's muscle and sinews and digging deep into the flesh in search of the bullet that had killed him.

It was grisly, gory work, but the shot had been clean, entering the big cat three-quarter on from the front and into the chest cavity, where it must have found the heart. Sean was glad Christine was not here to see the butchery going on, but he wanted to retrieve the copper-jacketed slug that had killed Casper. It could be important.

If it was a match to the empty brass casing he'd found, then they might be able to discover what weapon it had come from.

Of course, if Casper had been killed by one of David Li's hired guns, as a warning before an all-out assault on the farm, then it would be academic, but if the bullet pointed to someone closer to the team, then that might help them avoid attack from within.

Sean wanted more information before questioning Oliver or levelling any accusations at him, but time was running out.

He cut some more flesh then reached into the carcass with his free hand. Just as his fingertips found something hard, smooth and pointy, he heard Tumi scream his name. Sean grabbed the bullet, pulled it out of the lion's body and got to his feet. He pocketed the bullet and, knife in one sticky, bloody hand and rifle in the other, he ran back towards the hillock.

'Come, Benny.'

Benny was barking as he crested the rise in front of them before Sean. As he came up over the top he saw that Oliver had his hand on Tumi, grasping her by the forearm.

'Let her go!' Sean yelled.

'Get off me,' Tumi said.

Sean was about to order Benny to attack – the dog would get there way before him – when Tumi reached out, grabbed Oliver's free hand and, just as Sean had taught her in unarmed combat training – flipped Oliver, using the big man's oncoming momentum, so that he landed on his back. Before Oliver could get to his feet Benny was standing over him, growling, and Sean was soon with them.

'Are you OK?' Sean asked Tumi.

She looked shaken, but she nodded. 'I am. He tried to attack me.'

Oliver got up and brushed himself down. 'Nice move. I wanted to see how she handled herself in hand-to-hand combat. She didn't realise that I was trying to test her.'

'*She* knows exactly what you were trying to do,' Tumi said to him.

Sean moved between them and stared at Oliver, inches away from his face. He reached into his pocket, pulled out the bullet and held up his reddened hand. 'I'll talk to you about Tumi later. If she wants to lay a complaint against you I'll gladly hold it up. For now I want you to tell me where this bullet came from.'

Oliver squinted at the slug. 'Where did you get that?'

'Out of the dead lion, Casper.'

Oliver shrugged. 'Why should I know where it came from?'

Sean reached into the other pocket of his camouflage trousers and pulled out a clear zip-lock bag with a brass cartridge case in it. 'This is a 7.62-millimetre cartridge case found near the enclosure, and I'm pretty sure the bullet I took out of Casper came from it. Question is, which rifle did it come from?'

'Again, why are you asking me this?'

'Where were you last night and this morning, Oliver?'

'At home. You can ask my wife if you want.'

Tumi scoffed. 'I'll tell your wife what you're like if you want.'

Oliver glared at her.

Sean took a step closer to him. Without taking his eyes off Oliver he said, 'Tumi?'

'Yes?'

'Take Shikar and check the road again, please.'

She nodded, called her dog and set off.

Oliver squared up to him. 'Just you and me now.'

'Yes. What time did you get here, to the farm?'

'A couple of hours ago. I hitched a lift with one of the other Sabi Sand security guys.'

'Which one?'

Oliver shrugged. 'I don't know his name. He was heading this way, saw my uniform, and when I stuck my hand out he stopped for me.'

'Just happened to be going this way?'

'Yes.'

'And you had your rifle with you?'

'I was told to come ready for action, by Craig, and to get to the farm as quick as I could.'

'You spoke to Craig in hospital?'

'Yes, on the phone. I was worried about him.'

Sean rubbed his chin. He couldn't imagine Oliver being worried about anyone other than himself. He held up the bullet again. 'Did you shoot the lion with this bullet, Oliver?'

The other man clenched his fists and glared at Sean. 'No, I did not. I don't think these stupid lions or this farm are worth dying for, but I did not kill it.'

There was nothing Sean could do without further proof or a lie detector test. He was about to tell Oliver that he would have to submit to a polygraph when they both heard two gunshots.

*

Tumi was firing blind.

'Shikar!' Tumi dropped to her belly in the long, dry grass and Shikar, who had also been scared by the noise, ran back to her and lay down beside her.

Tumi remembered the drills Sean had taught her and crawled until she found some cover behind an anthill. Her heart was thumping. Someone had fired a bullet at her and the round had come close enough for her to feel the displaced air as it zinged past, but she had not heard the shot go off. She had raised her rifle over the mound and fired twice in the general direction the bullet had come from.

She peeked cautiously around the mound of earth. She could see nothing.

A second later Tumi was showered in termite-excavated clay and felt the air displaced not more than an arm's length away from her. It was from another bullet, but again she hadn't heard it. Tumi put her hand on Shikar, who was whining. 'Stay down, girl.'

Tumi rolled onto her back and took her phone out of her breast pocket and called Sean. 'Someone's shooting at me, with a silenced weapon! That was me, just now, firing back.'

'I'm on my way,' he said.

'No, Sean. Don't come to me. There's a sniper somewhere. He's got me pinned down. I can't move and if you come across the open ground he'll pick you off before you get anywhere near me. I'm by the western perimeter fence, not far from the locked access gate. Behind the big termite mound.'

'OK. I know where you are. Shit. Are you in cover?'

'For now, yes,' she said.

'I'll call you back. I'm going to get Christine and whoever else is here and we'll make a stand at the *koppie*.'

'Roger that,' Tumi said. Sean ended the call. She felt very alone.

Shikar was still whimpering. 'It's OK, girl,' Tumi said, though she felt anything but.

Tumi looked up at the top of the anthill. There was a furrow made by the bullet that had very nearly taken the top of her head off. She could tell by its direction that the sniper was firing at her from the south, roughly parallel with the fence along the main road. A car whizzed by, oblivious to the deadly game of cat and mouse being played out just across the barbed wire.

The land across the road was heavily vegetated. Tumi would find shelter there, but first she needed to get over or under the perimeter fence. This part of Christine's farm had been cleared for cattle grazing many decades ago and was covered in dry golden grass, with not a tree in sight to provide concealment or protection against bullets. About a hundred metres from her was the gate that provided access to this part of the property, but it was locked and Tumi did not have a key.

'Think,' she told herself.

To try to still her mind, she patted Shikar. When another bullet searched her out, skimming across the top of the anthill, she lay flat again. Tumi buried her face in the dog's coat, and when she shifted again she saw how the wind had picked up and was ruffling Shikar's hair.

That gave Tumi an idea. She picked up a handful of fine dirt and, as she had seen Sean do, she let it fall slowly from her closed palm. Tumi watched as the wind caught the tiny particles and blew them away from her and towards where the sniper was firing from and then on to the perimeter fence.

'Perfect.'

The problem with her idea was that she needed matches or a cigarette lighter and Tumi did not smoke. She thought about what she did have in her personal equipment. Mentally she checked off her gear.

She had a compass. Tumi reached into her cargo pants pocket and pulled out her Silva compass. The perspex housing could be laid over a map, as Sean had showed her, and there was a small magnifying window for reading small print. Tumi looked up, checked the angle of the sun and snatched up some leaves and dried stems of grass. She tilted the magnifying glass on the compass until a beam of light was concentrated on the pile of kindling.

The sniper fired another shot and Shikar jumped up and barked, searching for the angry bee that she probably mistook the bullet for.

'Get down!'

The dog obeyed but Tumi was shaking so much she had to use her other hand to steady the one holding the compass. She focused on the refracted light again and bent her head closer to the kindling so she could blow on it.

A tiny pillar of smoke started to rise.

'Yes!'

Shikar barked.

'Shush.'

Tumi kept blowing and added more grass and twigs to the pile as little orange flames started to rise. She moved her body and the breeze caught the fire and it started to blossom.

Nature took over and the fire started to spread away from Tumi, growing in ferocity as it devoured the long grass. As she had hoped, a wide pall of smoke was now rising ahead of the crackling flames.

She was pleased with her work. The fire was heading away from her on a forty-five-degree bearing towards the tar road. Tumi was no expert on fire management, but she was almost a hundred per cent sure this one would not jump the tar road and would safely burn itself out. With the speed it was moving, however, she needed to get up and get going.

'Come, Shikar!'

Tumi jumped up and ran behind the smoke, and as she charged, Shikar at her heels, she flicked the safety catch of her LM5 to fire, aimed the rifle in the direction of the person who had been shooting at her and started pulling the trigger as she ran. She hoped her wild rapid fire would at least keep the sniper's head down.

Legs pumping, she sprinted to keep the smoke between her and where the gunman was. Tumi knew from Sean's teaching that it took less than three seconds for a good marksman to draw a bead on a target. She was moving, which was in her favour, but soon she would be at the gate and that was where she would be most vulnerable, particularly if the fire burned itself out at the roadside.

Bugs took flight ahead of the flames and birds appeared as if from out of nowhere. Brilliant blue lilac-breasted rollers quacked and dived, snatching up insects in mid-air. Tumi registered a bullet passing by her. Perhaps the sniper could see her through the smoke or maybe, like her, he was firing blind and trying his luck.

She prayed that her desperate gamble would pay off, but it all depended on her being able to get through the locked gate.

Tumi judged the movement of the smoke as she ran, and she and Shikar made the gate just as the fire was reaching its crescendo. A wide swathe of blackened stubble was left in the blaze's wake. Fortunately, the local municipality had allowed the verge on the side of the tar road to become overgrown, and while the fire had taken hold there now, having raced through the chain-link fence, it was taking its time to consume the grass, shrubs and even trees on the roadside.

Tumi got to the fence, coughing from the smoke that protected and choked her at the same time. Her eyes watered and Shikar was barking crazily, her instincts picking up the danger of fire. Tumi had counted the rounds she had fired and knew she had five left in the magazine attached to her rifle. There would be no time to reload.

She moved along the fence through the smoke until she found the gate. A thick chain and padlock held it secure. Tumi had seen this done on television and in the movies but had never tried to shoot open a padlock herself.

Steadying the barrel of her rifle as close as she could to the lock, she pulled the trigger. Sparks flew off the metal but the lock stayed in place.

The smoke cleared. The sniper fired.

Chapter 24

Sean spoke on the hands-free phone to Christine as he floored the *bakkie*'s accelerator pedal. The rear of the vehicle swung out and he wrestled with the steering wheel as he took a corner at speed.

'Get to the lion enclosure, to the rocky hill,' he told Christine.

'Where's Oliver?' Christine asked.

'I left him at the *koppie*. I'm still not sure about him, Chris. Be careful of him – things aren't looking good – but for now I have to give him the benefit of the doubt. He maintains he had nothing to do with Casper's death, but the fact is he tried to assault Tumi, and when I checked his rifle I found it had been fired recently and left loaded and cocked, as though he was ready for action – maybe too ready.'

'Sheesh. I wish Craig was here as well. Not that I don't trust you, Sean . . .'

'It's OK. I'm starting to feel the same right now,' he said. 'Get to the *koppie*. I'll call you back.'

He came to the tar road and now the rear wheels squealed as he accelerated hard. Up ahead he could see smoke billowing.

Sean prayed he wasn't too late. He called Tumi's number.

'Sean! I can't get through the fence. I tried to shoot the lock off the gate but it didn't work.'

Damned Hollywood. He heard gunfire through the car stereo speakers. Tumi was firing.

'Hold on.'

'Shooter's to the south of me,' she said. 'On a rise, close to the fence.'

Sean raced up the road, along the fence line and up the rise towards the locked entrance gate. There was no one coming in the other direction so he swung over to the right and, as he came abreast of the gate, turned the wheel sharp to the left.

'Stay away from the gate, Tumi!'

He hoped she had heard him as he geared down and accelerated hard, engine and gearbox screaming as he rammed the gate with the *bakkie*. The chain snapped and metal screeched against metal, then something, maybe the swinging padlock, shattered the windscreen.

Sean glimpsed Tumi to his left and saw Shikar stand up in the grass and bark. He turned the wheel to the right and sped up the hill, bouncing over the uneven ground as he headed in the direction Tumi had indicated the gunfire was coming from.

Through the crystalline web of broken glass he saw a man stand up and bring a rifle to bear. Sean leaned over towards the passenger side, trying to keep his head just below the dashboard and his right foot hard down on the accelerator. The steering wheel bucked in his hands and Benny barked crazily from the back of the truck. He hoped the dog was OK.

Sean popped his head up and saw the man looming large. The gunman had left his shot till the last second and was diving to his right. Sean heaved down on the steering wheel.

He heard a thud and glimpsed an arm and a leg flying past the passenger-side window as the front nearside wheel went into a burrow and the *bakkie* rolled.

*

Christine drove to the lion enclosures faster than she ever had on the rough farm roads. *Please, please, please let Sean be OK*, she prayed. *And Tumi.*

Christine pulled up and got out. She couldn't avoid going to have one last look at Casper, but when she did she wished she hadn't. Her lion, her baby, had been eviscerated. It was Sean who had done this, looking for evidence, but she had imagined there might just be one neat hole. Her stomach turned and her heart ached. Why were people doing this to her?

She forced her eyes away and strode into the enclosure, to the *koppies*.

Oliver stood as she approached, rifle in his big hands. She looked around and saw smoke rising to the west by the perimeter of the farm.

'What's happening?'

He shrugged. 'Sean told me to stay here.'

'There's a fucking gunfight going on,' she said, 'and you're hiding here.'

Oliver's mouth was set grimly. 'He *ordered* me to stay here, to protect you, and said I must come fetch you if you didn't show up.'

Christine ran a hand through her hair. 'Of course. I'm sorry, Oliver.'

He shook his head. 'This is madness. We do not have enough people to stop a full-blown attack.'

Christine sighed. 'I know. I called the police, and the fire brigade, but they're all busy. Someone blew up some kind of armoured car on the road between Hazyview and Mkhuhlu. The road's blocked and they're all tied up.'

'Another explosion?'

She nodded. 'Coincidence? I think not.'

'So we are on our own?' he asked.

'For the time being at least.' He stood there looking at her, his last words hanging in the air between them. She shivered involuntarily.

Felix the lion, who had heard Christine's voice, came to the fence about fifty metres from where they stood. Oliver gestured to the cat with a flick of his head. 'These animals are not worth dying for.'

She put her hands on her hips. 'That's where we disagree. But if you want to leave now, you're free to.'

He held her gaze. 'I will not desert my post.'

'Did you kill Casper, my lion?'

He maintained his stare and she felt fear, looking into those dark eyes. 'I will not desert my post,' he said again, 'but you need to give the order for all of us to pull out. We should all go to Lion Plains. We will be safe there.'

'You didn't answer my question.'

It was his turn to sigh. 'I did not shoot your lion.'

'What's going on here, Oliver?'

'I risk my life, Christine, just as the others do, every day, to protect wild animals – lions, rhinos, elephants – and that is a job worth doing. These,' he made a sweeping gesture towards Felix, 'these are farm animals. Whether you like it or not, they were bred for the slaughter. What you are doing is *wrong*. These animals can never be released into the wild. They have value, because people in China will pay for their bones to be made into a potion and people in America and Europe will pay to have their heads on a wall. You can end this, today, and save Tumi's life, and Sean's. These are people you care about.'

She was confused. There was something more at play here. Hearing those arguments, from Oliver, a man she paid to protect wildlife, shook her. For a moment she questioned herself. Were the lions really worth their lives?

'Well?' he asked.

Christine looked back over to Felix. He was a beautiful creature, in the prime of his life, just as Casper had been. He was worth much more than the sum of his body parts. Even if he would never roam free, and that was the regret of Christine's life, he had still had a good life. He had always had food and sunshine and exercise and love. He and his brother had been fine ambassadors for their wild roaming cousins. If a lion had to live in captivity, for whatever reason, then this was the best one could hope for.

Even as she thought this through, however, Christine knew in her heart it was wrong. Casper and Felix should never have been hand-reared, no matter how lovingly. Christine wished for a world in which no lion – indeed, no animal – need ever be in captivity, no matter how noble the reason, but nor would she consign Felix and the other lions here on the farm to a premature death to save her own skin, or Oliver's.

'Do you want to be here, Oliver? Are you one of us? If you're not, then leave.'

'I was told to stay.'

'Go!' He was like any bully, she thought; if you stood up to them they crumbled.

'Christine . . .'

'I don't know if you're crooked or if you're a coward, Oliver. Which is it?'

She saw his hands tighten on the pistol grip and the stock of the R1 rifle. He glared at her for a few more seconds, but the will left him. He came to her and handed over the rifle. He unbuckled his webbing harness and shrugged it off. 'The ammunition is in the pouches. You are a very arrogant woman.'

She shook her head. 'No, Oliver, I'm just a woman in a position of authority and that is what you and too many men like you can't get your heads around. I'd rather have ten women like Tumi standing by my side than an army of men like you. Get out of my fucking sight, right now.'

He took a step towards her and she forced herself not to flinch, to stand up to his intimidation. He backed down.

'You will regret this.'

*

Sean was alive in the upturned *bakkie*.

The truck had come to rest a hundred metres from Tumi and she had run to it. To reach Sean, she'd had to peel out the shattered remains of the windscreen and half crawl in through the gap to pour water from her canteen onto Sean's face to help bring him around. He had a nasty gash on his head but he knew his name and what day it was. The problem was, he was stuck in the *bakkie*. Benny had jumped clear just as the vehicle started to roll.

'What's happening?' Sean asked.

'You hit the guy who was shooting at me. Can you feel your legs? Are you hurt bad?' Tumi said. Benny was barking now that Sean was talking.

'Hush, boy. I . . .' He touched the cut on his forehead, then moved his hands down over his body and tried wriggling. 'Yes, I can feel my legs, but the steering wheel's wedged into my belly.'

Tumi could see the problem. When the *bakkie* had flipped and rolled it had ended up on its roof, but on a forty-five-degree angle. It had come to rest next to a granite boulder that was bulging up through the grass on the driver's side. The passenger-side door couldn't be opened more than a few centimetres before it came into contact with the ground.

'What happened to the guy I ran down? Is he dead?' Sean asked. 'If not, you need . . . need to question him, Tumi. Find out how many of them there are.'

'OK. I'll check him.' Now that she had ascertained that Sean's life was not in danger she got up and went to the man, who she could already see was immobilised.

Tumi went to the prone form. He was alive, but badly injured. She knelt by him. He was African, dressed in black jeans and a matching T-shirt. He groaned and clutched at his belly.

'Who are you?'

The man looked at her and blinked.

Tumi stood, rage boiling up suddenly inside her. This bastard had been trying to kill her – and Sean, and Shikar and Benny – a few minutes ago. She pointed her rifle at him.

'Goddamn you, who are you and why were you trying to kill us?'

Sean coughed and called from the wrecked vehicle. 'Tumi!'

She looked over her shoulder. 'I'm going to kill him if he doesn't talk.'

'Stay calm, Tumi,' Sean called. 'Think. Don't do anything crazy.'

Tumi took a breath and looked down at the man. He was in terrible pain and she felt her rage dissipate a little. Lying in the grass, a couple of metres away where he had dropped it, was the man's AK-47. Keeping a bead on the man she moved and picked it up and tossed the rifle closer to the *bakkie*. She thought about how close the man had come to killing her. His fire had been deadly accurate, and it was only the moves that Sean had drilled into her over and over again that had saved her from being shot.

'Tumi? What are you doing?' Sean called.

'Thinking,' she said. Tumi replayed in her mind what had just happened and how surprised she had been by the first bullets that came her way. 'Oh my God.'

'What is it?' Sean called.

'The man who shot at me was a *sniper*, Sean. He was using a silenced weapon.' The realisation filled her with dread. 'This guy's got a standard unsilenced AK-47, so –'

'Shit, there must be another one,' Sean said. 'Quick, Tumi, call Christine, tell her there's a gunman on the loose. My phone seems to be working – I'll get us some help.'

'OK.' She got her own phone out and entered Christine's number. Tumi glanced at Sean while she waited to connect. 'Who are you calling?'

'Tienie Theunnisen. He owns a game lodge not far from here. Rich doctor, has a helicopter as well. Sometimes he helps out with hot pursuits of poachers and other emergencies. We're going to need air support.'

Christine's phone went through to voicemail and Tumi left an urgent message, telling her and Oliver to be careful as there was still a gunman loose on the property, armed with a silenced sniper's rifle.

Tumi ended the call and looked back down at her captive. 'Who sent you?'

The man just looked up at her.

'Tienie?' Sean said into his phone. 'Yeah. It's Sean Bourke here. We need you, man, if you can spare your chopper for a bit. I'm at Christine's farm, by the western boundary fence. We've got a sniper on the loose here and a badly wounded poacher.'

Sean carried on talking to the pilot and Tumi pushed the tip of the barrel closer to the man on the ground, until it was just a couple of centimetres from the spot between his eyes. 'Talk to me!'

The man blinked up at her. There was blood oozing out the side of his mouth. She touched him and he winced, then she glanced at Sean in the wrecked *bakkie*. 'What's the chopper guy saying?'

Sean ended the call. 'He's on his way; he'd already taken off. Turns out Craig's checked himself out of hospital and he talked to Christine and then Craig phoned Tienie. Apparently Craig's not far away and Tienie's going to pick him up on the road somewhere. Leave that guy alone, Tumi, and get me out of this vehicle.'

She looked from the wounded man to Sean. 'He tried to kill me. We need to find out who he's working for.'

Sean nodded. 'That would be nice, but you're not going to torture him, and we've got to get back into the fight.'

Tumi dropped to her knees next to the injured man and grabbed his shirt front in her hands, half lifting him up. He moaned in pain. 'You work for David Li, right?'

The man blinked up at her and tried to say something. Tumi lowered him down. 'If you live you're going away for life, for attempted murder. You know that, right?'

The man gave a little nod of his head.

'There is a helicopter on its way. I can get you on it.' She picked her rifle up from the grass. 'Or I can end your pain now.'

'Puh . . . please,' the man croaked.

'What is it?'

The man winced. 'Li . . . Li and . . .'

A tremor started within the wounded man, gaining in strength as it rippled through his body. Tumi put her weapon down now, suddenly, instinctively aware that this man was about to die in front of her. She got an arm under him, around his shoulders, and held him, tighter as the shaking increased.

'Who else?' Tumi pleaded.

But he was still.

'Damn it,' she said.

Tumi stood again and walked in a circle, trying to let the anger dissipate from her body and soul while she tried Christine on the phone again. *I would have tortured him or killed him*, she said to herself. The realisation was terrifying, and when she turned and looked at his broken, dead body, she doubled over and threw up.

Tumi heard Christine's voice, then wiped her mouth and replied. 'Christine . . . there's a sniper, and . . .'

'It's OK, Tumi,' Christine said, 'I've just got off the phone to Craig. Tienie's just picked him up near the farm and they're searching for the sniper. How's Sean?'

'A bit beat up and trapped – he rolled the *bakkie* – but we're both fine. We'll be with you as soon as I get him out.'

'OK, be careful,' Christine said, then ended the call.

'Tumi,' Sean called. 'There's a high-lift jack in the back of the *bakkie*. Get it out. You've got to try and lift the vehicle a bit so I can get out.'

'I can't take too much more of this, Sean,' she said as tears began to stream from her eyes.

He nodded. 'No one can. It's just a matter of time before we all break, somehow, some way. It's called being human, but you can do this. You have to help me and we have to get to Christine.'

Tumi took a deep breath and left the dead man. She went back to the truck; Sean was right, she needed to stay focused. This was what the training had been about, giving her the skills and the willpower to fight on when it all looked hopeless.

'I'm here, Sean.'

Chapter 25

Christine's phone rang and Craig's number appeared on the screen again.

'I'm overhead now,' he said, 'we're searching the bushy area between the western perimeter fence, where Sean and Tumi are, and your location. That's the nearest cover the sniper could have moved into.'

Christine used her free hand to shade her eyes and searched the sky. 'OK. You should still be in hospital, but I can see you and, man, am I glad you're here.'

'Be careful, Chris, we don't know how many of them there are yet.'

'I'm staying put, with the lions,' Christine said.

'Is Oliver with you?' he asked.

'He's gone. I just fired him. Shit,' Christine put a hand to her mouth, 'he's probably walking right into the sniper.'

There was a pause. 'Or he's joining him.'

Christine felt very alone, and scared.

'I'm coming to pick you up, Christine,' Craig said. 'We can fly away from this place.'

'No, don't,' she said. 'I'm not leaving my lions. You go get these bastards.'

*

Craig was in the co-pilot's seat of Tienie's little Robinson R44. The door on his side, like Tienie's, had been removed in order to improve visibility when the helicopter was being used in low-level game-capture work.

They flew over Sean's upside-down *bakkie* and Craig could see that Tumi was busy pumping the long arm of a high-lift jack. Craig knew Sean was trapped inside. Tumi paused to look up and wave. She was resourceful, and Craig had no doubt she would free Sean, but it would be slow work.

'We can come back for them,' Craig said to Tienie via the helicopter's intercom. 'Carry on towards the farmhouse; let's see if there are any more intruders down there, then we can come back and sweep the bushland again.'

Tienie had good eyes and pointed through the plexiglass windscreen for Craig's benefit. 'There's a man running down the hill, Craig, from the lion enclosures towards the farmhouse.'

'I see him,' Craig said. 'Circle him, Tienie, let me see where he goes.'

'Roger.' Before going to medical school Tienie had been a pilot with the old South African Defence Force, flying Alouette gunships in South West Africa, now Namibia, and Angola during the Border War in the 1980s. He was fearless, but not crazy. 'Hey, I know that *oke*. That's Oliver, your guy.'

'Yes,' said Craig, 'but we're pretty sure he's working for the bad guys and Christine just fired him.'

'Your call.' Tienie brought the R44 down low, flared the nose then circled the fleeing man and settled into a hover downhill from him, cutting him off from the route to the farmhouse and the main entry gate to the farm.

Craig brought his LM5 up into his shoulder and trained it on Oliver, who slowed to a halt, then pulled a nine-millimetre Star pistol from where he normally carried it, simply wedged in his belt.

'He's got a gun,' Tienie said.

'Roger that.' Craig held his aim.

Oliver fired and at least one of the three rounds he got off hit the chopper before Craig's second shot, through the heart, put him down.

*

Christine saw Tienie's little red helicopter fly over and while it gave her a measure of comfort to know Craig was up there, the sound of gunfire from down the hill a short time later made her jump.

All the talking to and fro had flattened her phone battery. She felt helpless again, but she lay down behind a rock and held the R1 rifle at the ready. Felix was pacing around her, the gunfire having put him on edge.

From her vantage point Christine saw the chopper bank again and fly off towards the western perimeter fence, over the heavily vegetated part of the farm. This, Craig had told her, was where the sniper who had been firing at Tumi had probably taken shelter.

Christine had no idea who had been shooting at whom, but when she peered over the boulder she was using for cover she saw a man she did not recognise running up the hill. He was dressed in green trousers and shirt and carried an AK-47. He must have been hiding in the long grass when Craig and Tienie had flown towards the farmhouse. Her heart started thumping in her chest.

The man dropped down and out of sight again. Christine rested the long barrel of the R1 in a cleft in the rock and took aim where she had seen the running man go to ground. She watched and waited for him to pop his head up again.

She cursed herself for not having the foresight to charge her phone that morning, but there was nothing she could do about that now.

She wondered if she could make a run for it, but she also realised she had probably left it too late. From where she was, the best she could do was to retreat over the brow of the hill she was on, through the security gate and into the lionesses' enclosure, next door to Felix and Casper's.

'Get down, boy,' she said, as Felix walked in front of her, spoiling her view, but he did not respond. He looked towards the bushy part of the farm, beyond the fence.

Christine got up on one knee to get a better look in the other direction, down the hill towards the farmhouse where she had just seen the man in green.

Felix roared, and she glanced at him, but when she returned her gaze down the hill she saw the man in green with the assault rifle running at a crouch towards her, along a dry creek that ran down the slope. She raised her rifle to take a shot, but the man ducked down again. He was less than two hundred metres from her.

She realised she had to get ready to take a shot at him next time he showed himself. Resting the barrel of the heavy R1 rifle back down on the rocks in front of her, she steadied herself. She was trying to locate the last place where she had seen the man when the rock she was leaning on seemed to erupt just centimetres from her face, and sharp shards stung her cheek.

Christine screamed and dropped to her belly.

Felix roared again, this time at the unheard shot that had just come from the direction of the forested bushland. 'Come *here*, Felix!'

The lion growled but came to her, and lowered its belly into the grass and rocks beside her. Christine realised the shot must have come from the hidden sniper who had fired on Tumi earlier, the man with the silenced rifle. With dread she realised she was facing enemies on two sides.

Terrified now, Christine crawled on her belly to another cluster of rocks to her left, and changed position so she was facing east, towards the bush. She raised her head.

Another silenced shot ricocheted off the stones in front of her and she ducked down again, her face in the dirt and grass. She used her toes, knees and fingers to ease herself backwards. She was pinned down and the helicopter, just a faint buzz in the distance, was searching on the far side of the bushland. Christine had no way of signalling to Craig and Tienie.

Felix was getting increasingly restless next to her. Another gunshot from the hidden sniper scored a furrow of dirt near the big cat and he jumped to his feet and ran in the direction the shot had come from.

'Felix!'

Even as she feared for her lion Christine saw her momentary chance. She got to her feet and ran as fast as she could away from both sources of danger, towards the far side of the enclosure.

Felix must have thought it was a game, because he turned within his own body length and came bounding after her.

He roared.

Christine, now at the brow of the hill, looked over her shoulder and saw Felix go down. At the same time, not watching where she was going, she tripped.

She rolled over onto her side and saw that Felix had got up again but was limping as he came after her. Another shot sent up a geyser of dirt next to him. This bastard was trying to kill her cat as well as her. She could hardly contain her fury as she crawled further away from the whizzing bullets.

Felix caught up with her and bumped his big head against hers.

Christine reached up and put her arms around his big shaggy head. 'Come here, my poor boy. Let's get away from all this.'

Now out of sight of both the intruders, Christine got to her feet and, with Felix hobbling along after her, ran to the gate that led to the lionesses' enclosure.

Chapter 26

'**H**ow's Sean?' Craig asked Tumi on her phone.

Tumi wiped sweat from her brow. She was exhausted. 'I managed to lift the *bakkie* with the high-lift jack and open the door and drag him out. He's drifting in and out of consciousness; he wasn't wearing a seatbelt and he took a bad knock to his head.'

'Stay with him, Tumi,' Craig said. 'I'll organise an ambulance, but someone blew up a national parks armoured car on the road from Hazyview to Kruger so it's madness out there right now.'

Tumi searched the sky. 'Where are you now? I can't hear the helicopter engine in the background.'

'I'm on the ground,' Craig said. 'Tienie was low on fuel when he picked me up; he'd been out doing game capture work and he had to leave me for now to go and refuel. I got a glimpse of the sniper running through the bushveld, but then we lost him, so I got Tienie to drop me off. He should be back soon. I'm making my way towards the lion enclosures. I keep trying Christine but her phone must be dead – at least, I hope that's the worst that's happened.'

'I'm going to check on Christine as well,' Tumi said.

'No. You stay there, wait with Sean. I've got this.'

Tumi heard gunfire. 'Is that you firing?'

'Shit, no,' Craig said. 'That sounds like it's coming from the direction of the farmhouse.'

'I'm coming to help you, Craig. Christine might be in trouble.'

'OK, sheesh.' Craig was relenting. 'Take Shikar and see if you can pick up the sniper's trail through the bush. There must be two guys out there. I'll circle around towards the farmhouse and see if I can see who was shooting from that direction. Just be careful, Tumi, and call me if you see the sniper.'

'OK, Craig. You be careful as well.'

Tumi ended the call and went back to Sean. Benny was sitting next to him, whimpering. She checked Sean's pulse and breathing and both were fine. Tumi hated to leave Sean like this, but she knew he would want her to go and help Christine.

Benny looked up at her, whining. 'I'm going to need your help as well, Benny. Come, boy!'

Tumi, Shikar and Benny headed away from the wrecked *bakkie* in search of the man who had tried to kill them.

*

Christine had managed to unlock the gate that led to the lionesses' enclosure, but when she tried to refasten the padlock a bullet from the silenced sniper's rifle pinged through the chain-link fence next to her hand. He was still tracking her. She screamed, snatched up the R1 rifle she had set down, and ran.

Christine had thought that if she could lock herself in with the lions she could hide from the two gunmen, but she was exposed standing by the gate. There was more natural vegetation in this compound and Christine sought refuge behind a stout marula tree. She peered around the trunk, holding up the rifle.

When she saw the man in green with the AK-47 slide open the gate she'd just come through she fired, but the rifle packed a punch and the end of the barrel bucked upwards. However, her two-shot salvo at least made him drop to the ground. Christine ran deeper into the lionesses' domain. As yet there was no sign of the female cats, but Felix was ranging ahead of her, still limping, and he would find them soon enough. She hoped she could at least put herself out of sight of the hidden sniper.

Christine expected to feel the thump of a bullet in her back at any moment. She worried for the others and longed to hear the clatter of Tienie's helicopter above. Then she heard a burst of gunfire and bullets were all around her. Christine dived behind a rock and pointed the rifle in the direction from which she'd just come. She fired three, maybe four times, not even sure where she was aiming. Her shoulder hurt from the recoil.

'Calm down,' she told herself.

Christine peered through a gap between two rocks and sighted down the length of the rifle's barrel. She knew enough about shooting to line up the foresight between the leaves at the far end inside the circular rear sight. She waited for the man in green to show himself.

When he did she took a breath and told herself to squeeze the trigger, as Sean had taught her, not jerk it.

Christine winced again at the kick to her shoulder. The man had disappeared, but she didn't know if she had hit him or if he had merely dived for cover as she had. She saw a movement and fired again.

For a moment all was quiet, and then on the breeze she heard a dog barking.

*

Tumi called Shikar and Benny back to her as she neared the lions' enclosures.

She was annoyed with herself and the dogs. She had cast around the area where she was sure the man Sean had run down

312

and the sniper had been hiding. Shikar had detected some spent bullet casings, and when she inspected them Tumi could tell they were not from an AK-47. So, she had found the spot where the sniper was, but the dogs had not been able to pick up his trail beyond the firing position. It was as if he had vanished.

Tumi had ranged up and down the edge of the bush area between the western perimeter fence and the lion enclosures, but still luck eluded her. Worried about Christine, she had pushed on through the bush. When she came close to the enclosures she ducked behind a tree and hissed at the dogs to stop when she saw a man in green fatigues carrying an AK-47. The man was on Christine's side of the enclosure fence and must have just entered – Tumi could see the sliding gate to the area was ajar. This was not the sniper, but it must, she reasoned, be the man whose rifle she had heard firing earlier. He had gone to ground behind a tree about a hundred metres ahead of her and the dogs.

Shikar and Benny settled down on either side of her.

Tumi knelt and took careful aim. She stilled her breathing. This would be an easy shot, but she was about to shoot a man in the back and he had no idea she was behind him.

She couldn't do it.

'Drop your gun!' she called to the man.

The man turned, but instead of complying, he swung his AK-47 around and opened fire through the diamond mesh fence. Tumi already had her rifle trained on the man, but when she squeezed the trigger all she heard was a click.

She dived to the ground as bullets zinged through the wire and flew around her. Benny and Shikar barked and whined. Tumi didn't know if her rifle had jammed or if she had a dud round, but she frantically crawled out of the line of fire, trying to get away.

The gunman was on his feet, advancing on her. He was at the gate. Tumi found a tree trunk big enough to protect her and called the dogs to her while she shook out a jammed cartridge, then reloaded. By the time she had crawled to a new vantage point and risked a look around, all she caught was a fleeting glimpse of the man's back.

In the time that she had taken to clear her rifle, the man had been able to close and padlock the gate. Christine was trapped inside.

*

With some difficulty Christine managed to remove the magazine from the R1. She looked inside and could immediately see she had only three bullets left.

She had felt a moment of hope when she had heard Tumi order the man to put down his weapon, then the burst of gunfire, but when she didn't hear Tumi calling out to her she assumed the worst. There was no helicopter, no police sirens, just an eerie quietness. Even Felix had limped off, in search of the lady friends he'd been denied contact with for so long.

As she ran through the bush, Christine wondered what had happened to Sean and Craig. But, mostly Sean. She hated the thought that she might die today without being able to say goodbye to him. As for Craig, she felt sorry that she hadn't loved him as much as he loved her.

Christine looked back over her shoulder as she ran, but her right foot hit an exposed tree root and she sprawled forward. The rifle fell from her hands and the skin of her palms was taken off as she hit the ground and rolled painfully onto her side. Christine tried to get on her knees and crawl to the R1 but her ribs had connected with a rock, winding her. She struggled to find her breath.

'Mrs Glover?'

Christine rolled over and looked up into the face of the man who had been following her, and the tip of his AK-47.

'Mrs Bourke, actually,' she wheezed. She was sounding braver than she felt. Christine thought of Sean, and what could have been, again, for them both. She hoped he was safe. 'Are you going to kill me?'

He shrugged. 'I have a message for you. I didn't think it would be this difficult to deliver it to you.'

She coughed. 'I've got no option but to hear it, I suppose.'

He smiled. 'The offer to buy this farm still stands.'

'You work for David Li.'

'I didn't say that,' the man said, 'but I have been instructed to tell you that you will be paid for the farm, and the lions, and no harm will come to you.'

'Christine!'

She looked past the man, who didn't bother turning his head. It was Tumi, calling from somewhere outside the enclosure. Christine couldn't see Tumi, but realised she must have been running down the outside of the fence.

'You're trapped in here, you know,' Christine said to the man.

He shrugged. 'Yes, and I have you hostage. I'm not worried. Tell her you are fine.'

Christine thought a moment, then nodded.

'Meg!' she called.

The man kept his rifle trained on her. 'Again. Tell this "Meg" that you are fine.'

'Meg, I'm fine,' Christine said, though not too loudly.

'Louder.'

She shook her head. 'No.'

'Do as I tell you, woman.'

'No. I don't want to scare the lion.' She looked to her left and the man's eyes followed hers.

There was a blur of tawny fur moving through the trees. The man swung his rifle and fired.

'Meg!'

The man looked back to her. 'What are you playing at? Who is Meg?'

315

Christine screamed, because she was in fear of her life and she wanted them all to know it.

From the trees where he had just shown himself, deliberately, to distract the prey, Felix roared.

The gunman, like a confused and not very bright wildebeest, looked in the direction of the primeval, terrifying sound.

From behind the man came the muffled thud of big pads pounding the ground. The three lionesses moved as a single unit, splitting into a classic flanking formation, with Amy going left, Pelo breaking right and Meg, the eldest and biggest of the lionesses, charging straight up the middle. Christine had known that if she called Meg, who responded best to her commands, then the others would follow her out of curiosity. Even though they had been hand-reared, together the girls formed an instinctive hunting machine.

They were all around him, on him, before the man had the time to fire a single shot, let alone realise what had just hit him.

Christine pulled herself to her feet and retrieved her rifle. She fired two shots in the air and the lionesses, who had been joined by the wounded Felix, momentarily looked up, their faces now red.

She had saved the last shot for the man who had tried to kill her, but it was too late. The lions went back to their feeding.

Christine backed away, towards the gate. While the lionesses knew her, and probably considered her as part of their artificial pride, she knew better than to get too close to them when they were eating.

'Chris!'

She turned and saw Craig and Tumi, both waiting for her on the other side of the gate. Craig was going through his master keys looking for the one for the padlock.

'God,' he said, 'I'm so pleased you're alive.'

'Me too,' Christine said, because she knew this fight was far from over.

Chapter 27

One week later

'Sean's gone,' Christine said.

Craig, sitting across the old wooden table from her in the farmhouse kitchen, shook his head in evident disgust.

'I can't believe it,' said Charles, who had only been released from hospital the day before. He was still on convalescent leave, but had come to visit. 'So much happened while I was away.'

Christine nodded. 'I'm sorry for what happened to you, Charles; I hope our company will still be in business when you are fully recovered, but I'll continue to pay your medical bills, out of my own pocket, whatever happens.'

He looked down at the table, then at her. 'You have your own troubles.'

'Yes.'

'I knew Oliver was cheating on his wife,' Charles said, 'but it's still hard for me to believe he was in bed with a poaching gang.'

'That's what the cops seem to think,' Craig said. 'Amazingly they were able to identify the guy the lions killed, from his DNA. He was a local criminal, with a prior conviction for poaching, and a neighbour of Oliver's.'

'I'm convinced Oliver was working for David Li, the man who wanted to buy my farm,' Christine said to Charles. 'The poacher the lionesses killed was delivering a message to me from Li, and even though he didn't actually name him, Tumi found evidence in Mozambique that Li was planning a hit on me.'

Craig folded his arms. His face was a mask of anger. 'The cops say they'll question Li, but, sheesh, he'll probably just say that the gold was his and the pictures of the farm were just him doing some market research before putting in an offer to buy, or some such *kak*.'

'Sure,' said Charles, 'but has Sean really run off?'

Craig thumped the table. 'We wouldn't be in this situation if Zali hadn't been so stupid.'

'Hold on,' Charles said, 'what did Zali do wrong?'

Christine got up, filled the kettle and put it on the gas stove. 'Coffee?'

Both men nodded.

'Zali thought she was helping us,' Christine said to Charles as she took out three cups. 'You saw online all the coverage of what happened here?'

'Yes, it was the talk of the hospital, I even saw you on TV. You saved the farm and you got a lot of coverage for the plight of lions and the trade in lion bones. The government says it is now reviewing the policy on allowing a quota of lion bones to be exported.'

'Yes,' Christine said, 'but it won't save our farm.'

'Why not?'

'After all the attention on social media and on TV and in the newspapers, we received quite a few donations. Zali was coordinating an appeal via an online crowd-funding site and when she arrived back two days ago from the US one of her guests at the lodge, a wealthy American software mogul, gave her a cash donation of twenty thousand US dollars. That would have really helped us stay afloat.'

'So what happened?' Charles asked.

'Zali gave the money to Sean, to bring to Christine,' Craig said, 'and we haven't seen him since.'

'So?' Charles asked.

'Sean has a problem with gambling, he's an addict,' Craig said.

Charles looked to Christine for confirmation.

Christine stared at the mugs and started to sniff as she poured. 'Yes, Craig's right.'

Craig got up and started pacing around the kitchen. 'We'll find a way through this. There's that other buyer who wants to invest in the farm.'

Charles's raised eyes conveyed his sudden renewed hopefulness.

Craig looked over at him. 'Yes. An American guy. He says he's serious about conserving lions and doesn't want to get involved in hunting.'

Christine sighed. 'Yes. He could be our saviour, Charles. Craig knows him from his days as a safari guide. Like David Li he wants to develop a lodge here on the farm. We'll need security people.'

'That is good,' Charles said. 'And where is Tumi?'

Christine held up her hands. 'Who knows? She went through a pretty traumatic time on the day of the shootout here at the farm and she took some leave.'

'I hope she is OK.'

Later, when Charles had gone to the bathroom, Craig set his cup down, folded his arms and leaned against the kitchen bench. 'We need to talk, Chris. You've been avoiding me all week since the gunfight, finding excuses to be away from me.'

She shrugged and looked out the window. 'It was all the media interviews and stuff. You saw how hectic it was.'

'Look at me,' he said. 'We haven't . . . been together for ages. What's changed? If you were falling for Sean again I think we both know that was a mistake. I love the guy, but he's a flake, Christine, he's gone and let you down – let all of us down – yet again.'

Christine sipped her coffee. 'We don't know that.'

'A leopard doesn't change its spots. Tell me, though, is it over between us?'

She looked to him. 'It's been a tough time for all of us. I just need a bit of space, OK, to think, on my own.'

Craig picked up his coffee and tipped what was left down the sink. 'We've still got a business to run, you and me, and I don't intend on letting you down. I've still got dogs to train; I'm going to town to pick up the food.'

Craig walked out and Christine watched him go. She hoped she was doing the right thing.

*

Tumi looked over her sunglasses at the man seated opposite her and sipped from a cocktail with a miniature umbrella in it. The Indian Ocean sparkled across the beach where Sean, dressed in a pair of rugby shorts, a T-shirt and sandals, played fetch with Benny and Shikar.

A warm breeze brought the scent of saltwater and the cry of sea birds into the open-sided bar perched atop a vegetated sand dune at Ponta Malongane in Mozambique. The man, with skin the colour of coffee and eyes as dark as sin, paid no attention to the goings-on below on the beach.

The only other patron in the bar was a man in his early fifties with fair hair and a beard turning to grey. He looked like an ageing surfer, dressed in board shorts and a black Dois M beer T-shirt, and he held a matching beverage in front of him. He was reading a paperback novel with a picture of hippos on the cover.

'Are you here on holiday, Mo?' she asked the man opposite her. He had told her that his name was Mohammed, Mo for short, but she knew it was Zohair.

'No, I live here,' he said.

'Nice place.'

'I like it.' He smiled, his teeth as bright as a shark's. 'I can't help but think we've met before.'

Tumi had gone to some length to disguise herself with an Afro wig, fine resort-wear clothing, big sunglasses and heavy makeup. Perhaps, she thought, he was naturally cautious.

'Oh, I'd remember a smooth talker like you, Mo.' She laughed and he toasted her with his Scotch. Men were easy to distract.

He took a sip, then set his glass down. 'Do you have plans for this evening?'

Tumi played with her fake hair. 'Not really. I feel like a lie-down, though, before I go out for dinner.'

He swallowed and his Adam's apple bobbed. 'Me too.'

She raised her eyebrows. 'Are you interested in some company, for your lie-down, that is?'

'Most assuredly,' he said without hesitation.

'Well, then, maybe you should get the bill, Mo.'

He called the waiter over.

After 'Mo' had paid the bill they walked, arm in arm, along a sandy path to the thatched bungalow Tumi had booked. The man couldn't even wait until they got inside. He put his arm around her shoulders, drew her close and reached for her breast.

'Hey,' she said.

'What?' he replied. 'You want this. We both know it.'

'Get your hands off me,' Tumi said.

'Is there a problem?'

Zohair looked around and Tumi saw him see Sean with the two dogs. In a heartbeat recognition blossomed in his eyes. Zohair turned but ran straight into the fair-haired bearded man from the sand dunes, who had pulled a big old 1911 Colt .45 semiautomatic pistol from his board shorts.

'Morning, Zohair,' the man said.

'Put that gun away. You have the wrong person. My name is Mohammed –'

'Save it,' the man said in an American accent. 'I'm Jed Banks, CIA, and you're Zohair Mohammed, former Taliban and ISIS bombmaker. We thought you were killed in a UAV Hellfire strike, Zohair, but it turns out, thanks to some DNA evidence, we now know you're alive and kicking and still up to your old tricks.'

'No!' Zohair cried. 'I will show you my passport, you have the wrong name.'

Jed smiled. 'I've seen your passport, with its phony name. That's how we found you, Zohair. We got a phone camera picture of you and did a facial recognition search – you might remember the Mozambicans take photos of all foreigners entering the country these days, even those on well-crafted fake passports. They didn't pick up that your passport was bogus, but they had your picture on file. On top of all that my colleagues here today identified you as the guy who took a real professional interest in the scene of a bombing in Maputo.'

Zohair spread his hands. 'I didn't plant a bomb in Maputo. I can explain.'

Jed kept the gun on him as Sean moved forward with a pair of handcuffs.

'Oh yeah, buddy,' Jed said, 'you're about to do a lot of explaining.'

Chapter 28

Three days later

The sights, the sounds and the smells were almost too much for Sean to bear.

Being in Emperor's Palace Casino, near Johannesburg's OR Tambo International Airport, felt like being drawn back into the womb; it was a place of comfort and solace where the tinkle and chime of the digital bells and the moody lighting and the touch of green felt under his fingertips produced the same rush as a first kiss.

Everything about it turned him on, and even as it did, his in-built alarm was going off. He *knew* how easy, how delicious it would be to just get on the merry-go-round and fling his arms out, to be like the alcoholic taking that first drink after so long, to hear the fizzle of a cigarette being lit, to be the coke head snorting that first line after rehab. The chips came with that same satisfying click, the same whiff of the high rollers' hookers' perfume.

He was home.

'You OK?' Tumi whispered. She had turned herself into a night-owl version of the beach bunny from Mozambique, almost as tall as him in red patent-leather stilettos and a matching satin jumpsuit. They had both gone shopping in Sandton with the cashed-in proceeds of some of David Li's gold especially for this evening.

He clenched his fists. 'I've got this.'

They were in the casino's lavishly decorated Privé Romana private gaming room and Sean put down two thousand dollars in greenbacks on the table as his entry fee.

'The girl's with me,' he said aloud. 'For now.'

The second remark elicited a small laugh from the others around the table. Behind David Li was not a girl but another Chinese man, though this one was solidly built and bald, as opposed to his boss who looked like an advertisement for Ralph Lauren's Hong Kong outlet store.

Li showed no sign of recognising Sean, which was not surprising as his fair hair was now black, long, and twinned with a beard. Pads in his cheeks fleshed his face out and the contact lenses had turned his green eyes brown. Instead of camouflage fatigues he wore a farmer's two-tone blue and khaki shirt, long chinos and sturdy buffalo-hide Rogue boots.

The other three players at the poker table looked, in turn, like a professional, a merchant banker and an entrepreneur-cum-cabinet minister. The croupier dealt the cards.

Sean nonchalantly drew a deep breath to steady himself. He picked up his cards, read them, then organised them into suits. He closed his eyes and willed his hands to stop shaking while he repeated his silent mantra.

I'm sorry, Christine, for hurting you, for stealing from you.
Please forgive me, Christine.
I love you, Christine.

Sean opened his eyes. He was supposed to finish by giving

thanks for something. *Thank you, Christine, for trusting me.*
He looked around and there, behind him, was Tumi. She smiled
and winked.

Thank you, also, for my friends, who are here for me.

'Place your bets,' said the croupier.

*

By the end of the evening, several hours later, it was just the two
of them. The others had folded or left.

Sean had won many hands, then allowed himself to lose.
It was funny, he thought, how easy it was to win when one
knew that the tables would eventually turn. The only difference
between now and his past life was that this time he was doing
it on purpose, and he knew exactly when to stop.

Sean laid his cards on the felt, knowing he would lose.

'Sorry,' Li said, as the chips were raked his way. 'Tell me,
Frikkie, what sort of farm do you have in the Free State?'

'Lions, man,' Sean said. 'But, *ag*, those things are worth next
to nothing these days.'

'I'm interested in farming,' Li said.

Sean saw the not-quite-concealed flicker in Li's eye.

Tumi had moved closer to Li's bodyguard through the evening,
and while he was good, he was only human. She had slowly
coaxed a few words out of the bald man, with little touches now
and then on his biceps. As Li had relaxed around Sean, so, too,
had the thug dropped his own guard.

'Let's go again,' Sean said.

'I think you should call it a night,' Li replied with a smile.

'*Ag*, no, man. Come on. Lungile, get me another Klipdrift
Premium and Coke.'

'Maybe we should go,' she said to him, following the script
they had rehearsed.

'Rubbish, my girl, get me a drink!'

'Hey,' Sean winked at David, 'if we meet outside of here, don't tell anyone what old Frikkie gets up to when he comes to Joburg, hey? The dominie at my local church would have a heart attack if he knew. Not if he knew I was with a Zulu girl, but if he knew how pretty she was.' Sean laughed long and loud.

Li chuckled politely. 'Do you have any money left?'

'Deal the cards,' Sean said to the croupier. 'I'm good for it.'

'Sir,' said the attractive woman behind the table. 'You'll need more chips.'

David looked at him.

'Half my farm. It's worth ten million rand. I've got more than two hundred lions and five hundred hectares.'

'I'll stake you two million for a half share,' David said.

Sean laughed. 'Five.'

'Two point five,' Li said.

'Three?'

'Deal.' The croupier counted the chips and slid them across the table. 'Let's play.'

Each slap of a new card in front of him was like the sounds of passion to Sean, a rhythmic tantric tattoo. He picked them up, his made-up face a mask.

*

The game continued, but it did not go according to plan.

Tumi watched Sean, and she began to worry. The scenario had been following the script – Sean won a few hands then lost, steadily, until he offered up half of his fictitious farm as collateral. From that point he was supposed to lose it all, and then he and Li would arrange to meet as soon as possible at a remote location in the Free State. There, with Sean wearing a recording device, they would try and get Li to state outright his interest in lions and their bones. Tumi did wonder if Sean simply wanted to get Li somewhere quiet and remote where he could kill the Chinese man, but she had gone along with the plan in any case.

But then Sean had started to win.

As the evening wore on, and Tumi tired of making flirty small talk with the bodyguard, Li became increasingly anxious as his fortunes fled him.

Sean laid his cards on the table.

Li threw his down. He had just lost five million rand.

'Enough,' Sean said.

Tumi looked up, relieved.

'Give me a chance to win it back,' Li protested.

'No,' Sean said, 'I'm cashing out.'

'But –'

'But it's late, and I've got an early flight to catch back to Bloemfontein tomorrow. I mean, today.' Sean raked up his chips, pushed his chair back and stood.

Li was angry, barely able to control his rage. Tumi saw his balled fists.

'Stop.'

'You know what they say on the advertisements,' Sean said, 'winners know when to stop.'

*

Even as he stood, Sean had the urge to get back in the game, to push his winning streak even further, but he had already set himself a limit, which he had reached, and part of this gamble involved him leaving the table, one way or another. If he couldn't lose all his money and entrap Li into trying to buy the lion farm he supposedly owned, then he would take Li to the cleaners as he had just done, and then hopefully the man would run true to form and show his criminal side by trying to get the money back off him. Sean had briefed Tumi for either eventuality and she knew her part.

'Well, that's enough excitement for me,' Tumi announced to the room. 'I'm going home to Soweto, unless you've got a better offer for me.'

Sean grinned and flicked her a thousand-rand chip which she caught one-handed. 'Get yourself an Uber Black home, gorgeous.'

'You going back to the Peermont Metcourt?' she asked Sean, referring to the cheapest of the three hotels at the Emperors Casino complex.

Sean shook his head, secretly glad she was keeping an eye on him, and reminding him it was time to leave. 'Nope, I'm upgrading to a suite at the D'oreale Grande now that I can afford it.'

'You *sure* you don't want someone to celebrate with?'

He shook his head. 'Good night. It's been nice having you around as my good luck charm, but like I said, I'm beat and I have an early flight. I've got to walk back to the Metcourt and get my bag.'

'Well then, gentlemen,' Tumi hovered a few seconds in a show of waiting to see if Li or the bodyguard made her an offer, then gave a little bow of her head, 'good night.'

Sean collected his chips and nodded to Li before tipping the croupier and walking out.

Once out of the room he met up with Tumi, who was waiting for him. He handed her his chips and she went quickly to a cashier. Because of the amount Sean had won he would have had to present valid identification in order to cash in the chips and, as a self-excluded problem gambler, he would have been denied the money. Tumi came to him and handed over the cash. Sean sent her on ahead while he took his time, going to the bathroom first, then walking out of the casino. The ding and flash of the slot machines made his heart race, but he kept on going.

Sean's phone, set to silent, vibrated in his pocket. It was Tumi.

'Li is following you. The bodyguard left via the first exit,' she said.

'OK,' Sean replied quietly. 'The goon probably went to get his gun.' There were metal detectors at the doors leading into and out of the gaming area to stop people bringing in firearms. 'You go out to the car park, get your gun.'

'Will do. We know where Li's Merc is parked. I'll watch the bodyguard.'

'Don't get too close to him. He'll recognise you.'

'All right,' she said, then hung up. 'And Sean, I'm glad you quit while you were ahead.'

'Thanks. Be careful, Tumi.'

*

Tumi walked out of the casino. It was cool outside; the evenings in Johannesburg were always chilly compared to the lowveld because of the city's elevation.

She made her way to the car park. Off to her right was Li's Mercedes. Their own vehicle, another double cab *bakkie* from Hunde und Katzen that Christine knew they had taken, was directly ahead. Tumi could not see the bodyguard and wondered if he had already retrieved his pistol and gone to the D'oreale Grande. She had only seen him a couple of minutes earlier, however, so it would have been almost inconceivable for him to have done all that in such a short time.

Where was he?

She increased her pace, but when she passed a parked delivery truck someone stepped out from behind and put one hand over her mouth and a strong arm around her neck.

*

Sean walked down a corridor lined with reproduction Old Masters' paintings and emerged into the sumptuous foyer of the D'oreale Grande hotel. He went to the reception desk.

'Good evening, sir,' an attractive woman said to him.

'Howzit. Have you got a room?' He raised his voice. 'Best you've got, a suite or whatever.'

'Just let me check, sir.'

While the girl gazed at her screen, Sean looked behind him. If Li was still following him he was holding back, not wanting to show himself. He didn't seem like a man of action, so maybe he was waiting for his hired muscle to return.

'Yes, sir, you're in luck. I have one grand suite left.'

'I'll take it.'

'Very good, sir.' She printed a check-in form and handed it to him to complete and sign. 'Do you have any luggage, sir?'

'I have a bag over at the Peermont Metcourt.'

'I'm sure we can get one of the porters to go with you to fetch it.'

'No, that's fine,' Sean said. 'It's not heavy and I need a walk. I've been sitting at the poker table for hours.'

Before he left, Sean sent Tumi an SMS. *Heading out now.*

Sean left the hotel reception not by the passage leading to the casino, but out into the fresh air. David Li was standing outside, waiting for him.

'Howzit,' Sean said with false bonhomie, 'can't sleep? Hitchhiking home?'

'Very funny, Mr . . .'

'Du Toit, Frikkie Du Toit. We didn't officially meet in the poker room.' Sean extended a hand. 'What can I do for you?'

Li kept his hand to himself. 'I want my money back.'

'You're a sore loser, Mr Li.'

'I don't recall giving you my name.'

Sean shook his head, thinking fast. 'You didn't, but I know who you are. A mutual acquaintance, who also runs a lion farm, told me you like the private poker rooms here at Emperors. He also told me he does business with you and that business is getting tough.'

'I have no idea what you are talking about,' Li said.

Sean shrugged. 'I get it. You're being cautious. We both know the trade in lion bones is going underground, so you need to be careful. But I've got two things you want: your money and a big stock of bones, present and future. I've got two hundred lions and they're breeding well. Canned hunting is drying up and I want to make some money out of my livestock while I still can.'

Like the gambler he was – and not a bad one – Li's body language was muted. 'So?'

'So I'm looking to get out of this business, and since I'm not going to give you your cash back, or give you a chance to win it back off me, I'm going to make you an offer. You can buy all my lions and make a very handsome profit on what I'm going to charge you. You'll make a killing when you export their bones or, if you're smart, you might sit on the stock, so to speak, and watch the value skyrocket as the legal supply of lion bones dwindles.'

'The government has a strict quota on the export of lion bones, so how could I hope to benefit from buying all of your lions?'

Sean smiled. 'OK, keep playing dumb. I'm going to change hotel rooms and get some sleep before my flight to Bloem later today. I'll find another buyer.'

He turned and walked away.

'Wait, Sean,' Li called.

Sean did not pause or show any other sign of recognition, but all the same he felt a chill shoot from his heart and fill him with dread.

'Very good,' Li called, taunting him, 'but you might stop and listen to me if you want Tumi to live.'

Sean stopped, but did not turn around.

'Take a look to your right, about a hundred metres,' Li said.

Sean swivelled his head, slowly. The face of Li's bodyguard appeared from behind a food delivery van and for a fleeting moment, just long enough to be seen before they went back into cover, he saw that the man was holding a gun to Tumi's head.

A few seconds later a BMW drove away at speed from the space beyond the delivery van. Sean assumed the car was being driven by the bodyguard. He watched the car head to the entry gates at the far end of the car park.

He swore under his breath, then did an about face. 'What do you want?'

Li smiled now. 'Oh, that is much better, Mr Bourke.'

Sean sighed, reached up, pulled off his wig and tossed it aside.

'If it is any consolation,' Li said, 'you had me fooled. I did not recognise you at all. Your disguise was very good, but then I guess it had to be – as a pathetic problem gambler you need to be able to slip into those casinos that you have been asked to be banned from. The girl was not so clever, however.'

Sean didn't say anything. He would let Li gloat while he tried to work out how to get them out of this situation. It would come down to money, but the trick would be for both him and Tumi to get out with their lives.

'You should stick to running with your dogs, Sean. You're out of your depth and have been from the start of all this. I know who you are and I know who Tumi is. Even though her face was pixelated in the news coverage of the explosion that injured her dog, I know more about what is going on at Christine's farm and in her business than even you, her ex-husband, knows.'

Smug bastard, Sean thought. 'OK, so what do you want?'

'Hand over my money, for a start. You play well, and I am impressed that you did not let your addiction rule your head.'

'Thanks.' Sean fingered the daypack full of cash.

'Throw it to me.'

The money could give Christine the lifeline she needed, and go some way towards repaying his debt to her. The problem was, he had won the money by gambling, something he had told himself – and her – he would never do again. He needed to earn her forgiveness. What burned, though, was that Li would also take the money donated by their wealthy tourist benefactor from Lion Plains.

'I'm keeping my twenty-thousand-dollar stake.'

Li laughed, long and loud. 'Oh, Sean, you are very funny. You gambled and now you lost – all of it. Give me every single rand.'

'You can have what I took off you,' Sean said.

Li pulled out his phone and made a call. 'Vincent?'

Sean watched him, wondering what would happen if he jumped him.

Li spoke again. 'Cut off one of Tumi's fingers.'

'No!'

Li held up the phone. He heard a scream.

*

Tumi was lying in the boot of a BMW sedan, a car other than Li's. She wondered if it had been stolen and for how long Li had known of their plan. Her hands were bound with duct tape and another piece was across her mouth. The lid popped open and the bodyguard leered down at her.

After the bodyguard had shown her to Sean he had thrown her into the boot and driven off, but it was only a short distance.

He held a pair of side cutters in his right hand and a phone in the other. He set the phone to speaker mode and placed it on the body of the car.

'Cut off one of Tumi's fingers,' said the voice through the phone speaker.

The bodyguard reached down and pulled the tape from Tumi's mouth. Next he grabbed her wrists with one hand and put the cutters against the pinkie finger of her left hand.

Tumi screamed, and as she did so the bodyguard's head exploded in a bright spray of red. Tumi gasped.

In spite of her shock, she managed to yell, 'Get him, Sean. I'm safe. Kill the bastard!'

*

Sean had no idea what had happened at Tumi's end, but he didn't need any further encouragement. He charged at David Li, and the Chinese man was so confused that when he turned to run he tripped over. Sean was on top of him, landing blows on his face, when two dark-suited Emperors Palace security guards arrived and pulled him off.

'Break it up, man,' a bodybuilder type with a blond crew cut said. His Zulu partner grabbed Li and held him to one side.

'This man robbed me,' Li said.

'I won it off him fair and square.'

The Afrikaner guard looked at Sean. '*Praat hy die waarheid?*'

Sean understood Afrikaans, but replied to the question in English. 'Yes, I'm telling the truth. Talk to your security people and the croupier in the Privé Romano room. I just won all this *oke*'s money from him, and he's pissed off. He just threatened to hurt a friend of mine if I didn't give him his cash back.'

'Rubbish,' Li said.

The guard glared at Li. 'Is he right?'

'I've got a digital voice recording I can play you, right now,' Sean said.

'Maybe we should listen to that, Hein,' the Zulu said to his partner. 'And call the police, let them deal with this pair.'

'No, no,' Li said. 'I was mistaken. I may have provoked this man, inadvertently, of course. I have no wish to press charges. But, please can you take me away from here. I am scared this man will assault me.'

'Wait a minute,' Sean began.

The Afrikaner guard held up his hand. 'Shut up, man. You were *moer*ing this guy and he has a right to leave here safely.'

'Thank you,' Li said.

'I've got the recording, Li,' Sean said as the security guards escorted him away. 'I'll call the cops if you come near Christine or her farm again. This is it, finish.'

Li didn't even bother to look back.

Sean's phone rang. It was Craig.

'Sean, get in the *bakkie* and leave the casino, now!' he said without preamble.

Sean watched Li disappear inside the hotel foyer with the security guards. 'Where are you? Tumi's –'

'Tumi's with me. She's OK. We're outside the Emperors complex, in the industrial area. Meet me at the Garden Court Hotel, in the car park. You know it?'

'Yes.'

He went to the truck, got in and started the engine. The hotel was only a couple of kilometres away and he found his way there easily. He was seething at what had happened, and how Li had been able to escape from him. Sean pulled up and saw Craig and Tumi standing by Craig's Land Cruiser.

Tumi came to him and he hugged her. 'Are you OK?'

She sniffed. 'Yes. The guy was about to cut off one of my fingers and then his head just exploded. Craig –'

Craig broke in over Tumi's tears as Sean held her. 'I called the car-tracking company, found out where you were heading in Christine's *bakkie* and followed you guys here.'

'Why?' Sean asked.

'Because you should have told me what you were up to,' Craig said. 'When Zali told me she had given you that huge cash donation I was sure you were going to take it and gamble it away. I guess I wanted you to, in a way, so that I could tell Christine that you were unreliable and that she would be better off with me. She's barely spoken to me since the shootout at the farm. I think it's you she wants, not me.'

Sean ran a hand through his hair. 'I could say sorry, but I'm not.'

Craig nodded. 'I was in the car park. I saw you come out of the casino, and then when I saw you were with Li I wondered what the hell was going on. And then I saw the bodyguard grab Tumi and bundle her into a car so I followed them.'

Tumi had composed herself. 'Craig shot Li's man, just as he was about to hurt me.'

'I can't hang around here, Sean,' Craig said. 'It will only be a matter of time before the guy's body is discovered.'

'You acted to protect Tumi's life.'

'Yes,' Tumi said, 'I'll swear to it in court, Craig.'

Sean pulled a small digital voice recorder out of his pocket. 'I've got Li on here, ordering his man to cut Tumi's finger off.'

'You've done a good job,' Craig said, 'though I wish you'd told me what you were up to. It turns out you needed me to back you up after all.'

'Thanks,' Sean said. 'Now, should we call the police?'

Craig looked him in the eye. 'I don't really think I want to get involved with the police over David Li or let on that I even know about that bastard and his evil plans.'

'How come?' Tumi asked.

From the direction of Emperors Palace came the *whump* of an explosion. They all looked towards the casino and saw a pall of black smoke rising from the car park.

'We don't need to worry about David Li any more,' Craig said.

Chapter 29

Sean and Tumi drove back to Christine's farm together and Craig travelled by himself.

Sean was tired from being up most of the night; that and the strain of the last couple of weeks was telling on all of them. Sean called Christine from the car and filled her in on what had happened.

'Craig assassinated David Li? Blew him up?' Christine asked, the astonishment clear in her voice.

'As far as we can tell,' Sean said. 'He didn't answer the question directly, but as he said, "you don't have to be a terrorist to rig up a car bomb".'

Christine was waiting for them at the farmhouse when they arrived there several hours later. When Sean got out of the *bakkie* she ran to him and threw her arms around him.

'I've got the money with me,' he said, hugging her tight.

She kissed him. 'I don't care about the money. I just want you. And you, Tumi, it's good to have you back safe.'

Tumi smiled and Christine led them into the house. 'I've made coffee.'

337

Shikar wandered inside from the yard and bounded over to Tumi when she saw her. Tumi patted her. 'Good girl.'

'Where's Benny?' Sean asked, dread tightening his chest. They had all been through so much he was still on edge.

'He's fine,' Christine said. 'Though I think he was pining for you. He's been acting funny since you two snuck off to Joburg. He was just sitting outside for hours yesterday, over there by the old Land Rover, like he was waiting for you. Eventually I half dragged him inside. He wouldn't stop barking and carrying on so I locked him in the laundry.'

'I'll go get him, in a minute.' Sean looked to the Land Rover, processing what Christine had just told him, then went to her and took her in his arms again. 'I love you.'

'Same,' she said, blinking. 'I'm proud of you.'

He shook his head. 'I won't let you down again, but I've got to go now. Tumi, come with me, please, let's get our rifles. We've got work to do.'

'I know. Good luck.'

'Don't go near that Land Rover for now.' Sean went to the laundry where Benny, having heard his voice, was barking like crazy.

*

Christine held her hand to her eyes to shield them from the sun and saw Craig's *bakkie* coming up the access road.

Li was dead, but her future was far from secure. She would need to replace Oliver, and Clyde the bloodhound, and it looked like Charles would be on convalescent leave and on light duties for at least another month or more. Everyone needed time off, but she couldn't afford to let anyone go.

Craig drove up to her, stopped and got out. He reached into the passenger side of the *bakkie* and produced two bottles of French champagne from a cooler box.

'We're celebrating? Seriously?' she said.

He shrugged. 'Why not? Li is dead, and –'

'About that, Craig. I never told anyone on my team to kill people in cold blood. You know our rules of engagement.'

'I know his bodyguard had Tumi in the boot of a car and was about to start dismembering her. Li wouldn't have stopped until he got your lions, even if it meant killing you. He came damn close with that attack by his guys on the farm, with Oliver as their inside man.'

She exhaled. 'I don't know how to handle this.'

'Live in the moment,' he said, his face serious. 'We never know how much longer we've got left. It's not too late for you and me, Chris.'

Christine looked behind her. Sean came out of the house, with Benny at his side. Tumi and Shikar followed. Sean and Craig nodded to each other.

'We still can't be sure we're safe,' Sean said, his rifle hanging loose by his side. 'Li might have made arrangements that we don't know about.'

'Agreed, *boet*,' Craig said. He leaned into the cab of his vehicle and put the champagne back in the cooler.

Sean turned to Tumi. 'Take Shikar up the western fence line. Check for any incursions. Take one of the radios from inside the farmhouse.'

'OK.' Tumi went inside, came back with a handheld radio, then headed for one of the farm *bakkies*. She and Shikar got in and Tumi drove off.

Craig put his hands on his hips. 'You taking charge now, brother?'

Christine looked to Sean and held her breath.

Sean locked eyes with his former best friend. 'I think it would be good if you could go take a drive around the lion enclosures, make sure they're safe.'

The muscles in Craig's jaw tensed. He turned his head to Christine. 'I'm still a part owner of this operation and, when I last checked, its manager.'

She gave him a small, sad smile. He was a handsome man, confident and assured. 'Please do as Sean *suggests*, then, Craig. I'd like you to go check on the lions.'

'Go inside to the gun safe and get your rifle,' Sean said to Craig. 'You might need it.'

Again Craig squared up to Sean, but just for a few seconds, before he turned on his heel and walked inside.

Sean went to Craig's *bakkie* and reached in through the driver's side window. 'Have you got the Land Rover keys?' he asked Christine.

She took them out of her pocket and put them in his outstretched hand. 'Are you sure you want to go through with this?'

Sean nodded and walked over to the Land Rover and Benny followed him. When they got close, Benny sat down and Sean knelt next to him.

A few minutes later Craig came out of the house carrying his rifle. 'Reporting for duty, *sir*.'

Craig made to walk past him, but Sean checked him by holding out Christine's keys. 'Take Chris's Land Rover.'

'That old banger? Why?'

'Because I asked you to,' Sean said.

Craig stared at him but walked on to his *bakkie*. When he looked inside he saw the keys were not where he'd left them. 'What are you playing at, *boet*? You even want the boss's Land Cruiser now?'

'Please do as Sean asks,' Christine said, her heart beating faster.

'Chris,' Sean said, 'can you please go inside for a minute and radio Tumi.'

'OK.'

Craig looked to both of them and shrugged, as if he did not

know what was going on. Christine walked to the door of the farmhouse, but stopped when she got there and turned around. She had to trust that Sean knew what he was doing, but she would *not* let Sean do something he might later regret. She stayed close enough to hear what they were saying.

Craig went to Sean, snatched the keys out of his hand and carried on around to the driver's side of the Land Rover. He opened the door and got in.

'Stay here,' Craig said, 'like a good doggy and take care of the boss lady. See you in half an hour or so once Tumi and I have finished doing our patrols.'

Craig started the engine and reached down to put the Land Rover in gear.

'Benny, *voetsek*, go to Christine!' Sean commanded.

'Here, Benny,' Christine called. Benny looked back at Sean, but reluctantly walked away from the vehicle.

Before Craig could drive off, Sean darted around to the front of the Land Rover, raised his rifle into his shoulder and took aim at Craig. 'Stop!'

*

Tumi stopped the *bakkie* by the gate that Sean had driven through to break the lock, the spot where they had both narrowly escaped death. Christine's farm workers had made a temporary repair of the gate and fence, but it was far from secure.

Shikar jumped down from the back of the vehicle, eager to work or play. Tumi's phone rang. When she looked at the screen she was surprised. 'Hello, Dad. How are you?'

'Fine, Tumi, and you?'

Where should she start? she wondered. 'Fine.'

'Your mother has told me what you've been up to.'

It was good to hear his deep voice again, after quite an absence. She assumed he was calling to order her to leave her job and come home and study some university course he approved of. 'Dad, I'm sorry. It's good to hear from you but I'm working right now. Can I call you –'

'Just hear me out, girl.'

'OK.'

'Tumi, you know I didn't approve of you studying vet science, and nor was I happy for you to become a dog *handler*, but your mother has convinced me that you are a grown woman now and you can make choices for yourself. Also, I have to tell you I've been worried sick since she told me what happened. How you were . . . hurt in that explosion.'

She thought she heard his voice catch. He was a proud man, traditional, and thought it weak for men to show their emotions. She was glad he didn't know about the events that had followed that first IED.

'Dad, I'm all right.'

'I know you are, Tumi. I just wanted to say . . . well, whatever you choose to do in life I just want you to be safe, and I will support you, including financially.'

Tumi felt her own words stick in her throat. 'I . . . thank you, Dad.'

'Now go back to work. We can talk again when you have a free minute for an old man.'

She laughed. 'I will, Dad, as soon as I can, tonight. I promise. Bye.'

She got out of the *bakkie*, smiling, and whistled to Shikar as she led the dog to the gate. 'Shikar, *soek*.'

Tumi and Shikar made a thorough search of this part of the fence, as it would be the easiest place for an intruder to slip through.

Finding nothing of note, Shikar came back over to her and looked up at her lovingly, panting. 'Good girl.'

They were on a rise and Tumi could see Christine's farmhouse about a kilometre away. Tumi took out her phone. She would, she decided, send Charles an SMS and see if he wanted her to visit him this evening, after she'd had a good long talk with her father and mother. She had a feeling Charles would be very happy to see her.

When she had pressed the send button she looked back over the rolling grassy hills towards the farm.

And then a voice suddenly blared from the radio clipped to Tumi's belt. 'Tumi, Tumi, this is Chris, over,' Christine said.

'Tumi here, Chris.'

'You can come back to the farmhouse, Tumi. The game's over.'

*

Sean kept the rifle trained on Craig as he switched off the engine and opened the door of the Land Rover.

'Put the rifle down, *boet*,' Craig said as he got out. Christine was striding towards them from the farmhouse.

'Take your gun out, Craig, slowly, and toss it to me,' Sean said.

'What?'

'You heard him, Craig,' Christine said. 'Do as Sean told you.'

Craig forced a smile and slowly reached for his pistol with the thumb and first finger of his right hand. He slid it from his holster and dropped it on the ground. 'OK, someone is acting crazy here. But I don't like having a loaded weapon pointed at me, *boet*, so I'll play along. What's going on?'

Sean followed Craig's movement with the barrel. 'I had to make sure.'

Craig stood by the front bumper. 'Make sure of what?'

'That you weren't trying to kill me,' Christine said, glaring at Craig from Sean's side.

'Of course I wasn't trying to kill you,' Craig said, hands out. 'Will someone please tell me what's going on?'

'Benny!' Sean called. His dog bounded over to him. 'Benny, find.'

Benny sniffed around the Land Rover, as he had been doing for the whole day, and sat down near the rear of the vehicle, ears up, tail straight out.

Craig looked to Benny. 'He's indicating like there are explosives under there. What is it?'

'Take a look,' Sean said, 'nice and slow. I've got you covered.'

Craig walked around the back of the Land Rover, with Sean and Christine following him. When Craig got to where Benny was sitting he got down on his hands and knees and had a look under the vehicle. 'Shit.'

'You got that right,' Sean said. 'Benny found the bomb, Craig, under the Land Rover. He was indicating all day and Christine just missed the signs. He was barking, which was unusual when he found explosives, because he was looking for me, to warn me. Chris just thought he was pining.'

'I still don't understand,' Craig said.

'Oh, it's not too difficult, *boet*. Someone, one of Li's gangsters, I think, fitted a bomb with a mercury tilt switch; the same type that Zohair Mohammed used on a few Afghan National Army Humvees in Kabul and Kandahar.'

Craig tried a puzzled look. 'Who's Zohair . . .?'

'Mohammed,' Sean said. 'He's the bombmaker that Tumi and I helped the CIA track down in Mozambique, when we disappeared. The Americans thought he was already dead, killed in a drone strike, but the hat Tumi recovered in Maputo had his DNA in it. The Yanks only had one blurry surveillance picture of Zohair on file, so they needed Tumi and me to confirm his identity. They used a photo I snapped of him in Maputo to trace the fake passport he was travelling on.'

They both heard the noise of a car engine, revving high and fast, but Sean kept his eyes and his rifle on Craig as Tumi pulled up and got out. She took her LM5 from the cab of her vehicle and aimed it at Craig, saying nothing, but covering him.

'Craig?' Tumi said to Sean.

Sean shook his head. 'No. I told Craig to get in the Land Rover and drive and either he's very good at playing chicken or he didn't know the bomb was underneath. At least we've cleared that up.'

'Of course I didn't place any bomb,' Craig said.

'That's not true, Craig, and you know it,' Christine said. 'You did set several IEDs, but in your defence you didn't mean to kill anyone, dog or human with those small IEDs in the bush, did you?'

Craig said nothing.

'But you *did*, almost,' Tumi said, raising her voice, 'and Charles is still recovering.'

'It's OK, Tumi,' Sean said, 'let's hear him out.'

Craig smiled and held his hands wide. 'Look, this is all a mistake. I don't know what you think I've done or why, and I'm sure we all have our conspiracy theories, but I'm not involved in any of this. You could have told me there was a bomb under the Landy before I got in. Now, let's stop this pantomime and work out who did actually set this device. I think you're right in assuming one of Li's guys did, acting on orders before I killed Li. You've got nothing to tie me to any bombs, Sean.'

Sean looked down, but only for an instant. He hated to say what he was about to. 'No, but the Americans have.'

'What do you mean?' Craig asked.

'Jed Banks, the CIA man Tumi and I went to Mozambique with, called me soon after we helped him capture Zohair Mohammed. The Yanks sweated him and he told them that as well as supplying bombs to David Li he was dealing with a South African, guy, a Shangaan, bald head, about six foot two, military bearing, fit.'

Craig raised his eyebrows, a little too theatrically. 'Oliver? We worked out he was a poacher and behind the attack on the farm, but I didn't suspect he was planting bombs as well.'

'Right. And you shot Oliver dead before we could interrogate him and find out who else he was working with.'

'What are you suggesting?' Craig said.

'Christine and I both spoke with Tienie after the gunfight at the farm,' Sean said. 'There was too much that didn't add up on that day. Tienie told me that he recognised Oliver from the air and told you, but you took aim at Oliver without even trying to talk to him; he thought that seemed like an odd thing to do to a guy you had worked with. I think Oliver realised you were going to double cross him and take him out, make it look like he was the real villain. Christine had fired him but she didn't have a confession from him or even much to go to the cops with, yet you took it on yourself to draw down on him. Oliver saw what you were doing and he tried to take you out.'

'Rubbish,' Craig said. 'He was a criminal and your bombmaker fingered him, he was clearly the big bald-headed guy.'

'There's more,' Sean said. 'Zohair was a cautious man – Tumi and I saw that for ourselves in Maputo, he tailed the people he was doing business with to make sure he wasn't being double crossed. He told the Americans he followed the African man and saw him with another guy, white, same height as Oliver, black hair, also fit. Just like you Craig.'

'Bullshit,' Craig said. 'That could be half the white male population of this country.'

'Could be,' Sean agreed, 'but then there's the dogs.'

Craig laughed. 'Got statements from them? I'm done with this bullshit.'

He started to walk, but Christine blocked his way. 'Stay where you are, Craig. The dogs are what really aroused Sean's suspicions about you.'

'Neither of them,' Sean said, 'not Shikar nor Benny, could pick up the trail of the mystery sniper you were supposedly chasing through the bush on the day of the gunfight here at the farm.

That's because *you* were the man shooting at Tumi, and later at Christine with a silenced rifle while you were supposedly checking yourself out of hospital. The dogs would have both picked up your scent, but they know you, as a *friend*, thanks to your program of selective detection training, your dirty socks that they've sniffed so often, so neither of them indicated when they picked up your scent. If there really had been a sniper in the bush the dogs would have found him straight away. Shikar picked up your empty shell casings, so she would have been able to follow an unfamiliar human scent easily.'

Craig looked to Christine. 'This is nonsense. Dogs –'

'Don't lie,' Christine said. 'Tienie told me he picked you up *inside* the perimeter of the farm not out on the main road on the way from the hospital, like you claimed. Before that you were firing at Tumi, well-aimed shots with a silenced rifle to keep her out of the way while your other henchman came after me at the lion enclosures to deliver Li's message and frighten me. Tienie said that after he picked you up he later dropped you off at your request.'

Craig shook his head. 'He needed fuel, Christine, that's why he put me down.'

'No! Stop lying.' Christine got in his face, her hands clenched beside her. 'Tienie told me that he said to you that he could fly for another twenty minutes before he would need refuelling and that you should stay with him in the chopper to search for more bad guys. *You* told him to put you down and that gave you time to take bloody pot shots at me. I trusted you. And now I remember you asking me if I'd consider selling the farm. Who was your mystery American buyer who was going to rescue the farm, Craig, just another hunter who would be happy to sell off my lions' bones once his buddies had mounted their heads on the walls of their trophy rooms? Why, Craig?'

He said nothing.

Sean kept his rifle trained on Craig. 'I am trying to work this out, Craig. We both loved the bush, when we were kids out of school training to be guides, so what made you the sort of man who would organise a bombing campaign against dogs and people and shoot one of your girlfriend's prize lions to force her to sell her farm? Was it just the money, Craig? I was fucked up after Afghanistan, but you . . . you were always the strong one, the one in charge.'

Craig exhaled. 'If only you knew the truth, *boet*. We sweated our arses off in Afghanistan, risked our lives, for what? You think the money we made was worth it? It wasn't. It seemed good by South African standards, but that place took our *souls*, man. Look at you. You're a fucked-up gambling addict. I got into heroin.'

'Seriously?' Sean said, taken aback.

'Yes, I kicked it. But I needed it for a while, after I was injured by that IED in Afghanistan. I couldn't stay in the field, like you, with a dog. I was burned out, so I took that managerial job in Kabul, but even there I couldn't keep it together without drugs. When I needed to score in Kabul there was a Pakistani guy who hooked me up. He'd had relatives in South Africa, got me to be a mule, a courier, and I brought that evil shit back here when we came home on leave. The Chinese triads were involved; that's who I delivered to. I got help, though – remember when I took two months off? I told you it was because my grandmother died.'

Sean nodded. He did remember.

'I was in rehab. I got clean. I turned my back on all that.'

'Craig . . .' He sensed his friend wanted to reach out, to confess, but he was stopping short of telling them everything. Sean wanted to believe Craig was innocent of the worst of this.

'I'm not saying anything else,' Craig said, 'because that is the end of this story.'

Sean saw how Craig looked away, unable to meet his eyes. 'Did they blackmail you, Craig . . . the Chinese, Li? Was David Li your contact who you delivered the heroin to? He wanted the farm, and you, romancing my ex-wife – was part of your plan to get your hands on our lions?'

'*Our* lions, *boet?*'

'Don't call me that any more, Craig.'

'She carried you, man.' Craig nodded to Christine. 'You don't deserve her. You're not half the man Christine needs. What she needs is someone stronger. A *man* who could get on top of his addiction and keep her satisfied, like I did, not a loser who gambled away everything she had worked for.'

Sean took up the slack on the rifle's trigger. He clenched his teeth, but despite the pain he felt he would not succumb to the anger that was part of the reason he had become addicted to gambling in the first place. 'I know what you're doing, Craig.'

'Tell me, you fucking loser.'

Sean controlled his breathing. 'You want me to kill you.'

'I'll kill him,' Tumi said. 'He nearly killed my dog, and Charles.'

Craig shifted his gaze to Tumi. 'I do believe you would. Sean taught you well. You're a real warrior now. I wonder what it would take for you to pull the trigger?'

'Just try me,' Tumi said.

'Why the IEDs that injured Gemma, Tumi and Charles?' Sean asked. 'Zohair supplied them to Li, but you and Oliver placed them. Did you think I'd break? Did you imagine I'd run away to the casino and self-destruct? Was that it? I'd be gone, you'd have Christine and the farm and what, with the business in turmoil you'd eventually convince her to sell?'

Craig stayed silent.

'And the firebomb in the hut?' Tumi said. 'The car bomb in Maputo – I assume you got Oliver to set that while he was supposedly on leave?'

Craig just glared at him.

'Pretty amazing,' Sean said, 'Tumi and I probably missed bumping into Oliver by only minutes. Did you do all this? You were trying to cover your trail and maybe you wanted Li dead. Jed, the CIA guy, said Zohair sold two car bombs to the African man, Oliver, and a couple of devices to Li to blow up the national parks Casspir. That was you trying to kill Li, twice, but not planting the bomb in Christine's Land Rover doesn't absolve you from all the others.'

Craig puffed his chest out. 'Prove it was me and not Oliver acting alone or with Li. You can't. Li was behind all the bombings, and other than a vague description of a white South African guy in cahoots with a black guy, you don't have anything on me. As for the horseshit about me being the sniper, well, maybe, just maybe, your dog and Shikar aren't as good as you think they are.'

Sean took a deep breath. He despised all that Craig had done, but he did not have it in him to assist his friend's suicide. Nor did he want to see him condemned to the living hell of prison in South Africa, but he had even more to pay for than putting their lives and the dogs at risk. He had murdered a man who trusted him.

'And Oliver?' Tumi asked, taking the question out of Sean's mouth.

Craig's defiance wilted and he hung his head, though he still admitted nothing.

'He worked for you,' Sean said. It wasn't a question.

'And you killed him,' Tumi said, her voice low, full of contempt. 'You were both criminals, and he was a pig of a man, but he put his trust in you and you shot him dead, in cold blood, from Tienie's helicopter to cover your tracks. Even if you didn't actually try to kill me, or Gemma, or Charles, or Christine, you murdered Oliver. He kept quiet about you and you . . .'

Craig looked up. 'I guessed that you had your suspicions about me, even though you can't prove them; that's why you kept me in the dark about your little trips to Mozambique and Joburg.'

'You killed Casper,' Sean said.

Craig hung his head now, his facade of defiance cracking under their onslaught.

'You bastard,' Christine said.

'For all his surliness, Oliver was a soldier,' Sean said, 'and professional with weapons. When I checked his rifle he had been wandering around with a bullet in the chamber, and it had been recently fired. That's because you had killed Casper and gave Oliver the rifle, just before you went into the bush to link up with Oliver's neighbour, who brought the silenced weapon, and you started shooting at Tumi.'

Craig looked from Sean to Christine. 'I did what neither of you could do, I got rid of Li.'

'Because it didn't suit you to work with him any more,' Christine spat back, 'because we weren't buckling beneath your bombs and bullets. You would have just tried to get me to sell to someone less obvious.'

'No,' Craig said. 'Li was the criminal in all this, man, not me!'

Sean looked down, but Tumi, he noticed out of the corner of his eye, kept her rifle trained on Craig, who remained still.

'What do we do now?' Tumi asked.

Sean raised his head and caught Christine's eye. She shrugged. Sean lowered his weapon.

'You're not going to shoot me, are you?' Craig said, and Sean thought there was a trace of disappointment in his best friend's voice.

Sean shook his head.

'You wounded yourself, didn't you,' Christine said to Craig. 'That night Zali and I were out. It was nothing, just a scratch on your ribs. You must have just held the barrel against your side and pulled the trigger. You did it to put us off your trail, didn't you?'

Craig just looked at her. Sean saw the anger rising up in Christine.

'You killed Clyde,' Christine hissed.

Craig lowered his head again. 'Clyde was dying of cancer.'

'And Casper,' Christine said, the tears trickling down her cheeks.

'You *knew* what he meant to me. And yet you killed him, to try and break me and make me walk away from the farm, and when that didn't work you tried to intimidate Tumi and me by firing at us with that sniper rifle.'

Craig looked at the sky. He turned away from them and started to walk.

Sean slung his rifle and went to Christine and put his arm around her. Tumi kept her weapon trained on Craig's back.

'We can't just let him go,' Tumi said.

Sean heard a siren and they all looked to the main road. A police car and a *bakkie* turned onto the access road to the farm.

Craig stopped, away from them, and stood still, looking up the hill towards the lion enclosure as the vehicles arrived and pulled up. An attractive woman in plain clothes with a blonde bob got out of the car. Sean, Craig and Christine knew her well; it was Captain Sannie van Rensburg, who ran the anti–rhino poaching unit at Skukuza, in the Kruger Park. She greeted Sean and Christine and cast a glance at Craig. Sean introduced Sannie to Tumi.

Sannie, flanked by uniformed officers who got out of the vehicles, took a pace towards Christine. 'You and your boys here have some questions to answer, Chris.'

'How so?' Christine asked.

'You maybe don't think so much of our bomb squad guys, otherwise you wouldn't have sent a hat to the FBI in America. That's a crime in itself, hiding evidence from the police.'

Sean held Christine's hand and gave it a squeeze.

'The fact is,' Sannie said, 'that the South African Police Service is not as disorganised as people like to think, and we *do* talk to our counterparts overseas. Although, between you and me, sometimes we are a little slow. I contacted TEDAC and told them I was investigating a bomb that was set to blow up a South African National Parks armoured car, which was full of rhino horn and lion bones. As you might have read, we foiled that attack. The guy who detonated the roadside bomb did so too early. The Casspir was damaged, but the crew inside were fine. They were stunned but opened fire on the bombers as they were trying to fix a limpet mine and then our guys responded and it was game over for the thieves. Shame, as we didn't get to interview them. Anyway, Christine, your friend in America, Ruth, was very helpful. In fact, she just got some new information back about some fingerprints that our forensic people lifted off that firebomb that Sean found in the hut. There were six prints in all from two people, none of them from the Pakistani bombmaker they have in custody, but the others all belonged to two South African men they had on file, contractors who had worked on US military or embassy properties overseas, specifically in Afghanistan.'

Sean looked to Craig, who had turned and was now facing their way.

Sannie took a piece of paper out of the pocket of her jeans and unfolded it. 'Those prints belong to Sean Bourke and –'

'Me,' Craig said. 'I –'

'You never touched that IED, Craig, on the day I found it,' Sean said. 'I took it to the police.'

Craig held up a hand to him, then looked to van Rensburg. 'Sean defused the bomb, but I planted it. I'm the one you want, Sannie.'

Sannie looked to the uniformed officer next to her. 'Arrest him.'

Craig walked towards the police, but stopped in front of Sean. 'With Li dead and me gone they won't come after you or Christine any more, *boet*, at least not for now.'

Sean nodded. 'If they do, we'll be ready for them.'

Craig reached out and clapped him on the arm. 'Yes, I know you will. I didn't mean any of that shit I said before about you being a loser. You're strong, Sean. You'll make it, *boet*.'

As Craig was led away, Christine turned to Sean and wrapped her arms around him. 'I love you. It's time to come home, Sean.'

Epilogue

The leopard got me in the end – the arse, that is.

Cat lovers, you might think that's poetic justice, 'cat eats dog', but let me tell you, it hurt worse than that bullet, or the homemade shrapnel from the bomb in Afghanistan.

Old Vin Diesel got into our enclosure one night a few months ago and he found me and he opened me up. Sean came out and he fired a few rounds in the air and chased the leopard away. Sean called up Tienie and he flew me to hospital in his helicopter.

Still hate helicopters.

Graham Baird, the veterinarian in Hazyview, stitched me up and saved my life. When I came to, Tumi was there. She was hanging around the surgery a few days a week, doing some work there. She'd bring her pet dog, three-legged, one-eyed Gemma with her. Gemma's nice, but her sister, Shikar, from the same litter, is still my favourite.

I still hate Graham.

When I came out of hospital I was officially retired from my work as a tracker dog. At first, I was bored. Sean and Christine got married again and I moved to the farmhouse. Its fenced-in yard became my world and I thought I'd go stir crazy. Maybe Sean did, as well, but he soon got used to a management role in the business. He doesn't seem to need to spend all his days in the bush any more.

Shikar's still tracking poachers, but she comes to visit sometimes, to play, if you know what I mean.

I got a new job myself, close personal protection – aka bodyguarding. My principal, which is what the humans call the turkey who has to be protected, is a tiny human called Sarah. She's about eight months old now. Anyone comes near her I bark like crazy and I'd tear their throat out if they tried to hurt her. She cries a lot, and Sean's favourite trick is to get me to go up to her pram and grab it by the handle with my mouth and rock it until Sarah goes to sleep.

Turns out I'm good with kids.

Got a few pups of my own, now. Ever seen a Malinois-Weimaraner cross puppy? Cute as hell.

The lions are all safe, by the way. Screw them.

I still hate cats.

ACKNOWLEDGEMENTS

At the time of writing *Scent of Fear*, the war on poaching is continuing in Africa.

While the human and animal losses in this conflict are alarming, it is a fact, as mentioned in this work of fiction, that dogs have proven to be something of a game changer in the fight to protect endangered wildlife. Man's best friend is proving to be a rhino poacher's worst nightmare.

Belgian Malinois, German Shepherds, Weimaraners and bloodhounds (and, interestingly bloodhound–Doberman cross dogs) are all being employed on a day-to-day basis to hunt down poachers and detect illegally harvested wildlife products, guns and ammunition. Their successes have been numerable – anecdotally, what's currently happening is that poachers seem to be shifting to reserves and national parks, which do not have a strong presence of dogs and handlers.

Several people involved in the world of canine operations helped with the research for this book, directly and indirectly. My friend Shane Bryant inadvertently helped by getting me interested in the world of working dogs when we co-wrote his biography *War Dogs*, about Shane's time as a civilian contract dog handler serving with US Army Special Forces in Afghanistan (the fictitious characters Sean and Craig share something of Shane's background). My leading dog Benny is named after one of Shane's working dogs, who served him faithfully during the war. You can still buy *War Dogs* by Shane Bryant with Tony Park as an e-book.

Another ex-military dog handler Marianne Hay, who served with the British Army in Afghanistan and later as an anti-poaching volunteer in South Africa, answered several questions for me early on in my research. On the ground in South Africa I was lucky enough to meet Vianna von Weyhausen who runs the international charity Canines For Africa (www.k94a.org) which trains and supplies dogs and handlers for anti-poaching work. The dynamic Vianna opened many doors in the canine world for me, and read and checked the manuscript. The fictitious Shikar is named after a real-life Malinois (not a Weimaraner as in the book), trained and funded by Vianna's supporters.

Through Vianna I met Conraad de Rosner (and many of his dogs including his personal favourite Anubis) who, through his company K9 Conservation, trains and provides dogs and handlers to private game reserves in South Africa. Conraad gave me an excellent overview of canine operations and training in the world of anti-poaching and introduced me to Rory Guthrie and his team from Eastern Wildlife and Security Services, who provide anti-poaching support to Singita Game Reserve in South Africa's Sabi Sand Game Reserve. Rory and dog handler Phillip Snyman answered my many questions and showed me their dogs at work. Phillip checked and corrected the manuscript for me. Thank you all for your help and for the fantastic work you are doing protecting Africa's endangered wildlife.

Several friends read and checked early drafts of the manuscript. I'd like to thank my good friend, Sydney psychotherapist

Charlotte Stapf (and her cats Casper and Felix) for her editorial input and comments on characters and their motivations; my go-to person for all things South African and Afrikaans Annelien Oberholzer (who still picks up typos the native English-speakers miss); dual Mozambican/Australian citizen John Roberts for his knowledge of Portuguese and his beloved Maputo; Fritz Rabbe for his firearms expertise; Maddie Duncan for helping out with publicity on the last few books; and Wayne Hamilton from swagmantours.com.au for his wide ranging knowledge of Africa.

Vin Diesel, aka Mbavala, was a real leopard whose territory encompassed part of the Kruger National Park and the area where my wife and I have a house in South Africa. Mbavala was an impressive animal, one of the biggest leopards in the park and famous enough to have his own Facebook page and following. We saw him many times, including around our home. He passed away from complications related to old age while I was writing this book so I thought it a fitting tribute to include him as Benny's nemesis.

The real Craig Hoddy is a good guy and an ardent supporter of African wildlife conservation, as is his wife, Kim, who paid for Craig's name to be used in this book at a fundraising auction for Perth-based charity Painted Dog Conservation Inc. Kim (who herself appeared as a character in one of my earlier novels, *Ivory*) also paid for real-life Lion Whisperer, Kevin Richardson, to have his name mentioned.

Getting people to pay money to charities for the right to have names assigned to characters is a good way to relieve me of the onerous job of thinking up names. Accordingly I'd like to thank the following good people and the causes they chose to support: Maryanne Bourke on behalf of my oldest friend Sean Bourke and their dog Fifty 'Fiddy' Cent (Painted Dog Conservation Inc.); Evan Litis on behalf of Ruth Boustead (Save the African Rhino Foundation, Australia); John Glover on behalf of Christine Glover

(The Askari Project, supporting elephants in Kenya); and Holly Longmuir on behalf of Zali Longmuir (Heal Africa, a hospital in the Democratic Republic of Congo).

Book talks and signings are notoriously risky events to arrange – sometimes I have a couple of hundred people attending and, once, one person (thankfully never none, at least not yet). Thank you to Paula Raath who was the sole attendee at a signing at Castle Hill in Sydney – for that I was pleased to name Clyde the bloodhound after her beloved dog.

I'd like to say I visited Huntsville, Alabama, to get information about the FBI's Terrorist Explosive Device Analytical Center (TEDAC), and claimed the trip on my income tax, but in fact I found it online at www.fbi.gov/services/laboratory/tedac

As always my unpaid editors – wife, Nicola, mother, Kathy, and mother-in-law, Sheila – all read and had valuable input into early drafts of the book. The paid team at Pan Macmillan Australia and South Africa, Cate Paterson, Terry Morris, Danielle Walker, Andrea Nattrass, Yvonne Sewankambo, Veronica Napier, Eileen Bezemer and Gillian Spain are more like family than publishers and I'd like to thank them all for allowing me to continue to live my dream.

If you've ever made it to the end of the acknowledgements section of one of my books, then you will know by now that it is you who is the most important person in the world of books. Thank you.

South Africa 2018